THE PROMISE

CHILDREN OF ANNWN BOOK ONE

Jennifer Owen Davies

Mainstream Romance

This was the first book I wrote. I hope you love it!

Jen.

The Promise

First book Publication: December 2014
Second edition September 2015
Cover design by Dawné Dominique
Edited by Leslie Fish
Proofread by Rene Flowers

All characters and events in this book are fictitious. Any resemblance to actual persons living or dead is strictly coincidental.

Dedication

Dedicated to my mother Josephine Owen.

Acknowledgements

I have a list of people that have helped me tremendously, and I have to say thank you because you enabled me to fulfil the promise I made to myself, which was to get this book published!

I have to thank my supportive and very patient husband Paul Davies and my mother Josephine Owen, whose constant reminders to get it finished, pushed me on when I wanted desperately to give up.

My brother-in-law Christopher Phillips who is a singer and songwriter and my friend Daniel P. Nakhoul, a musician, both took the time to educate me about the music business and helped me to understand a little of what a musician's life is like, for which I will be eternally grateful.

My dear friend Julie Ross who took great pains to help me edit, proofread, provide invaluable feedback, and was always the source of encouragement which I will never forget.

I have a whole slew of friends and family who have given me their unswerving support and have put up with my creative moods throughout. I want to thank my close friend Maryline Bellosguardo, who read through my first draft and still talks to me. My teenage readers Monique Stewart, Paige & Samantha Rodrigues, Kelly Phillips, Sara Willert, Makayla Richards, and Frankie Hearst who gave me such great constructive feedback on the characters, the flow of the story, teenage slang, and fashion which really helped to get me on the right track.

I must also thank my oldest son Jonathan Davies for his continuous creative ideas on the plot, and my writer friend Rachel Alesse Knox for sharing in my highs and lows.

There are still many more out there, and you know who you are whose kind words of encouragement raised my hope in times of doubt, thank you all.

A BRAND NEW DAY

Rest your head and close your eyes
All the world shall turn your way
For when you wake with the sweet sunrise
It will be a brand new day
Turn down the lights and pull me close
Feel our hearts beat as we lay
For when you wake to soft morning breeze
It will be a brand new day
Lie soft as I caress your hair
Let all life's worries melt away
For when you wake to warm summer scent
It will be a brand new day
Fall fast asleep and dream with me
Whisper "Love, I'm here to stay"
For when we wake in each other's arms
It will be a brand new day.

Author Aeni.

Prologue

Leaving Annwn

It was dawn, and in twenty-five minutes and thirty-six seconds, Mia would be human. Her hands trembled as she raised them, pointing out at the sea. As she stared at the raging waters, her heart raced alongside. Breathing in the saltiness of the sea, Mia called to her magic to still the rushing tide. When the water stopped, her uneven and irregular heartbeat settled.

"Are you ready?"

Mia turned at the sound of a deep husky voice, and gazed at Ryder, her betrothed. He was tall, broad shouldered, and his eyes were the color of roasted chestnuts. Their intense gaze reached into her soul, and managed to melt her worries while stirring her heart to a fever pitch. She accepted his outstretched hand and smiled. He was her heart, and the reason they both stood on the shores of their home, ready to cast aside everything they knew. Her toes curled into the silky grains of white sand like an anchor, but she knew she must let go and set sail.

"It's now or never," she said, giving him a brief smile.

Ryder smoothed a rough hand across her cheek, and she closed her eyes. Falling in love in Annwn came with a price, and she was willing to pay if it meant there was a happy ever after with Ryder, the man who possessed her heart. Once a couple took *The Promise*, an ancient law which pledged them to each other, they must complete a challenge that would test the power of their love and magic.

If their love did not survive they would remain mortal, and in a world where they did not belong. At this thought, her arms dropped to her side, and once more the waves thrashed upon the shore. The roar of the ocean as it crashed against the rocks echoed inside Mia Leronde's ears, and she stared as the white foam fizzled and dissolved into the sand. Usually the sheer power of nature revived her, but today there was nothing but despair.

Mia shivered as cold settled in her bones and icy tentacles locked inside her throat, rendering her speechless. The fierce wind whipped around them and Emrys, one of the Wise Elders, appeared. His usually kind face was devoid of emotion. He was pale, and dark shadows lingered like bruises under his blue eyes. The waves parted, and Mia looked into the distance. A land she had never seen before beckoned and bright lights twinkled.

"It's not too late to change your mind," said Emrys. "We can look at another way to complete your challenge—but once you enter their world, your memories of Annwn and Ryder will be locked away inside your mind until the awakening. The spell will be cast from the moment we leave, and I cannot say how old you will be. The magic in this area is unpredictable, but I will aim for you to be teenagers once more." Emrys dipped his head low, and his gravelly voice wavered to silence.

"So, we will be human?" She let go of Ryder's hand and grabbed his cotton shirt, tugging him closer.

"Mia, you'll be you, but as you step into the human world your immortality is relinquished, your magic suppressed. Memories of Annwn and Ryder will disappear. You will experience life as every other human, and face the challenges their world has. I will guide your path toward each other, but it's your love for Ryder that will help overcome the obstacles in your way to unity," Emrys said.

A flapping of wings and a wail of ear-piercing squeals filled the skies. Mia clasped her hands over her nose, and tears filled her eyes. It was Gerty and Jasper, Mia and Ryder's pet serpents. The two pale green and leathery-scaled creatures landed on the soft sand with a thump, their wings flapped and then settled, but their long, thick tails bashed against the ground. They furiously ducked and nodded their heads skywards, squealing continuously.

"They don't want us to go," Mia said as she approached the gentle-looking creatures that purred, nudging their heads against her waiting hand. Mia stroked first one, then the other. She massaged their baby-soft scales in a soothing circular motion, and the creatures batted against her palm in approval.

"They want us to go for a ride. They don't realize we're leaving," Mia said.

At that moment, a buzzing and whirring sound filled the air. Mia couldn't see Ryder as hundreds of swarming colorful fairies, the size of her hand, surrounded her. Their voices all merged together to say one thing.

"Don't go Mia. Don't go."

A flash of white light dispersed the fairies, and Mia saw Emrys and Ryder frowning. The fairies continued to voice their opinion, but silently.

Darkshadows. It's not what you believe to be true.

"Hush now," Emrys ordered. "It is time for Mia and Ryder to leave. Wish them a safe journey."

Ryder clasped Mia's hand and pulled her against his chest. She frowned as she listened to the message from the fairies. Could she be heading into danger?

Ryder lifted her chin with his finger, so she had no choice but to look into his eyes.

"You already look human in your clothes," he said, as his gaze took in her snugly fitted faded jeans, long-sleeved black T-shirt, and boots.

A smile lifted the corners of Mia lips. "I love their clothing."

Ryder's gaze swept over Mia from head to foot, and then rested on her face.

"I suppose, I could get used to it," he said, as he wrapped his arms around her waist and tugged her in close laying tender kisses on her lips.

Mia was one of the last of her kind, a Guardian of Annwn, a peacekeeper of her world and the mortals'. Only those with the strongest magic were given such a role. She glanced around, looking toward the cliff. The Otherworld, Annwn, was a realm on earth, shielded from human eyes by powerful magic. Its exact location a highly guarded secret, but legends and Welsh folklore suggested that it lay along the shores of Wales.

Mia smiled, recalling the history lessons about King Arthur and the Druids, and sighed because that was when everything changed for the children of Annwn. In those days humans told tales and whispered about the Otherworld, reciting scary stories of Annwn, saying that it was a place for the lost souls and that sometimes the inhabitants would steal into the human world to watch the mortals at play.

Annwn did have its share of lost souls, but it was mostly a beautiful land of plenty. The Wise Elders were at the helm, enforcing all the laws of the land, and the people lived in peace. Food was grown with the help of the land, and the people lived in harmony with nature. Of course, few humans believed in magic or Annwn.

Watchers from Annwn visited the human world to observe their exploits, but it was never with the intention of causing harm, but to help. However, evil resides in the most unexpected places. Mia shivered as she thought of the Darkshadows and the evil witch Rhiannon, about whom she knew very little.

After the fall of King Arthur, Annwn closed its doors to the humans, refusing to assist, and strict laws were created to maintain its privacy, peace, and security. One of those laws was *The Promise.* Mia stared briefly across the endless glossy water, and her hair danced wildly as the wind whirled around and then back at the headland.

Mist rolled off the grassy slopes on the hillside. The purple and pink slashes of light in the sky stained the sandstone, on the castle that abutted the cliff, a beautiful rose color. The majestic fortress stood guard over the menacing sea, a foreboding sight to any that dared to enter Annwn. The milky white sun peeped from behind the curtains of clouds as they rolled past, and she inhaled deeply, capturing all before her, soaking in the very essence of her home, hoping beyond hope that one day she would return and with Ryder.

“Come, it’s time. The portal’s ready,” Emrys urged, beckoning for them to follow.

It was too late to turn back, and as her heart hammered in her chest, Mia stepped forward.

Chapter One

Over seventeen human years later…

The bell over the front door at Felicities jingled every time a gust of wind blew, and Mia glanced over as tingles exploded down her spine. The diner hummed with animated conversation and the aroma from the bubbling espresso machine. All seemed normal, but she knew it wasn't. Something was lurking, whispering inside her head, and scratching under her skin to be free.

Which could only mean one thing: trouble with a capital T.

Her glance darted from the door to the hands of the clock. *Seven fifty-five*. The black arms on the chrome clock slowed, but the ticking became louder with every passing second. *Tick. Tock. Tick. Tock.*

Mia usually loved working in the diner. It was the one place where she knew was safe.

Not today.

Today the familiar signs were creeping around, and everyone would see her for the freak she was. Everything would change. Mia sighed and took a quick inventory of customers. Why today, when the diner was full of customers lingering because of the stormy weather? Her normally cool self was melting with a burning need. She willed her mind to reject the onslaught of visions that she knew was coming, but still her stomach heaved in rebellion.

A wave of nausea clutched her throat, and she watched the crowd to see if anyone was observing her descent into hell. Nope, everyone was too busy devouring their green salads and greasy cheeseburgers. Mia lifted her head to stare at the overhead television. A special report flashed across the screen. It was addressing the dramatic rise in male infertility, and Mia shivered.

A light snapped on inside her brain—and then fizzled out, lost in thought, and the news shifted to a weather alert. A reporter stood blown by the wind and rain, reciting the direction of a storm. The picture changed quickly showing a weatherman pointing at a map highlighting a flurry of red swirls and lightning bolts that converged around their tiny town of North Littleton.

New England weather was weird, but today it was downright eerie. Mia wished she was home. As soon as that thought left her brain, Sam, the silver-haired owner, dressed in a cook's outfit, pushed through the kitchen's swinging doors and announced they would close at eight o'clock.

Sam never closed early. Tiny hairs along the back of her neck prickled and stood up. A heat rose inside her and sparks fired in her belly.

Mia shook her head and moved to the espresso machine. As she touched the cold metal switch, an electrifying zing of pain shot up her arm. *Damn.* She snatched her hand away and sucked on her fingers. All of a sudden the lights dimmed, and there was a wave of low groans from the customers. This was it, the warning incoming vision, only no one except Mia knew. She didn't know whether to laugh or cry. Her head throbbed, and a wave of panic rose inside.

"Mia, the couple at table eleven by the door both want coffee and a slice of pizza. Do you mind?"

Monica, a young dark-haired waitress, was taking her apron off. Mia eyed the large clock on the wall. She wanted to run and hide, but couldn't. Instead, she swallowed her fears and pushed away from the counter. Turning around, she poured two steaming mugs of coffee, grabbed a slice of pizza from the heated tray, and headed toward the red leather booth by the door. Mia winked at Mr. Peterson on her left.

She took two steps and froze to the spot as everything became a blur.

Excruciating pain tore through her belly, and blazing heat stabbed her like a hot poker. Mia wanted to scream, but clutched the tray against her body like a life buoy and clenched her teeth. Blocking everything out, she forced her mind to obliterate the pain, and within seconds, it was gone.

Here we go.

Her heart thumped against her ribs, and her chest rose and fell in rapid succession. Mia moved slowly and bit hard on her lip, drawing blood. Her belly was on fire, and breathing was difficult as the air stayed trapped in her lungs.

"Ow." The coffee slid across the tray, almost spilling. Mr. Peterson grabbed it, just in time.

"Are you okay?" He reached for the tray and placed it on the table. Mia sucked in a deep breath, and adjusted her square-framed glasses.

"It's fine, honestly." Her cheeks flamed, for she was anything but fine. Blinking, she mentally pushed against the pain until her body was numb. She sucked on her lower lip, shook her head, and forced the tears away. Today had started like every other day in August, beautiful, perfect, until this crazy storm, and now distorted images raced through her head, too many to comprehend. *Please not here, not now.* The pain vanished, and she was able to move away. As she walked towards the young couple, she stared at the many faces in the diner.

Regulars, no one new.

She licked her lips and tensed her shoulders. The visions followed the same pattern. Pain. Terrifying images. Screams. She gave herself a mental shake. Elvis blared from the jukebox. The pain was temporarily gone, but the attack wasn't over. Her hands shook, and the tray slipped banging against the table. The young couple jumped apart and stared at her with rosy faces.

"Sorry," Mia said.

The bell tinkled, and Mia turned, catching a blast of warm air that kissed her lips. Gusts of wind swirled into the diner, whipping strands of hair across her face, making visibility impossible. The door slammed shut, and footsteps quickly passed her by. Mia shook her head to get a glance of a tall retreating figure. Words were on the tip of her tongue, like *we're about to close*, but a fragrance tickled her senses and a magnetic pull towards the hooded stranger rendered her speechless. A dark hood hid the person's identity, but Mia stared in fascination as water dripped from black hair and slid down a pale and stubbly cheek.

"We're about to close…because of the storm," she said.

There was no response, and automatically she edged closer.

"So okay, I only want coffee," a husky male voice replied—but he didn't turn to face her, and the door banged again, dragging her attention away. Wind howled through the diner, and sprinkles of rain made her glasses misty. Outside, large threatening gray and black clouds dominated the sky. The storm was coming in fast.

Mia wiped her glasses, and then tackled the door. The pain didn't return. Maybe she was wrong about the vision? After all, it was six years since her last one. Turning around, Mia walked toward the new customer, needing to see his face—but stopped. A clear image flashed before her. Pictures flickered inside her head. Each one showed snapshots of the diner.

The jukebox.

Mr. Peterson.

The pictures flooded her mind. She spun around and scanned the crowd. A rip-roaring crack of thunder shook the diner, making Mia jump. Someone screamed and the lights went out, plunging them into darkness, and there were more shrieks—but everything faded away in her mind. Mia couldn't breathe. Another startling image appeared, and this time it was Mrs. Fielding, a regular. Her big blue eyes stared, unseeing and her cheeks were a mottled gray. Mia covered her mouth to stifle a scream. The lights came back on, and Mia's brain buzzed with a million thoughts. Whirling around, she placed her hand on her racing heart.

Mia, don't.

An angry and distinctly male voice blasted inside her mind. Mia turned in a complete circle, searching the crowd for the owner of the voice, but no one was paying her any attention. Her hands itched and burned as she rubbed them against her sides. Images flashed like a green light, urging her forward. Thunder rocked through the diner, and a terrifying scream came from the back. One last look around, and Mia raced towards the sound—and found Sylvia, another waitress, holding a limp, elderly lady.

Mrs. Fielding.

"We need to lift her," Mia said, not wondering how she knew. They gathered her up, and Mia placed her hand on the frail lady's cool cheek. A clear picture of Mrs. Fielding choking on her food entered her mind.

Blinding white light streaked through the diner, and the lights went out once more. Screams ricocheted around the walls, and a small circle of people gathered around, watching in the shadowy-darkness. Mia was so absorbed in saving the lady's life that she was beyond caring what anyone would think. Her hand rested across the woman's chest, and heat flowed out from her fingertips, charging into the old lady's lifeless body. She guided her strength into the woman, and used her energy to force the blockage out.

A gasp escaped Mrs. Fielding, and she raised her head, struggling against Mia and Sylvia. Mia spoke softly to the old lady, soothing her fears, and eased her back into the chair. Tears ran down the old lady's face as she came around, and a rosy color flooded her lined cheeks.

"Thank you…I couldn't catch my breath, I'm not sure what happened."

Mrs. Fielding's hand trembled, as she touched Mia's arm. Their gazes connected, and Mia turned away from the old lady's intense stare and look of curiosity. Sylvia grabbed Mia's hand and was speaking loudly, but the words didn't register. Mia was captivated by a familiar fragrance and each breath in increased her desire to close her eyes. A warm trickle of fluid escaped from her nose, and she wiped it away with a tissue from her pocket. It was blood, and her knees buckled. People talked around her, but the sharp edges of the room folded. She was sinking.

Mia.

That voice from earlier was back. A hand connected with hers, and she jerked forward, needing to be closer to whomever it was that held her. A spark of heat ignited at her finger tips and flooded her body. *Hmm, so nice and warm...*

"Mia."

Mia closed her eyes and sank into the darkness that surrounded her. Breathing, Mia smelled an intoxicating scent, and her shoulders automatically relaxed. She wasn't awake yet, and was enjoying the sensations of the warm and fragrant air against her cheeks. The roar of the ocean and the twittering of birds played in the background, but still she didn't want to open her eyes. An insistent male voice called her name. His voice grew louder and more urgent by the second. Her mouth curved into a smile, and she opened her eyes—Mia jumped forward, touching her head, as stars danced around in a merry circle.

* * * *

"Are you all right?" A drop-dead gorgeous boy, with the most magnetic and dark eyes, cradled her in his arms. He dipped his head low and gazed at her. Mia pushed against his steel-like chest to gain some space, because he held her so close and she couldn't breathe. As she struggled for freedom, the boy frowned and reluctantly released her.

"Where am I?" she said, blinking and looking away from his intense stare. She stood up but wobbled, and he caught her to stop her from falling again. He held her around the waist with one hand, while his other roamed through her hair, exploring.

"What are you doing?" she said, needing to be free of his disturbing touch.

"No bumps, but you're weak," he said. "Stay still and I'll take the dizziness away."

Mia squirmed, as he placed his hands on either side of her face and shut his eyes. She looked up at his rugged features, taking in his long dark lashes, and gasped as he opened one eye and smirked. Mia stared into his muddy-brown iris, and had to tear her gaze away as her cheeks flamed. Something stirred inside, a memory, something familiar, a name perhaps...but then it was gone.

"Better?" He asked, and she nodded. Only then did he let go of her.

"Where am I?" she asked again

"You're in Annwn. It is shielded from human eyes by magic, but you were using magic, and you called out." He frowned, and eased his hold around her waist.

She searched around for a way to escape this boy who was talking about magic and humans as if he wasn't one. It was at this point that Mia stared long and hard at her surroundings, not recognizing where she was. At least, she didn't think so, but a shiver of something lessened her fear. Soft golden rays of light shone down upon her and the air hummed a soft tune. This was definitely not anywhere near the diner. Whispers beckoned on the breeze, words that sounded like Annwn. Listening intently, she heard the words grow louder. She watched the boy as the sound increased.

"You don't have a lot of time here. This isn't real, and you must go back," he said, reaching for her hand.

Mia saw that she stood in a beautiful garden, dressed in her black and white uniform from the diner, and everything was surreal. "Am I dead? Is this heaven?" she asked, fearing that must be the answer.

The boy smirked and shook his head. A willowy breeze beckoned her forward. Trees with small pink blossoms swayed, and the tiny flowers floated like butterflies around her. Mist rose off the green grass, and she held her breath. Screeches from above made Mia raise her face skywards.

Two gigantic winged serpents were flying closer and closer. Loud squawking filled the air. The serpents butted heads and then dived, flying straight at her. She stared, mesmerized, until she realized they were not stopping. A scream escaped her mouth, and she turned and began running like the wind. Not daring to look behind, she kept going—but the creatures' wild yelps rang in her ears, and her heart raced. The boy, with his shoulder-length inky-black hair, appeared alongside her and placed a heavy hand on her shoulder, urging her to stop. He laughed, and in-between deep breaths spoke.

"Mia, they're harmless. They merely want to play, and the more you run, the more they'll chase you."

The sound of her name upon his lips stalled her. Did he know her? Did she know him? A wave of déjà-vu invaded, and she shivered. The slender serpents hovered in front of them, flapping their wings and squawking once again before soaring high into the fluffy white clouds. They circled around and dove in front of them.

"I'm hardly dressed for flying." She wasn't sure what made her say that, or why she suddenly forgot that she was frightened, and pointed at her short black- and- white uniform.

He frowned, and his eyes narrowed. "There, much better."

Mia was speechless for a second. Gone was the revealing and short dress—now she was wearing a long black satin gown, with cap sleeves, that clung to her like a second skin. The neckline plunged downward, exposing cleavage that threatened to tumble out any minute, and slits on either side that revealed the length of her legs. She gasped and raised her arms to cover herself.

"What are you doing? How dare you!"

He chuckled and paused. Mia's outfit changed into a pair of jeans and a white T-shirt. She glared at him.

"It was what you wanted."

He was right. Feeling exposed in the dress, Mia had instantly wished to be in comfortable jeans and a T-shirt. How was that possible? A smile formed, and her shoulders relaxed. This must be some kind of dream, and a pretty good one at that.

Breathing in, Mia noticed that all around the garden and filling the field beyond were flowers in a riot of colors. There were roses, lilies, tulips, hyacinths, and many she didn't recognize. Color dotted the hillsides, and the fragrance they produced was sweet, intoxicating.

Mia stepped forward to study the ancient domed temple that lay before her, and wondered what treasures were hidden inside.

"Books," he said.

"What kind of books?" she asked.

"History books, spell books, and ones that are ancient and secret. The Temple of Ashwar houses them all."

"Where exactly am I? You said Annwn, but where is that?" Mia asked

"Mia, it's a highly guarded secret. Now come on. "

"May I just have a peek inside?" She walked closer to the temple.

"No…another time," he said, sighing heavily.

She took a step forward, and wavered. There were so many questions she wanted to ask, and looking at the temple, knew the answers might be inside. Mia was about to carry on, when she noticed how the boy ran a hand through his wayward hair, and his nostrils flared. He lifted his chin and stared at her. Mia sensed his exasperation or annoyance, but wasn't sure. However, when he lifted his square jaw and crossed his arms over his chest, it was definite sign of stubbornness, or maybe a challenge to defy him.

Seeing that pose, Mia decided he was definitely arrogant, and feared that any argument would be pointless. This was his world, not hers. A grin spread across his face as he towered over her. Even his dark intense eyes looked darker now, like liquid chocolate. Any desire to argue with him evaporated. He stood so close, his warm minty breath fanned over her cheeks. Mia's heart fluttered and she was embarrassed at her response. She didn't even know him… or did she? There was something knocking against her brain, as she studied every expression and movement he made with pure fascination. Her heart pounded in her chest as he lifted his hand and trailed a finger along her arm, setting her skin ablaze. Mia didn't resist as he lifted her chin upwards, meeting his penetrating gaze. She held her breath, waiting, as a purely wicked thought entered her head. Kiss me, she silently pleaded.

The boy lowered his head, so their lips were inches apart and stared at them. Needing to be closer, she pressed against him. His dark smoldering eyes flashed—but instead of giving Mia what she wanted, he stepped back and grabbed her hand.

"Come on, I want to take you flying."

Mia tightened her mouth, and tried to ignore his rejection as her cheeks burned even more than before.

"Not now," he said, softly. The boy clasped her hand and tugged her…upwards.

Mia's body lifted like a feather in the breeze. In seconds, they were flying among the white cumulus clouds. She giggled, and gasped, as she stared at the distance to the ground. His hand held hers tightly, pulling her onwards, and they glided above the tops of fir trees to fly level with the snow-capped mountains. A shiver ran across her body as she stared across at the never-ending sapphire-blue ocean, and Mia pictured herself falling from the sky.

Without thinking, Mia let go of his hand and dropped, plummeting toward the ground. Her arms flailed around, and she screamed. Out of the clouds, a strong arm clenched her wrist. He scowled, his face serious and focused on her.

"Be still. Do you really have so little faith in me? Don't look down, Mia. If you let the fear overtake you, then you'll be truly lost. You can do this, I know you can…"

Mia stared at him, unsure if his words held a hidden meaning or not, but she lifted her head and nodded. He released her. This time, she floated.

From up in the sky, she could see across Annwn—an immense island surrounded by an emerald sea. There were tall ice-capped mountains in the north, narrow gorges, impressive waterfalls to the east, mile upon mile of dark thick forests, fields of green pastures, multi-colored flowers, winged horses galloping for freedom and dolphins splashing in the ocean. At the heart of Annwn was a powerful-looking medieval castle built of white stone, with turrets at each of its four corners. All the surrounding houses were fashioned of similar stone, and the fields lay filled with corn and wheat. It was beautiful. The two friendly serpents drew level with them, and the boy eyed her with an eager grin.

"Are you game?"

He was right—she could do this, and she was no longer afraid. He lifted her hand towards his mouth kissing her fingers. Mia was mesmerized by his touch, and captured by his dark eyes which never left her face. Inside, she wondered why all her dreams couldn't be like this.

"All right, what do I have to do?"

Without warning, a monstrous fire-breathing dragon swooped in front of them. Upon the dragon's back sat a boy with long straw-colored hair, sharp blue eyes and a determined glare. The dragon roared and charged directly between them. Without thinking Mia screamed, and let go of the boys' hand suddenly hurtling towards the ground.

The wind surged around her, and the dragons' screeching rang in her ears. Out of the clouds, an arm ripped her out of the sky and hoisted her onto the back of the scaly gray and purple dragon. She thrashed out, kicking and screaming even biting the boy's hand. Instead of releasing her, though, his grip tightened, and his breath washed over her ears.

"Be still, or I'll do something far more dangerous."

Mia froze, willing herself to remain calm. She turned to steal a look at the boy, but soon turned away as he leered uncomfortably close to her face. There were no more words as the boy dug his feet into the dragon's underbelly and pulled sharply on the reins. The dragon howled and soared up into the sky. Where was the dark-haired boy?

Voices called to Mia once again, familiar voices, and everything shifted. The clouds broke apart and again Mia was freefalling. Everything slowed. The wind ceased. The colors faded, and it was dark once more.

Mia's eyelids fluttered open to a sea of faces, all staring at her. She sat up blinking and stared at the room. A large oak desk, framed awards for Best Diner littered the walls alongside pictures of her boss and the staff. She was back at the diner, in Sam's office.

"How are you feeling?" Sylvia's voice and frowning face told Mia she had given them quite a scare.

"How long was I out?" Mia touched her forehead, and forced her breathing to slow. She wasn't sure, how long she'd been asleep and didn't want to say more than she needed to.

"About twenty minutes. You scared me—well, us—half to death."

Mia gave a weak smile. Sylvia went on to explain about the storm and loss of power, but never once mentioned Mrs. Fielding, which was odd. Maybe, it was part of the dream. A rush of air entered the room as Sam appeared with his cell-phone plastered to his ear, his voice rough and yelling. He stopped talking as soon as he glanced at Mia.

"Thank god. I've been worried sick. I've been trying to get an ambulance, but with the storm, it's been crazy. How are you doing?" A muffled voice echoed in the background, and Sam lifted his phone.

"Yes, she's awake. Okay, finally—a bit bloody late, but all right." He clicked his phone off and strode toward her.

"They'll be here in two minutes. Sit down, you need to be checked over."

Mia rubbed the back of her head. Apart from feeling lightheaded, she was fine. Saving a life was amazing, and a first, even though no one remembered. Experiencing a vision as the event unfolded had never happened before, and slipping into the dream world was a rush, kind of wonderful and scary all rolled into one. The dream was over, but Mia shivered as if something momentous was about to begin.

Chapter Two

Back to school

A blast of *Fallen*, a new indie band, screeched from the radio on Mia's nightstand, and automatically her hand bashed against the mute button. Her head throbbed, and she wished more than anything that she could stay in her bed dreaming, but today was the first day of the new-school term. Mia still didn't understand why no one had mentioned what had happened with Mrs. Fielding. At the time, it seemed so real. Now she wondered if it happened at all. Was it all part of the dream? Since that night, dreams of the Otherworld and the dark, mesmerizing boy visited every night. All in all, the dreams left her restless and wanting.

Mia picked up her glasses and mentally checked off familiar landmarks—four white walls, a myriad of CDs, her converse sneakers dumped by her bed, black skinny jeans on the back of her swivel chair, mess everywhere, and posters of Johnny Depp.

Yep, definitely her messy room.

She tucked lose strands of her hair behind her ears. Real life sucked. A sudden burst of— what the hell—her latest ring tone, and she jumped out of bed. Only one person called her this early. *Danni*. The ringing sound stopped as Mia lifted her pillow. Nothing there.

Okay... She scrunched her eyes closed and pictured her phone. Walking around the room, she twisted her crystal pendant with her hand and stared at her desk where college booklets lay scattered. She paused, and smiled at a photograph of her friends. Last summer they'd created a band called Fusion. Now they were rehearsing every night, and it was the other reason she was tired. Blinking, she saw pictures flash in front of her. Each time she blinked a different picture appeared. She saw a small dimly-lit room, full of shadows, and filled with old books covered in dust.

Don't know what that's all about. As Mia blinked, an image of her room with clothes strewn across the floor and her desk appeared. Mia walked towards the desk, lifted and moved it away from the wall. There lay her phone, peeping out from under the curtain. Mia's talent for seeing lost items was cool, but it wasn't the only thing she saw. Her mother called her perceptive, and she'd take that any day over *freak*.

Many times she'd questioned why she was different, why she saw terrifying images of events that usually involved someone dying, when others couldn't. Over time, she had learned how to hide that part of herself that scared her the most.

Five minutes later, Mia was dressed in a pair of denim shorts, a white camisole, and loose Chambray shirt. She grabbed her bag, slung it over her shoulder, and walked out of the house. The cold air smacked against her skin and jolted her awake, whether she wanted it to or not. Walking past her glimmering Volkswagen beetle, she ran an admiring finger along its length—and then hurried away.

Danni, her closest friend, lived three houses down in a white saltbox, and it took all of thirty seconds to reach her front door. They were always swapping clothes and make-up, and painting each other's nails. Sharing almost everything—almost, because there were some things she couldn't share with anyone. Mia pushed Danni's front doorbell, and a loud *dingdong* burst into life, followed by a series of crashes, bangs, and loud swearing.

"I'm coming!" a high-pitched voice yelled through the door.

The door opened and a dainty pixie-like creature, bright and florescent, appeared, rubbing her knee.

"Are you okay?" Mia asked.

"Boys! You're so lucky you're an only child," she said. "They're *so* annoying."

Mia smiled. Danni's ebony hair was flicked out at the sides, and the ends were dyed a vibrant orange, which made it look as if it was on fire.

"What do you think?" Danni twirled around.

"I love it. You'll have to do mine. Why orange, though?" Mia said.

"For the fall," Danni said with a shrug.

Linking arms, they walked down the tree-lined street toward the high school. Mia pushed her glasses up, gave Danni a sideways glance, then looked around, shook her head, and ran her hand across her forehead. A sense of being watched drowned out Danni's lively chatter, and she glanced around, sure that someone was watching them, but the street was quiet and the roads empty. They walked through the school gates and across the parking lot. Cars were pulling in, and kids were milling around. The unsettling feeling disappeared, and Mia headed toward the modern two-storey brick building.

Danni nudged her. "Did you sort everything out with Alex?"

"Danni, we're friends, nothing more. Me and boys…it's just, well it's awkward. You know me. Ice princess. "She shoved her bag over her shoulder.

"Mia, come on. Alex is different. He cares about you." Danni touched her arm.

"It's me, not him. Seriously, the band stuff is fine. I just don't want anything else, okay?"

Mia let out a long sigh. It was easier to be distant than to risk anyone get close and then discovering that she was a freak. Anyway, no matter what she did, most kids thought she was plain weird and stayed away. And she was fine with that. Mia didn't have friends, not until Danni.

Lost in her thoughts, Mia stopped and glanced around, Alex was a thorn in her side. More than once he had tried to kiss her, but she'd pushed him away. It wasn't because he was unattractive. With his cropped blond hair and cool slate eyes, he was considered to be handsome by most and very talented. No, his looks didn't put her off. Mia didn't know how to explain, but whenever she was near a boy, a sinking emptiness consumed her. Her throat constricted and her heart would squeeze.

"I know he wants to do more than practice, that's what I know," Danni said, smirking.

Mia sighed, and stared at the ground. "I just think I'm better on my own." She lifted her gaze to stare at Danni.

"That's so sad, to be alone. What's that quote, it's better to have…" She smiled at Mia.

"'Tis better to have loved and lost than never to have loved at all.' Yes. Well, Tennyson was a man, and men don't feel pain the way we do."

She looked away. Maybe part of her reaction towards any boy was because of her parents. After all, she'd seen up close and personal how love ended badly for them, and if that wasn't enough of course there was the fact that she saw dead people, which would make anyone believe she was a mental case.

"Leave it, Danni. I'm just messed up," Mia said, staring at the ground and feeling her scars itch.

"No, you're not. You're special, quirky. Look, this is senior year, and you should have some fun. You know—love' em and leave' em." Danni squeezed her arm, and trudged up the steps before disappearing inside the school.

Mia stared as the door swung behind Danni. Her friendship with Danni was the best, but it was changing. At some point Danni would realize she was holding back, and their friendship would be over. Lately, Mia has sensed Danni was keeping secrets. Of course it was silly that she was so upset, because, deep down, she was keeping the biggest secret of them all. Mia took the steps two at a time, pushed through the double doors and stood in the main hallway of the school.

Kids converged and shoved against her. Around fourteen hundred students boisterously walked through the sun-filled hallways of North Littleton High. Their loud voices vibrated around the walls. Standing alone, she looked both ways but couldn't see Danni. Everything slowed to a stand-still. A tall dark-haired boy wandered passed and tingles of recognition raced through her mind pulling her toward him. She spun around searching, but everything was moving at full speed again. The boy had disappeared.

A tap on her shoulder made Mia jump. Alex appeared from nowhere. He grabbed her around the waist and planted a playful kiss on her lips.

"Alex, let me go." Mia wriggled, and then shoved against his chest. He grinned, and kissed her cheek, before he released her.

"It's only a kiss, and you looked kind of lost standing there all alone. I just wanted you to know that you're not…all alone." Alex let his arm hang around her shoulders, and coaxed her to walk alongside him. Sometimes he could say the nicest things, but he wasn't just after a kiss. Mia searched the crowds, as Alex chatted away.

"Mia, are you listening? You look miles away." Alex moved to stand in front of her and he gripped her shoulders.

"Sorry," she said, glancing around. His head was slanted to the side, and he was frowning. Mia forgot about the boy, stared up at Alex, and smiled. "I have a new song for tonight, for rehearsal."

His frown quickly turned into a beaming smile. He let go of her shoulders and moved forward.

"Great. For a minute, I thought you'd forgotten."

After they turned the corner, a tide of students stalled their progress. Mia caught a glimpse of Tyler, with his shaggy chestnut hair, standing sideways. His arm was raised up against the locker, and he leaned in toward a smiling Danni. Mia watched in fascination. Danni was oblivious to everyone, except Tyler. Mia wondered what words he was saying to make Danni's cheeks flush such a deep scarlet. Tyler lowered his head toward Danni, at which point Mia tore her gaze away, and she stared back at Alex. Filled with embarrassment, Mia tried to focus on him once again. It was ridiculous, she told herself. She didn't want a relationship, and had convinced herself that she couldn't trust anyone—and yet, watching her friend and Tyler, she was jealous. Mia flicked her hair over her shoulders and tapped Alex's arm.

"I didn't forget. See you later at lunch."

Alex paused for a second before nodding and moving away. She stuffed her bag in the locker and slammed the door shut. She stole another glance over at Danni, and guessed that whatever was going on with her had to do with Tyler.

Mia walked into her first class, which was biology with Mr. Brandish. Mia sat down, and stared at her ghostly reflection in the window.

Cheer up, you're not alone.

Mia swiveled around, smiled, and stared at Mike and Lisa, who gave her a blank look and carried on talking to each other. The deep soothing voice she'd heard made her pulse race, and heat spread throughout her body. She bit her lip. How could she hear that voice in her head, and whom did it belong to?

Soon, very soon.

Mia inhaled sharply as she searched the faces in the classroom, but everyone was chatting. What on earth was going on? Had she totally flipped? Was this some kind of nervous breakdown? Had she hit her head, and this was all part of a dream? For a moment, in the corridor earlier, she could have sworn a boy passed her that she knew—and now this.

Danni bounced in and launched herself into the seat next to her. Right then, Mia decided to tell Danni about the dreams, even if she ended up thinking Mia was crazy. Maybe she was, but she couldn't keep it bottled up any longer.

"You all right? You look whiter than Miss Carmela's teeth."

Mia stared at her friend. "Did you say something before?" she asked.

Danni opened her textbook. "No. Did I miss something?" She flicked through the pages, and raised her head to find Mr. Brandish glaring at her.

"Glad you could join us, Miss Kaya," he growled.

"Sorry, sir," Danni said. She peered sideways at Mia and mouthed the words, *talk later*.

Mia nodded, quickly scribbling a message on a piece of paper which she passed over to Danni. *Meet in the garden by the cafeteria at lunch. Have something important to discuss.*

Danni nodded.

As soon as the class ended, Mia and Danni went their separate ways and the rest of the morning dragged. Mia couldn't focus. Her mind wandered over the scene in the hallway and then the voice in her head. Was the boy in the hallway the voice in her head? She didn't know what to think.

As soon as the bell rang for lunch, Mia leapt out of her chair and headed for the garden. As she pushed through the double doors that led to the outdoor pavilion, her hands shook and her heart sprinted. Several kids sat on benches together, chatting away, their laughter breaking her thoughts. She glided past, seeking Danni. Looking about, she absentmindedly crashed into an impenetrable wall of muscle and heat. Mia snapped her head around, brushing her nose and mouth against the soft cotton of a boy's T-shirt. A round of applause and giggles sounded in the background.

"I'm sorry," she said as she pushed her glasses back up her nose and stepped back. Cursing her clumsy feet, she raised her head to stare up at her victim. The sunlight blinded her, and she dropped her head to gaze at a pair of scuffed black boots. The boy coughed, dragging her stare upwards as she studied his faded blue jeans and black T-shirt. Goose-bumps broke out along her arms, and her shoulders stiffened. At five feet six she was about average in height, but the boy was at least a head taller, which forced her to tilt her head back to capture a view of his face.

Staring at him for a second, she couldn't think or do anything else. Deep dark eyes stared back at her, and she swayed. Two strong arms reached out and grabbed hers. Mia opened her mouth to speak, but couldn't utter a single word. *Impossible,* her mind said as her legs trembled and threatened to give way. Feeling weak, she leaned into the warm body that held her, grateful she hadn't collapsed on the ground. Any minute now, she expected the scenery to change—but it didn't, and they were at her school. Mia dangled like a puppet, with no willpower at all. All the while, his dark eyes roamed up and down her body.

The boy pulled his mouth into a tight line, and his eyebrows dipped as if he was weighing up something in his mind, and then he stared back at her. The corner of his mouth lifted into a half-smile, but he didn't speak. The world around them paused. His warm breath touched her cheeks, and Mia closed her eyes. *Impossible. He cannot be real. Take a deep breath, and in a minute he'll be gone.* Slowly, she opened her eyes. He stood there, shoulders back, tall, menacing, and glaring at her.

Mia glanced toward the group of kids, and then back at the boy. He was breathtaking, gorgeous. Was he the boy from her dreams? What was his name? His black-as-coal hair was the same, only shorter. The rich earth-brown eyes, that seemed to penetrate her every thought, were the same. He pouted and then spread his lips into a lazy smile. Mia tried to concentrate, but under his scrutiny found it impossible, and looked away. Her gaze drifted down toward their hands as he laced his fingers with hers, and his skin felt rough as it smoothed over hers. Watching their fingers touch, she saw a bright white light spark like a flame between them, Mia gasped and tried to pull away. *What the hell?*

She snatched her hand back and rubbed it. Waves of recognition pummeled her mind, and she sucked in the air around her, needing oxygen. Stepping back, she wanted to run, but instead moved closer and once again stared at his face. Mia was drawn to him like a magnet, and wondered if he'd cast some kind of spell on her. She dug her nails into her hand and cried out. This was no dream. This was real. A wave of déjà vu engulfed her, and she shivered.

You're not real. You're not real. Just go away.

Once again, she closed her eyes. There was a series of fake coughs, and a splutter of laughter. Mia opened her eyes and stood there with her hands on her hips, ready to lash out. As if sensing her thoughts, the boy frowned and stepped back.

Just you try it.

A scream filled her throat, and she bit it back. How did he know she'd wanted to kick him? It had been an idea, one set to test if he was real, not some figment of her imagination.

Mia…I'm not a dream.

His words echoed inside her head, and as Mia looked around she saw that the only one that could hear them was her. Chills cascaded down her back and she shivered. He was the same magical, bewitching boy who dominated her dreams.

"What did you just say?" she said.

I didn't say a word.

His dark irises flickered with a golden flame as he glared at her. The words swirled around inside her head.

I didn't say a word.

* * * *

Reaching out to Mia was as natural as breathing air. However, Ryder knew it was a mistake the minute he sensed her reaction.

Fear.

Damn, his impulsiveness. He wished he was patient, and that he'd chosen somewhere private. In his defence, seeing her earlier, and being this close, made reaching out impossible to resist. She was a walking hazard, and appeared completely ignorant of the fact. Seeing her in the hallway this morning and without thinking, he stopped time wanting to say hello only to have to backtrack quickly before anyone noticed. However, afterwards, he couldn't stop himself from dipping inside her thoughts, which were swamped with confusion and loneliness. That was his undoing and the reason he was here. *Deep breath and be smart,* he told himself.

Since the end of summer, Ryder's impatience reached the boiling point. All his instincts told him that Mia was close, but he wasn't a hundred percent certain until last week at the diner that she was in fact his Mia. That night was a total disaster. What was she thinking? At the diner, he knew what she was about to do, and tried to intervene, to stop her, but was too late.

Eventually, after Mia saved the elderly lady, in full view of everyone, he was forced to stop time and clear up her mess, making it seem like nothing had taken place.

Mia's magic glowed around her like a halo as she worked to save a life, exposing herself to everyone, and he couldn't simply stand by. Watching her now, he frowned. Since, that night he stayed near, like a shadow, watching her every move in case he needed to intervene again. He wanted to awaken her fully, but she was constantly surrounded by either Danni or that idiot Alex, which left him no choice. Ryder dipped inside her mind and listened to her thoughts. Ryder knew she was scared and her emotions ran from panic, to disbelief, and terror.

His gaze wandered over her heart-shaped face as milky white as a lily, and wide blue-violet eyes that flashed wildly. It was Mia, and yet it wasn't. This Mia was distant and cold. She certainly wasn't standing there with arms wide open. What had he expected? He wasn't really sure, but after discovering her flaunting her magic in public, risking exposure, he was shaken to the core and at this point acting equally reckless. He was desperate. Staring at her, he feared his touch at the diner wasn't enough. She didn't believe he was real. Why was she so scared?

The rate and rhythm of her beating heart was frenzied and wild. Adrenaline raced through her veins ready to fight or flee. A deep laugh exploded as he realized *he* was the source of her fear. She was terrified of him. Her fear was like a block of steel against the awakening. Emrys had said it would be like an electric charge into her brain, and it would release her past.

Damn it Mia, let me in.

Taking a deep breath, he cursed and forced himself to be still, listening instead to Mia's thoughts.

It can't be possible, he's a dream. Nothing that looks that good can be real. Great, maybe I don't really have all that homework.

Ryder stepped closer, unable to stop the smile that spread across his lips at her words.

Jeez, I think I've totally flipped.

He searched around. Maybe, he should just whisk her away. Deciding that was the best option, he moved to grab her only to stop. He couldn't just take her. What if she started screaming? She was already terrified, and if she used magic in public again it would only cause problems for them both. They weren't supposed to use their magic here firstly, and secondly, he already sensed danger surrounding Mia. Exposing themselves in such a way would be irresponsible, and way beyond reckless. No, he would have to find another way of awakening her. He sighed and started to walk away.

"You, it's you…" He only moved several steps, but as her words registered he turned and walked back.

"Mia, please keep your voice lowered. Not everyone needs to know what passes between us," he said, raising his eyebrows. Mia stared, open-mouthed, and he moved closer.

"I know you don't believe I'm real, so go on and pinch me if you like." He lowered his voice to a mere whisper. Licking her lips, she stared at his raised arm and moved her hand to touch him. Mia wanted to test his theory, but stopped midway. Instead of touching him, she backed away, withdrawing her arm. Ryder touched her mind with his, and realized that even the thought of touching him terrified her.

At the diner, his touch must have unlocked something. He dipped into her mind again, and could see blurry images and a roller coaster ride of emotions, from cold shock to warm happiness, and then back to complete disbelief. He raked his hand through his hair. When his hand had touched hers at the diner, he'd sensed danger all around her. Staring at her wide eyes and unyielding mouth, Ryder worried over how to convince her that he wasn't the cause, that he was here to help.

"Mia, look at me. I won't hurt you." He inched closer and lowered his head.

Long black lashes fanned her eyes."I'm not afraid of you."

Her eyes reminded him of a rabbit caught in a trap. She was lying.

"Prove it," he said lifting his chin.

"I don't need to prove anything. I've gotta go." She clamped her arms around herself and started to walk away. This was crazy, and as he watched her stroll away he berated himself for being impatient, and knew he couldn't let her go. Ryder marched towards her, grabbed her arm and pulled her back to face him.

"Damn it Mia, it's not that simple. It isn't just about us. There are others. Things have changed, and I need to talk to you alone."

She looked down at his hand, and then up at his face.

"Alone? You're crazy. I wouldn't go anywhere with you—alone. Let go of my arm, or I'll scream." She yanked her arm, and he let go.

"Ignoring me isn't the answer…" He bit his lip. "The Darkshadows are watching you. They were at the diner that day, and started the storm. They're meddling with the humans, I don't know why, but they saw you. They saw what you did. Mia, you need to remember." Ryder knew as soon as the words left his mouth that he had said too much. He backed away and wiped his mouth, glancing around to see if anyone was watching. His words hadn't drawn any attention, but he could see Danni walking over.

Ryder gazed at Mia. "Later—" He walked away without glancing back.

Mia stood dumbstruck, watching the boy's retreating figure, certain he would simply vanish into a puff of smoke, *but he didn't.* What did he mean, the Darkshadows were watching her and there were others? Who the hell were the Darkshadows? She was going to be sick, and swallowed to settle the queasy sensation that rose inside her. Cold tingles erupted over her skin as she stared at his broad shoulders. When she'd bumped into him earlier, he was all muscle and warmth. How was that possible if he was a figment of her imagination?

"Hi, sorry I'm late. What's so important that we had to skip lunch? Mia, what's going on?" Danni asked.

Mia looked at Danni, "I'm going to be sick."

Danni jumped quickly out of the way as Mia vomited on the ground. Tiny white spots floated, and the world spun around. Shivers exploded throughout her body. A fire was raging inside her, and all she wanted to do was sleep. Muted voices filled her ears, and strong arms lifted her off the ground. In one full sweep, she was hoisted through the air as if she weighed no more than a grain of sand. She flopped against taut muscle, but a fiery heat pulsed through her body. Mia struggled against strong arms wanting to feel cool and free.

"Too hot, I'm hot, I need…" She pulled at her top, revealing her belly button. A hand caught her wrists together and she was imprisoned against a steel chest. Mia couldn't move.

"I know you're *hot*, but not in front of everyone, Mia." A familiar male voice chuckled. The minute Mia heard his voice, her body responded, jerking forward.

"Put me down. I feel better now."

Still his arms held her, and he rushed toward the doors. Her stomach heaved, and her body was melting as the fire inside consumed her. Using all the strength she had left, she dug her elbow into his ribs and heard him groan.

"Put me down! I don't need your help." Mia forced her eyes to open, but the bright light hurt. He was speaking, and the words came in gentle waves washing over her. She couldn't resist, and her head flopped back against him. She could hear them talking away as if she was invisible, and like they'd known each other forever. Which meant Danni could see him? Mia opened her eyes and forced her legs down. Finally, he gave up his hold on her. Mia stood on her shaky legs, and grabbed Danni's arms for support.

"Look, thanks for helping. What's your name, by the way?"

He walked with them and held the doors open, as they walked through and into the school.

"Robert. Robert Mathews." He kept on walking alongside them, and Mia staggered.

"I really think you need the nurse, before you collapse, Mia," Danni said.

"Your friend is right. Let me help." He moved in closer, and Mia almost screamed. Her head throbbed as she tried to understand what was happening. Nothing made any sense to her. His voice was hypnotic and his broody stare reached inside her making her long to be in his arms. The boy stared at her and she shook her head violently.

Please don't.

His eyebrows arched, and his arms dropped to his side. Mia blinked. *Did he hear me?* Mia tore her gaze away. Things were as far from normal as possible. Her visions were back, and now she was staring right into the face that appeared every night in her dreams. Everything, inside her mind screamed, *impossible*. Yet here he was, laughing. His touch was warm and electrifying. And, now he had a name. *Robert Mathews.* Saying, his name made him real, and their eyes met. He looked exactly like the boy from her dreams, whose name she couldn't remember. Why was that? And why could she hear his voice in her head? Wave upon wave of nausea rose up to greet her, but—nurses, doctors, needles, hospitals—there was no way she was going to any of them, even though a multitude of pictures flashed in front of her, and she clamped her eyes shut.

"I need the restroom, please."

You're so damn stubborn. You never change.

Chapter Three

The Homecoming dance

Mia slept for the next couple of days, as her body burned and raged with a mysterious virus. By the second day, she was feeling much better. In fact, she was feeling wonderful and tried to understand her encounter at school with the boy from her dreams, with little success. She suspected that this boy, *Robert,* was behind her illness. His touch elicited a response and it set her blood on fire. Since that day in school, her dreams were more vivid, like memories, which scared her even more.

Robert Mathews, a simple name, and it played over and over inside her mind. When he stared at her, it was as if he knew exactly what she was thinking. She shivered at the thought that he knew things about her which even *she* didn't know or understand, but his open stare seemed to tell her exactly that. Staring into his eyes was both mesmerizing and terrifying. Mia shook her head, dismissing the idea that this Robert Mathews and the boy from her dreams were one and the same. Just because they could be twins didn't mean that they were. Maybe there was a tiny part of her that wished him to be, but that was impossible.

Mia returned to school on Wednesday, and for the next two days everything was normal. Despite the fact that at every corner she expected to bump into *him,* she didn't. It was Friday evening before Mia caught sight of the elusive Robert Mathews again.

She was sat in Danni's car driving to the high school, humming the notes of her song for tonight's show. It was Fusion's first true performance, in front of their peers at the homecoming dance. Oddly enough, in between singing the words of her songs, images of Robert Mathews kept popping up. Any belief that he was merely part of her dream was shattered by Danni, as she recounted events of his sightings on the football field and around the school. Mia neither acknowledged, nor welcomed this information.

Sucking on her lower lip, Mia desperately needed to put everything that happened over the last couple of weeks behind her. Tonight was important, and not just for her, but for the band. As she stepped out of the car, it was pitch black and a bone-chilling breeze whipped around them. The parking lot overflowed with vehicles, and dark figures raced toward the stadium. The high school football team was playing. Bright white lights illuminated the sky, and the music vibrated through the amplifiers.

"You nervous at all?" Danni called over the bumper of the car as she climbed out and slammed the door shut.

"A little. What about you?" Mia walked around and moved in step with Danni.

"Piece of cake. How are you and Alex?" Danni grabbed Mia's arm and hugged in close to her as they climbed the steps in the school. There was a loud cheer, and they both looked back toward the stadium.

"Sounds like we're winning."

"Hope so. Danni, there is no me-and-Alex. You know that. To be honest, I'm thinking of quitting the band. Don't be mad. It's just that if I tell Alex how I feel he's going to hate me, and if I stay in the band with him I'm going to end up hating myself." They pushed through the double doors, and a fresh blast of rock music greeted them.

"Be straight with the guy," Danni advised. "And tell him to back off, or you'll leave. I bet he'll back off. He doesn't want you to leave the band."

"I will, just not tonight."

Danni slipped her arm back through Mia's, and they strolled down the hall. Bright autumnal colored lanterns hung around the borders of the hall, and huge banners were being secured into place welcoming the home team. Intermittent bangs came from the drums and the electric guitar screeched around the hall.

"One-two-three can you hear me, one-two-three can you hear me, testing," a male voice repeated. Mia's stomach lurched and she sucked on her lower lip.

"Wow, this is giving me the chills. This makes it real. I hope I don't snap a wire or lose my place," Danni said. They walked over to the stage, left Danni's violin, and checked the microphones. Evan, the drummer, was setting up the amplifiers.

"Watch the leads and don't pull anything out, okay?" He winked.

"Sure. Where are the boys?" Danni asked, looking at the empty hall.

"Hmmm, checking the lights with the stage crew, just making sure everything's ready. Any nerves yet?"

"A bit, aren't you?" Danni said.

"Nope. Been waiting for this for a long time. We've practiced so much, if we're not ready now, we'll never be."

Evan pulled out his drumsticks from his back pocket, and strode over to the drums. Mia smiled. It was now or never. Low in the center of her abdomen a flutter of butterflies started to rise, and she shivered. Kids started to filter in, and the lights dimmed. The DJ was set up on the side of the stage. He nodded in their direction, put his headphones on, and his body swayed back and forth.

"Just to get you all in the mood here's 'Empire State of Mind' by Jay Z and Alicia Keys."

Heads nodded. People embraced each other and laughed, as they entered. Music filled the hall and slowly people began to dance. The room swirled around Mia, even though both her feet were planted firmly on the ground. Were they really ready to perform in front of their friends? Staring at the swarms of people, Mia felt her heart accelerate. All the noise and chatter faded into the distance. Her mouth went dry and she couldn't speak. Instead she focused on Danni's voice.

"Mia, let's go and find the boys. It's starting to get busy. You look great tonight, by the way, but I thought you were going to try the lenses instead."

Mia looked down at her tightly fitted black T-shirt, denim shorts, and black sparkly tights. Around her waist was a black leather belt with a vintage silver buckle, and to complete the outfit she wore her comfortable converse sneakers.

"Next time. I need to get used to them, and I didn't want my eyes to be watering on stage. You look amazing too, and Danni, thanks for being such a great friend."

Absent-mindedly, she pushed her hand through her hair and glanced at Danni's sleeveless red sequined tank-top and three-quarter length black leggings with black ballet pumps. She was dazzling with streaks of red coloring her hair and matching her top.

They hugged, and walked to the back of the hall in search of Alex. People moved around them smiling and chatting. Mia stopped and stared at the crowd as a familiar odor pirouetted around her, and she froze. She moved her head slightly and took a deep breath.

Scanning faces, Mia wouldn't acknowledge who she was searching for, but there was only one face emblazoned on her mind. Her shoulders tensed, as her gaze swept the crowd, and cold air brushed against Mia's shoulders. He was here. Her heart lurched and then sped like a runaway train. She wanted to escape, to run away. Before she could move one foot in front of the other, the deep lilt of his voice reached her. It was pleasant, almost lyrical. His voice commanded attention and inadvertently she turned gazing at him.

Robert stood tall, with his shoulders back. A playful smile lifted the corners of his mouth. His hair was wet and looked a bluish black. Michael and Casey, his teammates, surrounded him, along with several very pretty cheerleaders. From their laughter, Mia assumed they'd won tonight's game. Fascinated by the scene, Mia watched as Robert joked around with the girls and frowned as they stared at him with obvious adoration.

Mia's shoulder's tensed as a need for Roberts's undivided attention swamped her and she couldn't move as her feet stuck like roots in the ground. Her cheeks flamed and she sank sharp teeth into her lower lip until it hurt. For a millisecond, Mia looked away, but couldn't resist another glance in his direction. His strong jaw tilted upwards as he laughed with ease, and his hooded dark eyes were ever watchful of the crowd. She was certain that very little, if anything, scared him.

Her gaze followed him as he mingled and was jostled by the crowds, totally oblivious to her interest, which allowed her free rein to study him. Robert moved with confidence, and when his hair flopped into his eyes, he ran his hand through it to settle it back into place, laughing at some girl's comment. Mia watched and licked her lips. Robert lifted his head, turned and gazed straight at her. The corner of his mouth lifted into a full smirk letting her know he was aware of her perusal of him. Mia clamped her mouth shut and turned away. *Damn him.*

Her cheeks burned with mortification at being caught, and even though she turned away from him, Mia could feel his eyes upon her. Mia forced herself not to turn around.

* * * *

Ryder watched her with weary frustration. His gaze washed over her waif-like features as she stood with shoulders back, proud, and beautiful, yet unaware of how she appeared to the world.

Innocent. Shy. Provocative.

Such an alluring mix, and she was *his,* even if she didn't realize that yet. He knew that she wasn't as unaffected by his presence as she pretended. Even now, he could hear her heart beating thunderously. It wasn't just fear that made it soar. Her eyes flared with attraction toward him. Watching that, Ryder almost reached out to her, again. Only, he knew it would be a huge mistake.

Too public. Too many prying eyes.

Her silky hair flew around her shoulders as she turned away, leaving him to stare at her long auburn tresses, and he imagined his fingers entwined in her locks. To ignore him was playing with fire. Ryder pushed his thoughts into her reluctant mind, willing her to listen to him and turn around, but he came up against an impenetrable wall. She was deliberately ignoring him, which made him smile. Maybe it wouldn't be so hard after all. In time, she would accept him—because after all, they were the same. Until then, if she insisted on goading him with these silly games, he was going to give her a reminder of who she was.

The dance hall was overflowing with teenagers striking poses and dancing to the music. Alex stood next to Mia, dressed in a blue plaid shirt and dark jeans. He whispered into her ear, and she nodded. Smiling, he lifted her hand, and led her into a sea of dancers.

Ryder wasn't going to stand idly by and let this human interfered with Mia. The music changed to a slow beat, and Ryder forced the image of them holding each other out of his head. He concentrated his thoughts on Mia, manipulating his fire elements to send a blazing heat directly into the palms of her hands.

Let's see what she makes of that.

As the swarm of dancers moved, he caught a glimpse, as Alex gently spun her around the dance floor and reeled her in close against his chest. Mia's face twisted in pain. Alex lowered his head close to her face. Ryder wanted to charge right over, but stopped as Mia's deep labored breaths flooded him. Her heart was beating way too fast.

Stop what you're doing and I'll make it go away.

There was silence, but Ryder saw her pull her hands away from Alex. Ryder heard her curse, and then his hands burned with a scorching heat. Clenching his fists, he frowned and his gaze flew toward her. Was she playing with him, or was this a side effect of their bond with one another? He wasn't sure. He hadn't meant it to be so painful, just a warning. Her beautiful violet eyes rested on him. Even when she was angry, she was beautiful. Full pink lips pouted, as she glared at him. Although, her heart slowed, he tasted her anger—and it was aimed at him.

Now, now.

An excruciating stabbing sensation penetrated deep in his belly, and he doubled over, his hand clutching his side.

"Robert what's wrong?" Cindy, one of the cheerleaders said. She laid her arm along his shoulder and bent to check.

"Cramp. I'm fine." He shook his head and waved her away. As Ryder looked up, he found Mia staring directly at him. The white glow of the disco ball highlighted her face and her eyes were the darkest shade of purple possible. Inside her head swirled confusion and regret.

Did I do that?

The pain vanished. His mouth spread into a knowing grin and he nodded.

You don't know your own strength.

For a second, there was nothing. Then she gasped, and her sweet, stubborn voice spoke clearly into his mind. Each word deliberately enunciated.

Leave. Me. The. Hell. Alone.

He took a deep breath.

Afraid I can't do that.

Ryder chuckled as she spun around, her hair flying on the breeze, and stomped away. Alex followed close behind, unaware of what had happened. Ryder moved with lightning speed trailing their footsteps. Mia climbed up the steps to the back of the stage. Fusion was about to perform. The crowd around him grew, but he positioned himself in the center to make sure that she would see him, and waited. Principal Grayson appeared from behind the long velvet drapes.

"Finally, ladies and gentlemen, please give a very warm welcome to our very own senior group called, Fusion, singing their debut song, 'Stargazing'."

With that, there was a cacophony of deafening screams and stomping of feet. The curtains swished opened, and for a moment there was silence, until Danni raised her right arm to run her bow across the violin. Tyler and Alex joined in, swinging their electric guitars back and forth strumming out the notes. Evan came in next, whipping it all together with his rhythmic thrashing on his drums.

The music began to pulsate around the hall, and the crowd moved to the haunting rhythm. Mia swayed to the sound. On stage she let go of her inhibitions, singing with all her heart and soul. Her voice reached out to the crowd, soft and yet powerful. Singing words of love. Mia stared into the abyss that was the audience. She smiled, and twirled around on stage. Ryder watched, completely entranced. On stage, she was unafraid, confident. Breaking into her thoughts, he discovered she was using all her strength to avoid looking at him.

Ryder smiled, sensing her pulling to look anywhere but in his direction. The more she tried to avoid his gaze, the more he willed her to face him. The tug of war didn't last long. Mia turned. Her gaze fell upon him, and then she was singing to him alone. She was captivating, and cast a spell over everyone who listened. Holding the microphone tightly in her right hand, she twisted, and glided, across the stage. Her left arm rose way up in the air. Her body danced to the beat of the song, beckoning for everyone to join in with the chorus. The words spoke about the power of true love. Under her own volition, she faced Ryder and brought the song to its conclusion. The music slowed its pace, and once again the violin intermingled with her voice.

"One life, one love, for always."

She closed her eyes and bent forward to say thank-you to the crowd. There was an outbreak of wild clapping and whistles. Mia straightened and watched the crowd. She didn't appear to be nervous at all. She fell apart and was jumpy in his company, but on stage she was like the Mia he once knew very well. The clapping and yelling carried on, until the curtains finally closed. Ryder stole away from the front and moved to the back of the stage, where he watched Mia with her friends.

"Dude, that was awesome," Tyler said.

"Amazing! That's the best we've ever sounded," Evan said.

Alex walked toward Mia, cupped her face with his hand and tilted it, so he could kiss her lips. He stroked her cheek as their lips touched. Instantly, she drew in a deep breath and stepped back. Alex stared at her as she moved away. Hidden by the curtain, Ryder watched and listened, waiting for a chance to speak with Mia.

"I couldn't take my eyes off you. You were amazing," Alex said. His hand moved to grip hers, not letting go of his hold on her. "You were all fantastic," he added, looking around at the others.

Principal Grayson appeared. "What a wonderful performance! Well done, everyone. It was a lovely song, and you have a beautiful voice, Mia. I'm looking for a band to play at the Thanksgiving benefit. Would you like to come back?"

"Oh yes, yes, yes!" Alex said.

Everyone nodded, and Alex launched into a discussion about more rehearsals. After that, Danni and the boys wandered off to thank the technicians. Mia looked around the now empty stage, and walked over the side and picked up her gray leather jacket. Ryder walked out from the shadows and stood behind her. He touched her arm and she jumped.

"Stop doing that! You're giving me the creeps."

He inhaled a subtle scent of roses, and laughed, "You've bewitched me, and I can't stay away." Instead of pulling away, she remained by his side. At least this was an improvement on her being sick.

"About the other day—" he said.

"There's nothing to say. I'm fine now." Her eyelids fluttered, and she looked away.

"Really…nothing. What about tonight in the hall?" He pulled up her hand, and turned it over. Raising his head, they both stared at one another. She bit her lip but stayed silent.

"Nothing to say?" He shrugged.

Mia was anything but fine. Ryder could hear the unsteady rhythm of her heart echo through his mind. He was aware of the rapid escalation, that his presence caused her. Sensing her fluctuating emotions of fear and delight, he smiled. She had every right to be angry with him, but she didn't look angry. He didn't mean to hurt her, but watching her dance with Alex, with her body close up against his, he couldn't stop himself. He tucked a stray strand of hair behind her ear. "I'm sorry. I shouldn't have hurt you like that. It was stupid. I was being stupid."

Damn this human world. He'd never experienced jealously, not really, and had certainly never lost control before. He was trapped in this confusing world, because of her, and she was prancing around acting as if he didn't exist—flirting, with a boy she didn't really care for. Part of him justified his display of impatience, although seeing and feeling her pain was another thing. In hurting Mia, he was only hurting himself.

But Mia had reacted with her own magic. Feeling the pain had been worth it to catch a glimmer of who she really was, even if she didn't fully realize it. That would be easily solved, and soon.

"Mia, we need to talk, don't you think?" he said, moving closer. "I can help you, Mia. I'll answer all your questions," he said, whispering the words against her hair.

"Why did you burn my hands, and how?" she said, loudly.

"You had them on *him*," he said. He nodded, and stood back a little. His stare reached beyond her shoulder and footsteps announced that they were no longer alone.

Not here, but we need to talk!

She heard his rushed, frustrated words and nodded.

"What's up, Mathews?" Alex said.

Ryder bit his tongue, and tried to stay calm. He'd already let his emotions get the better of him with Mia. He didn't want to start a fight with Alex, unless he had no choice. Ryder glanced toward Mia, and removed his hand. He shook his head and smiled.

"Sorry." He smirked and faced Mia," You sounded amazing up there. I wanted you to know that."

She stared over at Alex, and then her eyes settled on Ryder's face. "Thanks." In a flash Alex was beside her, and he draped his arm on her shoulders in a possessive gesture.

"You belong up there. You know that, right?" Alex said

There was an awkward pause. Ryder knew he should leave, and turned to walk away just as a pretty blond girl came running in, calling for him.

"There you are! Come on. Everyone's leaving and going to Mike's." The girl tugged on Ryder's arm. "Hi, you were all really great tonight," she said with a smile.

Ryder and the girl turned away and left, but he continued to listen to their conversation.

"Do you know him?" Alex said to Mia.

"Not exactly, I crashed into him," she said.

"Well, sweetie you made an impression," Danni said.

"What do you *mean*?" Alex said, scowling at Danni.

"Oh come on, it's late. Stop acting all cave-man, will you? You'll get your share of groupies, I'm sure," she said laughing.

"Yeah? Like, come on, everyone knows you two are together. The guy's a jerk," Tyler added. Mia headed toward the exit. Everyone had made up their minds about her and Alex.

Alex thinks he has a chance with you.

She stopped, and then carried on, leaving the others behind.

Get out of my head, you're impossible. They're right, you're a real jerk. Stop intruding in my thoughts and leave me alone. You're spoiling a magical night.

"Whoa, slow down, wait for me," Alex said.

Mia looked away and kept walking.

You've got that wrong. You're magical, Mia, not the night. Sweet dreams.

Chapter Four

Mia stood in the cobbled courtyard, staring with a faraway look into the water fountain. She gazed at her reflection in the water, which showed a young sad woman. Her tears dropped, causing tiny ripples, and the water swirled around like a tiny tornado. She watched, enthralled, and eventually the water grew still as glass. Across the flat surface, scenes replayed like headlines from the global news.

> *VOLCANO ERUPTS KILLING HUNDREDS: IS THIS THE BEGINNING OF THE END? PESTICIDES GENETICALLY ALTER FOOD AFFECTING THE HEALTH OF MILLIONS. INCREASING TENSIONS IN MIDDLE EAST AS OIL RESERVES DECLINE DRAMATICALLY. DIVORCE RATES HIGHEST EVER. TEENAGE PREGNANCY ON THE RISE. TSUMAMI CAUSES WORLDWIDE CHAOS. STOCK MARKETS COLLAPSE. MALE INFERTILITY IS CAUSING GRAVE CONCERN ACROSS THE GLOBE.*

Each scene told a story. Tears fell down her cheeks and her heart ached. She turned her head, and there stood Ryder. His eyes watched her with a hooded gaze, and he was frowning. Within seconds, he moved by her side and wiped away her tears with his hand.

"Mia, you must rest. These events are yet to pass, and some may never occur. You cannot do anymore than you already have. We've made our decision. Find comfort in that, at least."

He draped his arm along her shoulders and led her toward a wooden bench where Emrys sat. Ryder motioned for her to sit. Emrys' smiled and held Mia's hand. The walled garden was delightful and warm, but today Mia was chilled with unease.

"Ryder is right. I will help all I can, but even I cannot know beyond a shadow of doubt what will happen." Emrys was one of the Wise Elders, a group of highly respected wizards responsible for all the laws in Annwn. He was also their dearest friend. When he spoke, the deep lines etched across his face, and forehead grew. No one knew exactly how old Emrys was. Seated alongside him, Mia was dwarfed in comparison to his size. His mostly-white hair was neatly tied away from his face, and a long ponytail fell down his back.

"Each couple's challenge is different. The fact that your visions call you into the mortal world is indeed rare. The Elders worry that your existence in their world will endanger us again, but they realize we face an uncertain future and this venture maybe our only answer. I believe this is your destiny, but never, lose sight of the reason you're there." Mia listened to Emrys and silently nodded.

"Do not give in to the ways of the mortal world. It's full of lies, war, selfishness, promiscuity, greed, hatred, and evil. There will be many temptations, and their way is not ours. Although you will be mortal, you are a child of Annwn. The laws of our world were created to safeguard our existence. Humans diluted our bloodline, and the Elders created the law of the promise to ensure that only strongest matches were allowed—strong in love and magic, to ensure that magic always continued. Remember your promise to one another." Emrys placed something small into her hand.

Mia stared in fascination. In the palm of her hand lay a necklace made of silver. A clear crystal in the shape of a flower dropped from the center of the chain. As the sun shone against it, a rainbow of colors sparkled. It was beautiful.

"Love is infinite. Wear this. It has many purposes which will be revealed over time and acquaintance." He kissed her head and stood, casting his shadow over her, and walked away. Ryder took the necklace from Mia and placed it around her neck. It was cold against her skin, and she shivered. Mia watched him as he stepped back and admired the pendant. A tremor of awareness raced through her body and mind.

"Will our love survive in the human world?" Mia asked.

Ryder lifted her chin with his hand and Mia stared into his dark eyes.

"There is nothing you could do to stop me loving you. What about you? Will you still love me as a human?" Mia stared at his serious expression, watching his dark eyes flicker with a golden light.

"Only you."

Mia blinked awake, stared at the ceiling in her bedroom, and jolted forward, now wide awake. The dream faded as she pulled up her necklace and stared at the shiny crystal. The necklace was her only clue to her real parents. After she was abandoned as a baby, the necklace was found in an envelope. There was a note with a few details, but nothing that explained why she was left. Now that necklace was in her dreams, alongside a boy called Ryder. She blinked as the crystal flower sparkled.

* * * *

It was a wet and gloomy start to Monday as Mia walked through the corridors of school, brooding over her dream. Images of her necklace were interwoven with the dream, along with the promise to love this boy called Ryder. Although there were no fire-breathing dragons or serpents, this felt like a memory. Mia swallowed and looked around, feeling on edge as she remembered Robert Mathews' parting words from Friday's concert.

You're magical Mia, not the night.

She stifled a laugh. Magic? Was he being serious, or was this some kind of plot to expose her and tease her? Turning her small hands over and over, she bit her lip and stared at them. True, she wasn't like everyone else—that much she knew—but magic? Really! There was no such thing as magic. Walking down the corridors in school, she was here in body only as her mind was somewhere else entirely.

When Mia reached her locker, there was an explosion of shouts and whistles. An eleventh grader yelled, "Love you, Mia!" A boy she didn't know was blowing her kisses, and she laughed. Being in the spotlight was very strange. Until recently she'd been content to hide in the background.

Throughout the day kids commented on the concert and the band, asking questions about how long Fusion had been together, where did they rehearse, and where did they get their songs? By the end, her cheeks ached from the smiling. Danni and Mia walked out of their last class of the day, together.

"Like, I'm still reeling from Friday's concert. What about you?" Danni said.

"I loved it, more than I thought. But I wanted to ask you about that boy—Robert?" Mia admitted.

"I wasn't going to say anything until you said something." Danni stared at Mia.

"What do you mean?" Mia asked, holding Danni's arm.

"Well, isn't it obvious? There's something going on there. I can feel it," she said.

Mia wanted to deny it. She wondered how on earth Danni could see something between them, when all the while she was doing her best to ignore him. "There's nothing going on. He just keeps popping up, and he's a jerk, like the boys said." Mia stashed her books in the locker, grabbed her folder, and slammed the door shut.

"Mia, come on—this is me you're talking to. Your face hides it from most people, but this is me. I've watched you when he's around, and you're different." Danni closed her locker door and walked down the corridor.

"What do you mean?" Mia followed right behind her.

"Well, I know that most boys turn you cold, right?" Danni turned to face her.

"Yes, but…"

They walked out through the main doors and down the steps.

"But nothing. Mia, you don't outright freeze until they start to want more. I've seen you, like with Alex. You allow him to kiss you, even though you don't want to. But with Robert you're like a firecracker. You won't even look at him, let alone let him touch you." Danni strode off leaving Mia standing still.

"Hang on... What does that mean?" She ran to catch up with Danni.

"Well, I think it means you doth protest too much, mi' lady." Danni smiled. "I think he terrifies you in a completely different way—because, for the first time, you're scared you may actually like it."

"That's crazy." Mia shrugged and adjusted her bag as she walked.

"It's no crazier than Alex wanting to rip his guts out, just because he talks to you." Danni shrugged.

"Alex is trying to stake a claim. I get that, but it's annoying. He doesn't, own me, and besides, it's complicated," Mia said.

"Really, too complicated for me? We're friends, remember? And Alex wasn't like this until Robert turned up. I promise, anything you have to say is between us."

Mia studied her friend's face, and sighed, turning her head away. "I can't. I'm sorry." Tears threatened to fall, but she held them back. Keeping secrets was killing her friendship.

"Whatever. Maybe, I'm overreacting. I just think you and Alex are perfect for each other."

"Danni, I don't want a boyfriend."

"As I said, I think you protest too much. Your cheeks are on fire when he's around. He's fire to your ice."

Mia laughed and Danni joined in.

"Alex, isn't stupid you know," she said.

"Look, I'm going to quit the band," Mia said, all in a rush. "Don't say anything yet, but it's for the best. The only problem is that Alex had agreed to the Thanksgiving show."

"Hmmmm, quitting isn't the answer," Danni said.

They strolled out through the school gates. The loud rumble of a motorbike drew Mia's gaze toward the road. It was Robert Mathews. He was riding a black and chrome Harley-Davidson

Sportster, which made him look even more dangerous. He drove past and inclined his head toward them.

Soon, Mia.

Mia blinked.

Hell will freeze over first!

Her words spilled out before she could even stop herself, and his laughter echoed inside her head as he drove away: *I never had you pegged as a chicken.*

How dare he! Her back stiffened at his words. Mia wasn't scared of him, and yet everything about him terrified her. He'd said he would help her understand, but maybe she didn't want to discover the truth. Maybe the truth was something to be scared of. *I'm not scared, I don't know you, and this is madness.*

Part of her knew that avoiding the obvious couldn't go on forever. They were speaking to each other without words, for goodness sake! What did that make them? Maybe she wasn't the only freak. She stared at the now empty road, feeling lost.

Really, is that all you've got? Mia, you know me, better than anyone.

In an instant her lips were crushed and kissed by an invisible force. She gasped, and covered her mouth with her hand.

"What's wrong?" Danni stared at her and Mia's cheeks burst with heat.

"Oh Mia. You're in so much trouble girl."

Mia tore her gaze from the road, and gently touched her lips. She could smell a slight minty odor on the breeze.

I know you like me, Mia. I can tell by the way you react.

"That's not true." Mia shouted in outrage and then gasped, as she realized she had spoken the words.

"What's not true?" Danni turned and grabbed her arm.

Mia was racking her brains trying to remember what Danni was just saying.

"I meant to say that it's true, I'm in *deep* trouble."

You see, you can't even think straight when I'm around.

Reaching Danni's car, Mia opened the passenger door and threw her backpack into the rear. *You're annoying. I'm going to ignore you from now on, so leave me alone.* She sat down, as Danni switched the engine on.

You cannot ignore me, and we need to talk.

Mia didn't respond. Was her fear of him getting the better of her? What was she really scared of the most? A loud banging on the window made the girls scream.

"Hey, babe, don't forget me," Tyler shouted, and then squished his face against the glass. The girls laughed. Tyler opened the door and jumped in.

"Sorry…" Danni said, steering them to Alex's house for rehearsals.

Alex's dad, Stephen Fitzgerald, was a talk-show host at Equinox radio station in Boston, and he loved music. When Alex formed Fusion, his dad wanted to be involved. It was a short ten-minute drive, and soon they were getting out of Danni's Honda and running up the steps that led onto the wraparound porch. The front door to Alex's place was ajar, so they walked straight into the cavernous colonial house.

The smell of freshly baked cookies hung in the air, and led them straight into the kitchen. Mia's stomach rumbled. She watched as an animated Alex chatted with his mom, Mrs. Fitzgerald. Her natural blond hair was cut short into a bob that finished just below her chin. Her warm smiled greeted Mia as soon as she entered the room.

"Hi Mia, come here," Mrs. Fitzgerald said. Mia walked over and they hugged. "How's your mom? I haven't seen her in a while."

"She's good, but busy at the gallery," Mia replied.

"Well, now that you and Alex are dating, we'll have to get you over for dinner. Oh, Alex, by the way, I forgot to say that dad won't be able to make it tonight."

Mia shuddered. Had she heard Mrs. Fitzgerald say that she and Alex were dating?

"Okay," Alex replied.

Mia glared at Alex. He had told his mom that they were *dating*. She wanted to throttle him. Danni and Tyler began to tuck into cookies. Their laughter diffused her anger, and temporarily interrupted her giving Alex a piece of her mind. Mia lifted a double chocolate-chip cookie off the plate and stuffed it into her mouth, letting the gooey chocolate slip down her throat.

"Guys, stop making such a mess," Alex said. "Enough. Let's get started, else we'll never get anything done."

Each in turn grabbed a bottle of water from the counter and disappeared downstairs. The basement had been converted into a recording studio, and was Mr. Fitzgerald's and Alex's domain. The room was open-planned with high ceilings and crisp, white walls. Silver frames adorned the blank canvas with pictures of Elvis, Jimi Hendrix, and Eric Clapton. In the center, two large black leather couches faced each other, and further down there was a pool table, which came in handy when Alex and Tyler were arguing, because the rest would play.

At the very end stood Mr. Fitzgerald's prized collection of guitars, displayed on individual stands or hung on the walls. His very first electric guitar was a Kay hollow-body, a sentimental piece he said he'd never part with. There were also several Martin guitars, a Fender Precision bass, an old Taylor acoustic, a 1958 Gold Top Les Paul, and a 1960 Double Cutaway Les Paul electric guitar. They were striking, glossy, elegant—and not to be messed with.

To the left of the stairs were two separate rooms. The first one they called the White Room, and it was where they played their music and stored all the amplifiers, microphones, stands, the PA system, and all their instruments. The adjoining room was smaller, and they named it the Control Room. In this room the music was recorded, mixed, and perfected. Mr. Fitzgerald would help with the fine-tuning of their recording. It was where the final tweaking took place, which could take hours until they were happy with the finished sound of the piece.

Mia flopped down onto the couch and Alex sat down next to her. Danni and Tyler set up the pool table and Mia flicked through the song sheets. Evan, the fifth, and quietest, member of the band strolled in late, as usual.

"Glad you could join us," Alex said.

"Wasn't sure it was tonight, dude. Didn't see you at lunch and kind of forgot. I was halfway home, before I realized." He shrugged, shoving his floppy brown hair behind his ears before sitting down opposite them on the couch.

"Well, you're here now. Mia, can we go over the arrangements for *Dream Lover* and see how they sound?" Alex said.

"Sure. Can we also try this new song?"

Mia pulled out some rumpled sheets of paper from her backpack and gave them to Alex. He studied her writing and rough notes, nodding occasionally. As he progressed through her song he sat back and tapped his foot against the wooden floor. During the summer Alex and Mia had written several songs together about their dreams for the future, broken promises, and love. As they put lyrics on paper and played with the melody, eventually the arrangements and music came to life.

Alex leaned forward and began scribbling, crossing out some of Mia's notes and adding new ones. Mia shuffled closer, and as he started to hum a tune, she started to sing the words. Evan joined in tapping his drum sticks against the table and nodding his head to the beat. For about an hour, they played around with the beat and the notes.

"Okay, well it's a start. I like it. I really like it. You're on a roll lately." Alex knocked her shoulder playfully.

"It's just kind of there, in my head, you know," Mia shrugged.

"Well, it's good. Now, let's get started on *Dream Lover*. Come on." Alex grabbed her hand, tugged her off the couch, and walked toward the White Room.

"Tyler, hurry and finish the game! Come on," Alex called over his shoulder.

"Dude, I'd be glad to. She's killing me," Tyler said.

Mia waited for everyone to collect their instruments and check the equipment. Then she placed the headphones on her head and settled onto the stool. She wet her lips and picked up the microphone. Music filled her head. Taking a deep breath, she started singing.

You're always on my mind,
Always in my dreams,
You've cast a spell,
Bewitching me,
My dream lover. My dream lover,
Your eyes hypnotize,
And, I'm mesmerized.
Your words lift me up to the bluest skies
And have me reaching for the highest stars.
My dream lover, My dream lover.

Singing the words, Mia imagined Annwn. She remembered the time she was flying with the boy from her dreams, and her vocals came out with a remarkable depth of passion. The song moved her in a way she'd never dreamt possible. Maybe falling in love with the *right* person was worth the risk.

For the next several hours the band worked on the song, listened to the recordings, and stopped for food breaks. Then they worked for a while on Mia's new song, and headed back into the Control Room. Tyler had been mixing the music, and they listened, and discussed the performance. Mia gazed at the clock, and looked at Alex. He took a swig of water, wiped his mouth with the back of his hand, and faced the others.

"Okay, I think that final playback was the best. The bass was just right and the melody great. Your pitch was perfect, Mia. Great job."

"Totally, that last one, great sound," Tyler said.

Yawning, Mia couldn't believe it was almost midnight.

"It's late, and I need to get home. I still have homework," Mia said.

"Me too," Danni echoed.

Evan stretched and bowed. Danni hugged Mia, and then collected her violin. Tyler dragged her out of the door and gave the thumbs up as he left.

"I really liked the new song, Mia. G'night," Evan said, tapping his sticks across the wall, and then he disappeared out of the door.

Mia was alone with Alex. They gathered up the mess of empty chip packets and dirty plates. When they reached the upstairs there was a deep-belly laugh coming from the living room. Mrs. Fitzgerald sat, transfixed, watching the Three Stooges.

"Goodnight, Mrs. Fitzgerald. Thanks again for the food," Mia said.

"Goodnight. Was it a good session?" Cathy asked.

"Yes. It's just that Alex is a slave driver, and I'm really tired. Goodnight."

"A slave driver…" Alex smiled.

He grabbed his keys, and they walked outside. The moon lit up the sky like a disco ball. It was quiet, and a thin layer of fog seeped around them. Mia walked quickly to the passenger side of the car, and stepped in. She sat and hugged herself, shivering.

"Boy, its cold!" she said, rubbing her hands together, instantly feeling warm.

"The heater will come on now, or if you scoot over I could warm you up," Alex smiled. There was a pause, and after starting the engine Alex pulled the truck away from the curb.

"It was good tonight, don't you think?" he said.

"Yes," Mia agreed, in between yawning.

"Look, I know it's a lot, with school work and everything, but you were brilliant at the homecoming," Alex said.

"I loved the concert, but I thought that would be it—now, it's every night. I'm not sure I can keep up with everything."

There was an uncomfortable silence, and Mia stared over as Alex hand's twisted on the stirring wheel showing the whites of his knuckles. Several streets passed by in a blur, and Mia stared through the misty glass, sucking on her lip. The blue truck stopped right outside her house, and still Alex didn't speak. Mia glanced at him briefly before stepping out. Alex jumped out and whisked around, almost colliding with her. He walked alongside her right up to the front door, looking lost in thought.

"Mia," he finally said, "I know it's a lot of work, but the band is sounding better all the time. The concert was merely the beginning. Dad really likes our music, and he's keen for us to record—professionally. He wants us to go on the station. I didn't want to tell the others, because it's not definite, but he wants to help. He can introduce us to people in the business. I know it's a lot, but you're good—and together it can be great. It's not just about you, but the band. We need you."

As Alex spoke, clouds of white vapor escaped from his mouth, and Mia shivered. It was freezing, but she stood and listened. Walking away from the band was incomprehensible, because he was right; it wasn't simply about her, but all the members of Fusion.

"Mia," Alex said softly as he stepped closer. Mia closed her eyes willing herself to relax and not scream.

Is this what you want, Mia?

She twisted around in a circle, worried that Robert was there lurking in the shadows. Thick fog flowed in waves around them, so thick in parts it was impossible to see anything. Mia stared until there was a break and the garden cleared, but it was empty. Shaking her head, she turned to face Alex.

"What's wrong?" he asked.

"Nothing. It's chilly, that's all," she said.

Standing in the doorway staring at her hands, Mia didn't know what to do or say. She lifted her head and they stared at each other. Alex leaned forward.

"Mia, is that you?" her mother called from inside the house.

Immediately the lights switched on, flooding the porch with a bright yellow glow, and they moved apart. Mia sighed. She looked at Alex and saw his look of disappointment.

Mia, don't. This is foolish.

Fed up with Roberts's interference, she grabbed Alex's jacket, pulling him into her arms, and planted a kiss right smack on his lips. His arms instantly clamped tightly around her. She was trapped. No sooner had the kiss started than an overwhelming sense of claustrophobia clawed at her. Mia shoved against his chest to break them apart, breathless at her recklessness.

"Goodnight, Mia," he said, all smiles.

She shook her head in disbelief. *Now look what you made me do. Just leave me alone.*

Mia stared as Alex walked away humming a tune.

What I made you do?

She opened the front door and slammed it behind her. *Go to hell.*

Chapter Five

Spellbound

Mia disliked what she saw as she stared at herself in the ornate silver mirror. Robert was squatting inside her mind, and she was livid. She blamed him for the kiss. Her annoyance toward his presence was to blame for her impulsive kiss. *What a mess!* Alex would never understand her actions—one minute she was cold, and the next she was kissing him. She paced around her room like a caged animal. *Damn Robert Mathews!* She wanted to be truthful with Alex, not lead him on. *Unbelievable!*

The look of satisfaction that was plastered across Alex's face after the kiss made her heart sink. It was one in the morning, but she still needed to finish her homework. Pulling out her science textbooks from her bag, she let the heavy books drop onto the table and flicked through the pages until she found what she wanted.

After reading several chapters, Mia answered the questions about Newton's Universal law of Gravity, put down her pen and stared at the stars glittering in the sky. Sooner or later she would have to face Robert Mathews and listen to what he wanted to tell her. She could feel that time was near.

Feeling sleepy, Mia let her body drift toward the bed. Her eyelids drooped with weariness. As soon as her head touched the soft pillow, and the cool sheets settled against her skin, she plummeted into darkness.

Dreams pulled her into another world—Annwn, a world in which everything made sense and she was promised to Ryder. She told herself they were harmless because they were only dreams.

Opening her eyes, she saw that she stood in a cobbled courtyard, dressed in a beautiful silk gown of ivory and gold with an empire waist. Ryder stood next to her, watching the rise and fall of her breathing. Long scarlet roses grew in the bushes that bordered a small stone cottage, and their delicate perfume filled the air. Green ivy twisted and climbed up the walls, and birds chirped. Ryder leaned in, his hand rested in the small of her back, and he pressed her closer to him. A wave of delicious sensations ran through her body. She loved him, and her heart thumped in her chest.

"I love you too," Ryder whispered huskily.

He dropped feather-light kisses along her neck, and she moved her head to give him greater access. Each kiss tickled, and she let out a carefree laugh. His sensory exploration stopped, and he raised his head, frowning.

"Why, Mia? Why are you so certain that we must enter the world of mortals?" His chin jutted forwards and his lips were set in a thin line.

"You know I love you, but I cannot ignore what's in here, or here. My visions show a child, and she is leading me into the human world. There is something I must do, and in turn the future of both realms will be saved. I have no choice—I have to go."

Mia reached for his hand and placed it over her heart.

"The visions pull me into their world and I cannot ignore them. How can you expect me to?" She turned, brushing her tears away.

"You get so immersed in the visions, it isn't good for you. Emrys says, to be able to see clearly, you must stand back—but you jump right in." He shook his head. They spoke, and yet she didn't need words—she knew his thoughts before any words were spoken, and yet he still wished to change her mind.

"You have never doubted my visions before. Why now? I have to do something."

"It's not the vision I doubt, simply the interpretation. We have never left Annwn before and will be alone once we are there, leaving us vulnerable. Never before has it involved anything so dangerous, and I wonder why now, when there is unease with the Darkshadows and whispers of an allegiance with Rhiannon. Why have you chosen this as our challenge?" Ryder said exasperated.

Mia walked out into the field filled with tall grass that abutted the cottage, and glanced around. The fields stretched beyond for miles, and as the white clouds rolled slowly she could just catch a glimpse of the snow-capped mountains. It was peaceful, quiet, and yet she sensed everything was about to change. Ryder followed her and captured her hand in his. Without looking at his face, she spoke to the wind.

"You don't have to come." Mia regretted it the moment she said it. However, she needed to offer him an out. He could change his mind, break off the betrothal and stay—but no matter what, she would venture into the human world and follow the vision wherever it led.

However, if Ryder did join her, then he must agree with the challenge—or they were doomed to failure at the start.

"And how does that work, Mia? Tell me. Have you forgotten the promise we made to each other? We bear the mark of that promise. If I walk away from this, even if I want to, our future together is over. But to enter the mortal world, to start again... Do you not hesitate for one second, and think this is too much to ask of us? Their world is unknown to us..." He backed away.

"That's not entirely the case; we have always watched over the humans, and helped when absolutely necessary. This time we have no choice. If we cannot alter their fate, then ours too is sealed. There will be no more children, and mankind will end. If we walk away from this, we have no future. Don't you see? If we fail, we are left in the human world. If we don't go and try, there will be no future. I know it's a lot to ask, but I must ask it anyway. Do you love me enough to trust me in this?" She touched his arm softly and he turned to face her.

"Every time we have helped the humans, there was war and destruction. Maybe history is repeating itself again. Damn it, Mia, I don't want to lose you! Don't you see why this is so difficult? If I don't agree with you and choose this as our challenge, then I'll lose you anyway. So, we go, we find a way to be together, discover the reasons why children are not being conceived, and then what? If we manipulate the future there

will be consequences." His voice was husky and his words were resolute.

"I only know that the child is calling for me, and if I come, all will be revealed. Should I ignore that?" Never before had she felt so certain about what she must do, even if she didn't have all the answers.

"It would be like asking you to stop breathing, and I cannot."

Ryder pulled her into his arms crushing her lips with his, and Mia responded with a hunger of her own, wrapping her arms round his neck. He whispered against her ear, and she laughed.

* * * *

Like night and day, the dream ended. Mia shot forward, gasping, and her heart beat wildly. Sitting up, she shivered, missing the warmth that Ryder provided. Her hand brushed against her recently kissed lips. Mia was still aware of his touch and the unmistakable tingling in her belly. In the dream, Mia was terrified of losing him and yet fiercely determined to pursue her quest. The dream shocked her to the core. A challenge that affected both Annwn and the human world, did that make Annwn real? How was anyone able to alter the future? Something shifted inside her mind. In this dream, Ryder was angry and scared. He didn't totally believe in their quest! She shook her head. Ryder was afraid she was making a mistake to enter the human world.

Mia drew her knees upwards and hugged herself. Remembering the kiss, she swallowed hard. Mia had responded to Ryder with as much need as he had, and his kiss charged through her body, exploding little fireworks along the way. Craving more, her body leaned into his and she gasped. In the dream, she responded to Ryder as if she knew him—which was impossible, and yet seemed to make sense. Mia shook her head, dispelling that thought.

A persistent tap at the window drew her away from her thoughts, and she stared as a branch from the tree outside rattled against the glass pane. A chilly blast of air made her pull her sheets around her, and she noticed an odd fluttering in the middle of the room. A speck of dust flickered and quickly morphed into a smoky outline of a person. Mia darted back against her headrest, but couldn't pry her eyes away from the ghostly apparition.

As the figure solidified, it smiled. It was Emrys. She smiled back, and relaxed her shoulders. Mia crawled across her bed, and reached her hand toward the specter. It was an illusion. Her hand twisted, and turned, in the translucent mist.

"Remember, you have many challenges before you and the path may not always be clear." Emrys smiled. "Your loyalties will be tested, as will your feelings for one another. 'Tis all but a test, remember. Take this."

He extended his hand, and opened his palm flat. There, curled in the center, lay a silver pendant with a crystal flower. Her necklace. The apparition faded and disappeared.

The tapping noise at the window continued at a frantic pace. Mia peered at the window and was about to step toward it, when a face appeared, and she screamed. Two large misty patches formed on the glass, and the nose of an enormous dragon snorted against her window pane.

The blond boy was seated on the dragon, as he had been in her dream. The dragon's large paper-thin wings flapped, and he gave a long screech. Her heart skipped and missed beats as she stared at her bedroom door and considered escaping, but what if he followed? Looking back at the boy, Mia lifted her head. *He cannot harm you,* she told herself. *He cannot be real.*

"What do you want?" She glared at him, trying her hardest not to be scared, but all the while her heart pounded in her ears. His glacial-blue eyes pinned her to the spot and roamed over every inch of her. She clasped her arms across her chest and shuddered under his examination.

"Why, you, Mia. What else?"

Mia argued with herself that he was outside, on a dragon, and couldn't possibly enter the house—therefore she was safe. The boy hovered in the air on the back of a now quiet dragon like a page from a fantasy novel, with his head slanted to the side, studying her reaction. She closed her eyes and wished for the fearsome boy, and his dragon, to vanish. Hearing nothing but the stillness of the night, she opened her eyes.

Her heart was still flip-flopping, but they were gone. All Mia could see as she stared at the window was the blackness of the night. She breathed a sigh of relief—but all too soon her heart was churning as an excruciating high-pitched squeal tore through her bedroom. Mia covered her ears as the panes of glass from the window cracked and shattered into a million tiny pieces. Fragments flew across the room.

I've been watching you Mia, and you're strong and brave. I like that.

His words entered inside her head. He too could speak without words, and she was dumbfounded. Mia's breath stalled in her throat, and shards of glass sliced across her cheeks. Pain ripped through her, and she fell to the floor. She touched her cheeks and they were sticky and wet. Staring at her fingers, a wave of nausea rose inside her. Hysteria threatened to take over completely as she shook all over, but a face appeared inside her mind and Mia screamed out a name.

"Ryder!"

Many will suffer at your hand. You will fail, and the Darkshadows, will win, a nameless voice accused. Mia suddenly knew the nature of the boy on the dragon.

One minute she had been locking lips with Ryder, then watching a ghostly apparition, and to finish the night she'd been terrified by a Darkshadow. His chiseled angel face haunted her, and chills exploded down her spine. The dragon's high-pitched squeal kept reverberating around inside her head, and she willed the noise to stop. Her mother would no doubt believe the shattered window was caused by the wind and nothing more.

If only that was true.

After clearing away the broken glass, Mia cleaned the cuts across her cheeks, and then finally settled into bed. Sleep was impossible. The boy's cold eyes bore into hers every time she closed her eyes. She was terrified he would return. A million questions pummeled her brain, and she tossed back and forth. Dreams of the boy flying upon the dragon's back, flying over large fields and crops, sprinkling what looked like dust into the wind, steadily plagued her.

* * * *

"Mia. Mia, it's time to get up. If you don't feel you can, that's fine, but I have to go to work."

Mia's eyelids fluttered open. The cuts on her cheeks, throbbed, proving that last night was real. She groaned, "No, I have to go to school."

"Well, your cuts still look slightly angry, but they'll fade," Cerianne said, as she studied Mia's face.

"Mom, thanks for letting me sleep in here. I—"

"Mia, the last time you were in my bed, you were looking after me. It was good to be the mom for a change. Now, go, get ready, or you'll be late."

"Okay."

Every weary step was an effort, but she was desperate to find Robert Mathews. He would have the answers she needed. She was running late again, and breakfast was a quick bowl of cold cereal. Walking to school, she messaged Alex that she wouldn't be able to make practice for tonight—and straightaway her cell-phone rang.

"Alex, look this crazy thing happened last night, and I can't come over tonight, but I promise, I'll do the Thanksgiving concert. After that, I just don't know—" Her words gushed out.

"Whoa, is it because of me? Am I putting too much pressure on you?" he said.

"Alex, I—" she started to say, but before she could answer, he interrupted.

"Look, the Blues are playing again tonight. Why don't we forget practice and have some fun. You can tell me all about the crazy thing that happened to you. It's been pretty intense lately. You know me—slave driver, remember," he said.

She wondered if he was right. Maybe a night of fun was exactly what she needed. Perhaps she could even get Alex to back off, solving one problem, leaving only a zillion more to figure out.

"Okay, but we need to talk, really talk," she said.

"I thought you might say that," he replied.

* * * *

All morning Mia tried to reach into Robert's mind, to connect with his thoughts. After all, he was always dropping in unannounced into hers, so why couldn't she do the same? She tried concentrating, visualizing his face, but nothing happened. Every lecture was a blur. She couldn't focus. Her back ached and every time someone passed, or laid a hand on her, she jumped. *Where are you Robert Mathews, when you're needed*? Her pleas went unheard.

At lunch she sat with Danni, Alex, and Tyler, smiling at their lame jokes about her face. Mia ran her hand over the thin lines from the cuts until Alex lifted her hand away.

"You know Tyler's only messing, calling you Scarface. You can hardly see them, honest," he said.

Mia looked at him, and nodded. "I know. Me and no sleep equals one grumpy bitch."

"All the more reason to let me cheer you up and take you out. Tyler's game. Shall I pick you up?"

Mia looked over at Danni. "I promised Danni I'd go to the mall with her first." Mia wanted to burst. It was getting harder and harder to keep her secrets locked away, and she needed to talk to Robert, but today he was absent and silent. At times like these she wished she could tell Danni about Ryder, the dreams, the visions, and the Darkshadows, but feared losing her friendship.

Their last session was a free period. Mia left the school with Danni, but the disturbing memories and the boy's face from last night appeared in her head. She pushed the images away and tuned into Danni's voice.

"Have you sent off any college apps, yet?" Danni said. "Mia, can you hear me?"

"Sorry…yes, I've sent off for early action at Northeastern and Dartmouth. Mom was on to me, but I haven't heard anything yet," she said.

"Yeah, Mom wants us to go and visit some colleges. I'm applying to the Julliard School in New York, and also to the New England Conservatory of music. I don't think I'll get in either, but I want to try," Danni smiled.

"It's all going to change, isn't it? We won't be at the same college; our lives will go in different directions. Promise me, we'll always be friends, no matter what,"

"Of course. Nothing will come between us."

Twenty minutes later, they arrived at the Maple Tree mall. Once inside, they agreed to go their separate ways and meet in half an hour. Mia headed straight to Planet Music to search for a song that kept bouncing around in her head. She hummed the lyrics, *Across the Emerald Ocean.* Nothing showed up on the computer's search engine, so she moved to look among the racks. Stepping back, she collided with a solid wall, and once again found herself in the arms of Robert Mathews. All day, she had been searching for him, and now he was here. Could she trust him?

Mia met his inquisitive gaze as he searched over her face and his stare rested on her angry slashes on her cheeks, and she looked away filled with mortification. His hold on her tightened almost painfully, and a hurl of curses left his mouth. Without asking permission, he cupped her face with his hands and his thumb slowly stroked across the angry marks. Mia blinked and her breathing hitched at his tender strokes. An undeniable force made Mia gaze at him and as she stared into the dark depths of his irises, she replayed the events of last night inside her head and she knew as his eyes widened that he could clearly see what had taken place. *Damn him*. There was definitely no way of keeping anything secret from him. Hot pink spots flooded her cheeks and she pulled away from him rubbing her arms.

"Mia, it's all right, please let me in, I saw him, he's a Darkshadow." He tugged on her arm so that she faced him. Her face lost the rosy hue. She knew that boy was a Darkshadow even if she didn't know what that meant. She bit her lip, and fear, swamped her body as she remembered his parting words.

Many will suffer at your hand. You will fail, and the Darkshadows will win.

Ryder pulled her in close. Mia tried to push the memories of last night away, but her body trembled.

"Mia, you have to stop doubting what you see and feel. He's very real and very dangerous. I'm not the one you should be scared of. I'm not going to hurt you, I promise. I can help you."

Her long lashes lifted, and Mia stared at him. "He said he wanted me, that I'm strong and brave—but I'm not."

He relaxed his grip, and let her stand alone. "Mia, I can explain everything, but we need to meet in private—not like this." He glanced around the mostly empty store as if worried that someone might over hear them, and Mia wondered what the hell was going on and what part he played in it.

"Mia, this is ridiculous. The longer you take to decide whether you can trust me or not, the more danger you're in. The Darkshadows are not like us; they don't…feel, like us. If he said he wants you, then you have become his latest toy to play with. I'm sorry, but Darkshadows like to tease, to taunt. They're inquisitive by nature, and if they're interested in something, they don't stop until they find something more appealing. I suspect your magic has drawn them to you. I'm sorry, but you must trust me in this." Ryder lowered his head and sighed. "You won't find the song that you're looking for. That's why you're here isn't it?" he said lifting his gaze to stare directly at her.

Suddenly, it was too much. He could talk to her without words and read her thoughts before she even had time to digest anything of what he was telling her. Her body wilted like a dying flower almost reaching the ground until, he gathered her into his arms before she fainted.

“Am I the only one, who has this effect on you? I’m not sure I like it. Mia, you never change—strong in spirit, but not in body,” he said, in a hushed voice.

His arm held fast around her waist, and he guided her toward a small alcove at the side of the quiet store. He sat her down on the couch, and sat next to her. Ryder brushed her hair behind her ear and stroked her cheek.

“Feel better?”

“Who are you?” she said, staring at his face.

He smiled and shook his head. “If you would look inside yourself and stop being so damn afraid of me, you’d know…Sorry that came out wrong. It’s just hard being so close to you, yet so far away,” he said, sitting back and resting his arm along the back of the couch. He reached down carefully to lift her hand. Mia looked at how perfectly it fitted in his as he rubbed his thumb across her skin. Slowly, her tension ebbed away and her heart raced, but not with fear—with something else. Taking her gaze away from her hand, Mia raised her chin and stared openly at his lips. A wave of needed swept through her, and she leaned closer toward him, and their lips almost touched, but he turned away.

“Mia, you’re driving me crazy. Did you come here alone, or is *he* here?” he said sitting back and staring at her frowning.

“If you mean Alex, I’m meeting him later. Danni’s here somewhere,” she explained feeling suddenly cold and alone.

“Danni’s a good friend, Mia,” Ryder stated. She raised her eyebrows at his comment, and he smiled.

“I know she is, and Alex is not my boyfriend. Well, he’s my friend and he’s a boy, I...” she said stuttering.

He sat forward and pulled her into an embrace. His hands gently cupped her face, and he lowered his head to kiss her parted lips. His touch sent fireworks throughout her body, and Mia responded with an eagerness that matched his. Automatically Mia reached around his neck, and her hands tangled in his hair. At first, his kisses were innocent and teasing, but as she responded with increased urgency, the kisses deepened. Their bodies clung to one another. Then, as if dashed with a bucket of iced water Mia pushed away from him, shaking and hurling a mouthful of curses mortified at her reaction.

"What are you doing?" she said, shaking her head. She wriggled out of his arms and stood up.

"I would've thought that was obvious, Mia," Ryder said, grinning as he stood too.

"I'm not interested in you…like that," she said, crossing her arms against her chest.

He stared at her. She was lying. She was lying to herself and moved further away.

"Mia, you needed that kiss as much as I did. I know you're scared, and I wish I could change that. I'm sorry about last night. If I'd known, I would've been there. Maybe I could've even stopped it from happening, but because you told me to stay away, that's what I did."

"Ha, don't even try and make out as if any of this is my fault!"

"Mia, you need to see the bigger picture, trust me. And I don't believe you. You wanted me to kiss you. Your heart is racing, your pupils are wide, and…you kissed me back. You feel…something," he said walking to stand next to her.

"Stop that! Stop reading me—that's what you're doing. How dare you?" she said.

"You need to understand, and then you wouldn't be so scared," he bit out, his voice hoarse and angry. "Mia, you say you don't feel anything, but your body say's something quite different. You cannot deny what's there for everyone to see. I need to show you something, to explain. Will you come with me?" His arms lifted to grip her shoulders.

Mia stared at his arms which held her there, fixed to the spot and tried to pull free.

"You're wrong. I can't do this. I'm not…not who you think I am? Please, let me go."

Instantly, his arms released her. Ryder lifted his hand, and tapped her small nose and inhaled. “If that’s what you want… Just be careful, and don’t make promises you cannot keep. You do know me, and you’ll need to face it sooner or later.” Before he moved away, he kissed the top of her forehead tenderly. He stuck his hands deep in his pockets and kicked the can on the floor before striding away.

Before Ryder had left Annwn for the human world, Emrys explained that when the time was close a stir of memories would begin, which would help the awakening. Mia was resisting him, every step of the way. She didn’t trust him or herself. He cursed under his breath. She had called out to the Ryder of her dream when she had been in danger, but she didn’t believe that he was one and the same. Mia had always been stubborn, but something had happened to her.

Maybe living in the human world had changed her beyond recognition, and she would never truly accept him. After all, they had been babies when they entered the mortal world—a glitch in the magic, if there ever was one. Emrys had placed them with a family, and planned that they would be teenagers once more, but that didn’t happen. They had been in the human world far longer than anticipated. What human experience made Mia so cold and untrusting?

Chapter Six

Mia's body trembled. Her feelings for Robert terrified her. Ever since she'd bumped into him at school, she'd been more of a nervous wreck than normal. Her body was a traitor. All she could think about was the taste of his kiss and how she yearned to be in his arms. She was constantly aware of him and the effect he had over her. Ryder was a magical dream from Annwn, but this was different—Robert was flesh and blood.

Were they the same?

Somehow, in his arms nothing else mattered. They could speak to each other without words, and he could hear her thoughts—just like Ryder. Could she do that also? What was he? What did that make her? Then there was the matter of the Darkshadow. What the hell was going on? Why were her dreams turning into reality?

Weary with frustration, Mia removed her glasses and rubbed her eyes. She didn't like the idea of being this Darkshadow's latest curiosity. She couldn't take any more. An unnatural laugh escaped from her. Listening to Robert, she feared, would be like opening Pandora's Box. She needed to fight him, make him go away—or was she simply going insane? Mia knew Robert was the key to it all, but was she strong enough to face the truth? She shivered, and realized her phone was ringing in her pocket.

"Mia, I've been waiting ages. Where are you?" Danni's voice sounded.

"Sorry, I'm coming."

Mia hurried through the mall, and found Danni.

"Mia what happened?"

Mia stepped back and took a deep breath. "Let's go, and I tell you on the way."

There was a tense silence as Danni drove, gripping the steering wheel tightly, turning every now and then to stare across at Mia.

"Danni, watch the road."

"Sorry, go on."

Everything came tumbling out. Once Mia started, the dam broke and she couldn't keep the secrets locked inside any more. She told Danni all about the dreams, the visions, and Roberts's part in it—everything, except the part about the Darkshadow. Danni's expressions didn't change. She listened and gave the occasional gasp and nod, but she didn't speak. Mia held her breath waiting for her to say something, but there was silence. She was about to tell her to forget everything, because she knew it must have sounded like the ramblings of a madwoman.

Danni pulled up and parked. "I can't believe you," she said, shaking her head. "All this time, and you've been keeping these secrets from me. Aren't we meant to be best friends? Aren't we meant to tell each other everything? I guess this is why you're so preoccupied all the time?" Danni stared at Mia.

"Danni, I haven't told anyone until now. Besides, you didn't tell me about Tyler, and I didn't want you to think I was crazy!" Tears brimmed in Mia's eyes and Danni touched her arm.

"Mia it's crazy…but that doesn't make *you* crazy. I'm your friend. You should've trusted me. I'm sorry about the Tyler thing. He made me promise, and that's different. Look, you can't avoid it. You must speak with Robert. If he's telepathic, and you can hear him and talk back, then you are too. That means you're gifted, not crazy. You say he knows your emotions and thoughts. Can you sense his?"

"Danni, I've been trying to block out all thoughts of him, but he creeps inside and plays stupid games, like burning my hands. I became so angry, that I hurt him in return. What does that make me?" she said.

"Remind me not to get on your bad side." Danni opened the door and got out. "Anyway, you don't know that for sure. Whatever's going on, you two have a lot in common. Look, I'm totally freaked about what you just said. You know Robert, the boy from your dreams, now here for real. Totally friggin' weird. Psychic abilities, reading your mind—crazy, but I believe you.

You're my friend, and there's always something going on that defies explanation. But honestly, you need to sort this out with Robert—and Alex, because this is going to explode, trust me."

Mia stepped out of the car, and walked over to Danni and hugged her. Inside, she knew she had to talk to Robert—and then everything would go back to normal, right? She gave a half- hearted laugh. Her nerves were doing somersaults. She didn't believe that, not for a minute. In fact, she was certain everything was about to change. The conversation hadn't revealed a game plan—but as she looked across at her best friend, Mia's worries seemed less, and she smiled.

"We could've just gone to your place."

"I know, but I can't hide from them. It really helps me, that you know and that I can talk to you about all of this."

Roberts's words rang out loud inside her head. *Danni's a good friend*. She thought it was an odd comment to make, and even stranger now that she had revealed her secret to her. Danni was a good friend, and she would have told her everything eventually—but she hadn't, until he had spoken.

"Do you think I'm crazy, having dreams about kissing a boy and then crashing into him in school? Do you think he's the same boy?" she said. "And it's more than that. He behaves as if we have a history together…and I feel somehow connected to him. He terrifies me, because I'm being drawn to him whether I like it or not," she said. A shiver rippled down her spine as she spoke the words, and Danni put her arm around her.

"What does it mean?" Mia asked.

"I don't know, but he's just a boy," Danni shrugged.

"But that's just it. He isn't just a boy. How many boys do you know that can talk without words, read your mind or inflict pain with a thought? What's worse is that I think I can do the same, so what am I?" she searched her friend's face.

"You're Mia. Look, maybe there's an attraction between the two of you, and you pick up on things because of that. So maybe it's all just subconscious, you know, not really real. Like, I don't think you hurt him with your mind. He was probably being a jerk, and was just pretending. As for your hands, you're being hyper-sensitive."

"And if not?"

"Well, maybe, you do have a past that you don't remember. Maybe that memory has been stored deep away in your subconscious, and your conscious memory is trying to bring it back,"

"I can tell you enjoyed psychology. It sounds convincing," Mia said.

"Last year we covered the possibility of suppressing painful memories. There are some who believe that when people suffer a violent trauma, they can forget the event completely. They only remember it when triggered by something familiar, a smell or a place. Sometimes it's only over time, as they get better, that the memories and feelings resurface," Danni explained.

"Really, believe me, there are some memories I would rather forget—you know the rows between Mom and Dad—but I can't. As for any trauma, I can't remember any, but then I wouldn't, so maybe that's it. Maybe, he's a painful memory," Mia said, looking puzzled.

"I know your parents break-up was a nightmare for you. I was there. But maybe you have met Robert before, when he was younger, and you just don't recognize him—and his memory resurfaces in your dreams," Danni said.

"Hmmm, when he speaks to me, I know he's telling me something that's just for me. It's hypnotic and dangerous."

Danni laughed. "Hearing you speak that way is so funny. You were so worried that you were frigid, unable to love! God, Mia, what you're talking about is passion—infatuation or maybe love. Isn't that what you were waiting for? Remember, you said you needed tingles? Well, this sounds pretty close."

"I don't love him, we've barely spoken…" Mia said, walking away.

"We love with our hearts, not our heads. That's the battle you're facing. We can't control who we fall in love with. Come on, we'd better go," Danni finished and Mia just looked at her.

"I'm not in love with him," she whispered as they walked toward the stadium.

A warm breeze coasted along Mia's shoulders, ruffling her hair. Danni grabbed Mia's arm and pulled her through a crowd of spectators. The school's band marched onto the playing field in their smart red and white uniforms, and the big drum started booming as they played the theme tune to ET, and it was deafening. Mia put her hands over her ears to drown it out. She glanced over at the cheerleaders, with their short skirts and big smiles, as they took center stage on the field.

They paid for their tickets, and immediately the boys appeared. Alex came to stand next to Mia, and Danni walked toward Tyler.

"I would've paid for your ticket," he shrugged.

"It's okay," she said.

Mia looked into his face with his blue-gray puppy-dog eyes. His furrowed eyebrows and mouth stretched into a pencil-thin line. Alex grabbed her hand, and she let him lead her toward the bleachers. Explaining anything to Alex here would be impossible. They sat down next to each other, and Alex placed a scarf with the team colors of Blue and Black around her neck. As his hands briefly touched her shoulders she tensed, but accepted his gift.

"We have to show our support," he said. The smell of onions and butter wafted through the air as she inhaled. "Are you hungry? I could get us some dogs if you like," Alex said.

"Why don't we grab something later?"

Alex gave a wide smile. He seemed to like the word *later,* and she wondered if that was the right thing to say. Maybe she should get it over with right now and then go home. But she couldn't do that. His boyish face stared out across the field, oblivious to her inner turmoil. She had to make him understand why they couldn't be together.

Vendors were strolling in front of the stalls, selling glow-in-the-dark bracelets and necklaces. Alex suddenly leapt from one row to the next, until he was on the walkway and next to the vendor. He bought several necklaces in bright pink, blue, and green. Horns were being blown like trumpets. It was crazy. He came jumping back up to the top in the crow's–nest, and tossed some necklaces at Tyler and then placed two around Mia's neck. She laughed at his antics.

"You're crazy."

"Maybe a little. I just don't want to lose you in the crowd," he said

His eyes lingered on her mouth. For a moment Mia froze, certain a kiss would follow. Nothing happened—he merely lowered his eyes and looked away. She wondered what he was thinking, because for a moment he looked so sad.

Sitting at the top gave them a panoramic view of the field. The crowds were shouting out, "Come on, Blues!" for the home team, the Blue Crusaders. They were lined up against the opposing team called, the Black Knights.

Mia watched, not taking her eyes away from the game. The opposing team players looked like fearsome warriors, poised ready for battle. She held her breath and chewed nervously on her nails. The only way she could pick Robert out from the other players was by tracking the number on his jersey, number nine. She stared, captivated by his determination. Both teams fought hard to gain the upper hand. At halftime the score was a draw of seven to seven.

Every time there was an injury she winced, and Alex laughed, grabbing her hands to hold them. It was like watching David and Goliath, as Robert's team was continuously pummeled by the defense. As one player collided into another Mia stood up, unsure of who it was. The player took a heavy blow to the head. She cursed, and then watched as he stood up and carried on.

"This game is brutal," she said.

"Mia, with all that padding, they'll be fine," he laughed.

The game drew to a close, and it seemed that the gossip for once might be right—but then screams rang out, piercing the night sky, pushing and driving the home team. The Blues surged forward. Mia was transfixed with the action, and shouted for the Blues. The surrounding crowds erupted, releasing a cascade of wild applause and shouts of joy. The clapping rallied the team, imploring for Robert to take the ball all the way. He charged down the field and delivered what the crowd wanted, a blazing touchdown. His team then followed it up with a triumphant final kick in the last moments of the game. The Blue Crusaders had won!

Fourteen to Thirteen.

Mia screeched with joy, and hugged Alex. As soon as she realized what she had done, she let go and moved away. The crowd was delirious. People were jumping up and down out of their seats, chanting and shouting. Horns were honking left, right, and center. It was a riot.

"Let's wait while it empties. What a game!" Alex said, holding Mia back.

"I didn't think it would be so exciting."

Everyone converged onto the walkway trying to get out, but they were jostled back and forth by the sheer numbers of people. Then the players did a victory lap. Robert was positioned on top of several of the players' shoulders as they paraded him around, the pronounced king of the Crusaders. What a moment! Robert was their hero. Mia knew a night of celebrating would be in order, and wondered what that would involve. Reaching forward as much as she could, she only caught a glimpse before he was swept away by the team. His smile lit up his whole face, which was red and muddy. There was an odd stirring where Mia's heart was. Robert laughed as he tried to stay upright on top of his friends' shoulders. He certainly looked just like an ordinary boy—maybe Danni was right. The cheerleaders were all giggling and shouting his name. Mia's chest tightened, and unable to watch any longer, she turned away.

"Come on, let's go to Felicities," Alex said.

She was so engrossed in the game that she'd barely spoken more than a couple of words to Alex. Glancing across at him now, she saw he looked uneasy and quiet. Maybe, after they had eaten, they could talk. She nodded her agreement.

* * * *

The bell tinkled as Alex pushed through the door to the diner. The song *Viva la Vida* by Coldplay greeted them, along with the warm and cozy smells. Alex marched forward, searching for a table. Mia poked her head through the kitchen doors to see who was working the shift. Her friend Sally was there, and she came over to join her.

"Mia, are you working tonight?" Sally said.

"No, we're here to grab some food," she said.

"Well you're in luck. It's pretty slow at the moment. Who are you here with?"

"The usual, except Evan, I'm not sure where he ended up."

"Okay. Let me grab my pad, and I'll be right with you."

"Great."

Alex sat in the booth at the far corner, looking outward onto the street. Mia squeezed in beside him, watching the door, sensing that the football team would be here soon and wishing they had gone anywhere but here. Danni was cuddled up against Tyler, laughing, and their heads close together, scrutinizing the menu. Mia stared back at Alex, who was still quiet. His back was against the wall, and his right arm stretched outwards across the red leather booth. She faced him and he ignored her, staring at the menu instead.

The loud music was suddenly drowned out by the overpowering noise of people, as they entered the diner cheering and chanting. Robert's name was shouted out, and applause rippled through the diner as the Blue Crusader football team came in. Robert was once again hoisted high into the air and carried through the diner like some Roman god. Alex and Tyler stilled and watched the scene.

"Maybe I should have been a football player after all," Alex joked. His face betrayed a forced smile that didn't quite reach his eyes.

"Like, no way there wouldn't have been a band. They're just a bunch of crazed, pumped up, steroid-addicted showoffs, with not a brain cell among them," Tyler said.

"Hang on, there. I'm sure they don't all take drugs," Mia said.

Standing up for anyone on the football team was obviously the wrong thing to say, as both boys glared at her. Feeling as if she needed to further clarify her point she continued, even as Danni's eyes sent her an imploring look that said *don't*.

"I didn't know you knew anyone on the team that well," Alex nudged.

In truth, she didn't. Instinctively Mia thought of Robert, and even though there were many things that scared her about him, she knew he would never take steroids. However, why she was mentioning him at all was stupid. Danni broke away from Tyler and stared at her. The words wouldn't come and she flicked through the menu that she knew by heart, her face feeling strangely hot. She wasn't prepared to answer questions about Robert yet.

"Only the boy I crashed into," she said, trying to sound casual.

Alex looked at Tyler, who shook his head,

"Mathews, the one from the concert?" Alex looked directly at her.

"Yes."

"Robert Mathews, the quarterback?" he said sounding surprised.

"I've only talked to him a couple of times, but I don't think he takes steroids," she said.

Alex moved closer and sneered. "Mia, I think you're very naïve to think that you know someone so soon. There are a lot of seniors that are taking drugs, kids you know, but wouldn't think for a minute they were!" he said passionately.

"Look, I know that. All I'm saying is that Tyler's statement is a generalization, and I don't think all the players do, jeez."

Mia rose to leave the table; she didn't want to get into a heated argument with the boys over the football team or Robert. She quickly walked toward the restroom. As her hand touched the cold metal of the door, she could feel a warm breath against her neck, and turned around. She smiled, believing it would be

Danni. Instead Robert stood there with a big confident grin, completely aware of how disturbing she found his presence. His face was now clean and his inky-black hair wet, most likely from a shower. His powerful sweet aroma tickled her nose.

"I'm glad you came to watch. I was never in any danger of getting hurt you know, even though your worry over me was a bit distracting," he said, baring his perfect white teeth.

Her hot cheeks flamed even more. She was an open book to him. It unnerved her, and she tried to ignore him. Any minute Alex could walk over, and there would be a massacre. Added to that, she knew without doubt he was anything but an ordinary boy. His remarks confirmed it. Even at a distance and while playing football, he had known her thoughts. Danni was wrong. She stared into his warm brown eyes that reached right into her soul, pushing her angry words into his mind.

You have to leave me alone.

Abruptly, she turned to leave.

Mia, I cannot do that. I'm not going to hurt you. When will you realize that?

His words were gentle, but strained as they raced through her head. There was no escaping him. They were the same, whatever that meant.

"I have to go or Alex will come looking—" she said, looking over her shoulder.

"You cannot keep running away."

His hand blocked the doorway, and she turned to stare up at his taut face which was inches from hers. He let out a sigh, and slowly removed his arm. Mia gazed over Robert's shoulder and saw Alex standing close, watching them, his face set like stone. Robert turned around to let Mia step forward, and the muscles in Alex's cheek twitched.

"You did a good job out there. You played well," Alex said.

"Thanks. There's a party later to celebrate. Why don't you all come along?" he said.

Alex cocked his head to the side, inspecting Robert up and down through narrowed eyes. Mia held her breath.

"Not tonight, mate. I just came to get Mia. Our food is ready."

Alex reached for her hand and she let him pull her away, hoping to diffuse the situation. Mia's hair flicked over her shoulders as she passed Robert, and she knew it wasn't finished. She tried to remain calm, but could feel the storm rising inside him as it washed over her.

Please, not here.

Robert's anger only escalated, and it emanated off him in waves. She wanted to scream at him to stop.

"Mia, is that what you want?" Robert called.

Alex snapped his head around, turned and marched past Mia, to stand face to face with Robert.

"What is it with you, Mathews? Winning the game not enough? Mia's with me, are you blind?" Alex said.

Mia forgot to breathe. Robert wouldn't back down.

"Is that right, Mia? Are you with Alex?"

There was an awkward silence, and she wanted to disappear. What was Robert doing? He was behaving as if she belonged to him, and Alex was just as bad.

"You two are beyond disgusting! I'm not a possession. I'm going to eat." She started to walk away because their volatile conversation was attracting a crowd, but Alex didn't budge.

"Mia, I want to sort this out. What the hell is going on?" he said, turning her back to face his icy stare blocking Robert completely out of view. Mia wished the ground would swallow her up. Why was Robert forcing this situation? Right now, she could gladly thump him. She had intended to discuss everything—well almost everything—with Alex tonight, now they were becoming a very public spectacle.

"Alex, there's nothing going on. Can we just go eat?" she said, in a hushed voice.

The Blue Crusaders gathered around watching the scene, looking eager to jump in and defend Robert should there be a fight. She couldn't stand it any longer. There was a movement among the crowd, and a girl from the cheerleaders appeared. Mia didn't know her name, but she was the same one from the night at the concert, and here she was again searching for Robert.

"Rob, come on," she said. "I want to go to the party. Can we leave?"

Robert glared at Mia.

The girl was very pretty, and it was obvious that she wanted his undivided attention. The crowd erupted again, chanting. "Party…party".

"Sorry," Robert muttered.

Mia wasn't sure whom the apology was aimed at as he stormed out of the diner. Some of the tension between her and Alex left too, but inside she was empty. Sitting down at the table, she couldn't manage a mouthful of food, but Alex devoured his in silence without glancing at her. As they walked out of the diner Mia turned and grabbed Danni's arm.

"Alex wants to drive me home to talk. Do you mind?" Mia said, as they stood outside in the parking lot.

"No, absolutely. You need to sort this out before they kill each other. Call me."

Mia hugged Danni before wandering off to find Alex.

As soon as Mia sat in his car, he began. "Mia, I don't think you're being honest with me. Please don't lie, or you're going to lose me," he said. "We've known each other for a while, and I've slipped into thinking of you as my girlfriend..."

"Alex…"

Before, she could utter another word, he carried on.

"No, let me finish. I need to say this. I know, I've never really asked you out, but we've spent so much time together, I feel…I love you, Mia…I want you to know that. I want you to know how I feel, because I want others to know it too." He took hold of her hand as he was driving, and she stared over at him.

"Alex, I know." She turned her gaze away and stared out the window, wishing for something impossible to happen, to make it easier. "Alex, you've always been my friend. You're like a…"

As if sensing a rejection, he immediately let go of her hand. "Don't say it, Mia. That's crap," he said. "I want more than friendship, you know that. We have more than friendship. You make me crazy, and I need to know where I stand."

"I'm sorry. I don't love you, not the way you want." Mia stared at her lap. She was being as honest as she could, but knew she was hurting him.

"Do you think it will ever change? I mean, I don't want to pressure you. Maybe you're not ready now, but in time?" he said.

Mia didn't want to leave the door open for misinterpretation; it was hard enough going through this once. Why was everything so complicated? He would never understand the truth. Hurting him now would save him in the long run.

"I'm a disaster. I don't want a boyfriend. I'm being honest. You don't really know me, and you're better off without me."

"Isn't that for me to decide? And, you're wrong, I know you. Look, I know you went through hell with your parents, and Danni said..."

Mia huffed, and lifted her head to stare at him. "What do you mean, Danni said?"

"She said to be patient."

Mia wanted to scream, but instead took a deep breath. "Alex, I can't do this. You're a friend, and I wish it was different, but it isn't."

"What if I give you some time?" he said.

"I'm sorry, I've got to go," she sighed. No matter what she said, he wouldn't listen. Opening the car door, she left. What else could she say? He revved the engine, and she watched as he tore off down the street.

Chapter Seven
Moonlight

Mia opened her front door and walked in. A sliver of light filtered through from the room beyond, signaling that Cerianne was still up. Mia crept in to see what she was doing. Her mother stood in front of a large drafting table, staring at stacks of black-and-white portrait-sized photographs. Cerianne turned, and smiled at her. "Hi, sweetie. Did you have a good night?" she asked.

"It was fine. I'm just a bit tired, that's all."

Cerianne stared long and hard at Mia. "Are you sure you're okay?"

"Mom, I'm just tired, honestly."

"Mia, I'm always here if you need me. You know that?"

Mia nodded.

"Okay, before you go, what do you think?" Cerianne spread her hands out toward the photographs, and Mia walked to stand over the table.

The pictures were of ordinary people, strangers, all ages, races and sexes. She had managed to capture their deepest emotions, and they left you wanting to know more.

"They're incredible. I love them."

"Thanks, love. They're for the exhibit," she said.

"They're amazing, mom," she said.

"Thanks, Mia. I needed that. Look, remember I'm here, if you need to talk about anything, okay? Goodnight, sweetheart."

Mia left her mom and ran upstairs. She wanted to forget all about Alex and Robert, and yet it was all that plagued her mind. Was that pretty blond his girlfriend, and if she was, why on earth was he messing around and interfering in Mia's life? She remembered the look of defeat on Robert's face as he left. He could have anyone, so why was he interested in Mia, anyway? The girl obviously liked him. What did he want her to do? Mia turned to stare at her window as a loud knock sounded against the glass pane. She gulped—*Not again!*—and froze to the spot.

Mia, I'm outside, and I need to see you.

Her unsteady heart refused to settle. It wasn't the Darkshadow. It was *Robert*. A quiver of excitement shot through her as she crept through the darkness to hide behind her curtains. Peering into the garden below, she saw a black silhouette standing in the shadows of the great oak. Her heart beat leapt at the sight of him. Robert stepped directly into the glow of the street light, and Mia stepped back from the window, hoping he wouldn't see her. Her face was in flames, and she smiled.

Mia, I know you're there. I can hear your heart racing. Do I need to come and get you?

Mia knew it was impossible to hide from him, ever, and the last thing she wanted was Cerianne being dragged into this.

Okay, I'm coming.

In a matter of seconds, she was downstairs and heading silently out the back door. Robert stood there, as dark and mysterious as the night. He gazed at her and smiled.

"Come with me, I want to show you something." He extended his hand toward her.

She stared at him, and then back toward the house.

"What are you afraid of? I won't kiss you, unless you ask, and you know I won't hurt you," he smirked. The effect his kiss had on her senses was alarming, but in truth, it was what he wanted to reveal that terrified her.

"You overestimate the power of your kiss. Besides, I thought you were going to a party."

"I was, but I knew I couldn't," he said.

"Why?"

He stepped closer, and she turned to flee.

"Because it's you, I want."

Robert's words stole her breath, and she turned staring into his dark and smoldering eyes. In one swift motion, he pulled her into his arms, holding her against his chest as her heartbeat thundered inside her ears. Mia was trapped and couldn't move.

Slowly, he dipped his head so that their lips were only a breath away from touching.

Mia was certain that he would kiss her, and this time she would welcome it. A smile lit his face, and Robert pushed her long hair behind her shoulder, tracing a line along her jaw with his finger. Tiny shivers exploded down her spine, but she couldn't stop gazing at him.

"Do you still doubt what you feel with my arms around you?"

Everything was surreal in his presence. It was as if he was casting a spell over her, making words impossible to find. Mia peered up at the black-as-treacle sky, staring at the bewitching spectacle as the stars sparkled and the moon glowed.

"I know I should run as far away from you as my legs will take me, but I can't."

He held both of her hands in his, and lifted them toward his mouth, brushing delicate kisses on her fingertips. The kisses sent heat flooding into Mia's cheeks, and she stepped closer. Lifting her head, she nodded.

"I said, I wouldn't kiss you again, unless you asked," he whispered against the soft skin of her neck.

"Kiss me," Mia whispered. His eyes looked almost black as his head descended to capture her lips with his. Mia clung to him, kissing him back with an eagerness that terrified her, and yet she didn't want the kiss and delightful feelings to end. Her hands raked through his hair, and he pulled her closer. Moments later, Robert pulled away, but he didn't let her go.

"No more running. Come with me, and I'll explain everything," he said, gently tugging her hands.

"Okay." Despite her fear, she needed answers.

Robert led her toward his motorbike, grabbed the spare helmet, and placed it on her head. He put his own helmet on, climbed onto the bike, and started the engine.

"Get on and hold tight."

Mia glanced back at the house. An hour ago, she told Alex that she didn't want a boyfriend, and here she was about to drive away with Robert, while her newly kissed lips still tingled. She should feel guilty, but she didn't. It was like in her dreams when she was with Ryder. He was scary, yet an unstoppable force, and she had no choice but to give in. Tearing her eyes away from her front door, she stepped over the bike and took a deep breath.

Relax. I won't let anything bad happen.

She leaned against his broad back and clutched him tight. Soon the neighborhood was a distant, hazy shadow. Robert drove fast but safely through the back lanes, and before long they were at Lake Cochichewick. The stars twinkled above, and the moon looked enormous up in the black ocean that was the sky. Its shadow glimmered on the silky, calm water of the lake. Robert parked, killed the engine, and reached for Mia's hand to help her down the path to stand in front of the lake.

"Finally," he said. "I know you have many questions, but first, you must be still and hold my hand."

Robert held her hand and closed his eyes. He stretched his other hand out toward the lake. An electrical charge pulsed through her, tickling her. Mia laughed, jumped and snatched her hand away. His eyes immediately opened.

"You shocked me!"

"Mia, you need to stay still…please."

She nodded, too nervous to speak in case she laughed again. This wasn't what she had expected at all—not that she had known what to expect, but not this. Once again, she held his hand and resisted the urge to pull away. Closing her eyes, she waited. Their hands clasped, and Robert began his strange performance again. Mia gave in, determined not to be afraid. A familiar voice called to her, and bursts of memories of herself at different stages of her life filled her mind.

Mia opened her eyes and stepped forward. This was like one of her dreams. As she walked, memories assaulted her—voices, faces, feelings, and wave after wave of familiarity flooded her. As each memory appeared, her body reacted. Each memory brought emotions gushing to the surface. Tears fell down her cheeks. She laughed out loud and hugged herself. Mia twirled around, absorbing the sensory invasion, and breathed in between gasps and sobs. Still memories poured in. She saw the moment of her birth, but her parents were different. She was a young girl, with long hair blowing in the wind as she ran across a field filled with flowers. In nearly every vision, Robert was there—impossible and yet making perfect sense.

It was another world, and a different life. She had existed before, and belonged somewhere else. How was any of this possible? Mia trembled, and the memories stopped—but as she tried to stay upright, the earth tilted and she almost crashed to the ground. Robert caught her just in time. For a moment, she let his strength be hers and she rested against him in silence.

"What did you do to me?" she said, shaking even more.

"It's called the Awakening. The first time I touched you, was an accident and it didn't work. At school you resisted, and it made you ill. In order for the awakening to work, you must have an open heart and mind. You had to be ready. I simply jolted your brain to reawaken your deepest memories of our life together. We are from the Otherworld. Annwn is real, and has existed for centuries. Our people created the magical realm to protect us and our way of life. We once lived alongside the humans, but when men realized the magic we held and the power it could yield, they became corrupted and sought to use it for evil purposes. A powerful spell shields Annwn from humans, and the Wise Elders worry that if magic is weakened in Annwn, the shield may fail. You need to remember who we are," he said, rubbing her arms.

Mia peered at the trees, bushes, flowers, absorbing the cries of the night as her head throbbed. Her heart was racing. Inside her mind there was a part that was relieved because she knew he spoke the truth. And yet...

"I don't understand. I have new memories, but how can this be true. What am I? Where is Annwn? I've visited a place in my dreams, but it's a fantasy. It can't be real!" A burst of uncontrollable laughter escaped from her lips, and Robert eased her into his arms and held her tightly.

"It's a lot to take in. You're in shock, and I've scared you again," he said, brushing her hair aside. "I once said to you that

I would do anything for you, and that I would not lose you. I meant it. We made a promise to each other, a long time ago. Mia, it's all real. We're from a land by the great sea, and only those who know how to call on the magic of our people can enter. We have always watched over the humans. Mia, look at me. We're not like others—have you not felt it?" He cupped her chin with his hands.

Numb, that's how she felt. A chill was settling in and twisting around her bones. She couldn't stop shaking.

"All my life I knew, I was different. I saw things as a child, and everyone thought I was mad. I thought I was mad. In school, the visions appeared all the time, and the kids were scared of me. My parents...my adoptive parents, didn't know what to do with me. I could see things, and words like freak and psycho were bandied about." Mia stopped talking and sobbed. Turning away from Robert, she took off her glasses and wiped her mouth with the back of her hand. Her sobs broke into a torrential flood of tears.

"Let it out. Mia, you're not a freak. You're amazing. Our people have always possessed magic. Some call us witches, but we are guardians. We're gifted with mind-speech, we foresee the future and make predictions. We can influence our surroundings, change the weather, and cause a storm." He spoke while stroking his hand down her back.

"You're telling me I'm a witch?" She gave a strangled laugh.

"Humans love to label things. When we lived among them they called us witches, but truly we are Guardians. We are here to preserve and watch over mankind. We're not here to cause harm. We harness the energy of the natural elements, and live at peace with the earth and nature. However, throughout history as humans became aware of our powers, we've been called many names."

"The boy at my house, what is he?" Her voice lifted a notch, showing her fear.

"I guess not all memories of the past have returned. Some of our people are Watchers. They are different from us, cold, calculating, and they observe the humans' gathering intelligence. To humans, they appear as shadows—hence their nickname, Darkshadows. In Annwn we tolerate each other, but it's an uneasy alliance and has been for some time. Before we left, Emrys spoke of increasing tensions between the Darkshadows and the Wise Elders. The fact that a Darkshadow is stalking you, and allowed you to see him, is unheard of. He knows you're different. When we first met, when I touched your hand, I sensed danger all around you. The only way we can exist for any length of time in the human world is to become human—that was the spell that Emrys cast—but it makes us vulnerable. You see, our lifespan in Annwn is undetermined. Here, we could die from the common cold—or a kiss." His shoulders sagged as if he had off-loaded a heavy burden.

"Your name is not Robert, is it?"

"No, it's Ryder."

Ryder watched Mia as she stepped back and twirled around and around. As her body moved around in a circle the yellow, brown, and red leaves lifted off the ground and danced around her. There was so much for her to remember. His name was different, but he knew who he was. Watching Mia, he wasn't sure she would ever be the same. Would the Mia he'd loved ever be returned to him?

Dizzy from the assault of memories, Mia laughed, and collapsed onto the soft plush carpet that was the forest floor. Ryder sat down next to her. The world stopped spinning and Mia tried to gather her senses, unaware of how much time had passed. Feeling nervous, she clasped and unclasped her hands. Ryder reached across to hold them still. She was trying to understand everything she had heard and seen. Facing him, she realized that if everything was true, he had known her. They shared a life together. Looking away, her face flushed with a roaring heat.

"Mia, don't be embarrassed. Our world is different. We were promised to each other from an early age, and even though we are betrothed, we left Annwn to come here. What I'm failing to make clear is that what you think has passed between us, hasn't. I would have hoped that if it had, you would have remembered."

Mia's face burned even more, if that was possible and there was an awkward pause. Ryder caught hold of her face to turn it toward his.

"Mia, do you remember our laws about the promise?" he asked.

"No," she said, gazing into his earth-brown eyes.

He let go of her face and took her hands. "Annwn is magical, but there's darkness too. It has always been that way. In any world there is good and evil, but things changed when the blood of our people mixed with mortal blood. In Annwn, once a couple is promised to one another, they're given a challenge to test their love and magic. There's a ritual, a ritual that marks the couple, to show they're promised to one another. "He folded back his shirt sleeve to reveal a thick and bold black tattoo.

"Oh…you've got to be kidding me. I don't have one!" Mia said, quickly.

"Your magic hides it, but it will appear if you focus on me. You're in control of your magic, you and no one else. You can switch it on and off, sometimes without even knowing it. Close your eyes and let your body relax. Trust me, Mia. Open your mind to me. This is who you are."

Mia stared at him, uncertain of her next step, but closed her eyes. "This isn't going to work. I don't possess magic."

Mia, you have no idea of what you are capable of. Remember the homecoming, and your hands. That was magic, and you retaliated with magic.

She gasped. *But I didn't know!*

"It's okay. I shouldn't have used magic the way I did. Talking the way we do, it's like breathing air. Once we were so close we barely needed words, because we were in tune with each other's thoughts and feelings. I could sense you all the time, and vice versa. It's about control, and just as you stopped the images, you can stop me talking to you or reading your thoughts. It's up to you. Now, let's work on your tattoo," he said.

Ryder didn't want to push Mia. She was having a rough time trying to digest her memories, and at some point he knew she was going to burst. To her, the seventeen years she had lived like a human were real, and it had changed her. Human years were no more than months in Annwn, but that didn't matter anymore because he had to deal with the Mia, he faced.

"Emrys warned us this wouldn't be easy. To enter the human world and take form, we needed to become human and relinquish our immortality—but he knew in doing so that it was a huge risk. The spell that he cast went too far back, making us babies."

He watched as she shook her head and raised her eyebrows.

"Mia, there's no need to be scared."

"I still think you have the wrong girl, but I'm not scared. What do I have to do?"

"You're my Mia. Emrys left instructions that your name wasn't to be changed—I think to help you remember who you are. As for me, I've always known who I was. Anyway, let's stand by the lake. I'll jump-start your batteries if you like, by pushing my energy into you. You may feel a burning sensation or a tingle, but it won't last. Try to relax and let go, see where your magic takes you. It's in there, everything you need to know. You just have to focus."

Ryder led her toward the water, and paused. "Whatever happens, I'm here and I won't let go. I promise," he said, taking her hand.

Mia closed her eyes. The wind stalled, and even the creatures of the night hushed. All she could hear was her heartbeat as it raced like a wild stallion. Crackles of energy fizzed around her, and Mia jolted and bucked as it surged through her veins. Mia held on as the powerful force sharpened all her senses, and Ryder's soothing voice urged her to let go and give in to the sensations she was feeling.

She was weightless and floating. The sun warmed her face, and the air was sweet and fragrant. Mia opened her eyes. She was in Annwn. Gliding along with the breeze, she smiled. She passed over a range of snow-capped mountains, narrow valleys with spectacular waterfalls, dense and secret forests. There were wild splashes of color from flowers and their heady scents, perfumed the air.

The sky was a water-color mix of bubblegum pinks and hazy purples. Mia stared across the turquoise sea where dolphins played chase, and her body settled on the earth. Birds cooed her name, and she laughed as she recognized the familiar scene of home. Her toes settled into the translucent water of the great sea, and curled into the sand. Breathing in, she knew this was where it all started.

Standing, as the warm water sloshed against her toes, she remembered the promise she made to Ryder before leaving Annwn. It all came rushing back—Annwn, Emrys, her life, her decisions, her visions of the future of mankind—everything with a pulsating clarity. Ryder had spoken the truth. A chill crept over her, and the sky turned a stormy gray. The sun vanished behind thick clouds that invaded the sky. A sense of dread rose up inside her, and she shivered. In the back of her mind, she heard Ryder's call to her, and once more her body lifted, and she was swept away.

She opened her eyes, aware of his strong arms holding her. "That was amazing. I was in Annwn. I've been visiting there since the summer, I thought it was a dream," she said.

"What better place to visit than Annwn, to kick-start the magic? It's called astral projection. Your spirit leaves your body and goes where it needs to, or is called to. You're not there physically, although it feels that way. Even here in the mortal world, we're tied to Annwn. We will never truly belong here. We are granted time and space, but it's not meant to be forever. Now, what about that tattoo?" he laughed.

Mia's heart was racing, and she was bouncing with an excess of energy as if she had been drinking shots of caffeine. A million thoughts were charging around all at once. She wanted to dance—hell, she wanted to jump out of a plane, fly through the air, everything, seemed possible. Wave after wave of sensations, ripples of pleasure, tingles, and shivers of fear, coursed through her. She could sense Ryder's thoughts and feelings clearly, and it made her smile.

"Whoa, I can hear everything—I mean everything. It's like the amplifier is on maximum in my head, and I can hear everyone's chatter. My brain is buzzing, and I feel invincible like I could come up with a cure for cancer or climb Mount Everest. This is amazing," she said, twirling around again. She reached forward, licked her lips, and grabbed his shirt. Ryder placed his hands on her waist as she wobbled.

"Mia, what you're feeling won't last. Your senses are awakening to the magic inside. The energy in magic is extremely powerful. Once it settles, you'll adjust and it won't feel so intense. You won't be able to hear the humans' thoughts, that will stop, but you can choose to hear mine. All your neurons have been highly charged, and your endorphins have been boosted big time. Eventually, everything will fall back to a more normal awareness."

Mia clung to him, leaning against his body and gazing at his lips as if hypnotized.

Kiss me. Kiss me Ryder.

Her arms coiled around his neck, and she breathed in his scent, and kissed him. Gently, her lips pushed against his, and his soft lips kissed back. She had never experienced anything so intense before. A desperate need to crawl inside him swamped her. A fever was building, and building…

Mia, stop.

His voice was low, insistent, and he sounded breathless. Ryder moved away, and struggled to compose himself. Mia stared at him, confused as to why he had stopped.

"What you're feeling is the magic—everything is heightened. We couldn't function like that continuously. It takes a lot of energy to channel our magic, and when the magic is spent we need to recharge."

Mia went to him and pulled his arm, turning him around to face her. "I didn't want you to stop. I wanted you. Wow, I feel so weak. I feel…" Mia closed her eyes, and the world disappeared.

Ryder darted forward as Mia keeled over. He reached out and gathered her into his arms. "Should've known that was going to happen. Mia, my love, you have your tattoo."

As he spoke, a dark twisting Celtic pattern of interlacing knots emerged on the underside of Mia's right wrist—matching his exactly: his family crest.

Mia's eyelids fluttered open, and she grinned up into Ryder's face. "That was such a rush," she said.

"It's intense. I'd like to think the effect was due to me alone, but I know better. Do you feel all right?" he asked.

"It's quieter, and I feel…" she paused, "Absolutely fine."

Ryder eased her gently to the ground and let her stand. "Good. It takes a bit of getting used to, and you have to take it slowly."

The wind picked up pace and whistled through the trees. It was getting cold now. A shiver ran over her, but she didn't want to move or speak.

"Here, put this on, you're freezing. We should go. Enough for one night," Ryder said.

Her heart was still floating up in the night sky, overcome with all that she had learned. How could anything be normal, ever again? Her life and all that she had known had changed. She looked into his eyes and started crying.

"Mia, it's okay. After the rush, as you said, there's the fall, the doubt. I know there's more you want to know, but it can wait," he said.

"You were right after all," she added.

"About what?" he cocked his head.

"I do know you," she said, as her hands entwined in his hair, and she pulled his head towards her face.

"Mia," he groaned.

She kissed him.

Ryder devoured her mouth, kissing her as if starved of oxygen, and she was fresh air. A rush of sensations took her breath away. The air crackled with electricity, and she clung to him, desperate for his touch, unwilling to let go. He held her face and brushed his thumb against her jaw. Breathing came in small gasps. Her hands brushed against the hem of his T-shirt, and as she touched his warm skin underneath, a searing heat shot through her whole body, down to her toes. Mia's hands roamed across his back, and as their bodies touched, they lifted off the ground and levitated.

Raindrops fell around them like misty drizzle. Neither of them stirred until the drops increased in size, drenching them. Only then did they become aware of their surroundings and drift back to the ground. Clasping hands, they ran laughing wildly toward the motorbike. They clambered on and drove, laughing, through the soft rain. They were just pulling up at Mia's house when the rain eased, as if somehow timed just for that purpose.

"It's just as well we left," Ryder said, wiping the wet hair out of her face. "I don't know what would have happened. We could've ended up in space. I've missed you so much."

"I've got so many feelings at this moment, racing around inside me. Am I the same Mia from Annwn, or Mia from this world? I feel happy and sad," she said, lifting her hand to touch him.

"You're both. Existing here has changed you, but you are still Mia. You're exhausted," he said, moving her hair out of his own eyes.

"I want to understand it all," she said, her teeth chattering.

"You're freezing." Ryder motioned for her to go into the house.

"I don't want to go yet. We are betrothed, aren't we?"

"Yes. Your tattoo appeared when you fainted. Look."

Ryder grabbed her right arm and turned her wrist over. Mia inhaled and froze, as she looked at the intricate seamless twists that lay engraved on her skin. The design, a triangle with a series of arches all interlaced and connected—it was striking, and her throat tightened as Ryder stepped closer.

"I would never lie to you, Mia. Your memories will settle, and it won't feel so overwhelming. We'll take each day as it comes. I know your feelings are not what they were, but I also know the effect I have on you… It's a start."

"I know how I feel…and then I don't. But, I dreamt of you. Did you do that?"

"Mia, you're beat. Haven't you had enough for one night? Your magic has been reaching out for some time. That day in the diner—the first day I saw you—you had a vision, didn't you?"

She nodded.

"Emrys said our magic would be suppressed, but it seems you're too powerful, and your visions have continued. You were always pulled into the emotional element of the visions. Your nature is always to help," he frowned. "When Emrys heard your predictions for the future, he went to the other elders and spoke on our behalf. To enter the mortal world, and use that as a testing ground for the promise, but there was a divide in consent. He held her hand and a wave of prickly heat ran through her. A scene unfolded before her eyes.

Deep voices were yelling and shouting inside a white stone-clad and smoky room. Several men gathered around a large wooden table, deep in a heated discussion. She recognized Emrys straight away.

"Even the Darkshadows predict the same future," he was saying. "The human race is in grave danger. Ryder and Mia are promised to one another—so let this be their test. They volunteer to go and help, and I believe it's their destiny. We must do all we can to assist them."

"What does it matter to us if mankind passes?" A man slammed his fist on the table, and his cheeks flamed a fiery red.

"You have to understand that, if their world ends, then so may ours. We gaze up at the same stars at night. Please, think it through for the sake of Annwn."

Mia blinked, and the scene vanished, revealing her empty garden once more.

"Emrys gave me this necklace," she said, as she pulled the chain forward showing the delicate crystal flower to Ryder.

"That's a blue serenity flower, and they grow everywhere in Annwn. They're very delicate, yet exceptionally strong, and bloom for most of the year. They were your favorite," he said.

"I remember their sweet fragrance, because it reminds me of Annwn and you. Emrys said I would have to overcome many hurdles, but that this would help me. What did he mean?" she asked, feeling confused.

"I don't know, but that necklace is a link to our home. Get some sleep, and the answers should come." His hand rested in the small of her back, but she twisted around, and jabbed a finger in his chest.

"Hang on. You've been pestering me for weeks to listen, and now that I know, I want to know it all. What are you hiding? Surely, there can't be much more. I mean, in one night I've discovered I am not human, but a guardian-slash-witch from the realm of Annwn. We are betrothed, and marked with a tattoo that binds us to each another. Ooh, wait, I'm missing out the part where I'm here to help mankind, but I don't know how." Mia looked wild, and her blue-violet eyes sparkled. Ryder knew she wouldn't let go.

"Where did your glasses go?" he asked.

"I don't know, but I can see. My vision is clear…I can't believe it." She blinked several times and smiled in wonder.

"Mia, you never needed glasses in Annwn."

"Oh…right. I didn't."

He sighed, "You're always so impulsive, yet so undeniable. Emrys took risks for us. You have to understand, we made the decision to enter the human world—we were not forced. You felt strongly that, if we entered the mortal world, we could alter mankind's fate. The Darkshadows and some of the Elders felt it was for personal reasons. They thought the risk was too great."

"But we're here," she said, spreading her hands out wide.

"Mia, you're so stubborn," he said, looked at her, knowing she was freezing. He placed his coat around her shoulders, resting his hand across her abdomen.

"We came because, in your visions, you saw a child you believed was ours. You saw her, in your visions, leading you into the human world to help save the mortals from extinction. You suggested to the Wise Elders that this be our challenge."

Mia was dumbfounded that it was *her* decision that led them into the human world. That meant the dreams she had were real. Looking at her belly, she pushed Ryder's hand off and moved away from him.

"You didn't make me do it. I would never have let you go through anything alone. Do you understand?" he said behind her, answering her question before it reached her lips.

"So, we're here, because of my visions of a child that's meant to be ours. I don't believe it." she said.

"Mia, when we left Annwn, we were promised to each other. The next step is the challenge, and then it would have been marriage. Your emotions at the time were, shall we say, ready to accept this if it was possible. Having a child in Annwn was becoming rare. Your vision seemed to offer hope—not just for mankind, but for Annwn. You believed this more than anything," he said.

Mia froze, unable to take any more in. She blinked at him, feeling exhausted. Mia knew she was different, but never in her wildest dreams did she imagine quite how different. Glancing at her sore wrist, she scratched the tattoo—and cringed. She was betrothed. In one night, her world had become unrecognizable. Mia frowned and tried to sift through which part of the night freaked her out more—the fact that she wasn't human but a guardian of Annwn, here to save the humans, or that she was betrothed to Ryder and visions of their child had led her into this world.

Chapter Eight

Revelation

After the revelations at the lake, Mia decided to avoid Ryder for a while, but his agitated and worried thoughts pummeled her mind. Staring at the mirror, she imagined Ryder's handsome face looking back at her. It was true, he looked like a young Johnny Depp and he made her heart skip and beat uncontrollably. The power of his kiss was undeniable, but seriously, *betrothed?* In a lot of ways he was a stranger to her, and the thought of being committed to one person stole her breath. She wasn't even sure that true love existed, and if it did, it certainly didn't last. It hadn't for her mortal parents. Was it really any different in Annwn? She never questioned it, until now.

The memories of loving Ryder were disjointed and hazy. Mia questioned whether that love was even real. Yet staying away was unbearably hard. Pulling her pajamas out of the chest of drawers, Mia quickly undressed. Ryder was the first and last thing on her mind, making her desperate to settle the conflict that raged deep within her. Give into the magnetic pull that Ryder held over her, or walk away? In choosing the latter she would remain mortal, living in a world where she didn't truly belong, and lose him forever. Remembering his kiss, and how it scorched her soul and sent it flying way up high under all the glittering stars, it was hard to think of fighting him—and her itchy tattoo was a constant reminder that she was promised to him. Lifting the plum duvet, Mia slipped between the sheets. Once in bed, she let her heavy eyelids close—and straight away she stepped into a vision.

Mia was no longer in her room or anywhere familiar. Her skimpy pajamas clung to her like a second skin, and the humidity slicked her cheeks. Mia was temporarily blinded by thick gray clouds that dominated the air, and blinking did nothing to change the view or her situation. Sucking in a breath, she gagged, and her eyes streamed with tears.

She had projected inside the vision.

She was actually here, wherever here was, and the air was suffocating. Mia coughed and gasped for fresh air. Her mind told her to act, and fast. Lifting up her short-sleeved top, she covered her mouth, and staggered haphazardly in the smog, barely able to breathe. After a few steps there was a clear space, and she took a deep breath lifting her head skywards.

Soft, dusty, gray flakes fell from above and fluttered against her skin. She raised her hands in the air, and tiny velvety scraps floated down and covered her. Ash. Her heart stalled. Ash, billowing smoke, and some weird noxious smell meant there was a fire somewhere, but sniffing the air and gazing around, she knew that explanation didn't quite fit.

Her body jumped to life. Real or not, she was in trouble—big trouble. Her feet shuffled forward, and she ran. She was running barefoot across the rough and uneven terrain when she stubbed her toe and lost her balance, falling hard against the ground. Her shoulder ached, and she lay there too stunned to move. Eventually Mia lifted her head up and gazed around. Forcing herself up, she was hit by a wave of dizziness. She was going to be sick, but the air thinned—and now she could see hazy outlines of trees, buildings, and maybe life. A spurt of energy moved her forward, and she darted in the direction that was free of smog. Beads of perspiration trickled down her face and she wiped them away. Mia wondered—if she died in the vision, would she die in real life? Not waiting to find out, she raced through the smog, the view before her suddenly clear.

Before Mia lay complete devastation. Row upon row of teetering charcoal frames, once homes, and burnt-out shells of cars, lay smoldering. Apart from the crackle of wood breaking and the hiss from steam, there was silence. Clouds of smoke filled the air again, and she called out, but there was no answer.

Edging toward the first dwelling, Mia searched for clues that would tell her where she was. A flash of blue caught her gaze—a scorched teddy bear. Her scream shook the desolate town, and she couldn't stop—until a small hand squeezed hers. She looked down. A child stood there. Long black curls fell down the girl's back, and huge violet-blue eyes sparkled at her. Before she could utter a single word, the child vanished, and the world around her fell away.

She was back in her own bed. Her visions were usually like photographs from a disaster or murder scene, which was horrifying enough, but this time it was as if she was there. Even her shoulder ached.

It was after two in the morning, but her phone vibrated. She picked it up.

"Are you all right?" Ryder's voice sounded.

"I was there. I couldn't breathe, I—" Her head pounded, and she couldn't quite get the words she wanted to say out. She gathered her sheets against her for comfort, and sobbed between words, retelling the events in her vision.

"Slow down. Hey, shall I come over?" he asked, waiting.

To have him near, to hold her, was just what she wanted—but Cerianne wouldn't understand or be pleased.

"Just stay on the phone with me, until I fall asleep."

"Mia, I saw your vision, experienced your terror—and I saw the girl. She's so brave and beautiful, just like you." Even though he was only on the phone, a warm sensation embraced her.

"Is that you?" she whispered.

"I need to do something, so I'm emulating what it feels like to be in my arms. It's not quite the same as being there…"

"It feels so good. My last vision was at the diner. I hadn't had one for six years before that, and there was no warning. It just came out of the blue, right then and there. But this was different. I was *there.* I couldn't breathe or see. I thought I was going to die… I hate them. I hate these visions. They make me feel so helpless. What am I supposed to do?" she said in a tearful whisper.

"Your magic has been awakened, and it's like a floodgate opened. I guess you were sucked into the vision, just like when you astral project to Annwn. The visions used to unravel slowly, piece by piece, like a jigsaw puzzle. By the end you were physically and emotionally drained… Hell, there are no easy answers. This is what we did together, in Annwn. We would decipher what all the visions meant. In the end, I used to think your gift was more a curse."

Mia closed her eyes, and listened to his soothing voice.

"I think of our child—and I don't know if she's real, or just a good way of making the visions easier to manage."

"You've seen her before?" she said, twisting the sheets with her fingers.

"None of this is easy. Knowing you were here. It seemed incredible, as if everything was falling into place. We have moved three times in the last several years. Emrys said he would help to lay a trail of events that would enable us to meet. Don't ask how, because I don't know. But each time we moved, the sense of you was stronger. I dream too, Mia. I have lain awake remembering how we were, and your face haunted me—the way Catherine haunted Heathcliff. You nearly drove me mad. Arriving in North Littleton, I knew you were here. I could hear your thoughts. But, I doubted it even then, until I had a dream and the girl from your vision was there. We have to believe we can face whatever is coming together, Mia. To me, she is a symbol of the power of our love. Real or not, you have to believe in love, or there's no point."

"Keep talking…I love the sound of your voice," she pleaded.

"You really should sleep, but I know you won't. I can tell you a story if you like—it may help you sleep. Most of our history is in the temple in Ashwar, in *The Red book of Rhydderic,* and it recalls the days of King Arthur."

Mia settled back against her pillow, closed her eyes, and listened to Ryder's soft lilting voice. It was like a drug, but soon his soft voice shifted into a deep baritone that was competing with several loud, angry voices.

In Mia's mind, she saw a magnificent room and in the middle stood an enormous, circular, oak table that could easily fit thirty people. Several men with shoulder-length hair and long beards sat there. They wore chain-mail vests underneath long red tunics. Logs crackled in the large open fireplace, and shadows danced across the walls.

A man whose silver-white hair fell to his shoulders raised his voice above the others, commanding attention. He appeared to stand heads above the others, and upon his red tunic a large striking dragon was emblazoned, labeling him as someone to fear. The man who stood dominating the scene was King Arthur, and next to him stood the wizard Merlin.

"Annwn. It's thought to be a place of magic. No one's even sure it's real," King Arthur said, watching Merlin, and drumming his fingers on the table.

"My liege," said Merlin, "For centuries, it's been a place shrouded by magic. Its magic hides it from mortal eyes, and its exact location is secret. Some say it's a place of great evil, a place where death is in control. I know firsthand that is not true. The myth of Annwn and the lost souls is a tale that has been spread throughout the land to instill fear and terror. This was a trick to keep any mortal from wishing to enter, but men who crave power find a way to overcome the obstacles in their way, and now important artifacts have been stolen from Annwn. A book called The Red book of Rhydderic, and a precious artifact called the Gilgamesh have been stolen by one of your knights. Prince Elgin will help you one last time in battle, if you find and return them," Merlin said, as he walked over and stoked the fire.

"Once they're returned, why will this Prince help me?" King Arthur said.

Merlin watched the faces of the knights as they agreed with Arthur.

"Prince Elgin's first concern is for his own people, but he always fights for the good of mankind—because he acknowledges that we need to help each other in order to survive. The future for your world and ours will be in grave danger if the balance is disrupted."

"Merlin, it's your magic that has helped me in battle. Why do we need his help now?" Arthur asked.

"I have seen your future. You are to fight the knight who stole from Annwn. He's no longer an ordinary man, and you alone cannot defeat him or his ungodly beasts. My powers are not enough. You need more."

"Who has betrayed me? What is his name?"

"I do not know his name or who he is now, but he will become known as Attor the Great. No land is without evil. An evil darkness from Annwn possessed him and claimed his soul. In the mortal world, he will be able to control the minds of men. He seeks power, desires riches, and with the Gilgamesh he can become immortal. If so, he will destroy mankind and Annwn. He must be stopped. My brother is the only warrior that can defeat him."

Merlin continued to plead with King Arthur to call for help from the Otherworld. King Arthur shook his head, and banged the table with his fist.

"If my time is at an end, then so be it, but to enter into a contract with this Prince from the Otherworld, even if he is your brother... How can I know it won't cause further harm? No, I will not ask for any more help. I have had my fill of magic and its repercussions. Let that be an end to it."

Ryder's voice stopped, and the scene evaporated. Mia sat up and opened her eyes.

"Merlin eventually persuaded King Arthur, but it wasn't easy. King Arthur made the deal with Prince Elgin."

"What happened?" Mia said, gripping the phone.

"King Arthur was right after all. For all his powers of foresight and magic, Merlin didn't see what would happen as a result of his interference. Prince Elgin entered the human world with his men and fought in battle. He defeated Attor the Great with one blow of his mighty sword, but was badly injured. Merlin managed to save his life, but many of the men from Annwn died."

"Did they get the treasures back?" Mia asked.

"Prince Elgin was never the same again. His last act as Prince was to demand that King Arthur replace each person from Annwn whose blood was spilled with a mortal. Arthur surrendered fifty of his men, who were never seen again. After this, he lost the loyalty of his army and in the next battle, was mortally wounded. *The Red Book of Rhydderic* was returned, but the Gilgamesh was lost. Merlin returned to Annwn needing to bring stability, as there was a shift in power."

"I remember, from a history lesson, that instead of there being a royal family to rule over Annwn, the Wise Elders were appointed. They were a group of twelve extremely strong and powerful wizards to govern the land, one of whom was Merlin. I remember, although his name wasn't Merlin, but…Emrys," Mia said, before yawning and closing her eyes.

"Merlin was his mortal name. When Emrys returned to Annwn, he refused to take control, and Prince Elgin lost his mind. Emrys decided to form a council of elders. The people of Annwn grew and life went on, but now the children were not just of magical blood lines, but a mix of human as well. Everything changed, and new laws were created to protect Annwn and its people. It was decided that Annwn would never again interfere with the mortals."

There was silence apart from the steady beat of Mia's heart and the slow rhythm of her breathing.

"Goodnight, Mia. Let's hope history is not repeating itself. Sweet dreams. I love you…" he whispered.

* * * *

Waking up, Mia stretched out her arms. She could've sworn that she'd heard Ryder say the L word last night, but she wasn't sure of anything anymore. It was Saturday, and Mia had work. Looking out the window, she saw that it was gray and the rain fell in sheets. Going to the diner was the last thing she wanted to do. After her vision last night, all she wanted was to see Ryder. Dragging herself out of bed, she quickly got ready, and ten minutes later strolled into the kitchen.

"G'morning. Would you like some breakfast, coffee?" Cerianne said, putting her newspaper down.

"No, thanks. I'll have a banana, and I'll grab something later… Oh, Mom, when is your show?"

"Two weeks, and you can bring some friends if you like," she said, lifting the paper once again. "Mia, I just want to let you know that the Fitzgeralds are coming over for lunch tomorrow. I saw Cathy at the beginning of the week, and we got talking. Hope you don't mind."

Mia choked on the banana. "Mom, do we have to? I really wish you had said something before you arranged it." She turned to grab her bag, and started to walk out.

"Mia, Cathy and Jonathan are my friends. It's only a meal, and you and Alex are friends, aren't you? Or is there something you're not telling me?"

Mia swallowed and shook her head. "No…I'm sorry. Dinner will be fine."

Staring at Cerianne, Mia knew it was wrong to be so moody with her. After all, Cerianne had no idea what was going on her in life. Reaching for her raincoat and umbrella, Mia darted outside. Ever since the night at the lake Mia was snappish with her mom, and it needed to stop. She walked alone through the torrential rain, and let her mind wander toward Ryder and how he had comforted her last night. As she smiled, the rain slowed. By the time she reached the diner the sun twinkled in an aqua sky, and she didn't need her umbrella. The bell tinkled as she opened the door to the diner and walked in. For a second Mia was blinded by the brightness in the diner, and was then dazzled by the mesmerizing figure that stood before her.

It was Ryder, looking utterly perfect and staring, with a grin, right at her.

Mia removed her coat, and began self-consciously re-arranging her hair and tugging on her short dress. Ryder raised his eyebrows as he watched her.

"Nice outfit," he said.

"I could thump you for that. Hey, I think I just stopped the rain!"

"Mia, shush. We don't want to draw attention toward us. Maybe I forgot to stress that using magic here is not allowed. You cannot simply go around changing the weather and not have anyone notice…"

"I didn't realize I was doing it."

"Look, we have to be careful, Mia," he said.

Her smile vanished. "I wasn't trying to stop the rain. It just kind of happened."

Ryder stepped closer, and spoke quietly. "Your magic feeds off your emotions, and you need to be in control of them, always—or god help us all when you're in a bad mood. I guess you were having happy thoughts?"

He kissed the tip of her nose, and her cheeks flushed.

"I know, I said I'd keep a distance and give you some time, I just couldn't help it. I wanted to see you after last night," he whispered hoarsely.

Staring at his black jacket and crumpled shirt, she wished they were anywhere but here.

"It's okay. I wanted to see you, and thanks for last night. No one has ever been there when I've had a vision, and I've never had one like that. I've gotta check in, and Sam the owner will be annoyed if he sees me fraternizing with *you*, instead of a customer."

Sam was in his middle sixties, and his wife had died several years ago after a long illness. After mourning her, he decided to do something that he had dreamt of doing his whole life, which was to run his own diner. Sam named it Felicities, after his late wife, and it became an overnight success. Outside, it resembled an old silver railroad carriage, but inside a fifties diner gleamed with black-and-white checkered floors, gleaming silver tables, leather seats, and cozy booths that all vibrated to an eclectic mix of old and new hits on the jukebox. The diner served all-day breakfasts, and had won several awards. Last year it expanded out the back to include a fresh bakery.

"I was always there for you, and I always will be. Besides, I am a customer. I'm here with my dad. He's a terrible cook. We nearly always end up eating out, and I thought I'd bring him here to meet you," he said, smirking.

"Dressed like this? You could've at least warned me," she said, raising her eyebrows in mock horror.

"Mia, he'll like you no matter what."

"I'll go and sign in, and come and take your orders," she said, as she pulled at her uniform once more before turning to leave, but Ryder gripped her arm to block her moving.

"Why the bandage?" he asked.

She sensed his tension as he stared at her arm, knowing he knew the answer without her saying anything, but she spoke anyway.

"I needed to hide the tattoo, and the cover stick didn't work." She raised her face to stare directly into his brooding and dark eyes.

He stifled a laugh by covering his mouth, and she thumped him playfully in the stomach.

"The tattoo, I see. Hmm, well, you can hide it with the bandage, but it's always been hidden until now, by magic. If you really want to hide it, you will," he taunted. "Anyway, don't fidget, you look great. Although, I'm not sure I like everyone seeing you like this."

"I'm actually quite accident-prone, especially with customers who get too friendly."

She smiled as she walked toward the kitchen. Pushing through the swinging doors, Mia could hear the chef shouting and the cooks busy preparing food. It was organized chaos. The smell of bacon sizzling made her hungry. Her friend Sylvia smiled when she saw Mia squirming in her uniform and walking toward her.

"Argh, I hate this uniform! I feel so exposed. Why won't Sam change them?" she said.

"Honey, I get it, but you're young and pretty and Sam wants to flaunt that. It's good for business. Anyway, I'll take all the dirty looks I can get, because I'm not getting any younger," Sylvia laughed.

Mia grabbed the order-book and pen, and shoved it behind her ear. "The boy, the one I told you about? He's here, with his dad."

Sylvia smiled. "How old is his dad?"

Mia laughed and then walked back into the diner. Ryder was sitting in a corner booth with an attractive man in his late forties.

"Hi, I'm sorry it's taken me so long to get to you. Can I get you a drink to start?" she said, aware that her cheeks were burning.

"Mia, this is my dad, Dr. James Mathews."

Her eyes flicked from Ryder to Dr. Mathews. They were strikingly similar, although they weren't related. Dr. Mathews was about her mom's age, and he wore modern black-rimmed glasses, but his dark eyes looked at her with such warmth that she instantly relaxed.

"It's nice to meet you, Dr. Mathews," she said, as they shook hands.

"James. Please call me James. It's good to meet you, and to know Robert has friends. He talks about you a lot. You should come over to the house." His eyes narrowed, as he held her gaze and smiled.

"I'd like that, thanks," she said, smiling back, liking Dr Mathews. She took their orders and left the table.

"Mia," Ryder called behind her. "I hope you didn't mind us coming here?" He strode up close to her.

"No, your dad seems really nice."

"He is, he's just always busy, and we live on takeout. There's only so much General Tao's chicken you can eat." He shrugged.

"You should both come for dinner when things settle. My mom is a great cook."

"Sure, that would be great, but dad rarely goes out. He's obsessed with his research."

"What is it in?"

Ryder shrugged his shoulders. "He thinks he's discovered a technique to enable time travel."

"And has he?" she said watching him closely.

"I honestly don't know. But…I think Emrys choose him because of his science background. Maybe he thought it would help, I don't know. But who we are and where we're from must remain a secret. No one would understand, Mia," he said.

"I'm not sure I understand. Sometimes I don't believe it. Maybe I've lived here for too long. I've got to go, otherwise I'm going to be sacked."

Ryder's hand shot forward and he grabbed her. "How can you say that when you just stopped the rain? Anyway, Sam would be a fool to let the best-looking waitress go. Can I see you tomorrow?"

"I'd love to, but—" Mia bit her lower lip, and stumbled to explain, and before she could, Ryder had slipped inside her mind, and discovered why.

"Damn it, Mia, you're seeing Alex?" He shook his head and moved away.

"Look, it's not like that. I'm sorry, but Cerianne invited him and his parents for dinner, and I can't get out of it. We could meet up afterwards. I really want to see you."

"Mia, you have to sort this out with Alex. Otherwise he's getting the wrong message." Ryder turned and started walking away, but she pulled him to face her.

"You have to be patient. Alex is my friend, and I tried to explain the other day, but he doesn't get it."

"He loves you, Mia. He doesn't want to face the fact you don't feel the same. You need to make a clean break—unless you do have feelings for him, which would change everything." He stared at her and then turned to walk away.

"It's all happening so fast," Mia said.

"To let him think he has a chance is wrong. I won't force you into anything, but I will not stand by and watch as you play around with him. You must decide. It has to be your decision." Then he strode away without looking back.

After the other night it was as if a light had been switched on, and almost everything seemed to fit into place. It all made sense, even when she questioned what she had seen. She and Ryder had been real. But when he talked about this Mia from Annwn, insecurity rose. The girl he talked about was so strong, brave, knowing what she wanted and going for it, willing to risk her life for the rest of mankind—and this didn't sound like her. The only time she was strong and confident was on stage, and then…well, then she was someone else! This world's Mia was no warrior. The smell of blood made her queasy, and faint. Fear was her middle name. She was just a girl who was too scared to have a relationship in case she broke her heart. Yet, when he talked, everything made sense and nothing else mattered. It was madness and yet wonderful.

A memory burned behind Mia's eyes. She was wrapped in Ryder's arms.

"I love you, and promise nothing will change. I'm yours." As the words left her lips, a dark twisted shape appeared on her wrist. The same design lay bare on his upper arm.

"So let it be. Mia and Ryder are promised to one another. May they both be blessed with strong magic and happiness."

Ryder swept Mia off her feet and swung her around as the crowd cheered. They had made a promise to love each other, no matter what, and now they were reunited. A gasp escaped from within her. Mia knew she belonged with him. She had to let Alex go.

Chapter Nine

Sunday Roast

Sitting at her desk, watching the people walking down the street outside her window, Mia played with her hair. Today was Sunday, and there was a misty drizzle outside which matched her melancholy mood. Last night after work, she remembered Ryder's words about the tattoo and using her magic to hide it. She tried to hide it, focusing her energy on the pattern, but nothing happened. The skin itched and she rubbed her wrist, undoing the bandage, which only made it worse. Dropping the bandage, her fingers smoothed over the inky design.

Be gone from sight, be gone.

The tattoo was still visible, and she sighed, reaching for the bandage once more—only to abandon that as an image of Ryder appeared inside her head, and she put all her energy into his smile. She closed her eyes.

For now be hidden.

Cerianne shouted from downstairs. Mia was meant to be studying for a biology quiz on Monday, plus she had an English assignment, but she couldn't focus on anything. She leapt up and ran downstairs. Her mom stood in the hallway wearing a bright pink apron over her black Capri trousers and white shirt.

"Do you think you could help set the table, and are you all right about Alex coming over now?" she said.

Mia stepped down and stood next to her mom. They were almost the same height.

"It'll be fine…but please, no baby photos or putting us together."

"I've never seen you so nervous. What's going on? Have you met someone else?"

Mia winced, was she that obvious. She shook her head and turned away. Mia had not talked about boys for so long with Cerianne, and now there was no way to explain Ryder. Mia took a deep breath. She blamed herself in part for her parent's breakup, and her mother's depression. The visions caused many arguments. However, lately Cerianne was happy, and she didn't want that to change.

"There is, isn't there? I can tell."

Cerianne walked to face Mia, who didn't know what to say. She bit her lip, flicked her hair behind her and moved toward the dining room. "I can't do this now."

The front doorbell rang, saving her from any further interrogation. Mia turned around, as Cerianne opened the door, and Mr. and Mrs. Fitzgerald and their daughter Louise walked in. Louise had her headphones plugged into her ears while furiously texting. She briefly lifted her head and mumbled a quick, "Hello."

Mia was about to ask where Alex was when he burst through the front door, large as life, holding a huge bunch of Calla Lilies, which he handed to Cerianne. She smiled, giving Mia a quick sideways glance, before ushering everyone into the kitchen.

The kitchen dominated the downstairs. It was sleek and modern, and the last piece of remodeling that had been done in the house since dad had left. The white units and sparkly granite counter-tops made the kitchen bright on any given day.

The adults were chatting about work and cooking, while Cerianne poured glasses of wine, so Mia excused herself to go and finish the dining-room settings. Alex followed hot on her heels, and she turned to face him, almost bumping into him.

"Sorry—" she said.

"Look Mia—" he said, running his hand through his hair.

"Alex, this dinner…it wasn't my idea." She turned away, and continued to lay out the cutlery.

"I figured as much. So, why?" he asked.

"Mom. Alex, we've been friends for so long, can't we just go back to the way things were?" she said.

Alex opened his mouth only to snap it closed. The dining room was softly lit with fairy lights, which surrounded the windows, and the long rectangular wooden table was laid with a crisp white tablecloth and silver chargers. In the center there was a small arrangement of fresh red roses. Cerianne carried the roast chicken dinner into the room. A veritable feast was laid out—of roasted vegetables, parsnips, Yorkshire puddings, and chicken gravy.

Cerianne lit the candles, and they all sat down to eat. It all looked inviting and welcoming, and yet the look between Alex and Mia, as they sat across from each other, was anything but friendly. The adults talked about the past, and in particular the good times they had shared. Louise continued to listen to her music in her own world, and Mia talked to Alex about the only safe topic she could think of—the band.

As soon as dinner finished, Mia rose from the table and gathered up the dirty plates. Alex collected some plates and followed her into the kitchen.

"Mia, stop. I honestly feel I don't know you anymore, it's like you're not the same person. What's changed?" His eyebrows bunched together and he continued, "Have I upset you?"

Mia held the tea towel, twisting it, as she spoke, "Alex, it's not you, it's me."

She stared out through the window. Her head turned, as the sounds of laughter reached them from the dining room. She turned to face him.

"Why can't we just be friends? I…" Her face was on fire, as she stumbled over her words.

"Damn it, Mia. The trouble with you is you don't know a good thing when you see it. I would've been good for you, and looked out for you, and you need someone like that." He leaned back against the kitchen units, gripping the tops with his hands. "I wanted things to change between us, but instead of getting closer, you've gone. I'm not sure where," he said, moving away.

"I didn't mean to. It's complicated," Mia said, avoiding his look.

"Complicated, right. You mean *Robert*?"

There was an edge to his voice, as if he chewed on the name and spat it out. Mia could hear her heart beating faster and faster as it skipped over beats. She said nothing not wanting to talk about *him*, but lifted her head, and caught Alex's look of anguish. He continued to stare, waiting for her to speak.

"Look, it's—"

"Complicated. Jeez, you must take me for an idiot."

He swore under his breath, threw the dishcloth in the sink, and stormed out the back door. The door swung on its hinges, and a blast of arctic air swirled inside. The warmth vanished with Alex, and Mia's heart pounded. A noise startled her, and Louise strolled into the kitchen, headphones in her hands.

"That Mary Kate is such a bitch," Louise said, to no one in particular. Staring around the kitchen, she turned, eyeballing Mia.

"Where's *Alex*?" Louise shivered catching the draft from the cold air, and Mia went to shut the door.

"He's gone," Mia said.

"Why? He wouldn't just leave. What did you say?" she asked, raising her voice.

"Not now!"

"You know, Mia, everyone thinks you're so nice, but I have to listen to him when he comes home, slamming the door. I've seen the way you are with him. I've told him you don't care about him, the way he wants. But, you wouldn't leave him be, would you." The words shot out of Louise's mouth like venom, and they stung.

"He's my friend, and I never intentionally led him on. I never wanted to hurt him," Mia said.

Cerianne walked in frowning, and behind her were the Fitzgeralds. The angry shouts must have been louder than their laughter.

"What's all the yelling about? What's wrong, Mia? You look…"

Louise stood in the middle of the kitchen and pointed at her. "*She*'s dumped Alex, and he's stormed off."

"It wasn't like that. I was never…actually…going out with him," Mia said, looking straight at her mom, pleading for her to understand. "I'm sorry, but I don't want to talk anymore."

"It's okay, love," Cerianne walked toward her and stroked her arm.

"Your mom's right. He's gone off in a huff, but he'll be back. We were your age once—in love one day, and out the next. It's time we went. Thanks, Cerianne, for a lovely meal," Mr. Fitzgerald gave a small smile, and then kissed Cerianne on the cheek. Moments later the hallway was deserted, except for Mia and her mother.

"I'm not going to pry, but I hope when you're ready, you can tell me what's going on."

"Thanks."

Mia wished she had told Alex after the first kiss, but she didn't want to lose him as a friend or hurt him, yet she'd managed to do both. Why was everything so complicated? She ran upstairs. He deserved to be angry. She was angry. Standing in front of her window, she held back the voile, watching gray clouds gather outside and the wind pick up speed, tossing the leaves around. There was a flash of white lightening across the sky, and she counted. One. Two. Three. Four. Thunder boomed overhead, the sound deafening and terrifying. Her cell-phone rang, and she answered ready to scream.

"Mia, I know you're upset, but stop with the light show," Ryder said.

This mess was because of him. Everything lately was to do with him, and she didn't want to speak to him for fear of what she might unleash. Thunder boomed loudly in the background.

"I'm not in a good mood. Alex walked out after we talked. I've really hurt him, I feel horrible," she said. It was true. Her body was stiff, cold, and she was shaking all over. Another huge crack of thunder boomed like an explosion, and shook the house.

"I'm coming over. Don't move," he ordered.

Before Mia could object there was a click, and he was gone. He knew that talking was the last thing that she wanted to do, but he gave her no option. How dare he? She twirled around in a panic, and ten minutes later strode out the back door of her house. Ryder must have been on his way when he called, because he was already there, astride his motorbike. The rain was torrential, but she didn't care. He was parked a short distance from the house, and Mia walked toward him, pulling up her zipper to keep the cold out. Ryder motioned for her to get on the bike, his expression invisible in the darkness, but instead of stopping, she ignored him and walked on.

I told you, I didn't want to talk.

Her feet moved, unsure of their destination, as the thunder roared overhead, and she jumped.

Stop the theatrics Mia, I'm not impressed.

She ignored him and carried on, lost in her thoughts.

Mia, stop.

His words screamed inside her head. The rain increased, and she walked faster ignoring the roar of the motorbike at her back.

"Mia, stop! This is stupid," he shouted. "This won't help anyone."

Mia turned to glare at him as he drove alongside at a snail's pace. Thunder ripped through the sky and a branch near where Ryder was snapped and fell to the ground, narrowly missing him. Louise's words rang aloud in her head. *Everyone thinks you're so nice*. Mia sensed Louise's anger and Alex's sense of betrayal. She stood drenched, oblivious to the flood of rain.

"Stop." Ryder parked his bike and walked to stand in front of her, gripping her arms. He shook her and when that did nothing, he pulled her into his arms and held her against his chest.

"Quit the fireworks. At this rate we'll either drown or get electrocuted."

Somewhere, along the walk her hood had slipped off her head and Ryder tried to wipe wet strands of hair out of her face. She was shivering. The thunder continued to pound the dark skies, and he ushered her in the direction of a deserted house. A For-Sale sign was staked out in the wild and overgrown front garden. Ryder held her hand and with his free one pushed against the front door, which clicked and opened.

"Come on, you're frozen. Any arguments and I'll throw you over my shoulder and take you home. Do you hear me?"

Something registered within her. "Not home—"

A musty odor greeted Mia as she walked in, and shadows stalked across the walls. Every now and then yellow headlights flashed in from passing cars. The room was a dark, empty shell, devoid of any life, but it was dry. Ryder took off her sopping coat and wrapped her in his leather jacket. He gently pushed her onto a wooden moving crate. Mia was beyond his take-charge attitude, and stood up ready to yell at him, but he caught her chin with both of his hands and kissed her.

The numbing coldness vanished, and a blaze of heat filled her. For a moment, she absorbed it, and then remembered why she was angry at him. She stood, thumped his chest and punched his jaw. The lights flickered. Ryder rubbed his jaw, moving it back and forth, but remained quiet.

"How could you, after what I've just done?" she screamed. The lights burst into life with each high-pitched tone in her voice. Her eyes briefly flicked toward the ceiling, but she kept going. "Are you completely heartless?" she said, knowing, as she spoke the words it wasn't his fault alone.

"Mia, I wanted to break the daze you were in, which worked, but next time I'll remember to move quicker! You pack one hell of a punch for someone so small," he said. "If the band doesn't work out, you could take up boxing." He watched her for a response. Anger makes you warm and strong. It gives you the strength to fight back, and bright amber light flooded the room.

"What do you mean? Alex is upset with me, not the band. This won't change anything for him! Once it's settled down..." She was shaking, and realized how clever Ryder was.

"Exactly! When Alex calms down—which, believe me, will be quicker than you—he'll see reason, and everything will sort itself out. You were right to do what you did. You have to give him time, and things will work out. Trust me. Are we done arguing? Because any more light shows, and the police will be here."

Mia let out a long breath—and the lights switched off, plunging them into darkness. Ryder stepped closer, lifted both her hands and kissed the fingertips, which sent a warm, fuzzy sensation racing throughout her body.

"Thank you," she smiled, as her teeth chattered. "Why do you push?"

"I knew you were angry, and you blame me. I feel your pain, and it doesn't go away until you're happy. Mia, in Annwn, we could reach each other's thoughts and feelings even if we weren't in the same room. We were connected. It's like that here, only I get a quick—usually painful—burst, and then nothing, because your feelings for me run hot and cold. We used to be able to comfort each other." He brushed a stray wisp of hair out of her eyes. "You're not a bad person."

She stared at his long dark lashes, which framed his beautiful chestnut-brown eyes. Their rich color drew her in. He was spellbinding. She couldn't breathe, and watched, mesmerized, as he lowered his head to brush his lips over hers. Shivers exploded down her spine, and her heart rocketed into space.

"I don't want to be hit again. Are you sure?" he said, raising an eyebrow and laughing.

Yes, kiss me, but if you don't stop messing with me, I will hurt you.

The heat level in the room rose, and the air stilled, as his steely gaze washed over her body and he pushed her against the wall. He captured her hands with his and kissed her lips. Small kisses to start, then deeper, more urgent ones, and Mia yielded to his possession. He leaned into her and pulled her closer, so that his tongue explored and tasted her. Lost in the overwhelming ripples of sensation, she wrapped her arms around him, and breathed his intoxicating scent in. Cocooned against his strong body, she never wanted it to end. Finally, she lifted her head, only because she needed to breathe. Ryder was grinning at her as she touched his face in wonder and smiled, her anger long forgotten.

"Tell me more about our life in Annwn," she whispered.

Ryder stroked Mia's cheek with the back of his hand and smiled. He let go of his hold on her and with an eager grin grabbed two empty boxes, which he pushed together. Glancing back, he winked and smiled. Then he closed his eyes, and mumbled some words under his breath. The air crackled with electricity, and the boxes vanished. In their place, a modern gray love seat appeared. Mia laughed. Ryder grabbed her hand, and they sat down.

Ryder sighed, "We aren't meant to use magic here, as I've said, but every now and then it serves a purpose. It's hard to resist and being here with you it's like old times, almost. I could've stopped you hitting me, but you needed to let go of your emotions, rather than stay angry. Your anger could've burnt the house down, or worse."

He grabbed her hands and Mia listened intently watching his face as his smile turned into a frown. A throbbing pain exploded in her temples and a scene from long ago surfaced. Her face drained of color, and she turned away. *Colorful flashes and distorted pictures filled her mind. Mia was at school and there was a girl, struggling to breathe.* Ryder's hand pulled her face toward him and his gaze was hypnotic. He was doing that thing again, probing her mind. She shut her eyes and shook her head. Instantly his hands slipped away. Mia chewed on her lower lip unsure as to how much Ryder had seen and that particular memory was not one she wanted to share with anyone, especially him, because it terrified her. It showed a side of Mia that scared her more than the Darkshadow and she wanted nothing more than to change the mood and forget it had ever happened. She touched his shoulder and smiled.

What spell did you use to change the boxes?

Her words ricocheted in his mind, and he stared long and hard at her for a few moments before he spoke.

"I know you are keeping secrets from me, and I won't push you, but I want you to know that when you're ready, I'm here for you. As for the boxes, I used a simple transformation spell. I simply wished for a sofa instead of the boxes, and *voila*." He placed his arm along the back of the sofa and gazed at Mia. She relaxed, but was unwilling to share what had happened in school, wanting to know more about the spells instead.

"But you were mumbling," she said, moving closer. She pressed her hands across his chest, and he stared at them. His hand rubbed the bristles on his chin.

"Oh, that. That was a protection spell. I was worried the police would turn up, because of all the flashing lights. I set up a one-mile perimeter safety spell. No one will disturb us, at least for an hour."

Ryder shifted his position resting his elbows on his legs as he sat forward. "Look, I know, I'm being blasé about using magic, something under normal circumstances I wouldn't. Emrys would be furious, but you drive me crazy. I want the old Mia back." He shook his head, and swore under his breath. "There are parts of our lives you either still don't remember or simply ignore, and you're blocking your thoughts from me. We never kept secrets from each other and it's very frustrating. I wish you would trust me." Impatiently, he grabbed her hand.

"Just hang on, okay? Don't let go. I know you've astrally projected several times alone, but I want us to go together. This requires more concentration and for both of us to use our magic. Please, let me guide you."

Mia's heart was beating fast, and she nodded squeezing his hand.

"We're going home." He stared at her with his big brown eyes and her insides melted.

Ryder's voice was hypnotic. Everything, inside Mia's body slowed, and her spirit lifted as light as air. This whole visiting another realm was beyond cool, but somewhat unsettling. Her stomach dropped, and for a moment she felt sick, but then it was amazing. She knew she wasn't actually up in the sky, but asleep on the couch. Even so, as they glided across endless blue sky and passed over the odd low flying white cloud, her body responded as if it were real and she shivered.

Mia gazed at the majestic mountains of Glynn Cunn, and the enchanted dark woods dominated by row upon row of evergreen trees. The wind bent the trees, and they looked as if they were bowing to them. The sun radiated its golden sparkling rays across the meadows and valleys of Annwn. Green grass stretched as far as the eyes could see, and eagles twice the size of Mia accompanied them all the way.

Her body lowered, and her feet landed on the soft grass. They were near the Temple of Ashwar by the great sea. Mia let go of Ryder's hand and walked to the edge of the hill to stare at the view.

"Annwn is beautiful, is it not?" he said, standing behind her. She turned her head to face him. His broad shoulders and wide chest seemed even more powerful here in this magical realm. He drew his thick brows together and stared at her with his beautiful, dark, earth-brown eyes.

"Of course."

A glowing sparkle covered her arms, and Mia lifted them in surprise. She stared at the clothes that she was dressed in. Ryder had changed her outfit, and she stood dressed in a beautiful silk gown of royal blue that fell to the ground. It was sleeveless, and the bodice was cut suggestively low. She huffed at that, but in touching the soft material admitted to herself that it was pretty. Ryder pulled her into his arms, and kissed her lips before she could resist.

"You're in Annwn, and I'm sick of seeing you in jeans…" he scolded.

Mia imagined him naked, and sure enough his clothes disappeared. He stood in just his black boxers. Mia thought it would be funny, and that he would be embarrassed, but of course, he stood brazenly with his shoulders back and wearing a smile from cheek to cheek. Mia's mouth watered as she studied his flat and taut abdominal muscles. Ryder was built like a Roman god or Calvin Klein model—and Mia's pulse raced. Her cheeks flamed as her gaze glided over every inch of his powerful physique. His eyes locked with hers, and he gave a smug smile that made her insides quiver.

"Is this what you dream about, Mia?"

Turning away, Mia gazed at trees swaying in the field to distract her mind from his gorgeous body. With the perfect image of his body gone, Mia changed back into her jeans and a black long-sleeved T-shirt. Ryder grumbled, "I prefer the gown."

He reached for her hand, and as she turned around she saw he was dressed in a white linen top and soft moleskin trousers that hugged his legs. "Man-made fabrics are too rough," he explained.

Mia stifled a laugh. A comfortable silence followed as they strolled around the elaborate gardens that bordered the temple. The only sound was the crunch their feet made as they walked on the tiny white stones of the paths. Tall hedges made an intricate maze, and flowers of many colors fringed the corners of the long rectangular garden.

"They call this the Lovers Path, because once inside the maze you can be in there for days and…" His thumb caressed her hand.

"I remember, Ryder," she said, as she willed her heart to slow, because his touch was eliciting such wonderful sensations

"And yet, not everything is the same." He stepped closer to hold her chin. Her eyelids dipped at his scrutiny, and she looked away.

"Nothing stays the same. We've both changed." She broke free of his hold and walked toward the castle steps.

"Yet it seems that we make the same mistakes. Annwn was never perfect, Mia. What place is? Yes, certain rules were made to protect us and our way of life. After the mortals entered our world, they had to be made to protect our future. Yet, here we are in the human world again. Do you not already feel the darkness that surrounds us?"

She crouched down low to pick a small serenity flower, and stood up as she examined it.

"Mia, I could have refused this challenge, but I knew we had to see this through. I knew you would never believe you had done enough unless you tried. Now, I wonder if you had doubts about your feelings for me before we left, and maybe that was part of the reason for choosing such an impossible challenge. Mia, we belong in Annwn, not in the human world, no matter what you think. If you don't open your heart, we'll never be able to return."

"Ryder, I feel the love I felt for you inside, but we were raised together from such a young age. I don't even really remember my parents. Don't you see? Our future was planned, and our fate sealed from the beginning."

Ryder stared at her opened–mouthed, and then let out a deep sigh. He let go of her shoulders and stormed ahead, shoving his hands deep in his pockets. Storm clouds gathered, matching his foul mood. Mia raced after him, and reached the wooden arbor just as the rain burst from the sky. She blew at her hands to keep herself warm. Ryder stood on the opposite side staring at the rainbow that filled the sky as the rain stopped.

"We are not human. Humans are weak, deceitful, and savage. No promise is kept. Men and women are equally to blame. In fact, it's hard to distinguish the men from the women. They share everything, even the clothes. Do you not find that in the slightest bit odd?" His eyebrows furrowed in confusion.

"Why do you have such loathing for humans? Our people are part human. Do you feel contempt for them as well? No one is perfect, Ryder." Her voice was distant and serious.

"Mia, I do not have contempt for the Shades. The children of the humans were raised in Annwn. We are all children of Annwn, but the Shades are different from us, Mia. Their magic is not as strong, but I do not loathe them. You know, I have friends who are Shades. "

"So, it's merely the humans you dislike. Honestly, Ryder, you're so conceited. In the human world, you have the freedom to have a relationship without a commitment."

Moving quickly, he stood in front of her and leaned in close, placing his hands on either side of her face. "Is that what you wish for…freedom…from me?"

Frustration flooded her, and something else—loneliness. That wasn't what she had meant at all. She wasn't sure entirely sure what she did mean.

"I'm scared, and I've been scared for so long that I don't know how to be any different. I don't know who I am, and I don't know what I'm meant to do."

Ryder pressed his body against hers, and brushed her lips. "I know, but you're not alone, and you're wrong Mia. You always had a choice. No one forced you. We made decisions together, we argued, but you used to listen to me and I to you. You've forgotten how headstrong you could be. You always knew your own mind, and were driven by your visions. In the end, they consumed you. When the visions showed the end of the human race you saw a time when, for all their advances, they seemed to lose their compassion and need for love. The divide between rich and poor grew wider. There was global unrest, and the world teetered on the brink of war, but the most pressing problem you saw was infertility. Maybe, it is the humans' passion for self-destruction that I loathe Mia—not the people."

Mia walked on, holding his hand firmly, as memories of the vivid scenes flashed into her mind. A renowned Professor of infertility, William Harding, was interviewed on television to explain why birthrates were drastically low. In the beginning, his research was dismissed as merely scare-mongering. Afterward his report was demonized—until more reports and studies were released, and they confirmed his research findings. Infertility was reaching epidemic proportions, after which the end of the world was predicted in every newspaper, sending millions into panic.

They were at the cliff head again. Mia stared across at the ancient fortress that stood on the adjacent cliff. The imposing castle, with its tall towers which stood like sentinels on guard, was once home—and now it seemed so alien to her. She turned and stared out at the never-ending sea, watching the ferocious waves crash along the rocky shore.

"I remember the pain of couples unable to conceive. The reason I withdrew was because this sickness, this epidemic. I saw it happen in Annwn as well, and I couldn't bear it. I saw a time when we would suffer too. Nothing's changed. That future is lying in wait. I don't know how we can change it, but I know we must try."

The ocean roared, and the spray from the seawater splashed up into her face. Her shoulders dropped, and something eased inside her. It didn't resolve the conflicted feelings toward Ryder, but she knew this was more important than their relationship.

"Look, maybe I'm not the Mia you used to know—we've both changed, but as you say, the reason we're here hasn't. We have to focus on that. The rest will take time. Part of me accepts you and everything you say, but there's a part of me that wants nothing to do with any of this," she said, shoving the tattoo in his face.

"All I know, is that until this moment, I was scared of who I was—terrified even. However, since I bumped into you I have been trying to accept that I'm different for a reason, and that I have responsibilities. To you. To Annwn. To the humans. I'm just not sure how I can help! Emrys said he was concerned that something else was working against the humans. In the global commission that was set up, it highlighted a multitude of issues behind the infertility. One was environmental, another was an infection that rendered males infertile. The human race's DNA was changing, making pregnancy unlikely. Do you think the Darkshadows could be involved?" Mia's body trembled at the thought. In the field beyond, she watched as winged horses took flight, and soared into the purple hazy skies.

Ryder remained unmoved. "Mankind is reckless. As guardians of Annwn and Mankind, we believe it has always been about balance. When our bloodline was weakened by human blood, the Wise Elders feared for our future and the strength of our magic. They feared that the magic that shrouds and hides our world would weaken, and our world would disintegrate. They created, the Promise to ensure the strongest of matches. I agreed to help the humans, to keep our world safe and ensure that the future you see doesn't happen. But I worry about the cost." Mia knew she wasn't the same girl he had known, living as a human had changed her, leaving her insecure and fearful.

"I know. I made the decision to come based on a vision, of a child I believed was ours. As laughable as it may be to me now, I know I felt I had no option but to go. Our lives are intrinsically linked with the future of the humans, because our people are partly-human and what happens in this world could happen in Annwn. Even if that wasn't the case, I would still need to help." Mia would've made the same decision again, even though she didn't understand how she could change anything.

"Mia, I know, and it's why I love you," he said, caressing her wrist where the tattoo was clearly visible. Wolves howled in the distance, and Ryder quickly glanced at the horizon near the forest and then back toward Mia. She was studying her tattoo and lifted her chin to face him.

"No matter what you think, Mia, we don't belong in their world. Being there is only meant to be temporary. You've been away from Annwn for too long, and are more human than I imagined. Come on, we have to leave."

Ryder held her hand, but Mia knew he was frustrated. The trees and tall grasses swayed. A sound like a lullaby sang on the wind. It was as if Annwn was saying good-bye. Emrys said it was her destiny to help mankind. Had he known she would feel such conflict in the human world? He once hinted at how different and challenging it would be. As she let Ryder guide them home she knew they were promised to one another, but a more pressing challenge lurked.

Annwn was real. Until now it seemed impossible, but as her hands ran along the bushes and she breathed in the air, familiarity stirred. Letting go once more, their spirits rose up into the skies. Even though Annwn was on Earth, it may as well have been on a distant planet, it seemed so far away from the human world.

Chapter Ten

Knowing the serious challenge ahead, Mia found the mundane task of surviving the Monday morning school gossip a welcome relief. She walked through the school halls with Danni, ignoring the glares and pointed fingers.

"Alex's ego's hurt, that's all. He'll survive," Danni said, quietly.

Mia tugged at her sleeve to cover her wrist. The tattoo's visibility mirrored her indecision over Ryder.

"What about you and Robert?"

Mia hesitated for a second as the name caught her, and then she smiled. To her, he would always be Ryder. "We're friends."

"Just friends?" Danni swung around to face Mia.

Mia opened her mouth, and then shut it unwilling to reveal anything more.

"Why can't you just admit you're seeing him?" she said, and then stormed off. Mia stared back at the onlookers, who burst out laughing.

Monica Goldman, a tall, broad-shouldered girl with raven-colored hair and blood-red lips, was at the center. Mia needed to move but stood glaring until the girl walked past her. A wave of intense hatred washed over her as Monica shoved against her.

"Lover's tiff, hm?" Monica sneered. "You've got the whole *ménage `a trois* thing going on, don't you? Personally, I don't see what either of them see in you, freak."

Mia pushed away from her and silently walked away, while her heart thumped against her chest. Monica and her groupies chanted the word "Slut!" Each step she took, the volume increased and her cheeks were in flames.

Don't Mia. Anything you do now puts you in danger.

Ryder's words calmed her, and she walked quickly, ignoring the laughter and name-calling. "Danni wait please," she said, trying to catch up with her.

Danni stopped and turned around.

"All right, we've been seeing each other, but we're trying to be discreet, which is almost impossible in this place."

"I knew it. Why are you keeping it a secret from me? You know you can trust me?" Danni said crossing her arms.

"It's not you—" Mia said, looking around, not wanting anyone to hear their conversation and not wanting to meet her friend's gaze.

"Oh, I see. Tyler… Well, I wouldn't have told him." She smiled and Mia smiled back.

"I didn't want you to have to keep a secret. Anyway, please don't say anything to him."

"I promise. What was all the laughing about back there?"Danni shrugged.

"Monica. She's always hated my guts—ever since middle-school, remember?"

"Yep. Like, how could I forget? But that wasn't your fault."

Mia remembered how she'd imagined Ryder in pain, and then he was doubled over in agony, how her temper made the thunder crack and the lights almost blow up. Now she was convinced that she was responsible for almost killing Monica that day, not so long ago, when they'd argued.

"I'm not so sure. Come on, we're going to be late."

For the rest of the day, Mia was a bystander in her own life. She smiled, nodded, and answered questions, coasting through the day until the bell rang, signaling that school was over.

There, that wasn't so bad, now was it?

The lilt of his voice was like a caress. She smiled.

No, not so bad. Mine, at five. Don't be late.

Mia heaved her books up and threw them into her backpack. The classroom emptied until she was alone. As she stepped toward the door, the distance seemed to increase, which made her stomach drop and a shiver of goose- bumps trail along her arms.

Ryder.

Taunting whispers echoed around the classroom, making her dizzy. Frosty kisses blew against her shoulders and she whisked around expecting to find someone standing next to her, but she was alone.

"Get a grip," she muttered under her breath.

Mia hugged herself. The normally toasty temperature nose–dived, and it was like being at the North Pole. A crackling noise at the window caught her attention, and she turned staring at them as a frosty film moved over the glass misting the windows hiding any view outside. A shaky scrawl of letters appeared on the smoky glass.

Dinner smells delicious.

Mia inhaled an odor of tomatoes and garlic that surrounded her. Cerianne's laughter echoed inside her head, and cold fear rattled her heart making it skip beats.

Ryder the Darkshadow has Cerianne!

Swiveling around as a hot burst of fury engorged her body, she ran for the closed door. Twisting and pulling the handle so hard, Mia ended up holding it in her hand and still the door wouldn't open. She yelled and screamed, banging on the door for help, but no one came.

Ryder!

Flashing before her eyes was Cerianne's normally friendly face, drawn taut, and her eyes flared in terror. Another picture flashed in her head. She could see the pathway and her mother stood smiling at the front door. A young man appeared, with hair the color of wheat and striking blue eyes. Mia's heart jumped. She knew that face, and time paused as she pushed against the door. There was a click and the door swung open, and Ryder ran toward her. He crushed her into his arms, reassuring her that Cerianne would be fine.

"We have to find her," Mia pleaded.

The drive took less than ten minutes, and after leaving the motorbike in her driveway, they ran into the quiet house.

"Mom!"

Walking through the empty hallway, all she could hear was the pendulum swinging back and forth from the tall grandfather clock. The house was devoid of any life. Mia crept toward the kitchen and Ryder searched upstairs. After walking through the empty kitchen, she entered the study. She sighed, and chewed her lower lip. Her mother wasn't home. Glancing around, she stared at a black-and-white photograph that lay on her mother's desk. The face of the man that stared back at her was the one who visited her house on his dragon.

The Darkshadow.

It was him. Floppy dirty-blond curls framed his chiseled and distinguished face. His eyes glinted at hers. She picked the photograph up and held it closer to examine. A sinking feeling invaded, and before she could control it she was on the ground, the photograph dropped from her hand. Mia sat, too weak to rise, but drew her legs up to hug her knees. Cerianne didn't deserve to be mixed up in this. Ryder was calling her name, but she couldn't summon the energy to respond.

"Mia, it's not your fault," he called as he walked in. "This Darkshadow is messing with you, playing some kind of game. Maybe, he wants to test your weaknesses, or see what you'd be willing to do. I don't know," Ryder said, shaking his head.

"Look at this picture," Mia said, as her hand reached out, searching across the floor. Jumping up, she nearly knocked herself out on the table as she began to look for the photograph.

"Mia what are you doing?" he said

"It was here, it was a photograph of him. Did you pick it up? It was just here." Mia frowned.

"Mia, I haven't touched anything," he said, as his arms pulled her into a hug.

At that moment, her cell-phone burst into song. She quickly looked at the screen, flashed Ryder a smile, and pressed the phone to her ear.

"Mom, where are you? Really? Oh my God, are you all right? Hm, yes. Don't worry, just please be careful and drive safely." She fixed her gaze on Ryder, frowning as she replaced her cell-phone in her pocket. Mia sucked on her lip and walked into the kitchen. Ryder followed close behind her.

"Cerianne's fine, like you said—a bit shook up, but fine. Apparently, a man grabbed her bag and ran off with it in the mall. She tried to follow, but another man intervened and chased after the man and got her bag back. Cerianne said the man had brilliant blue eyes and hair the color of straw. Ryder, it's the Darkshadow. What am I going to do?" She turned around staring at him for an answer. Ryder swept a hand through his hair and frowned.

"You can't let him know. I think he's waiting to see your reaction. Don't. He can't hurt you, Mia. He's only allowed to watch, not intervene. He suspects you're different, like I said," His eyes narrowed and his lips pressed into a straight line.

"I need to get hold of Emrys. In the meantime, have you ever thought about getting a dog?" Ryder led her to the back door and opened it wide. He stuck two fingers in his mouth and blew a whistle. Out of the bushes, a small, shaggy, beige-and-silver-haired mutt bounded up with its tongue hanging out and wagging its tail.

"Oh my God, he's adorable, but Cerianne will have a fit. She'll never let him stay, and I'm sorry Ryder, but he's hardly a guard dog!" She knelt on the ground patting her thighs, and straight away, the dog dived onto her lap. Bouncing up, he licked her face and eventually nestled in against her.

"Size isn't what counts. Samson isn't just a dog, Mia. He's a Scrivim. Not only can he emit really odious pheromones that the Darkshadows find unbearable, but he changes into a blood-sucking monster with a thirst for Darkshadows, but only if he needs to."

Mia gawped with her mouth open, suddenly uncertain as to whether she should stroke the dog, but he licked the palm of her hand and she smiled. "Well, Samson, you've got my vote."

* * * *

Later that night, as Mia lay in bed Cerianne came into her room and sat on the edge of her bed. Samson followed closely at her heels.

"Mia, about this stray dog—"

"His name is Samson, and Mom, you'll hardly know he's there. It's only for a while. When Stella moves into her new house then she'll take him back, but they won't allow pets in the apartment. She brought over all his food and his bed. Look at him, he's so cute."

As if on cue the dog sat still, wagging his tail and resting his chin on Cerianne's knee, soliciting a smile, and she ruffled his hair.

"All right, for now, but you have to take him for his walks. Sorry that I didn't get to meet Robert. Why don't you invite him over for dinner tomorrow?"

"Mom, you have nothing to be sorry about. Robert left because he thought you would be a bit shook up after what happened at the Mall. We can have dinner another night. I'm just glad you're okay."

Mia reached for Cerianne's hand and squeezed it. Her mother nodded her head and then gave an awkward smile, her brown eyes flaring widely.

"It was my fault. If I hadn't been rushing—but he came out of nowhere, and just ran at me. I couldn't react quickly enough."

Mia edged closer and hugged her. "It wasn't your fault. He saw an opportunity and grabbed it. Lucky for you, there was someone nearby that was able to help. Did you catch his name?" "No, it all happened so fast." Cerianne was smiling at the dog. "He handed over my bag and just told me to be careful. He said the world is full of dangerous people." Cerianne lifted her head and gazed at Mia.

Mia huffed and sat back. "Well, that's another reason for having Samson."

Cerianne raised her eyebrows and laughed. "He's not exactly what comes to mind when I think of a guard dog!"

"But he should make a good burglar alarm."

Samson jumped up, barking loudly as he pirouetted around like a dancer, and they both laughed.

* * * *

The next day after school, Ryder was at Mia's house for dinner. The smell of garlic and tomatoes wafted through the hallway as they headed toward the kitchen. Shivers exploded down her spine as the Darkshadow's words from the other day came to mind.

"Ryder, I know you said he's playing a game, but I'm scared. I feel as if he's watching me and Cerianne. Does he know who I am?"

Ryder breathed in, lowered his head, and sighed. "I'm not sure. I have my suspicions, but you have to act normal, and not use any magic for him to see. Mia, if he knows he can upset you, it will incite him even more. He's not behaving like a typical Darkshadow. Why he's playing you, I don't know—we're not enemies. We'll talk to Emrys and sort it out, I promise." Ryder stopped by a photograph that hung on the wall in a black frame.

"You all look happy together." He studied the family picture and stared back at Mia, holding her hand in a firm grip.

"We were." Mia tried to move, but Ryder held fast.

"Were you close to your father?" Ryder's eyebrows drew together as he waited for her to answer. The picture had been taken while they were on holiday in Hawaii.

Yes, we were close.

Mia was too choked to speak. She stepped closer and stared at her father. He was tanned, relaxed, and yes…happy. She hadn't spoken to him in such a long time. Hawaii was their last family holiday.

"Do these pictures upset you?"

"No. My dad left us, and that made me angry. Now, I don't care," she said, walking away. Painful memories resurfaced in her mind. She scratched her arm, then gasped as Ryder touched her hand. *Images and feelings raced through her head for him to read. Angry voices blasted out, and Mia crouched on the stairs as Cerianne screamed at her dad in the kitchen. There was shattering glass and Mia raced to her room, covering her head with a pillow and crying herself to sleep.* Absorbing this memory of hers, Ryder pulled her against his chest and stroked her hair.

They were arguing over dinner, but it could have been over anything. They just weren't in love anymore.

Mia sobbed against him, getting his shirt wet, but she couldn't stop. He kissed her head and held her tight until her sobs ceased.

I'm sorry

"It's not your fault. Moving from Wales to New England was meant to be a new start for us. Dad promised, but instead they grew apart. He left, and Cerianne fell apart. Within a year they were divorced."

Cerianne hasn't been the same since. Loving someone is not worth all that!

Mia moved away from Ryder, needing the space and drew in a deep breath. Part of her still blamed herself for her parents' split and her old insecurities returned. She blocked further thoughts from Ryder—there were parts of herself she didn't want him to see. Ryder was behind her in seconds.

Is that truly what you believe Mia? In Annwn, love is the most precious gift we can give to each another. To love and be loved—is that not what existing is all about? If not to be loved, then what?

"Living here, I grew up terrified because I was different from other children and it caused a lot of problems." Mia shrugged and tried to move away as a feeling of self-disgust rose inside her. She sniffed and glared at him.

"You have to deal with this, Mia. It's why you're the way you are," he said, pulling her into his arms.

"And *what* way am I?" She struggled, not wanting to be held captive, not wanting to give in, but looking at his dark determined glare, and feeling his thumb caress her cheek, she softened.

"Damaged, defensive, and very stubborn," he said, smiling. He held her in his arms and whispered against her neck. "I don't want you to hide this away from me. Your father let you down, I get that, but he still loves you, Mia. People make mistakes, but you cannot give up on love. You weren't to blame, and you have to stop thinking that. This was their mess, not yours."

Mia let his warmth comfort her. "It's more complicated than that. He, I—" Mia broke off and let some of her memories enter into his mind. *They played out before him, and Ryder saw Mia as a child sitting in the kitchen, crying. Her parents were talking to her about school and a picture she had drawn. The picture showed people, lying scattered on the ground covered in blood. Cerianne was sobbing, and her father paced up and down shouting.*

The memories continued. Mia was older, dressed in a white hospital gown, strapped down onto a slim silver table as doctors sedated her. Her violet eyes were wide, and tears fell down her cheeks. She was terrified, and inside her mind was numb. One last scene flickered to life in which Mia's father loomed in front of her. He gripped her hands, twisting them, and then let them fall away. He stalked away raking his hands through his hair.

"Mia, this nonsense has to stop. It's causing too much upset," he said.

The volume of the television increased, and Mr. Childs swiveled away from her to face the screen. A news report described a fatal plane crash. Moments before, Mia had told him it was going to happen. His mouth opened, and he jerked his head around to glare at Mia. All she could see was her father's disgust.

Ryder shook his head as the images left him. He frowned, and rubbed his temple. The shock and betrayal Ryder felt washed through Mia. She waited and stared as he squeezed the bridge of his nose with his fingers. Finally, he lifted his gaze to meet hers.

"I'm finding it extremely difficult to put into words exactly how I feel right now. Your father, I think, he knew you were gifted—but he was scared, as most humans are."

Mia had never considered that possibility before. After the plane crash, Mia mastered the trick of blocking the visions with pain, by cutting herself. It was the only way she found to stop the visions. But after a while she didn't need to physically hurt herself—she simply remembered the pain, and that was enough to stop the visions. She couldn't explain any of this to Ryder, because he would feel pity for her and that was the last thing she wanted. Mia lifted her hand to smooth it across his cheek and his eyes darkened. A ripple of awareness flooded her as his gaze rested on her mouth, and their bodies molded against each other. There were no words, just a pulsing warmth and intimacy that surrounded them.

"Well, you must be Robert," said Cerianne, as she looked at Mia and Ryder.

Letting go of Mia, he stepped forward and shook her mother's hand. "It's nice to meet you, Mrs. Childs. Mia's been telling me all about your work at the gallery."

Cerianne smiled and nodded at him. "Oh, has she now? Well, Mia's been keeping *you* a bit of a secret," Cerianne said smiling.

"Mom," Mia groaned.

He smiled, "Dad rarely cooks, so thanks for inviting me over."

"Oh, come to think of it, your dad is more than welcome to join us. I don't know why I didn't think of it before," she said.

"You sure? I'll try, but he may not pick up," Ryder said, walking into the hallway to try his cell-phone.

"Mia, he's lovely—polite, and handsome…" Cerianne said.

Watching her mother, Mia realized, just how far she had come since the divorce. After dad left, her mother turned into a ghost of herself and seemed to go into mourning. There were times when she came home from school to find Cerianne still in bed. Mia was the parent, comforting her while Cerianne sobbed in her arms, making her get dressed and forcing her to eat. For weeks, Mia tried to act normal in school. However, one day all her pent-up frustration and anger burst out.

Mia was used to being ignored, living in the shadows as she did, but this day was different. Whispers of her parents' divorce were at every corner of school. Monica, a known school bully, pushed into her as she passed by and yelled out.

"Watch it freak, or have you been drinking like your loser of a mother?"

Muffled laughter surrounded Mia, and she lifted her head to glare at Monica. There was total silence, and before she thought about her actions Mia was in front of her. Heat pumped through her body, surging through her veins, her heart bashed against her ribs, and her hands burned. Monica's mouth was moving and further taunts bellowed, but Mia shook her head, ignoring the words. Her hands twitched and throbbed with pain. A burning heat built inside Mia as Monica's freckled face pushed into hers, and she pushed her hand against Monica's chest, slamming her into the wall. The girl grabbed Mia's arm and twisted it around and something inside snapped.

"What ya got to say for yourself? Mom's a drunk, Dad's left town, and you like to cut yourself. Won't be long before they cart you off to the loony bin, and give you some shock treatment, you freak!" Spit splattered over Mia's cheeks as Monica hissed her venomous words.

In that moment, Mia smacked Monica across the face, stunning the girl into silence. For a second there was no response, but Monica's upper lip curled and she charged forward, grabbing handfuls of Mia's hair. War broke loose, and everyone joined in screaming and shouting. Tears streamed down Mia's face as she wished Monica Goldman dead. The very next second, Monica struggled to breathe, and her body jerked. She was coughing, wheezing, and strange rasping noises came from her throat. The light in Monica's eyes dimmed, and she dropped to the ground. It happened so fast, one minute Monica was standing and the next she lay on the ground lifeless. The crowd gathered closer, and shouts sounded out, which turned into screams. Mia stood by as people rushed around her, and she willed Monica to breathe, to move.

A roar from the crowd announced that Monica was awake and breathing. There were looks in Mia's direction, but the bell rang and when Monica stood, red-faced, everyone dispersed. When Mia arrived home later that day, as soon as she entered the house, she sank to the ground leaning against the doorframe. Tears fell, and she was shaking uncontrollably as they poured from her. A cold hand touched hers, and Mia lifted her head to find Cerianne kneeling next to her, fully dressed, with tears trickling from her eyes with her arms extended. For a moment, Mia hesitated and then fell into them. They clung to each other like shipwrecked sailors to a life raft.

"It's going to be all right. I'm so sorry," Cerianne said, as she rocked her back and forth.

Staring at Cerianne's smiling and confident face now, Mia realized, she had kept her word. She hugged her.

"Mia, I've never seen you looking more radiant and confident. If this is the affect Robert has on you, he has my vote." Cerianne brushed a stray strand of hair out of Mia's eyes. Mia gave a tentative smile and wondered if Ryder would feel the same way about her if he knew she had almost killed someone. Until recently, Mia wasn't sure that she was to blame over the Monica incident, believing it was an accident, but now she knew differently. Ryder was simply too good for her.

Chapter Eleven

The Warehouse

Mia sat in the back of Danni's Honda, listening to Tyler's exasperated conversation with her.

"*Danni*, watch the road! You nearly hit the mailbox." He wasn't a nervous passenger. It was a fact that Danni's eyes wandered as she drove. Ignoring him, Danni looked at Mia in the mirror.

"Everyone's going to The Warehouse, tonight. Why don't you and Robert come?" she asked.

The car shuddered to a halt at the curb right outside her house. The Warehouse was in the industrial part of town. It was an enormous and derelict mill building, yet to be renovated. Every month there were raves and illicit parties.

"Oh, I don't know—small problem, namely Alex," Mia replied.

"It's been weeks. Anyway, he's not hiding Laurie," Danni said.

"Yes…but," Tyler said. Mia knew he didn't think she should go, it was written all across his painfully still face and tight lips.

"It's a guy thing, I get it. I don't want to rock the boat. I'll see," Mia said.

She started to get out of the car, but before she touched the handle, Ryder pulled the door open. He nodded his head at Tyler and Danni. As Mia stood in front of him, he grabbed her backpack and swung it over his shoulder.

Danni stuck her head out from the car, "So, are you going to come to The Warehouse or not?"

Mia rubbed her eyes. She couldn't give two hoots about going or not, but she sensed it meant something to Ryder. His eyes rested on her face.

Come on, be brave. We have to face him sooner or later.

Mia bent to look at Tyler, who looked straight ahead. Ryder was right. They couldn't hide forever. How much trouble could it cause?

"No more hiding. We'll be there."

Tyler sucked his breath in, but Danni was ecstatic. "Great, we'll see you there, then."

The car pulled away, and Mia stood wondering whether she had made a huge mistake. "Well that's that then!" she said, stunned that she'd actually agreed to go.

"Mia, we have to face people. I've had enough hiding. We can't avoid him forever. It's time."

He lifted her hands and kissed them. Ryder made everything sound easy and straight forward, whereas she always saw pain and heartache. They walked side by side into her house, and ran straight up to her room. Mia showered and changed into a clean pair of faded jeans and a new T-shirt. Her hair was damp, and she added some mousse running her fingers through her long strands. Ryder sat on her bed watching her preen herself, totally engrossed. Finally, she smeared some lip-gloss across her lips and sprayed a small amount of perfume along her neck. The perfume was called *Miracle,* and that was what she needed tonight. Her shoulders ached, and a prickling sensation filled her stomach.

Mia studied her reflection in the mirror and gazed across at Ryder. He was pretending to be asleep, but every now and then, she caught his stare and smiled. The girl before her was barely recognizable. She looked older and taller. Her heart-shaped face was fresh and glowing. She was happy.

Ryder sat up. "You look wonderful," he said as he jumped up and came to stand behind her, folding his arms across her chest. Mia stared at their faces in the mirror and couldn't breathe. Ryder looked so strong and handsome. His cheek rested against hers and he wore a smug grin. Next to him, she was tiny. Brushing aside her hair, he kissed her neck.

"You smell wonderful too." His voice was hoarse, "If we don't go now, I may never let you leave." With his hand on her waist, he guided her out the door. Comfortable and secure with his arms around her, Mia forgot her fears.

Downstairs Cerianne was also getting ready to leave, and was in a state of panic looking for her keys. She was going into Boston to the theatre with Dr Mathews, strangely enough Ryder's father and her mother had hit it off straight away at dinner the other night, and now her nerves were showing.

"You look lovely Mia. Be careful, and have a great time. You haven't seen my keys, by any chance?" she said, rushing around lifting papers and searching around. Mia smiled and thought about Cerianne's keys and the tiny wooden spoon key ring that held them. An image of the kitchen appeared.

"I think I saw them by the kettle. Mom, we have a key rack. You really should hang them up," Mia smiled. She knew that Cerianne was nervous.

A moment later Cerianne walked out of the kitchen waving the keys in her hand.

"I love you, be good," she said. A horn beeped outside. Cerianne smiled and walked toward the door. Just then Samson brushed past Cerianne's legs and started to whine. She crouched down and stroked the mutt under his chin while his tail wagged.

"He's really taken to you. Have fun Mom, and relax."

Cerianne stood up and left Samson, threw Mia a kiss, and walked out the door. Samson barked as the door clicked closed. Ryder stroked the dog's head and he wagged his tail.

"We should go too," Ryder said as his hand linked with hers.

Bright stars twinkled like glitter in the night sky. It was beautiful. The warehouse was on the outskirts of town and it was regularly used for rave parties. It was far enough away from any residential buildings that the noise was not going to disturb anyone, except some stray deer or coyotes that ventured in from the nearby woods. Ryder drove up in his dad's old Range Rover, and the strobe lighting flashed out through the cracked windows. The music was booming and pulsating out of the brick mill building. People were streaming in and out through the open door at the end. There were also clumps of people sitting around an array of empty beer cans and bottles. Mia climbed out of the car and looked across as a boy stumbled out of the Warehouse. He swayed and then dashed toward the bushes, where he fell to his knees vomiting in the grass. She stared across at Ryder.

"Not a good sign," she said, "Do you still want to go in?" Mia sucked on her lip wishing they could turn around and leave, but at that moment Danni strolled over to them.

"You came, then! Great," she said, bouncing and smiling.

"Hmm, I'm not sure this is such a great idea," Mia said, gazing at the boy on the ground.

"Well, it's a bit crazy inside, but you don't have to stay long, do you?" she offered.

"She's right, Mia. We can go as soon as you want," Ryder urged, grabbing her around the waist and giving Danni a sideways glare.

Inside, it was even worse than she imagined. The warehouse was huge, but it was filled to capacity. You could barely breathe, let alone move. Sweaty bodies were gyrating against each other. The air heavy with a strong odor and it was sweltering hot, like a sauna. There were hundreds of twisting bodies dancing and grinding to the music. Couples were kissing and exploring each other's bodies in dark corners. As they weaved their way through the crowds, Mia watched as a group of boys pushed and shoved against each other. Ryder led her toward the clear space at the back where it was cooler and less noisy. Danni wandered off to find Tyler, and the rock music changed to a slow love song. Mia stood against the exposed brick wall and licked her dry lips.

"Let's dance," Ryder said, as he gathered her in his arms. Mia snuggled into his body and tried to relax.

He whispered into her ear, "You smell so delicious. What is it?"

"It's called Miracle." She looked up at him realizing, he was her own wonderful miracle.

He laughed and kissed her lips. When the song finished, Mia took a step back. Ryder's chocolate-brown eyes smoldered with intent as he gazed at her. She moved closer and nudged her lips against his and kissed him.

"Shall we go?" he whispered in her ear.

"Yes," she whispered back.

Ryder put his hand in the small of her back and guided her toward the exit.

Right by the door there was a scuffle as a boy bumped into people. He was laughing and slurring his words. As the crowd scattered away from him, he turned and came face to face with Ryder.

It was Alex!

Ryder and Alex stared at each other for seconds, and then Alex glared across at Mia. He looked like an angry bull about to charge, and she couldn't help it, but her cheeks burst into a furious blush. Watching her cheeks flare with color was like a red flag, and Alex launched at Ryder like a missile. Ryder pushed Mia aside, as he moved to avoid Alex.

"You bastard, you stole her from me!" Alex roared, as he missed his target.

"Alex, this is stupid," Ryder said as someone tried to hold Alex still. "How can I take something that was never yours in the first place? You know that."

At that, Alex growled and pulled free of his captors. Tyler was one of them.

"I won't fight you, Alex," Ryder said.

The crowd gathered around, yelling for Alex to fight. Ryder's gaze searched the crowd for Mia, but in the sea of faces, she wasn't one of them. He tried to reach into her thoughts, worried that she had left on her own, but there was nothing. He shook his head and cursed. Mia was right, they shouldn't have come. He sniffed the air and wondered what that odor reminded him of? A familiar sensation was once again snaking its way down his back and thoughts of Mia and the smell vanished. That shiver of awareness meant only one thing. He glared at Alex, wishing there was another way, but there wasn't. Alex ripped away from his captors, bellowing, "That's okay, because I'm going to kill you!"

Hearing the rough scrape of metal, Ryder glanced upward at the steel joists. A huge lever and pulley swung ominously. As he ducked Alex's second charge, Ryder pushed his energy into the surrounding area and quickly came up with a plan. The roars from the crowd increased as did the speed of the pulley. Eventually, it broke free and crashed into several wooden crates, narrowly missing him. His head snapped back to peer at Alex intently.

Some things never change.

Ryder smirked, which incensed Alex and he charged straight at him pushing him against the wooden crates. Alex's fists came upwards aimed for Ryder's face, but Ryder quickly ducked and moved away. Rebounding quickly, Alex turned around and attacked Ryder, pummeling his abdomen. They wrestled and crashed into the stacked crates. Several fell haphazardly to the ground and smashed, scattering the crowd. Still they fought, Ryder let the force of the punches push him to the ground and Alex tumbled with him. Ryder grabbed his fists, willing him to stop. An army of black bats emerged from the ceiling and flew among the crowd, flapping their wings and screeching. Girls screamed as the bats skimmed the tops of their heads.

The lights flickered erratically. Crackles and sparks burst out from the electrical circuits at the sound-mixing board. One yellow-orange flame leapt its way up toward the beams, and in seconds a fire raged. The flames raced over the ceiling, igniting everything in their path. The far wall was consumed by fire, and smoke filled the warehouse.

Alex pushed against Ryder and managed to free his hands. He kneeled over Ryder and was about to hit him in the jaw, but Ryder bucked forward and punched him back. Alex's head jerked and he fell backwards. Ryder jumped up and, wanting the fight over, knocked Alex again. With a thwack, Alex collapsed on the ground. He wiped his bleeding nose with the back of his hand and bent over his knees taking a deep breath.

Flames spread quickly, and screams shook the building downing out the music. A stampede of bodies hurtled toward the exit leaving the derelict warehouse empty and still. Ryder searched around checking the vicinity to make sure he was alone with Alex before willing the fire that was consuming everything as he had planned, to stop. Once the flames receded, he went back to Alex, gripped his hand, and let his magic flow into him. Alex's body twitched, and his eyes snapped opened. As soon as Alex saw Ryder, he jumped to his feet and rubbed his head.

Be still, you crazy idiot.

"What the hell? *What* did you do to me? My head's on fire, and I feel sick. Man, I'm hot. What's going on? I can hear you in my head," Alex said.

"Damn it Alex, hold still. Let it happen, just open your mind. It takes a lot of energy to create all of this to distract everyone, and I need you to focus." Ryder touched his shoulder and waited as Alex frowned.

"What the—" Alex muttered. He swayed as he sat down on the ground cradling his head. He scrunched his face in pain, and then he smiled. Finally there was understanding. Ryder gripped hold of his hand and pulled him up. Sharp pricks of electricity soared through Alex, and he closed his eyes.

* * * *

Mia was cold, and wave after wave of nausea engulfed her as her head bobbed against someone's back. The man had tossed her over his shoulders. She tried to call out and when that didn't work, she screamed, silently.

Ryder!

Her limbs were heavy and numb. Panic reached up inside her throat, which constricted and she made choking noises, gasping for air. The man who was carrying her stopped, lifted her off his shoulders, and let her stand. He kept a tight grip on her, and she had to lean against him as she stumbled. She was as weak as a kitten. Blonde short curls, ice-blue eyes and a wide grin faced her. It was him. She tried not to react, thinking only of Ryder, but the Darkshadow smiled and lifted an eyebrow.

The next thing she knew, he pulled her into an embrace. His lips smacked against hers for a fraction of a second, and then he let go, dropping her onto the hard, frozen ground.

You taste so sweet, like strawberries.

Mia gasped and wiped her mouth. *You're disgusting.* Damn, she was not supposed to react to him, let alone talk to him like that.

His laughter filled her head as he ran into the night. Her head throbbed and she was dizzy. Lying there, Mia could just make out two woozy figures running toward her, but all she could do was sob.

"I'm going to kill him," Ryder cursed, heading toward the woods.

"She needs you. I'll go," Alex said, as he ran past him. Ryder nodded, and Alex took off for the woods. Ryder raced back to Mia, and pulled her into his arms checking her all over. She nuzzled her damp face into his neck and continued to cry. He rocked her back and forth, until her body stopped shaking.

Mia, did he hurt you?

His words sounded fuzzy inside Mia's head, and she opened her eyes. *I'm not sure.*

Ryder brushed the dirt of her jacket and his gaze washed over her face and body. She blinked up at him unable to speak and watched as his face clouded with fury.

I shouldn't have taken my eyes off you.

Ryder helped a shaky Mia stand. He lifted her chin and brushed her hair out of her eyes, but she swayed, and he dived to catch hold of her once more.

"I'm going to be sick…" she said as the world spun around her.

"Mia, have you been drinking?" he said quietly. He shook his head, and his words faded in and out as did the view of the world. Mia was only able to stay upright by the strong hold of Ryder's arms around her waist, as he guided her toward the car. However, her legs buckled, and instantly she was hoisted into the air, and Ryder carried her the rest of the way. Reaching the car, he laid Mia along the back seat and covered her in his parka jacket, stroking her hair.

You're safe now.

She managed a weak smile and he frowned scratching his head turning to look over his shoulder into the darkness. Mia struggled to keep her eyes open and desperately wanted Ryder to hold her in his arms, but he stepped away from the car kicking an empty beer bottle toward the barn, where it smashed. He crouched down and ran his hands into his hair, staring at her and she slowly sat up. "It isn't supposed to be like this," he said.

Out of the forest came a breathless and panting Alex. "Man, he was fast! He just disappeared." He bent over gasping for breath.

"Was he alone?" Ryder said, as he jumped up.

"I'm not sure. When I said he was fast, I meant really fast. Ryder, he was a Darkshadow."

"I know. Sorry, I didn't have time to fill you in. He's been stalking Mia."

"I am really going to be sick," Mia groaned from the car. The boys turned to look at her, as she vomited over the back seat.

Chapter Twelve

The Watchers

Snapshots of the Warehouse, and her abductor, flashed into Mia's mind as she tried to sleep. When she woke up on Saturday morning, even lifting her head up to get out of bed took tremendous effort. The clock flashed eleven. When she managed to stand, three things happened at once. Her head throbbed with a blinding pain, making her squint. She reached for her necklace, and realized it was gone. Her phone burst into life with *Strawberry Fields* by The Beatles. What the hell?

"Hello," she yelled into the phone.

"How's the head?" came the voice that she already knew would be on the other end.

"It hurts."

"I'll be there."

Ryder loved to do that, and today she wasn't going to complain. Mia dragged herself into the shower. The water relieved some of the soreness from the bruises that littered her back and shoulders, but the headache remained. In fact, if possible, it was worse. Walking down the stairs, she couldn't understand why she was so weak. The doorbell rang, shattering the silence. Even after she opened the door, the ringing replayed inside her head and she wanted to fall asleep. Ryder was there. He rushed in and hugged her tightly. Mia lifted her head to stare at his pale frowning face.

"Do you remember much about last night, Mia?"

Her head thumped and she wanted to go back to bed. Parts of last night she remembered, but not everything. One thing she was sure of—it wasn't her fault.

"Stop it. I didn't want to go in the first place, remember? And stop asking if I was drinking! You know I wasn't," she said, hearing his thoughts and not wanting to fight.

"*I know,* and yet I could smell it. And we had to face everyone sooner or later. Less for people to gossip about,"

Ryder said. His rationalizing everything wasn't making her feel any better, and she looked away.

"If you want me to go, I'll go, but there are some things you should know."

"I wasn't drinking, Ryder, and you know I don't want you to go," she said, rubbing her head.

Ryder relaxed and gazed at her puffy eyes. The way she squinted told him she was in pain, and he could feel it too. Ryder pictured the Darkshadow from the memories that filled her mind, and he drew in a long breath.

"Come on, let's get you some coffee and painkillers. You look awful."

He pulled her toward the kitchen and made some strong coffee.

"I could smell alcohol, but I could also smell something familiar too," he said, leaning up against the sink.

"Ryder, I've told you, I didn't knowingly take alcohol—but it's all blurry. One minute you were there, then everything kicked off, and people were pushing. I was pushed to the back. I fell and someone lifted me up, but I didn't remember his face until later. Outside, when he dumped me, it was the first time, I realized who it was—and he kissed me. And have you been playing with my ring tone?"

"He *kissed* you?" Ryder frowned and moved closer.

"I couldn't stop him." She fluttered a look toward Ryder.

"I'm sorry, this is my fault. I never thought this would happen." He opened the cupboard, picked up a glass and filled it with water. "Drink this. It will help."

He handed her the glass of water and placed two white capsules in her hand. As she swallowed she remembered something, and looked at Ryder who was pacing like a caged animal, mumbling.

"His eyes were funny at the beginning, and he gave me a drink. I remember that. Also, my necklace is gone, the one from Emrys," she said.

Ryder stopped and looked at her, "Are you sure about the necklace? I mean, maybe you took it off?"

"I never take it off," she said stroking her bare collar bone.

"How could the Darkshadow kidnap me, in front of everyone? Why does he want my necklace, and why on earth would he mess with my cell-phone?" she said cheeks heating with color.

Ryder gritted his teeth. He reached for her and held her in his arms, holding her tight. He didn't know the answers to any of her questions, but was starting to believe there was more to the Darkshadow's presence.

"Apart from a major hangover, you're fine. That's the main thing. I think this Darkshadow likes you," he snarled.

"What?"

"Well, he kissed you, didn't he?" Ryder asked as he rubbed her back, trying to ease her tension. Her head flopped against his shoulder, and she closed her eyes.

"Yes, but oh, that is so nice," she said, smiling. "You're better than any painkillers."

Ryder turned her around so they faced each other, and brushed a soft kiss on her lips. They simply stayed holding each other. Once, she was calmer, he pulled her toward the sunroom.

They stood before the windows that overlooked the back garden. It was like a wilderness out there, leaves covering the surface of the garden like a carpet. He held her hands and stared at the swirling leaves.

"The Darkshadows are different from us, Mia. They specifically visit the humans and observe them. They are not to interact or disturb human behavior. They are meant to watch and record. What little I know of them is through Emrys, who says that they see no value in emotion or love. They were tolerated because of their intelligence. They are pure–blooded, and exceptionally gifted with recall and the ability to memorize any document instantly. These skills made them perfect to act as our eyes and ears in the human world." He shrugged.

"Why did I think they were old? The Darkshadow that's stalking me isn't old, and if they don't have any feelings, why did he kiss me?"

Ryder shifted his position and stared into the garden, "I don't know. They're a secretive people that seclude themselves in the enchanted woods. I've heard they have a hatred for the Shades and often cause mischief in their village, but I've never met one officially." His lips held a tight line and he bowed his head. "However, this one is breaking the rules, and for what purpose I'm not sure."

"What does he want with me or my necklace?" She walked away from the window.

"I won't let him near you again, but you need to try something. You need to reach out for his thoughts! You have a connection with him, and I wonder if you can reach into his mind. It will help us discover what he's after." Ryder watched as Mia's face paled. "Emrys didn't trust the Darkshadows. When we left, there was a lot of dissent about us going into the mortal world. The Darkshadows were against us going. They tried to convince the Wise Elders that we would alter the future for the detriment of everyone. Emrys thought there was an ulterior reason, and because of that he told me he would send us friends to help. Their identity was to be secret until the right time. At the warehouse—well, before actually—I knew that time had come."

Ryder stepped back from the window and grabbed her hand. "Also, there's an elixir called Loxus. It's very powerful. It takes away all inhibitions, control, and you have little memory afterwards, but you'll have all the symptoms of a hangover. Loxus has been used as a truth drug on rare occasions by the Darkshadows—in extreme situations. Otherwise, it is never used. Once the victim ingests the liquid, it renders them semi-conscious, their minds are easily probed, and information can be extracted without anyone being aware of what happened. It isn't meant to be used freely, but…" Ryder said as he looked at her.

"You mean that creep gave me this Loxus, and then ransacked my brain? This just gets worse. I could kill him." she said, letting go of Ryder's hand. She touched her lips and wanted to scream. Ryder watched and stalked away, then turned back.

"Did you want him to kiss you?" he said glaring at her.

"How can you even think that? I don't even know him." She reached to touch his hand.

"That's what you said about me, when you bumped into me at school. What if you do know him?" He stepped closer.

"Ryder, I've never met a Darkshadow until now. They don't live in the city in Annwn, and when they visit the Wise Elders it's always behind closed doors. I've never sat in counsel, but I have seen him in my dreams. The same ones you were in."

"I wouldn't ask you to reach out to him if there was another way. If you can hear him, we'll know he's near and you can block him from reading your thoughts. At the moment, he has the upper hand, and we need to turn things around. We need to start pushing him. I wish there was some other way. And I think he was emitting Loxus into the atmosphere at the Warehouse. I don't know why, but I could smell it." Ryder ran his hands through his hair and then gripped her shoulders.

I don't want you any closer to this Darkshadow than you have to be, but this is the only way. I didn't sense him at all, and usually when we're near one of our kind I get a tingling sensation, an awareness.

"Is he here to harm me?" she said.

"Mia, they've been watching *you* for some time. Back in Annwn, Emrys believed they saw us as a threat. Which begs the question, why? And we need to discover what he's doing with the humans. He's subjecting them to Loxus, which makes them lose all inhibitions. You saw the crowds. Some were ready to strip naked and have sex in front of the masses. I don't think that was just for us!" Ryder didn't understand why the Darkshadow was focused on Mia and her necklace unless he knew who she was, but that only seemed part of what was going on. He had no fondness for them as a group, but they worked hand in hand for the same end. Yet this one had broken one of the laws of the Council.

"When we first met, you said the Darkshadows were watching me and that I was surrounded in danger," she said trying to understand what was happening.

"Mia, I was at the diner. I was drawn there for several reasons. One of them was you. The other was the weather and the incredible energy surrounding it. Someone or something was manipulating it. When I saw you save that old lady, for a second I sensed another Watcher—but the aura of their magic was different. It was Dark magic. When we use magic, there is a bright white aura, but this glow was heavy and dark. Saving that woman in public would've exposed you. Using the energy of the storm to increase your magic sets off signals, a spike in energy so phenomenal that anyone who's watching for it will know. As soon as I sensed the dark aura had left, I intervened and used magic to stop time—to cover up what happened. I could've been wrong, but now I know I'm not," he said bluntly.

"Ryder, I couldn't just let her die. And what's the point of having this gift if I can't use it?" She stared at him as she sucked on her lower lip.

She looked so forlorn and innocent, his tone softened.

"We're in the human world. People die every day. You can't save them all. I think that Darkshadow set a trap, just to see if you would react—knowing if you did, a flare like a firework would go off, revealing yourself—and after using your magic, it would leave you defenseless. Last night at the Warehouse wasn't his first attempt at taking you. Do you see how you put yourself and those around you, in danger?" He sighed.

"You stopped time. That's why no one knew I saved the old lady. I thought I had imagined it, and I did what I had to. I've never had a vision on the day of the event—but I didn't know that it would set off an alarm, or that I would faint. At the Warehouse, it wasn't him and then it was, and I couldn't have stopped him. He was too strong. He just took me. I could be dead now," she said gasping for air.

He moved closer and pulled her to face him. "He must have used a masking spell to disguise his identity, easy enough to do—but your magic is equal to his, if not more powerful. You just need to tap into it and believe. It's doubt that makes you weak. This time he had the element of surprise, but from now on we need to be prepared. We'll find out what's going on and protect ourselves. I know, I said we weren't to use magic openly, but this changes everything. We need to protect ourselves and contact Emrys." Ryder gripped her tightly, raking his hand through her hair gently, soothing her.

"We're in this together, you're not alone, and you *have* to believe in us." He lifted her chin so she looked into his eyes.

"I'm not the same girl anymore. She was fearless, that's not me. None of this is me. Since you've been around, it's been crazy. I've hurt Alex so much, and now this creep out there wants to—What, Ryder?" she said, walking away from him.

"Mia, I know you're frightened. Just slow down. Let's take one thing at a time, okay?" he said. She was confused as she looked at him with a pleading face. "Everything's going to be fine. You're much stronger than you realize, and you have a great heart—always thinking of others before yourself—and it's why I love you. I know you can't quite accept your feelings or even say the words, but I'll wait."

Mia sucked on her lip and hugged him, listening to his heart as it beat to a steady rhythm.

"I just don't know what to do. Yesterday, I was afraid of who I was, but I was coping. I was trying to be an ordinary girl in a band, going to school," she said, as she traced the outline of a happy face on the window.

"Mia, you were never ordinary," he said. His finger touched the glass and misty flowers, trees, mountains, and the ocean—Annwn—filled the window. He reached for her hand and she looked at him. He was unafraid, so sure of himself.

Together we can overcome anything, and all of this will be a dream.

A tantalizing echo of laughter bounced around in her head.

He's wrong.

Familiarity made her stiffen.

Stop it. Leave me alone.

Mia frowned. Her eyes blinked at Ryder who looked puzzled. Mia shut Ryder's thoughts off and heard the Darkshadow's laughter. He was eaves dropping on their conversation. *How dare he!*

My name's Greyson. I know you've been wondering, sugar lips.

Her mouth opened only to snap closed. She couldn't think straight. Should she tell Ryder about Greyson sitting inside her head, or was this something the old Mia would sort out herself? Mia swept her hair back, and pushed pain in the direction of Greyson's laughter, until she no longer felt him there. She smiled at the thought she could gain control over this Greyson, just like Ryder said. Being aware of her magic and using it for her own purposes was strangely satisfying.

"How's the head?" Ryder asked, his gaze fixed on her frowning face.

"Better. You said Emrys was going to send us friends to help. Who?" she said, whilst still focusing her thoughts on Greyson.

Ooh, you little minx. I can see I've finally got your attention. Be careful what you start, Mia.

Mia reached forward and grabbed onto Ryder's shoulders. She couldn't think of anything else to do to drown out Greyson's voice. She clutched Ryder's face with her hands and pulled him toward her lips, kissing him with a desperate need. In response, Ryder wrapped his arms around her back so their bodies touched, and he could kiss her more thoroughly.

"Hm, that was nice," he said as he led her toward the couch. "Sit. You're not going to believe me if I just tell you, so I think the only thing I can do is..." Ryder reached for his cell-phone and started dialing. Someone answered, and he began to talk quietly as he walked away.

Mia sighed, knowing that Greyson had finally left. Part of her wanted to explore who this Greyson was and discover what he wanted, but she was terrified that it was another can of worms, best left untouched. Ryder returned to find her sitting on the couch with her eyes closed and yawning.

"You need an early night," he said, as he sat down next to her and put his arms around her shoulders. Mia snuggled against him, relishing his warmth and strength.

"Maybe we could just watch a movie—something funny, something normal," she said, opening her eyes. Ryder nodded. "So, this friend, do I know him or her? Did they come here the same way we did?" she asked.

"Yes," he said smiling.

"Why didn't you tell me before?" she asked.

"I only very recently discovered who it was. I've had my suspicions, but I wasn't sure until the night at the Warehouse, and before then I was too busy trying to convince you," he said, shaking his head.

"Why can't you tell me?" she asked, touching his shirt and twisting her fingers in the material.

"Be patient. Would you like something to eat? You must be hungry," he said, trying to change the subject.

"Last night, how come you didn't know I was in trouble?" she asked.

Ryder lowered his head, knowing she was hurt that he hadn't stopped her from being taken.

"I was somewhat preoccupied. I'm sorry. I didn't see the danger, but I promise it will never happen again. When we're close and open our minds to each other, our thoughts flow back and forth—but if we're distracted, well, I couldn't reach you. Whether it was because you were drugged or angry I don't know. Sometimes I know you hide your thoughts purposely from me, and it's very frustrating," he said.

"Preoccupied? You mean fighting with Alex, trying to rub his face in the fact we're together," she said, annoyed that they had gone to the warehouse at all, and blaming him.

"Mia, you amaze me. Do you hear yourself? That is the first time you've actually said out loud that we're together. Are we?" he smiled, and cocked his head. "That's not what I was doing by the way. I didn't want to fight Alex, but we had to sort things out. Anyway, it doesn't matter now," he said, looking at her face.

The front door bell rang, and Ryder rose to answer it, "Stay there and don't move. Can you do that for me?" he said, before leaving the room.

She nodded, still feeling achy and tired. Mia heard whispers and hushed voices in the hallway, but couldn't make out who the visitor was, so she sat feeling ready to burst with frustration. When Alex strolled in, he was the last person, she expected to see.

"What are you doing here? Did you come to apologize?" She bounced up, watching his face. He smiled, and his eyes narrowed staring at her. Alex grabbed her and swung her around. She couldn't help but laugh.

"I'm here to help, Mia," Alex said, all smiles leaving his face.

He touched her hand, and a familiar warm, tingling, sensation coursed through her—flashes of broken memories of their entangled lives together in Annwn. As all the memories invaded her mind, restlessness settled. Her anxieties about Alex vanished. She understood why she had felt the way she did. In Annwn he was called Tristan, and he was a friend, and a Guardian. Ryder and Tristan were best friends, and squabbled like brothers.

"Tristan, it's you! Why couldn't I see that before? I remember all the teasing, all the fights…I'm so glad you're here," she said, laughing.

Ryder and Tristan were always goofing around, and yet there was an unspoken bond. When they were young, with hormones raging, they had fought over Mia's affections, but Ryder always won. She hugged Tristan. This was how it was meant to be.

"Is it safe?" Ryder asked as he sneaked in the room. She left Tristan's arms to embrace Ryder.

"This is wonderful, but why didn't I see it?" she said, hugging him.

Ryder held her hands and stared at her and then Tristan.

"When you were awakened Mia, only certain memories were released, so as not to overwhelm you. As we reunite with each member, so those memories are unlocked. I am the only one with full memory, otherwise none of this would be possible. Until last night, Tristan *was* Alex. It's as simple as that. At first, Emrys wanted you to accept who I was. After you adjusted, he said to engage the awakening with the others—but not to begin until the group was needed, to ensure that their identities were not compromised. Knowing about Alex, I couldn't leave it any longer—and I was worried," he said.

"It took a fight to get my attention. I guess he knew that. I'm sorry I wouldn't listen to you, Mia. I just felt so connected with you, and now I know why. It was always the way. You only ever had eyes for him, never me, Mia?" he said, smirking and stroking Samson who strolled in from the kitchen. Mia looked from one to the other and laughed.

"I never had a choice," she stated.

"What do you mean?" Ryder frowned and pulled her to look at him.

"Ryder, not now. In a short space of time so much has changed, can you just not ask for anything more?" she said. Mia simply didn't wish to explain that in Annwn, even when she could have chosen another and that Tristan cared for her as more than a friend, her heart had always belonged to Ryder. Taking a sharp intake of breath, she let that knowledge settle inside her mind and body. She had always loved Ryder.

"Getting back to the Darkshadows, we need to find out what they want and what they're up to. When Emrys said he would send help, he didn't tell me who—only that when the time was right it would be revealed. I still sense someone else, and I have my suspicions. I just have to find the right time," Ryder said staring out the window. Mia and Tristan stood alongside him.

"We need to speak with Emrys." Ryder said. "Together our magic is stronger, and we need to find out what is going on with this Darkshadow—last night was too close for comfort. Just now, I could enhance your memories of Tristan without touching you—and the two of you only had to connect to remember, which means we're getting stronger. We should meet at the lake. It's a powerful energy source, and it will make contacting Emrys easier." He touched Tristan's shoulder, and they all agreed. "Tomorrow then, but for now I think we should let Mia rest."

"What about the band? Does this mean we carry on?" Mia said eagerly.

"Hell, yes. I believe the band has a role to play in all this, else why would we have created it? And don't worry about the Darkshadow. You have the two of us looking after you now," Tristan said, knocking Ryder's chest playfully.

"Tristan's right, you have us both watching over you," Ryder said.

Mia hugged them both, resting her head on Ryder's chest and comforted by the addition of their friend. Maybe Emrys had a plan after all, and everything was going to work out.

At that moment Cerianne walked in, "Okay, will someone please explain what is going on, Mia, Robert, Alex?" she said.

Chapter Thirteen

Emrys

Mia stuttered, laughed, and then explained to Cerianne how the boys had agreed to be *nice* to each other for her sake and Fusion's. Cerianne stared at Mia and the boys. "Well. I'm glad," she said. Mia knew, from Cerianne's weak smile and confused thoughts, that she wasn't convinced but accepted it.

Tristan stayed for a while, but by early evening Ryder and Mia were alone. Cerianne returned to the gallery to finish setting up her work for the show.

Mia stretched her arms and yawned, barely able to stay awake.

"I should go. You need some sleep," Ryder whispered.

"Please don't, not yet," she said, tugging his sleeve.

"I'll stay until you fall asleep," he said.

Mia awoke the next morning, smiling. Stretching her arms she laughed, realizing that Ryder must have carried her up to her room. Tonight, she was meeting him to go to the lake, to contact Emrys. Memories of the eerie lake made her shiver. She was beginning to get the jitters just thinking about it, but they needed answers. There was a knock on her door.

"Can I come in, Mia?"

Mia dragged the comforter right up toward her neck to cover her clothes. "Of course."

"Mia, I just wanted to check that you're okay. Yesterday, things were a bit strange," Cerianne said, sitting down on the bed.

"I know, but we've sorted it all out. The band must go on, and all that. Tri— er, Alex has a new girlfriend, and I think that really helps," she explained quickly covering up her near mistake.

"Oh well, everything is so quick these days. You will be careful, Mia, won't you? I like Robert—don't get me wrong—

but you're still so young, and there's a big world out there, just waiting for you."

Mia knew exactly what Cerianne was saying, and why. Cerianne was scared for her, seeing a reflection of herself at her age—trusting, foolish, and in love.

"Mom, please don't worry. I really care about Robert, but we're not going to do anything silly, trust me," she said.

Cerianne nodded and left.

With that, Mia jumped out of bed and took a shower. She was working a shift at the diner before she met up with Ryder, and hoped that meeting at the lake would relieve some of her worries.

Felicities was chaotic, which was good, because time passed quickly. Sylvia was not in tonight, but Sally was, so they worked together.

Ryder knows you're curious about me.

The dishes slipped through her fingers, but she grabbed them just before they smashed to smithereens on the floor.

Greyson.

She dumped the dishes in the kitchen, undid the ties to her apron and flung it by the sink. It was almost time to leave. She smiled at Sally, counted her tips, and tried to push Greyson out of her head.

Nice…you're very popular in the diner.

Mia ignored him—until a heavy pressure pushed against her lips. She froze and wiped her mouth with the back of her hand. Her hand viciously swatted the air in front of her.

"Are you okay, Mia?" Sally was staring at her. Mia turned to stare back, gave a short laugh, shaking her head, and ran for the restroom.

You disgust me.

She pictured smacking Greyson's face with as much force as she could muster. A loud slap ricocheted in her head, followed by string of oaths.

I guess I deserved that.

Greyson's deep-honeyed voice sounded sincere, which caught her by surprise. Then there was silence, and she knew he was gone. Stepping out of the restroom, Mia adjusted her T-shirt and pulled her sweater down over her head. Mia knew that Greyson was gone, but a prickling uneasiness persisted.

Arms grabbed her shoulders—and she struggled, thrashing her arms wildly, ready to hit or thump whoever was there. Turning around, she found a rather serious and unsettled looking Ryder.

"Sorry, that was stupid of me," he said, frowning.

Mia stared at him and thumped his shoulder, "You scared me."

"We'll fix this. He'll never get that close again, but… did you tell me everything about the other night?" He waited, his hand gently resting across her shoulders and his warmth radiating down her shoulder blades.

She sighed. "His name's Greyson, and he keeps popping up in my head." She blinked, knowing that Ryder already knew his name and he was angry she had not told him.

His arm dropped away from her body, "I saw *you* kissing him." He strode toward the door.

"I told you, he kissed *me*—not the other way around." She followed right behind him.

"Where's your coat? It's bitter out here." He held the door while she grabbed her black parka off the hook. With her thick jacket surrounding her, she walked outside, and he reached for her hand. He stopped and zipped her parka up, and their eyes met.

"I don't like feeling jealous, but I was. When I left you last night and put you into your bed I caught a sense of the Darkshadow and the conversation he had with you. I'd say, he definitely has a *thing* for you." He tapped the end of her nose and pulled her along to walk with him.

"Even if he does, you have no reason to be jealous." She tugged his hand to make him stop.

Ryder pulled her in close and gave her a soft kiss. "You're right, come on."

After a short bike ride, they approached the lake. It was an eerie place at night, especially when shrouded in fog. Mia dismounted from the bike and gazed around. She jumped as a figure popped out of the swirling mist. It was Tristan, shining a bright light straight into her eyes.

"Tristan, put that out! We don't want anyone knowing we're here."

"Sorry, I just can't see a blasted thing out here." Tristan shrugged and the light clicked off, plunging them into a misty darkness.

Mia stared up into the sky. The stars were hidden, but every now and then a sliver of moon appeared. Mia trembled and her shoulders tensed, sensing something amiss.

"Mia, are you okay?" Ryder asked.

She studied his face and let her fears enter his mind. He moved closer and glanced around, searching their surroundings. The fog came in thick waves, which then dispersed to reveal bushes and trees. Even close to his body, Mia's stomach twisted in knots and she gripped his hand.

"Tristan, can you sense anything?" Ryder pulled Mia closer. Tristan stared into the distance peering into the smoky bushes.

"I'm not getting anything except damp. Come on, it's too friggin' cold for a cosy stroll. Let's do what we came here to do."

Mia let go of Ryder's hand and breathed, "Sorry. I guess I'm still nervous from the other night."

Ryder brushed a stray strand of hair away from her face. "I'll, never let that happen, ever again." He kissed her forehead. "Okay, whatever it was, it's gone. We need to move closer to the lake and, like last time, stand together and hold hands. Don't let go, whatever happens. We need to concentrate. Think about the last time we were all together with Emrys. Are you ready?"

Mia and Tristan nodded. Her body stiffened and she tried to shake off her fears, but she couldn't forget the helplessness of the other night. Images of being carried away and then dumped filled her mind. An image of Greyson kissing her, and his rough hands ripping her necklace from around her neck made her shiver. His greatest weapon, so far, was intimidation and fear. A deep-rooted anger bubbled, and she was determined that Greyson wouldn't win this game he was playing with her. Mia dipped her head, realizing that Ryder was reading her thoughts. She hadn't thought to block them.

"It's not your fault. I believe he's watching us, reading our thoughts and taking advantage when he can. It's a game to him," he said, lifting her chin.

Mia looked at Ryder. There was no one she trusted more. She placed her hand in his and walked to join Tristan.

They lined up on edge of the shimmering lake. Screeches erupted from the forest. The frogs croaked, and the bushes rustled. Ignoring everything, all three joined hands—and there was a magnetic pull that joined the group with an electric snap. There was silence, and yet she could hear the thoughts of the others clearly. Her body jolted her forward, but she was aware of Ryder's firm grip as she sank into the hot charging sensation that pulsed through her. Even though her eyes were closed, Mia saw Tristan and Ryder standing next to her as a strong wind whipped up around them. She stared at Ryder—and then her hand was ripped away from his grip.

Whoosh! Whoosh!

She was hurtling through the air, pulled somewhere unseen. A cold wind slapped against her cheeks and blew through her hair. Her body trembled as she turned her head right and left searching for Tristan and Ryder, but she was alone. Why weren't they with her?

Her body drifted to the ground, and now bright sunshine surrounded her. Yellow, black, and lilac butterflies the size of her hand fluttered and hovered around her. One landed on her shoulder, and as she watched, a tiny, beautiful face lifted and smiled at her. It was a fairy.

"Mia, darkness has followed you!" the tiny creature trilled. "They are to blame for what's to come!"

Mia opened her mouth to ask questions, but the fairy vanished and in her wake stood Emrys. His gray hair was tied behind him in a ponytail, and his fierce blue eyes shone.

"Take this," he said, holding something unseen. "When you need help or question your purpose, use this to call upon me. I will guide you for as long as I can. Now go, fulfil your destiny. "

Her hand reached to touch his. "Please, I have so many questions to ask." He embraced her, and as she stood back her necklace was once again around her neck. The coolness of the metal rested against her skin. The crystal flower hung in its usual place, and a rainbow of colors sparkled in the sunshine.

Whoosh!

A dragging sensation pulled Mia backwards. "No!" she cried, but was pulled away.

She was flying again. The force that carried her was strong, and her body plummeted as if she was falling from a great height. She let out a scream. The light faded and there was darkness again.

"Mia, are you okay?" Ryder shouted.

Mia opened her eyes slowly. A familiar mix of euphoria and dizziness swamped her, along with an incredible thirst. Ryder held her in his arms. They were crouched on the ground, and the fog surrounded them like a cool blanket. The fog lifted and revealed an enormous hunter's moon. Tristan was on his knees next to her as well.

"I'm so thirsty. What happened?" she said, before sipping the water Ryder handed her.

"Don't get up yet. You gave us a heartache, that's what happened. You left us, and we couldn't wake you up. I wasn't sure what was going on," Tristan said.

Ryder stared at her and said nothing.

"We saw you go. One minute we were linked together, then you slumped against the ground and the connection broke," Tristan said.

"I felt that, but I didn't intentionally let go," she said.

"I tried to call you back, but I couldn't," Ryder bit out, as she placed her hand on his arm, sensing his frustration.

"I'm all right. I revisited the last time I spoke to Emrys. It was just before we left, when he gave me the necklace." Her hand reached to touch her neck, which was bare. The boys watched her as she stood up and adjusted her clothes brushing the leaves off her jeans.

"Emrys said something, something I had forgotten. We need the necklace to speak to him."

"Enough for one night," Ryder said, turning away sharply.

"Did you hear me? I'm fine, but we have to find it."

He moved closer and stood inches from her face. "You were out cold for nearly fifteen minutes. Do you realize that?" he said, gripping her arm tightly only to drop his hold and stand back.

She didn't realize she had been out for so long. Surely, it was only seconds? Mia tugged on his sleeve. "I'm sorry if I scared you, but I had no control, I just left."

Tristan spoke as Ryder glared at her. He kept his voice quiet and slow, all the while watching Ryder, and then he turned toward Mia.

"It can be dangerous when we're all connected like that. We didn't know if you had projected or not. Damn it—look, I think we should call it quits for tonight. I, for one, have had enough of standing here in this cold smog. What do you say?" Tristan said.

"We still need to find—" She would not let the necklace issue slide.

Ryder was beyond any patience with her. "Mia, that's it for tonight. No arguing. At this moment, I want to throttle you. I was ready to jump on your chest and start C.P.R. Your heartbeat was barely there, and you were out, stone cold. We're going home."

He stomped away, and a brisk wind blew across her. Mia opened her mouth, but realized it was pointless. Once Ryder's mind was made up, there was no changing it.

"Leave it. We need more light, and it's way across town," Ryder threw back over his shoulder, reading her thoughts. Tristan glared at her and walked to join him. Mia could hear their feelings about the night loud and clear. She pouted, but realized their reaction was out of concern for her.

"I'm sorry, I didn't realize. I've travelled alone before and I didn't think. I guess, I got caught up in the exhilaration of it," she said. Ryder charged forward, headed for the motorbike, and then turned around to face her head on.

"That's just it, Mia. You don't think! We're a team. We came here together, to reach Emrys. This wasn't a solo act—" He stared at her with his arms folded across his chest.

Mia walked over to Ryder and touched his shoulder.

"We'll go and search the fields after school tomorrow, and if it's there, we'll find it." He sighed. A branch snapped and an owl squealed. Mia bumped into Ryder's body and he grabbed hold of her, pushing her behind him. There was silence, but someone else was definitely there. She could hear whispered thoughts as Ryder held her hand and they huddled together.

Don't say a word.

Mia nodded. Her heart beat so loud, she was sure everyone would hear it. She sucked on her lower lip and focused on the garbled mix of voices that were nearby. One stood out, and shivers cascaded down her spine. *Greyson.*

They were too close and I dropped the necklace.

Shh!

The voices stopped, and the surrounding area came alive with the sounds of natural night life. The Darkshadows had left.

"Did you hear what Greyson said?" Mia said as her hand reached upwards, to her neck.

Tristan stared at her and frowned. "Greyson. Since when did you know his name?"

"Long story. I'll fill you in later," Ryder said.

"Might be nice," Tristan mumbled, frowning at Mia.

"I didn't know his name until very recently. But it was Greyson who snatched me, and he was the Darkshadow at my window." She wrapped her arms around herself and Ryder stepped closer lifting her chin.

"None of this is your fault. I'm not angry at you. It's this weasel Greyson—he's attached himself to you like a parasite. How else would he have known we were here? We need to discover *his* weaknesses, but we need to work together. I hope your necklace is the key, and that we can find it. In the meantime, you're not to project alone. It's too risky alone. Do you understand?" he demanded.

Mia wanted to yell at him, he was being so bossy—but she knew his mood, and decided against it.

"Damn it, Mia, stop being so stubborn! It's for your own safety," he said.

"Mia, he's right. Together we're a force to be reckoned with, whatever the game he's playing," Tristan added.

"When communicating to each other telepathically, we should keep our thoughts to trivial things, just in case he can read us all. That shouldn't be too hard for you, Tristan, should it?"

"Hey." Tristan jabbed Ryder playfully in the chest.

"Greyson wasn't alone," Mia said.

"I know. I heard three male voices. Whatever their plan is, somehow it involves you and that necklace. Mia, I will do everything I can to protect you," Ryder said.

"He's right. You've got two strapping beasts here to protect you," Tristan said, beating his chest. Mia laughed.

"You have to trust me," Ryder finished.

They walked out of the forest and back to the motorbike.

"We'll find the necklace." With that Tristan disappeared into the forest.

"Mia, listen. Being together again makes it unbearable to think of losing you. You said you weren't strong, but Mia, you were always much stronger than me, prepared to give up everything. I won't let you do that," Ryder stared at the ground before lifting his head to meet her eyes.

"We're in this together. No secrets. When you project, you use a lot of energy and it leaves you defenseless. I could've forced your mind to open, but that can cause a severe trauma. If you hadn't projected, if you'd collapsed, then I wouldn't have been able to help. Forcing me to sit and wait—*Don't* do that again." His worried look drilled into her.

"Ryder, I'm so sorry, I do trust you," she said, touching his shoulder. There was no one she trusted more. She stood up on tip toes and kissed him, gripping his shoulders for balance. His lips softened, as did his posture. Ryder brought his arms around her back and tightened them around her. Mia felt the warmth of his body against hers. He lowered his head, deepening the kiss, claiming her. A desperate need arose inside her. Her hands raked through his hair and then cupped his neck, pulling him closer.

How does his kiss compare to mine, beautiful? An unwanted voice teased.

Chapter Fourteen

The Necklace

Monday morning. Mia hated Mondays, and today was no different. Her head was swimming with Greyson's parting words.

How does his kiss, compare to mine, beautiful?

Ryder hadn't reacted, so she presumed the thought had been for her benefit alone. She couldn't decide whether she should tell Ryder or not, because she was certain that Greyson was trying to goad him. Remembering what he said about keeping their minds empty of anything that the Darkshadows could use, hers wandered toward school. She groaned, collecting her books and stuffing them into her bag. Everything was now out in the open, as the boys were no longer enemies. This was good—no more hiding. Ryder said he wanted to spend as much time with her as possible, which she liked, but she knew really he was making sure that she was safe. Knowing that he was worried about her made her feel warm inside. She couldn't stop thinking about him, and she was starting to realize why.

Mia entered the kitchen to find a note from Cerianne, telling her to eat before she went to school. Smiling, she grabbed a Pop-Tart. This weekend was her mom's first exhibition at the North Littleton art gallery, and Ryder, his dad, and her friends were coming. The roar of the motorbike made her wipe her mouth free of the strawberry jam and grab her bag to walk out the door. He stood there in blue jeans, a black t-shirt that hugged his broad chest, and a white long-sleeved shirt, looking disheveled yet gorgeous. On closer inspection, she could see gray smudges under his eyes. He held out the spare helmet for her.

"Now there's a dream walking. Morning." He bent down and kissed her cheek before he placed the helmet on her head. "Any more dreams?" he asked as he sat down on the bike.

"No. What about you? "

"All good, ready?"

Inside she knew he was lying. There was a reserve about him. Slipping over the bike, she clung onto him and the engine roared into action.

It took them no more than five minutes to arrive at school and park the bike. Mia walked hand in hand with Ryder, and Danni charged toward them with a face full of smiles.

"Alex was telling me he's cool about you two, because of the band. He really can be a good guy," Danni gripped Mia's arm and smirked at Ryder.

Holding his hand and strolling across the school grounds made it official. Mia smiled as she glanced at Ryder sideways, watching him as he talked.

Don't go getting too comfy, Mia. You may think you belong with him, but you don't. What would he think if he knew about Monica?

Mia inhaled a sharp breath of air. Her back stiffened and she glanced at Ryder who was laughing at Danni's joke. Monica was a sore subject, and one she should have explained to Ryder. If only they could skip school, but they both had papers due and a test.

He would understand. Now, leave me alone.

Mia's hands stretched out and her finger tips pointed at the ground. Greyson's words made her heart churn and her stomach heave. A sudden gust of wind swept up the leaves from the ground and they swirled around Mia in a circle. Her hair flapped over her shoulders and the force of the wind pushed Ryder and Danni away. Ryder rushed forward and grabbed her hand.

"Mia!" Ryder called her name in a low voice, but stern enough to pull her out of her reverie. She curled her hands and dug her nails into her palms. Staring at Ryder, she saw his cheek twitch and his pupils narrow. Anger poured off him in waves, as she watched him the leaves fell to the ground and the wind ceased. Danni stopped too.

"Did you feel that? It must've been one of those micro-bursts. Mia, you've gone a funny color. Are you all right?"

Ryder ignored Danni and dragged Mia toward the school entrance, not giving her any chance to explain, not that she could. His eyes flashed and their usual earthy brown was more like black peat. She tried to read him, but he was giving her the silent treatment, shutting her out. This was bad, very bad. He marched her into school, with Danni following behind.

"Really, if you two wanted to be alone, you only had to say."

Ryder turned and smiled at Danni. "Sorry, I'm always rushing around. Be good, girls. See you later." He released his hold on Mia and hesitated. His eyes flickered with a mix of emotions and his lips were still stuck together in a pencil-thin line as he stepped in closer.

"Especially you. See you at lunch." He tapped her nose and left.

Mia heaved a sigh of relief. The last time she'd let her emotions run riot was with Monica. Just hearing that name made her lose control, and Greyson had used that. He was starting to affect her, bringing out a wanton, uncontrollable rage. Her first class was calculus, which she hated. The lesson started and she peered out the window in a trance.

Time faded away and she stepped into another reality.

Mia stood surrounded by screams. Men and women haphazardly ran past, looking like warriors covered in gray war paint. It was the ash that fell from the sky like snow. She wiped her forehead, and sweat trickled down her back. Thick smoke clogged her throat, making her cough and gasp for air. Everywhere she looked was disorganized panic. Cars lay abandoned. People trampled over those that had fallen, desperate for escape.

Breathe. This wasn't real. This was just a vision, she kept telling herself—and Ryder was going to kill her when he realized she had projected once again. The heat was unbearable and making rational thought almost impossible.

Think! Think of the classroom, boring calculus and Mr. Smith. The smoke thickened and she called out. Ryder! Tristan! She blinked, and tears dropped from her eyes. The area up ahead cleared, and suddenly she could see the cause of the chaos. Not a fire, as she had suspected before, but something far more terrifying.

A volcano.

The brief break in the clouds revealed a monstrous volcano vomiting up its fiery orange lava. Smoke billowed out from the caldera, and filled the sky. Her heart galloped like a runaway horse. She wanted to scream for help, but what good would that do? She wasn't really here. Spinning around she looked for an escape route, but there was too many people running to nowhere. A scream rang out and shook Mia as she realized it belonged to her. The heavy clouds rolled in, and people dropped to the ground. She could feel herself sinking, and she closed her eyes.

At once, the smoky humidity vanished. The sound of whispers and chairs scraping reached her ears. She was back in class.

"Next Monday, we'll be having a test, so make sure you're prepared. Any questions? Great, then get your homework for tomorrow"

The math class was over. She couldn't believe she'd missed the whole lesson. Mia pushed away from her desk and stood up grabbing her books. An overwhelming weakness ran through her, and she wobbled as white stars flickered before her eyes. Then there was darkness and she dropped to the ground.

Moments later, she felt someone nudging her and she opened her eyes. Blinking, she tried to focus as her head throbbed. Mr. Smith was peering at her. His thick bushy eyebrows dipped in a frown and he was mouthing words, she couldn't hear. Mia tried to stand and his arm steadied her, but she stumbled again. Little by little the world settled and she could hear his voice.

"Miss Childs, how are you feeling? You gave me quite a turn. I'm not as young as some of the others, or as strong. You fainted. Can you hear me? I think we need to get you to the nurse's office. You didn't hit your head. Pauline came to the rescue, catching you just in time."

Everyone was watching. Some were giggling and making comments. Great, another round of gossip! Mr. Smith told everyone to go to the next class.

"I'm actually feeling much better now," Mia said. "I think it's because I skipped breakfast."

He peered closer, and his frown deepened. "If you won't go with Pauline, I'll have to take you myself."

Ten minutes later, Mia lay on the couch in the nurse's office reciting what made her faint. She explained to the nurse that she had not eaten before school, and was fine now. However, the nurse would not let her go until she took her vitals. Closing her eyes, Mia ignored her arm squeezed tight in the blood-pressure cuff.

What the hell's got into you today?

Ryder was fuming.

You don't listen to anything I say!

Mia wanted to laugh and cry at the same time. Did he really think she was doing this on purpose? Maybe she was missing something, but she hadn't planned for the vision to happen—it just did. The force that pulled her into these visions was stronger than anything she had ever experienced, and she couldn't stop it. She sighed. Maybe it would be better to stay in the nurse's office rather than face Ryder.

"Well, your blood pressure is a little bit low, but nothing drastic," the nurse was saying. "I want you to rest here until lunch, and then you can go. Be sure to eat plenty of protein."

Mia nodded and listened as the nurse lectured her about stress, studying for senior year, anorexia, and the importance of staying healthy. Mia stared at the clock, wishing more than anything that she could just leave, but as she closed her eyes once more she fell asleep.

An hour later a small nudge woke her. It was the nurse, and she was telling Mia that she could go.

As soon as Mia left the nurse's office, Ryder appeared, looking as dark as a stormy sky. He caught hold of her arm and whisked her away.

"What the hell are you doing? I was just going to come in and see if I could take you home." His eyes never left her face.

"Ryder, I know you're angry, but I'm really not in the mood. I'm fine now, really," she said, trying to smile, but his drawn lips and frown told her he wasn't in the mood for her flippancy.

"Mia, that's something you're saying a lot lately, and I don't want to scare you, but maybe you don't remember how you were before. Having all the visions, it took its toll on you, I remember, and I…" He shook his head. Reading her thoughts, he realized he was not helping the situation, and changed tactics.

"Come on, let's go eat. You need to eat, right?"

They walked into the cafeteria where there were long lines of people waiting for lunch and chatting away. About halfway across the room the conversation died and everyone turned to stare. Some nudged each other, and there was muffled laughter. Mia turned to leave, but Ryder held her firmly.

"We're not leaving. You go and sit down. I'll get lunch."

Realizing that it was better to face whatever comments might be slung at her, she walked to take a seat with their group. Tyler was seated next to Danni, along with Tristan, Laurie and Evan. No sooner had she sat down that it began.

"So, are you okay? Everyone's talking about it. They said you fainted in math." Danni sat next to her. "I was going to look for you, but Robert said he would."

News traveled fast.

"Well, if you had calculus, you'd be sick too. Honestly, I'm fine. I'm just hungry," Mia said laughing.

"So you're not—" Danni said, almost as a whisper.

Mia shot her a quick, short look of exasperation. "We've been here before, and nope, still not having sex," she said rather loudly. She realized then that Danni would not be the only one wondering. If she hadn't been starving she would have just left, but she needed to eat. The group, especially Tristan, glanced toward her, "You okay?" Laurie stared at her.

"Nothing a baguette won't fix. I'm fine," she answered, looking around.

"She should be going home, but she refuses, so here we are…some food," Ryder said as he sat down next to her. "Promise me, if you feel ill again you'll let me know, and I'll take you straight home, okay?" His arm rested on the back of her chair. Tristan nodded, and Danni looked at both, frowning.

"Okay, now stop it. Enough attention. Danni here thinks I'm pregnant, along with everyone else." Her face was a bright red, highlighting her embarrassment. Evan began to choke on his food, and Tyler had to pat him furiously on the back. Laurie continued to stare at Mia accusingly.

"Well that's definitely not the case," Ryder said with ease, biting into his turkey roll.

"Right, so now that's settled, can we please change the subject?" Mia said, munching into hers.

Lunch was over quickly, and as they walked off to class, Ryder pulled her aside. "Mia, I think we should cancel tonight's little expedition. You've had enough, for one day."

"No, I'm fine. I fainted because I had a vision, and I hadn't eaten very much. My blood sugar goes low when I use up so much energy. I guess I need to eat more. I get it now."

Ryder sighed, "I can't believe you, not after last night. After me saying not to go it alone, you do exactly that. Projecting in school is downright idiotic and dangerous. You have to gain some control, and you can. You're in command of these visions. You can switch them off."

She made to move away, not wanting to argue with him any longer. "I had the visions under control before you arrived. Now, it's a mess."

Ryder searched the corridor. "I know you think this is all because of me, but it isn't. Mia, you're like a receiver and you *can* turn it off, at least until you're in a safer place. You're controlling your thoughts, because when you transferred today I didn't sense it. You blocked me out."

"Look, I'm doing my best. When I reach out for Greyson's thoughts, I have to block yours out, and it gets so confusing. In the end, I think it's easier to keep you all out. These living nightmares just creep up on me, and I'm sucked in. Maybe I'm not as in control as you think, but I'm going to work on it. Just don't get in a mood. We have to go tonight. We have to find the necklace. Please. How can I make it up to you?" She teased, kissing his lips softly several times. He could never resist her, and she was right—they had no choice. It was their only lead to Emrys.

"Okay, on one condition. You do exactly what I say. Okay?"

"Of course."

"Come on. So, tell me about the vision," he said, as they walked out and headed to their next class.

* * * *

It was getting dark earlier now, so when they left school at the end of the day, Mia knew they wouldn't have much time to look in the field. The sky looked a moody gray and black, threatening rain any minute.

They had driven over in Tristan's car and they each were armed with a flashlight, just in case they lost the light. Standing by the barn, they tried to decide where to begin.

"Let's start where we found you. Tristan, you search up north where he headed after he left Mia, and we'll search here," Ryder said, taking charge.

"Won't it be quicker if we all split up?" Mia looked out across the field. It was a big area to cover.

"Mia, what did I say?" Ryder insisted.

"I will, with everything else, but this doesn't make sense." She stared at him until his mouth relaxed and he smiled.

"All right, I guess it will be quicker, but let me know the minute you feel that something isn't right," he said

"I will. I promise."

Tristan and Ryder joked with each other about how stubborn she was, and she laughed.

"Just like old times, everyone teases Mia. Fine. If I sense something, I'll let you both know. Now, can we get on with it?"

Ryder walked over to kiss her lightly.

"And you think you're weak. Never. Easy to tease maybe, but even when you're mad, you look gorgeous. Be careful, okay?" He smirked, "And, I know you can handle yourself. I've been on the receiving end of your temper, remember?" he said, touching his cheek.

Of course she recalled when she had hit him, but it seemed so long ago.

"The Darkshadows are dangerous. We've seen a little of what they're capable of, so keep your senses sharp," Ryder said, and then reiterated into her head not to be stubborn, just to listen.

Mia nodded and they each made their own way, combing through the fields of grass and corn.

It was painstakingly slow. There were so many leaves scattered around, it was like trying to find a needle in a haystack. Mia forced everything else out of her head. She pictured the delicate blue crystal flower and silver chain, feeling the coolness of it against her skin. The ground was mushy in places from the last rainfall, making her grateful for the boots she had brought. She lifted her head and watched the gray heavy clouds roll by.

Instantly Mia was pulled straight ahead. Her fingers twitched and the fingertips itched. She let her fingers lead her. She also picked up thoughts from the other two.

Do you think we'll find it? Tristan doubted that they would.

If Mia feels strongly that it's here, and with her ability to find things, yes we'll find it!

The magnetic pull led her through the field of corn. Mia huffed. Maybe Tristan was right and this was a waste of time, because she was much farther out than she had been with the Darkshadow. The boys were quiet, as they concentrated their efforts on searching the field inch by inch.

A glimmer of rainbow colors flashed before her. Her necklace.

I can feel it! It's here!

There was a rustle amongst the bushes and Mia stood still. She listened and held her breath. *He* was here. She could sense *him,* even though he was quiet. *Ryder!* Seconds ticked by and then Ryder appeared.

"Greyson's here." She looked into the distance.

"I had a feeling he might turn up."

"What should we do? Because after saying we wouldn't use telepathy, I can hear everything you're saying—and I'm scared Greyson will too." She moved to stand close to him.

"Just checking in… Oh great, water. Well, I say let's give it half an hour and then that's it. Sorry, Mia, but if it's not here, we aren't going to find it," Tristan said.

"We haven't got half an hour," said Mia. "I can sense them, so no more telepathy. Let's find the necklace and go."

Just then a flock of birds squawked overhead, announcing someone's presence.

We're out of time!

Mia dashed into the cornfield. She sped through the tall corn with no care for which way she turned. Her body just moved, following the pull of the necklace. At the stone wall, she stopped and bent down. At that moment, the sun decided to show itself fleetingly, peeping from behind the clouds, long enough to make something in the mud sparkle. She could hear footsteps, but she didn't care. She reached her hand out, knowing it was there. There was a shift in the atmosphere as if the wind held still, and standing there was Greyson. Her hand touched the cold metal at the same time her eyes connected with Greyson's. Her fingers closed around the necklace and she withdrew her hand, keeping her palm closed.

"Anyone would think you wanted us to know where you were. Not very covert. Where's the muscle, where's your boyfriend?"

He moved closer, and for the first time Mia acknowledged that he was even taller than Ryder. He towered above her, wearing a ripped pair of blue jeans and a white t-shirt. His muscles filled them, displaying a powerful physique. His cold blue eyes took her breath away. Almost absent-mindedly, she shoved her hand into her back pocket.

"I need your necklace, Mia, and I'm not leaving until I get it this time."

She didn't move, and tried to lock into Ryder and Tristan, but nothing happened. Wherever they were, they couldn't help right now. Her heart stalled. She had been so scared before, and yet now—looking at Greyson—even though he was stronger than her, she was certain he wouldn't actually harm her. At least, part of her believed that.

"Why do you want it?" She smiled in an attempt to look braver than she felt. He smirked and stepped closer, which made her gasp.

"No longer scared, are you? Well, I would be if I were you. Very scared." His words breezed over her mouth and her lips parted. Her knees buckled and before she knew what was happening, she was wrapped in his arms. She knew, he was going to kiss her, and she didn't resist. Warm forceful lips pushed against hers and her head began to swim. Inside her body a powerful force was building, and she willed it to flame and roar like a fire—and pushed it outward. *Ryder! Tristan!*

A gust of wind ripped them apart, and she dropped to the ground. Greyson vanished, just as Ryder and Tristan darted through the bushes, pale-faced and panting. Ryder didn't speak but grabbed Mia's hand to help her stand.

"Well, you two were great, just great." She brushed off the leaves and pulled her T-shirt down, feeling in her back pocket. She pulled out what was hidden there and stared at it, smiling. It lay so innocently twinkling, as she turned it from side to side—silver and crystal, beautiful, untouched, perfect. Ryder solemnly took the necklace from her hand and placed it around her neck once more.

"Mia, I'm sorry. I don't know what to say. I couldn't move..." Ryder said.

"Neither could I." Tristan moved closer and put his hand on her shoulder.

"He knew exactly what we were doing. He was listening to us. I don't know how he's always one-step ahead, but this time I wasn't going to let him take this. Whatever it does, it must be important," Mia said.

Ryder observed Mia's face and read her thoughts. "Damn it," he swore, and moved away as she followed reaching to touch his sleeve.

"I didn't want his kiss."

He spun around and ran his hand through his unruly hair. "You didn't stop him, either. This time, was different." He stood glaring at her.

"I was playing for time. I thought, if I kept him occupied, I could figure out where the hell you and Tristan were. My head was about to explode trying to locate you, and then I used my energy to shatter the spell that held you."

Ryder walked away only to turn back around. "Every time he touches you, he learns more about you—and us. You want to know how he's always one-step ahead? Well, it's because *you* tell him."

Mia gasped and backed away as if he'd hit her. "I needed you, and you weren't around. If I hadn't freed you, what would have happened? He would have taken the necklace, and possibly me. I wasn't going to let that happen again." Mia wiped her lips with the back of her hand.

"He kissed you *again?* I'm missing something. When did he kiss you before? Why am I always the last to know?" Tristan looked at Mia.

"Oh, shut up." Mia and Ryder said in unison.

"Well, I only asked, because it's obvious that for all you spout on about us being a team, we're not." Tristan stormed off with his hands deep in his pockets.

Ryder looked at Mia. "He's right. This is a mess. Come on, at least we found your necklace." They walked back and found Tristan leaning up against his Jeep.

"We're sorry, Tristan. Greyson is meddling with Mia. The night he snatched her, well, he kissed her—and just now, he kissed her again."

Tristan opened the car door and sat down. Ryder slid into the passenger seat and Mia climbed into the back. Tristan stared into the mirror and looked at Mia.

"So, tell me again how finding your necklace helps us contact Emrys, because it doesn't look like a telephone or a time machine to me." He smirked and started the engine.

"I have absolutely no idea; I only know that somehow the necklace will help us to talk to Emrys. He didn't say how."

Mia, you won't get away so easily next time, and I'll want more than a kiss.

"Uh." She sat up abruptly, her cheeks flooded with heat. Greyson filled her head with a mental picture of himself undressing her.

"Okay. Well, we have the necklace and Emrys said we can use this to reach him, so there must be a way! We just need to figure out how." There was a lull in the conversation and Ryder stared back at Mia. "Are you all right?"

She was staring out the window. Rain started to splatter against the glass, small drops at first, then larger splashes. The darkness was setting in, and there—in the middle of the field where they had been—stood two figures and a herculean–sized, rock-muscled, green-clad monster with the sharpest teeth she had even seen, and wings. *A behemoth!* A gasp escaped her, and Tristan braked. Ryder stared in the direction that she was staring.

"Tristan, step on it."

You can run, but you can't hide from me. You haven't seen anything yet, baby, and I won't tell your boyfriend that you think he's tame compared to me.

Ryder clambered into the back of the car stretched out his arm and pulled her in close.

"You're shivering, let me warm you up."

He pulled her face toward his and kissed her slowly, drawing her closer into his arms. Mia clambered onto his lap and wound her arms around him, needing desperately to feel that everything would be all right. She kissed him back with an urgent demand. Her shivering stopped.

"*Really...C*ut it out, you two." The car sped out of the field, swerving as it went, and the wheels skidded on the road, smoke escaping from the tires.

Chapter Fifteen

The Gallery

Seeing a mammoth-sized behemoth in the mortal world terrified Mia. How was it possible? These gigantic, winged, mythical monsters did not even exist in Annwn—and yet it was here. Neither Ryder nor Tristan had any answers.

After the mayhem that was Monday, the rest of the week was uneventful. Rehearsals ran every night, because the Thanksgiving concert was only a couple of weeks away. Ryder was Mia's constant shadow, in school and at her house. As the days passed by she pushed Greyson's taunting words to the back of her mind. However, the vivid picture of him undressing her kept surfacing. Letting him kiss her had been a ploy to distract him, not something she wanted. Now it was backfiring, and she couldn't help feeling jumpy at Greyson's insinuations.

Mia was desperate to talk with Emrys and had tried a variety of ways. Rubbing her necklace until her fingers throbbed was one, and focusing on Emrys till her brain ached was another, but nothing happened. Emrys was silent.

Today was Saturday, and the day of Cerianne's exhibition. All morning Cerianne was rushing around with rollers in her hair, yelling out a list of instructions. Mia tried her best to infuse waves of calm into her mother's mind, but the stress simply bounced back at her, making her frustrated. Mia stood in the empty hallway, checking her watch. Any minute now the taxi would be here to pick Cerianne up. A clatter of heels swept across the tiled hallway and Mia turned to stare at Cerianne.

She was beautiful. Her hair bounced along her shoulder, with flecks of gold and amber highlighting the chestnut-brown locks. Cerianne smiled and twirled around in a blue silk cocktail dress, which fitted her slim frame like a glove. Mia stood watching her as she turned from side to side, cursing under her breath. Mia collected her coat and lifted her cell-phone from under the stack of mail, and handed them over to Cerianne.

"Mom, you look stunning. It's going to be brilliant tonight, I just know it," Mia said.

"Thanks Mia. I just need to settle my nerves. You look so grown up and beautiful." Cerianne gave her a kiss—and then a horn blasted out the front, "That must be the taxi."

Cerianne hugged her and hurried out the door. Mia smoothed her hands down her own dress and gazed at her reflection in the mirror. The dress was made of fine black lace and the shift underneath was a shimmering iridescent blue that hugged her curves. Looking in the mirror, she saw her cheeks flush as she glanced over the exposed skin at the neckline that dipped suggestively low. Her pendant hung just above her breasts and sparkled like a blue diamond. Mia's hair fell in waves down her back, almost reaching her waist. A final touch of raspberry lip gloss, and she was ready.

The sound of a car engine grew louder and she smiled. Mia whisked around and headed toward the front door, but it creaked open before she reached it, and in walked Ryder looking like a catwalk model. Her heart fluttered in her chest. Seeing him dressed in a black tux took her breath away. His eyes appeared even darker than normal, and they zoned in on hers, holding her captive.

"Do you always leave the door ajar? You're far too trusting, for your own good." He held his hand out, and she accepted it. He twirled her around, and she laughed. Then he stopped, pulled her in close, and lowered his head.

"You're so beautiful—" The deep timbre of his voice startled her. His arms held her in a tight embrace, while his lips caressed her neck with tiny kisses. Chills erupted down her spine and a heat started to climb into the pit of her tummy. A tidal wave of need swept through her and her hands tangled in his hair, holding him close. Ryder lifted his head and groaned in approval. She watched as he licked his lips.

Kiss me.

For a second, Mia saw a silvery streak in his eyes as he lowered his head. She breathed the scent of him in. He smelled of leather and smoke. An alarm bell ran through her, but too late. Ryder gripped her back and pushed her against the wall. His lips crushed against hers. A surge of adrenaline gushed from her and she ignored her worries, gripping him tightly in response. He pushed his tongue into her mouth and it touched hers. Her emotions were spiraling out of control. She wasn't sure if they were still at her house, or if they had projected to somewhere far away, because everything around them disappeared. Her hands were feeling their way across his chest and reaching under his shirt to touch his hot skin.

An incontrollable desire pushed her forward and her body quivered as his fingers stroked against her neck and trailed across her collarbone. Her heart pounded and breathing came in short quick pants. Something was very wrong, and yet everything was gloriously right.

Mia are you ready? I'm almost there.

Her mind was fuzzy, but the words echoed clear and strong inside her head. It was Ryder—and yet how was that possible? Her body froze, and she shoved hard against the chest that only moments ago she had been caressing. Mia pushed and moved away as far as possible from the person who kissed her so intimately, clutching her stomach, feeling sick. He looked identical to Ryder, but the spell was broken, and once the shield was down he transformed back into his real image. *Greyson!* Instead of dark smoky eyes, icy-blue ones sparkled at her along with his unmistakable high cheek bones and lascivious smile.

"Hm, delicious, but what *would* Ryder say?"

Hearing his words, Mia pounced on him. Her nails ready to claw his eyes out, but he laughed and grabbed her wrists.

"You disgust me!" she shouted. "You tricked me. I wasn't kissing you, I was—"

Greyson tightened his grip and dragged her in closer. "My dear, you were kissing me and melting like liquid in my hands. I could have taken you, right on the floor. Whether you admit it or not, you respond to me. As prince of the Darkshadows, I lay claim to you, as is my right! Ryder is no match for you. You're wild, impulsive, and when you get mad there's darkness too. I can help you harness your magic, and make you powerful beyond your wildest dreams. You've been marked, and I claim you."

Mia sagged hearing his words, and he loosened his grip. What he said could *not* be true! She dug her nails into his hands until they drew blood, but his eyes flared as if her response confirmed his words. She tore herself out of his arms, fleeing for the door, but stopped mid-flight and turned around summoning all her energy into a fiery ball of hate, ready to hurl at him—but he vanished. Staring at the vacant space, all her fight left her, and she dropped to the ground in a crumpled heap crying.

After letting the sobs out and knowing the real Ryder would walk in any minute, she spurred into action. Leaping up, she straightened her dress, and wiped her mouth with the back of her hand. Getting rid of his kiss was easy, but removing the memory of his words much harder.

It'll take more than that, sugar lips.

The door creaked again, and Ryder stood there. Mia hesitating for a second, but when he winked, she jumped into his arms.

"Do you always leave your door unlocked?" he said, hugging her.

"I'm so glad you're here." She clung to him, burying her face in his neck, not wanting to move away. His hand stroked her back and he sighed.

"What a welcome. Are you all right? You're shaking." His hand swept across her forehead. "No fever. I guess you're just happy to see me. It's a shame we have to go out. You look beautiful," he said, reaching for her hand.

Mia couldn't speak. Should she tell him about what just happened?

He lifted a blue taffeta shawl off the hallway dresser and wrapped it around her shoulders. Before he moved any further, he lifted her chin and planted a delicate kiss on her lips. A tremble ran through her and her mouth was about to open. Ryder was dressed exactly as Greyson had been. His dark suit was immaculate. Now was not the time to talk about this claiming—it was more likely some joke that Greyson was pulling, and meant nothing at all. A chill touched her neck and she rubbed the spot with her hand.

"Come on. Dad's in the car," Ryder said, as he tugged her out the door.

"Ryder, I need to tell you something—" He stopped to study her face, but a horn beeped, and she shook her head. Images of her kissing and responding to Greyson's touch flashed into her head. Self-disgust rose up inside her as she remembered how her body ignited with desire at his kiss. Maybe Greyson had bewitched or drugged her? She snatched up her purse from the hall table, clutched Ryder's hand, and walked to the waiting Range Rover.

"Mia, you look lovely in your dress. Did Cerianne get off all right?" James Mathews said, as she sat down in the back seat.

"Just. She was a bit nervous!" Mia said, as she snuggled up against Ryder, pushing all other thoughts of Greyson out of her head.

"You know, Mia, you and Cerianne should come over the house for Thanksgiving," Dr Mathews said. Ryder stifled a laugh and began to cough instead. Mia jabbed him in the ribs.

"Dad, what are you going to cook? Or were you planning takeout?" Ryder smiled at Mia.

"I'll ask her, and we can always help," Mia stuck her tongue out at Ryder.

"I can cook when I need to—" Dr Mathews said, reeling off a list of dishes, he could cook. Mia laughed and Ryder gave her a whisper of a kiss by her ear, speaking softly. "I love you." Her eyelids fluttered and a heat stole across her cheeks.

He wouldn't love how I make you feel when we kiss. Now would he, sugar lips?

Mia shivered, and Ryder pulled her closer.

The drive to downtown Littleton didn't take long. Millions of dollars had been spent regenerating the industrial part of town, and it had transformed the once derelict red-brick mill buildings, that had harbored illicit deals and criminal activity, into a glittering array of designer shops, restaurants, coffee-houses, and art galleries.

In the center was the largest of the three brick mill buildings, and it housed the North Littleton Art Gallery. They drove past, and the music spilled out onto the sidewalk, and lights flashed through the full-length panes of glass. The traffic along this stretch of the road was bumper to bumper. Dr Mathews dropped Mia and Ryder off farther up the street, and left them while he went to park the car. Walking along the sidewalk, Ryder slung his arm around Mia's waist and directed her across the street.

"I'm not letting you out of my sight tonight," he said.

She laughed as they ran across the road. Ryder pushed opened the door, and they walked in. Everywhere she looked, people strolled around holding glasses of wine, pointing at the pictures as they chatted animatedly. Exposed wooden beams gave way to a vaulted ceiling, and white floating walls allowed the visitors to amble and weave their way around the beautiful open space, admiring all the works of art. Glasses clinked, and laughter bubbled. Lights flashed from several cameras, as a crowd of photographers took pictures and reporters interviewed the owners and artists.

Cerianne was right at the hub of it all. She stood with the Director and co-owner of the Art Center, Paul Walters—a tall, solid, and distinguished looking man—a local boy made good through booming stocks and shares, who was now a self-made millionaire. His name was also usually associated with some sort of scandal or other. The latest one hinted at an affair with a much younger model. However, tonight his wife of twenty years, Monique—a beautiful woman with naturally blonde shoulder-length hair—stood next to him in a shimmering golden gown, wearing a brilliant white smile. Cerianne glanced over and waved, beckoning for Mia to join her.

"Where's James?" she asked, looking around.

"Trying to park," Ryder said.

"Oh lord, I knew that might be a problem," she sighed, looking at Ryder and then Mia as they held hands.

"You make a lovely couple. Mia, some of your friends are here somewhere… Oh, here he comes," she said, waving James over.

"Sorry, outside is a mess," Dr Mathews said.

"So, how's it going?" Mia asked Cerianne.

"Well there're a lot of media here, which is good. People are looking, but it's early. Let me get you a drink, James," Cerianne said.

"No, let me," Dr Mathews smiled.

At that point, the director came over, said hello, and then guided Cerianne toward a group of media people. The reporter from the *Boston Globe* wanted more photographs. Mia strolled around the gallery with Ryder, looking for their friends. As they mingled, they stopped to study the photographs. Some of the photographs were colored, while others were in black-and-white print. Each one showed a snapshot of life and death. Tears brimmed in Mia eyes as she stared at a portrait of an elderly man kissing his wife a last goodbye as she lay on her bed in hospital, looking asleep.

"Cerianne is very good at observing people. I love this one," Ryder said, pointing at a photograph of an elderly couple walking, each with a Zimmer frame. They were smiling and laughing together. Mia nodded.

"Cerianne took one of us. She wanted to put it up tonight, but I said no. I'll have to show you," she said, as Danni bound over with Tristan.

"I'd like that," he replied.

"Hi, guys! The photographs are brilliant. Your mom is so talented," she said.

"Thanks. Where's Tyler?" Mia said.

"Sick. So, Alex brought me," she said smiling.

"No Laurie?" Mia asked.

"Nope, not tonight. Just me, guys," Tristan said.

Danni and Mia linked arms, laughing, taking in each photograph, and discussing the scene. Amongst all the noise and surrounded by her friends, Mia forgot her anxiety—but as her body bumped against Danni's, a fluttering sensation crept up her neck and sent shivers down her spine. Mia began to watch her surroundings, fearful that Greyson was at work. Small electric shocks coursed through her, and disjointed flashes of two girls together appeared in her mind. Unsure of what she was seeing, Mia searched for Ryder—who must have sensed her unease, as he appeared at her side offering a reassuring smile. Tristan was close behind.

Ryder's gaze left her and travelled over toward Danni. Mia's eyes followed.

"What's going on with you two? You're looking weird," Danni said.

Ryder and Mia smiled at her, and even Tristan winked at her. Ryder touched Danni's arm, and then had to let go as a crowd of people came pushing into the group. He moved away, and the others followed until Mia and the rest were gathered into the corner at the back.

"What's wrong with you two?" Danni said, glaring at Mia and Ryder.

"Nothing. It's getting hot and crowded in here. Why don't we go back to my house? Do you think your mom will mind?" Ryder asked Mia. He stared at her face, but his gaze shifted to her neck and in particular her pendant, which was glowing. The four of them were stood close together, as the gallery filled with more people. Ryder whispered in Mia's ear, "We need to leave."

Mia nodded and heard a heated, unspoken, exchange between Tristan and Ryder concerning her necklace. Her neck was hot, and she looked down at her chest. Her crystal was glowing like the flame from a candle. There was a sharp intake of breath and she raised her head, catching Danni staring at her necklace.

"Mia, your necklace—oh, my god," she said, loudly.

Ryder broke Danni's comment by grabbing her arm and leading her toward the exit. Mia stared at Danni's back, and then walked away to search for Cerianne. She found her surrounded by a group of smiling faces, but as soon as Cerianne spotted Mia she broke away from the group and headed toward her.

"Mom, I'm so pleased for you. Everyone is raving about your work," Mia hugged Cerianne, "I hope you don't mind, but we're going to head over to Ryder's. It's getting crowded in here, and Danni's feeling claustrophobic. Is that okay?" she said.

"Of course. I was going to come and find you. We're going out for dinner afterward, and I'll be home late." Cerianne brushed a stray strand of Mia's hair away from her face. "I love you, and be careful," she said, giving her a big kiss.

"I will." Mia turned and hurried away.

Walking outside, she found Ryder with the others. It didn't take her long because Danni's high-pitched and angry voice greeted her as soon as the door closed behind her.

"What the hell was that all about?" Danni said her hands on her hips.

"Look, I'm sorry. It was getting crowded and I thought Mia was going to faint," he said.

Danni took a sideways glance at Mia and headed for Tristan's car. Ryder and Mia followed.

"So you dragged *me* out! Mia your necklace it…" she said, her gaze fixed on Mia's neck.

"I know. It does that sometimes," Mia explained.

Huffing, Danni sat down in the car and stared out the window. Tristan slid into the driver's seat next to Ryder.

She'll be all right once we explain. Ryder's words filtered into her head.

Mia stared at Ryder's tentative smile and wasn't sure what he was up to, but a warm feeling was building inside her.

Ryder's Victorian house lay in complete darkness. He opened the front door, walked inside, and flicked the switch. Mia stepped in, and a huge crystal chandelier greeted her with row upon row of sparkling glass droplets. Walking through the black-and-white checkered hallway, Mia followed Ryder into a living room with dark wooden floors, tasteful paintings, and soft-stuffed chairs. The furniture was modern but comfortable.

In the adjoining study, bookcases adorned most walls and a long table in the center of the room was covered with books and papers. A white board occupied one wall completely, and was covered in mathematical equations.

"Wow," Tristan said.

"We'd better close the doors. Dad won't be happy if we mess with his work. He reckons he knows where everything is," he smiled. Ryder led them through to the kitchen, and beyond into a cozy den. The walls in the den were painted a rich warm red, and on each side of the room was a brown leather love-seat. The far wall was a stone fireplace. Ryder threw some logs and kindling in the fireplace, rubbed his hands, and closed his eyes.

There was a small flicker at first, and then a roar as flames started to burn and consume the wood. The fire made the room glow, and Mia brought some bottled candles from the shelf. Each candle, as it touched the table, automatically lit. Danni watched the pair speechless.

"Wow, how did you do that?" Danni asked.

"Magic," Ryder replied with a straight face.

Danni laughed.

"What would you like to drink?" Ryder asked turning to go in the kitchen.

Mia followed, leaving Tristan and Danni talking. Once, in the kitchen, she began questioning him as to what they were going to do.

"We have to awaken her here. As for the necklace, I don't know what it means—but when we were together, it switched on and started to glow."

"What if Danni isn't one of us? What do we do then?" Mia asked.

Ryder stared at her. "You'd better pray she is." He took her hand, not giving her time to ask anything more, and she sucked on her lip as they walked back in the room.

"Well, where are the drinks, guys?" Danni said, looking at them as they entered the room. There was silence now, as Ryder walked and stood next to her.

"You're doing that strange thing again, and it's freaking me out," she said, watching them both.

"Danni, I need to try something. Do you trust me? I won't hurt you, I promise," Ryder said.

"You're not going to ask me to do a threesome, are you?" Her eyes wide and a big grin plastered across her face. Ryder, Tristan, and Mia burst out laughing.

"Well, just checking," she smiled

"He won't hurt you, Danni, honestly," Mia said.

"Come on, then. You guys are crazy, but of course I trust you. What do I have to do?" Danni asked.

"Just stay still. We're going to hold hands," Ryder said, as he looked at Mia and Danni. "Try not to let go. You may feel something to start with, but that will pass. Ready?"

"Ready," she said, looking at Mia and winking.

Ryder nodded toward Tristan, and he joined the group as well. "Well, I was feeling left out," he smirked, standing up to take his place.

The four of them stood, holding hands. As their fingers touched, the candles dimmed and the flames from the fireplace grew into long tongues of fire. As the fire roared, a wind whistled around the group and the force pushed them backwards, but they all held on tight. Mia's hair was flapping over her shoulders.

Don't panic, Danni. Stay still. Danni lifted her eyes her eyes narrowing at Ryder who closed his eyes.

Everyone focus on Danni. Remember who we are.

The necklace illuminated the group. Danni stood transfixed, looking at each of her friends in turn with a fixed expression, and held their hands tightly. She jolted forward as a creeping tingle passed from Ryder and surged into Danni. Ryder held her hand firmly watching her all the time assessing her response as she accepted the sudden increase in energy inside her body. Her eyes widened and she paled. The awakening wasn't painful, just surprising and took some getting used to. Everyone let go together as each experienced the surge in memories, and then the emotions that came with them. It was breathtaking. Danni stood still as memories continued their journey home, flashing through her mind as if each neuron was being electrically charged, blowing the dust away until her brain was full of new thoughts and experiences. She flopped into the nearest chair, and held her head in her hands.

Mia went to her side. "Danni, are you okay?" she asked.

"Give her some space," Ryder said. "You know what it's like when all those memories burst into life. It's pretty overwhelming. Why don't you get her some water?"

Mia disappeared into the kitchen collecting several bottles of water and some chips. When she returned, Tristan was crouched next to Danni talking quietly.

"Is everything okay?" she asked.

Danni looked up, blinking, and rubbing the back of her neck as she stood up. "Finally, a drink." She guzzled some water, and then wiped her mouth. "I'm good, really good," she said looking from one to the other. "So, Emrys was as good as his word. We made it, and here we are. I know who you all are—Mia, Ryder, and Tristan. What I don't get is why you're all looking at me like a pack of rabid wolves," she said.

The boys stepped back, laughing.

Mia was taken aback and speechless at how quickly Danni adjusted to the knowledge of her true identity. It hadn't been like that for her. "I'm so glad," she said letting out her pent-up breath and hugging her.

The group was complete! Emrys had sent their closest friends to help and protect them. With the four of them united, their magic intensified and they would all grow stronger.

"This is going to get confusing, calling everyone by different names. How are we going to keep track?" Mia asked the group.

"We only use our real names when we're together." Ryder explained.

"That's fine. I hate my name Brianna, anyway," she said.

Out of everything that she could have worried over, that was it. Mia laughed and hugged Brianna, wondering what her friend would make of the Greyson situation. She pressed her fingers to her temple and stared at Ryder. Emrys had confided in him, that he was sending their friends to help. Why did he choose to keep it a secret from her? She sighed, hiding her thoughts from the others.

"It was an easy choice to make, Mia," Brianna answering her unspoken question. "We wanted to help. Isn't that true, Tristan?"

Tristan nodded and smiled at Mia. Their compliance did little to lessen the weight of responsibility that hung around Mia's heart for their presence in the human world. The more they talked about how their lives had been in Annwn, the more they all agreed that living in the human world had changed them. The question was, how much—and for the better or worse? Each looked at the others, as if to digest what had happened.

"I find it extremely hard to remember clearly what I was like in Annwn," Mia admitted. "I mean, I have all these memories—but I'm here, and I hear *Coldplay* on the radio and mom shouting at me to get a move on, and Annwn seems like a million miles away." Mia lowered her head and looked away. "I keep telling myself that what happens in the human world isn't real, and that when we leave everything will return to what it should be, but how is that possible?" Ryder sat down next to her, and lifted her hand.

"Emrys explained that we would fill in the gaps in people's lives, that each family or person like my dad would adopt us and absorb us into their lives, but that afterwards every memory they had would be erased. Their lives would return to their correct paths. He promised no one would be hurt, as much as he could predict, but altering history and manipulating human events is not an easy task. He also said that we can leave a mark without it necessarily being traced back to us. A whisper can start a war—that sort of thing."

"Okay! But, what are we going to do about Mia's stalker Greyson?" Tristan said.

Hearing Tristan mention Greyson made Mia suddenly want to throw up, and she turned away so that the other's couldn't see. "Who's Greyson?"

Mia's cheek's burned and she turned around to stare at Brianna. "He's a pig, that's what he is." She got up and stormed off, Brianna following quickly on her heels.

"So why are you feeling so guilty, Mia? I can smell it a mile away." Brianna said, as she gently closed the door behind her.

Chapter Sixteen

The Message

It was early in the morning before anyone decided that they should get some sleep. Tristan and Brianna settled down on the living room couches, and Mia and Ryder snuggled up in his room. They lay together on his bed, wrapped up in each other's arms, talking.

After telling Brianna all about Greyson, Mia played her words over in her head. "Just be honest, and tell him exactly what happened." A deep sinking feeling pulled at her insides. Would Ryder understand?

Ryder talked about Annwn, the band, and Emrys, as he stroked her hair. Mia closed her eyes, barely able to stay awake. She wanted to tell him about what had happened last night with Greyson, but feeling warm and deliriously happy, she drifted off to sleep.

Mia shivered as she walked down the aisle, in a short black satin dress that hugged her like a second skin and revealed her longs legs. A veil of black lace covered her face and was secured to her head with a ruby-encrusted tiara. It flowed down her back and trailed along the ground behind her. Breathing was difficult, as the bodice was pulled so tight to emphasis her moderate cleavage, and Mia couldn't catch enough breath to speak. Her bright red lips were held in a fixed line, and she knew her face was as white as snow. She marched slowly to a tune that was more befitting a funeral than a wedding.

Was she getting married?

Mia stared around and shivered again. Damp stone walls were closing in around her. The crowds of onlookers were shouting, and their jeers echoed up to the tall ceiling. The ancient chapel, with its tall ornate stained-glass windows, was filled to capacity with the inhabitants of the Shadowlands.

"Make her scream!"

"Make her beg!"

"Make her suffer!"

Dark ghostly shadows, the soul-catchers, flew around the ceiling, wailing. Demons and goblins bickered, and brandished their axes and swords in the air, as they chanted curses. The Darkshadows stood silently in their long rich robes, as the rest stamped their feet to a frenzied beat. At the front of the church stood Greyson watching her with a smirk littered across his face. He stood, dressed in a fitted brown leather outfit, with his hand outstretched. An elaborate sword was secured to his waist by a black leather belt. His cold blue eyes sparkled dangerously.

"You came, then." He grabbed her around the waist and pulled her roughly against his broad chest.

"Did I have a choice?" She knew the answer but asked it anyway.

"You know you did, and I'm glad you made the right one. I promise he'll be safe, anything, for my beautiful bride." Greyson leaned into her and kissed her lips roughly. The sound of wild applause drowned out her sobs.

"Mia, there are worse fates, my dear, than being my wife. Listen to them—they want me to hurt you, but that will never happen while you're under my protection. I will take care of you. I will love you."

Mia pulled against his tight grip, looked at his sword, and lifted her head to stare into his gaze. "You know nothing of love."

She bit the words out as a tall man, dressed in a black habit secured at the waist with rope, recited the wedding vows.

"Then you will teach me, my dear. But first a word of warning. If you let your pretty little fingers so much as touch the metal of my sword, I will be forced to react in a very public way—and while I may enjoy the act, you may not. Do you understand, my queen?"

She gasped as he lifted her chin and brushed his lips against hers.

"Do you take Mia Leronde to be your lawful wedded wife?"The man demanded as his hood fell backwards—to

reveal a face covered in red, oozing boils. Mia screamed, but there was no sound, and the service continued.

"I do." Greyson gripped her around the waist as his sword dug into her hip, and held her hand in a fierce hold. Her heart burst to life once more, but as she looked around the church, there was no friend in sight.

"He cannot save you, Mia. Only I can do that. My people want your blood, so say the words or the deal is off."

The dream ended and Mia sat up, gasping for air. Her body was shaking, and her cheeks wet from tears. She was alone in Ryder's warm bed, but the dream chilled her to the bone.

Brianna, where are you? I need you! She called silently.

The smell of breakfast wafted up from the kitchen, and her stomach growled. She threw the bed sheets back and stepped onto the cold wooden floor.

I'm downstairs. What's wrong?

Mia wasn't sure what to do. She pushed her hair back and tied it into a ponytail. Staring at her face in the mirror, she kept picturing herself in the sexy black bride's outfit. Her feet wouldn't move because inside something felt very wrong.

I'm not sure. I'm coming now.

Mia walked downstairs after a quick shower, still filled with dread. Pausing at the kitchen door, she watched the domestic scene as Ryder poured the batter onto the griddle to make pancakes, and Brianna poured coffee into Tristan's mug. A feeling of being disconnected, of not belonging, swamped her—which was ridiculous, because they were the same and friends. Taking a deep breath, she walked into the kitchen.

"Morning, sleepy head. I don't cook that often, so take a seat." Ryder planted a light kiss on her cheek—only to jolt backward, hissing. "Ouch, that hurt! You just burned me." He frowned, and drew his eyebrows together, watching her reaction as his hand smoothed his lips.

"Oh God, I'm sorry! It must be static or something. Let me make it better." Mia moved closer and kissed him on the lips, but he winced, and held her away from his body.

"Damn it, Mia. What are you doing? It's like getting branded by a hot poker." He touched his sore lip and a large purple welt appeared. Mia inhaled, staring at the mark that she had caused, and tears threatened to fall. Tearing her gaze away, she shot a glance over toward Brianna and then back at Ryder. She stretched her hand out to soothe his lip, but a voice stopped her.

Mia, I can play these games all day, but I'm not sure that he can. If you touch him again he will get hurt. You've been marked, you know that. You're mine, so don't forget it.

Mia gasped as the three glared at her. Ryder rolled his lips back and bit out, "I heard that, what the hell is going on? What does he mean, you're his?"

After holding her breath for what seemed like hours, she sighed and lowered her head, not wanting to face his hurt look.

"I tried to tell you last night, but there was so much going on and I didn't know how to explain—"

Ryder ripped off his apron, throwing it on the table, and turned to face Tristan and Brianna with his hands on his hips.

"You have to go. I need to talk to Mia now."

Brianna opened her mouth, but closed it and simply nodded. Tristan glanced at Mia sideways, and then grabbed his jacket off the back of the chair and walked past without saying a word. The front door slammed behind them leaving the kitchen silent as Mia stood facing Ryder. Mia hugged herself feeling so alone.

"Ryder, please let me explain." She wished he would hold her, and tell her that everything was going to be all right, but his scowl and waves of anger made her back up against the wall.

"Believe you, me, I'm waiting," he said, barely containing his anger as his cheek muscle twitched.

"I didn't mean for any of this to happen. I'm not even sure how it happened, but he tricked me. Now, he's revoking the Promise and has said he's claiming me as his. Can he do that? I've never heard of this claiming. It's such a mess. I started to tell you, but with Brianna's awakening I couldn't. I thought Greyson was simply lying, messing with my head, but the dreams tell a different story—and I can't hear your thoughts..." She wanted to sound more in control, but her heart was churning and Ryder stared at her like a stranger. None of this was her fault, and yet, sucking her lip, who else could she blame? Ryder stared at her face and cursed under his breath, his face finally softening. "Just start from the beginning."

* * * *

Ryder drove her home in an awkward silence. There was an impenetrable barrier between her thoughts and his. Mia knew, without being able to read his mind, that he felt betrayed. She tried to reassure him, but every time they touched each other Ryder's face twisted in pain. A line had been crossed, and she wasn't certain if he would ever forgive her, or trust her again. Mia wanted to shake him and make everything go back to the way it was, only she couldn't. His knuckles were blanched white as he gripped the steering wheel of his dad's car. Every now and then, she stole a glance hoping he would speak, but he didn't. The car stopped outside the path that led to her front door, but she sat still.

"We'll fix this," Ryder finally spoke. "I promise you we'll fix this. You're right, it isn't your fault—he's been manipulating you the whole time, and maybe we know why now. Look, I don't know what we've got ourselves into, but we all decided this morning we'd meet up at the lake and try to contact Emrys. Our energy is much greater than before, and we need answers, now more than ever. Just don't talk to Greyson until we figure out what to do."

Mia forced a smile as he spoke. If Ryder was right, the Claiming was an ancient law that superseded the Promise—and only a person of royal descent could use it if they so wished, but the subject still had to agree. The subject was her, and she didn't agree, not with any of this. She wanted Ryder. She longed for his strong arms to hold her, but he stared out through the windshield and his voice seemed far away. Mia nodded, tears threatening to come crashing down.

"Why is he doing this? Why me?" A single tear fell down her cheek, which Ryder brushed away, grimacing as he did so.

"That's not a fair question, because I'm biased."

With that he pulled her chin forward and gave a butterfly kiss where the tear had fallen. He dropped his hand and Mia saw the pain etched across his face. Ryder blinked and then grabbed her wrist turning it over. He bit his lip and stared at her, dropping her hand to let it fall into her lap.

"What…what did you see?" She pulled her wrist and flicked it back and forth. The tattoo lay there untouched. She stared up at his face but he was silent. He had seen something, she couldn't.

"I've gotta go, Mia. See you at seven."

Feeling dismissed and dejected, she descended the car and walked away, rubbing her wrist and brushing away the tears.

I hate you, Greyson! She thought. *I'll never be yours. I'll kill you first.*

A fiery anger burned low in her belly, and she walked in the house without looking back and slammed the door behind her.

I like a girl who's not afraid to show her feelings, she heard. *We're more alike than you realize.*

"Argh!" She stamped her feet and put her hands over her ears.

"Mia are you all right?"

Seeing Cerianne, she ran straight into her arms and the tears exploded. Her mother smoothed her hair and held her as she sobbed into her arms.

"What on earth's the matter? Is it Robert?"

Mia nodded, unable to speak, but needing to let go until the tears stopped like a dry well. Feeling drained and empty she reluctantly let go of Cerianne.

"I'm sorry, but I feel better now," she said moving away—only Cerianne held her hands and examined her face.

"Did he hurt you?"

"Mom, Robert would never hurt me. It's me. I'm just so confused." She pulled away.

"You'll find your way, Mia. I know you, you're the light in this often dark world. You're all good."

"But what if I'm not? What if I'm cursed and I'm bad, really bad?" She stared wide-eyed.

"It's just not possible. I know you."

But you don't! Mia smiled at her, and then ran upstairs heading for the shower.

After stripping her clothes off, she stood under the steaming water and scrubbed her skin until it was red. Tears fell unseen in the pouring water. The shower relieved some of the tension she'd been feeling, but she knew sleep was what she needed even more.

She slipped under the covers, nervous at first that she might dream of Greyson, but finally her eyes closed.

There were no dreams. No Greyson, or Ryder—just sleep.

Waking up to the sounds of her ticking clock was comforting. She stretched her arms, and her stomach rumbled. Mia dressed into a casual Henley T-shirt and light-blue wool sweater over her black leggings, and padded downstairs to get some food. After a chicken salad sandwich, Mia wandered back to her room to finish some homework. At six-thirty, she closed her science textbook, and sat back in her chair sucking on her pen.

How were they going to fix Greyson? What did they even know about him?

She scratched her wrist, and for a second the pattern changed from the interlacing Celtic knot to that of a swirling dragon. Her heart stood still. That was what Ryder had seen. What did it mean? Mia clenched her teeth. *Damn him to hell!* She wanted control over her life back, and that meant making some drastic changes.

Starting with Greyson.

He couldn't make her do anything. Her will was her own, and she was going to end this now. Mia brushed her hair until it shone like silk, and applied her plum-colored lipstick to her mouth. She wanted to look irresistible. One last glance in the mirror—and a car horn beeped. Mia grabbed her parka and left the house.

"Ready?" Ryder's eyebrows lifted. "You look great. Feeling any better?"

She pondered over this and reached for his hand, deciding not to let Greyson win or spoil anything that she had with Ryder, no matter what.

"Much better."

He tugged his hand away and gasped. "Sorry, it still hurts."

Mia frowned, but nodded.

As they approached the lake, she could see Brianna and Tristan. It was damp and already cold as they stepped out from the car. Brianna walked next to her. "Things sorted?" she asked, grabbing her hand and pulling her along.

"No, not really. I can't even touch Ryder without inflicting some kind of pain. It's like Greyson has possessed me—and my tattoo is fading. And this place gives me the chills," Mia said, hugging herself as her hysteria rose.

"Well, we'll have to perform an exorcism then, because he can't have you." Briana smiled at Mia.

"I see him in my dreams, only I'm not sure if they're dreams or a vision of my future. It's me, and yet it's not." Her eyes were pleading with Brianna.

"Even if it's a vision, it hasn't happened yet, has it? Ryder won't let it happen. I won't let it happen." She held her hand and they walked toward the lake.

"But what if it does?"

The boys walked behind, locked in their own discussion, and the only other sound was the crunch their feet made as they walked across the leaves. The lake was calm and quiet, and the half-moon reflected neatly on the canvas of still water as the four of them stood together. Mia's necklace began to illuminate brightly, its energy pulsating.

"Your necklace has a life source of its own, which is rare and powerful. I think it's going to work this time," Ryder said.

He reached for Mia's hand. Inhaling, she willed herself to stay calm. A picture of Greyson appeared before her, and she cried out. Before she could even stop to think, anger bubbled and spewed out from her, and she aimed at Greyson.

Don't touch him or...

The wind picked up and lifted Mia's hair, blowing it wildly around. Her body froze as she focused on Greyson.

Or what?

Sucking in a deep breath, Mia blanked her friends out as she channeled all her fury toward Greyson. Her necklace grew brighter and burst into a yellow flame. She imagined flames licking their way over Greyson's body, limb by limb. A brief shriek of agony echoed in her head and then silence. The wind stilled.

"Mia, what's going on?"

She tossed her hair over her shoulder and walked over to Ryder. "I want to hold your hand and not hurt you."

Ryder placed his hand into hers—and there was no pain. "How?" He raised his eyebrow.

"Does it matter? Shall we get started?"

He gave her a puzzled look but nodded. She smiled at Brianna, pleased that she had managed to win a small victory over Greyson.

The four of them stood holding hands and a charge of electricity surged through them, jolting their bodies. Mia heard their rapid heartbeats galloping like runaway trains, and their jumbled thoughts whipped around like the wind. They stared at one another.

What if we can't get through? What do we do then? Can anyone sense the Darkshadows? Mia, tell me what you did—I need to know. Can you feel that? Yes. I did what I had to.

Closing her eyes, she heard Emry's soft voice. The ground shook and a whirring noise started. Mia's body twitched with the energy that rippled through her. A bright white light encased them, protecting them from the rest of the night. In the center of the circle a stirring began, and the wind around them whirled, holding the four of them as they called to Emrys. In the eye of the storm, Ryder opened his eyes. A hazy outline appeared and again, they called out to Emrys.

Emrys, Emrys, Emrys...

The ghostly figure solidified. Tristan blinked, the wind rocking him back and forth. Finally, it settled and Emrys stood before them. In their tiny circle the sun shone, and the grass was green.

"Ryder, Tristan, Mia, and Brianna. It warms my heart to see you all together here, but I know you have questions and I'll try to answer them."

Mia could not stay silent any longer, "Emrys, something terrible has happened. A Darkshadow called Greyson has been watching me, I think for quite some time. First of all, he threatened my mother. Then he tried to abduct me and steal my necklace. Now, he says he's claimed me. I don't know what this means, except every time I try to get even close to Ryder, there's an unnatural force that pushes against me and hurts Ryder. I'm having dreams, but they're horrible, and I cannot see Ryder's thoughts anymore or he mine…" It all came out in one big heap of fear. Everyone stared, especially Ryder, who looked toward Emrys.

"Mia, you are and always will be in command of your destiny," Emrys insisted. "No one can make you do anything you do not wish. You need to look inside yourself and realize what it is you truly desire. Your challenge was not meant to be easy. Since you left, Annwn itself has been put at risk. There are rumors of an uprising from Rhiannon, and that the Darkshadows support her cause. The fact that their prince is here vying for your hand seems to confirm this." He frowned and shook his head.

"I don't understand, Emrys. You said that the Darkshadows don't have emotions like us, that they're cold and unfeeling. What does he want with Mia?" Ryder asked.

The lines across Emrys's forehead deepened, and he motioned for them to sit on the benches that appeared alongside a long wooden table filled with all manners of fruits, cold meats, and bread. Brianna and Tristan tucked in, while Mia and Ryder sat unable to eat.

"Ryder, just because they don't feel or love like us does not mean they do not desire or envy those that can. They see the power of love, and what it can overcome. As for the Claiming, it is an old law that was in place before *The Promise* and only used by royalty. The suitor proclaimed his intent, but in doing so he must obtain your consent. Unfortunately, there is another part whereby your essence can be extracted."

Mia paced back and forth, her heart beating erratically and her cheeks in flames. "Essence? What do you mean?" She stood directly in front of Emrys.

"Your essence is your magic. It's like your specific DNA. That's why you cannot hear Ryder's thought or he yours. Did you cut yourself, or were you ill?"

Mia stared at Ryder, whose face had lost all color and he remained speechless.

"No, I haven't been ill or lost any blood…but Greyson kissed me," she said staring at Ryder who turned away.

"More than once?" he asked. She nodded, tears streaming down her face. Emrys sat down and motioned for her hand.

"Mia, there is a game at play here. Greyson is here for a reason, and claiming you is only part of it. You can fight this, if you want to."

Ryder swiveled around. "But what do the Darkshadows want, ultimately? You said, before we left, that you had suspicions about them."

Emrys shifted his position, gazed across at him and sighed. "Rhiannon is the most powerful witch in all of Annwn. At one time, she would have been our Queen. She's using the Darkshadows to undermine the Wise Elders, to destroy the fabric of Annwn, so she can take power for herself. I'm certain that Mia's a pawn in this game. Perhaps, she promised the Darkshadow Prince more power in return for his loyalty. Whatever it is, she's not to be trusted. Rhiannon is pure evil. What is certain is that the Darkshadows have been travelling back and forth into the mortal world, acquiring wealth and knowledge, and they have been manipulating events to suit their purpose."

"Why now? Why Mia?" Ryder asked.

"In the human world, you are vulnerable. It's possible, he feared he would not be able to get close in Annwn, whereas here he has the upper hand. Whatever their ultimate purpose, they are causing grave unrest—as the Wise Elders are predicting that you are now the cause of your own vision, a self-fulfilling prophecy. They fear the Darkshadows will destroy mankind and Annwn."

"But I didn't see any of this. What are we to do?" Mia whispered.

"They have a talent for manipulation. I believe they created your visions, forcing you into the human world. They have to be stopped, and Rhiannon must not be allowed to gain control."

"But we're not supposed to use our magic here. How can we defend ourselves against them?" Tristan spoke.

"The rules have changed. Annwn must be protected, and so must mankind. You must find a way, and at the same time keep yourselves protected."

Ryder stepped in closer. "And what of our challenge?"

"The rules to that haven't changed. If you fail in your challenge, your union is dissolved and you will remain here. Your memories will fade, and it will be as if you never met. However, the greatest concern is the danger the Darkshadows pose to mankind and the threat to Annwn."

"What of the child?" Mia said.

"Mia, you believed this child was leading you here and telling you to help mankind. Being here could be more important than any of us ever realized. You were led here, and I believe for a reason. This is your destiny! Your challenge! You must follow it and in turn follow your heart." Emrys shifted in his seat. "What starts as a small ripple builds into a colossal wave. Unity is power. Remember, even the actions of one can affect a nation." Emrys popped a grape into his mouth and smiled at them.

"You're not in Annwn now, but remember what is in your heart. Protect our way of life. I will help as much as I can. Now, I need to speak to Ryder alone." He stood and walked a short distance away. Ryder glanced at Mia and then joined Emrys. Mia wanted to talk more, there was so much about the Claiming she didn't understand. None of this was fair. She didn't choose it. She didn't want to belong to a Darkshadow, to Greyson.

"Why must they speak in private? It's so annoying?" she said, as she wondered what they were discussing that couldn't be shared.

"I'm sure Ryder will let us know," Tristan said, rubbing her shoulders.

Emrys called to them all as his image started to fade.

Mia wanted more answers. "Emrys please stay! My visions—are they real? I just don't know anymore!"

"Your visions show a possibility. Some can be changed, others cannot. Many visions have been ignored throughout history. The planet itself relays warnings, telling man that it's changing, and that unless humans adapt too, they will not survive. You have to make them listen."

With this said, his image weakened and then he was gone. The ball of white light, that provided a safety net, disintegrated—and the net of energy that joined them broke apart, letting them fall to the ground.

For a while no one moved, but then Ryder sat up and stared at Mia. She captured his look of stony indifference, and pushed her thoughts into his mind. She desperately tried to call out to him, but there was nothing. Mia was miserable.

"Ryder, do you blame me for all of this?" she said, sitting up clutching her knees.

Brianna and Tristan gazed across at Ryder.

"Look, Mia, like Emrys said, I believe the Darkshadows tricked you, and have set a trap. I knew something was off, right from the beginning, I just didn't know what. We've all been played. I believe they lured us here because it's easier here for them to play their little games. No one, not even you, could have anticipated that this Greyson would stake a claim on you. I..." His hand raked through his hair. "I wish you'd have listened to me more before we came, when I told of the visions being so vague about what we needed to do—but there's no point arguing. We're here, Annwn is in chaos, the humans are in danger and so are we. My feelings haven't changed, but that was never the issue. What I take from Emrys is that the choice is yours, and has always been yours. I don't know how, but whether you accept this Claiming is ultimately up to you, no matter what he does. So, the question is, have your feelings about me changed?"

Brianna and Tristan stood up, brushing the leaves off their clothes.

"Look, maybe we should go and leave you guys to talk?" Tristan motioned to move.

"No, you're here because of us. What happens affects you both," Ryder said.

"So, you do blame me?" Mia asked.

Again there was silence. Mia shook her head and wanted to scream. She could hear both Tristan and Brianna's confused thoughts and fear. Tears that had been held in check began to fall.

"Stop it," Ryder snapped. "Whatever you think Mia did, she believed it was the right thing to do. Yes, she's impulsive and stubborn, but she puts everyone's safety before her own." He turned to Mia. "That's why Emrys wouldn't tell you about Brianna and Tristan tagging along, because he knew you wouldn't agree. As for Greyson, I told you to listen for him. Maybe I let him get too close, and he fell for you." He shook his head and cursed. Pulling her off the ground, he wrapped his arms around her and hugged her.

No flinching.

No pain.

Mia sighed and rested her head against his fast-beating heart, simply soaking up his smell and the strength of his arms. She'd missed that.

"I can understand why he likes you, hell, why anyone would like you. You have a good heart." He wove his hand into hers. "Mia, look at me. Greyson cannot have you. He's playing on your emotions, distorting your visions, and playing dirty, trying to seduce you. Never again, do you hear me?"

Her cheeks burned at the thought of what Greyson said in her hallway.

"You think I was blinded by the vision of our child, and that nothing else mattered," she said.

"Mia, it would be tantamount to impossible not to fall in love with the idea of her. But we came to help mankind and, whether she's real or not, that's our focus. Perhaps our music is the key. We are only a few, but music reaches everyone. We use the band, and our songs. Emrys said we have to look from within ourselves—but there's also the issue of why the Darkshadows are using Loxus on the humans, and I asked Emrys. He thinks they are using it to make the humans lose their inhibitions, to make them have sex randomly," he said, glaring at Brianna and Tristan.

"Shit," Tristan said.

"There's more going on here than just the Claiming, Mia. The Darkshadows are manipulating the human's fertility."

"I knew they held no love for the humans, but why?" asked Brianna.

"To control them. They think of humans as bloodsuckers of the universe, stripping all that is good from the planet. They want to eradicate them. At least Emrys believes this. Our songs will not stop the Darkshadows, but the songs can send a powerful message. Our songs will show the world that love is the greatest power of all—but we need to put an end to Greyson," Ryder said.

"How? We don't know how many there are or if it's just here or all over the world. How do we tackle that? This is a disaster," Mia said.

"Mia, we face many problems, but that just made the game more interesting. We cannot let him or the Darkshadows win. You see, it isn't about our child or us any longer. We don't know how long they have been experimenting and messing with the humans. Your decision to come here was right. We are the humans' only hope," Ryder said.

Mia tried to read Ryder's mind, but hit a blank wall. Staring at his face scared her and she broke free of his hold.

"What are you asking?" She shifted her weight and stood still, waiting for his reply, a sinking feeling invading her body. Brianna shook her head and bit her lip staring at Mia.

"There has to be another way." Brianna moved to stand in front of Ryder.

"Man, this isn't the way," Tristan moved closer to the group and stared at Mia.

Mia searched her friend's faces and knew whatever Ryder was planning, she wasn't going to like.

"There isn't, believe me. I have been to hell and back thinking over that one. Mia, you have to find out what's going on and the only way to do that is to get close to Greyson, without actually getting *close,* if you get my meaning. Mia, are you listening?"

Ryder's words swirled around, and Mia's body turned to stone inside. Surely, she had been mistaken. Not even twenty-four hours ago, Ryder had promised he would fix this and not let Greyson touch her again. So how could he be telling her to get close to him? Did he have any idea about the dreams in which she was walking down the aisle? Of course not, but…maybe he wouldn't care? Maybe Ryder had made some kind of deal with Emrys, so that when she failed he would get to go back to Annwn. Her body trembled. This was up to her. No one could make her do anything she did not want to do, but how on earth was she going to get close without getting *close*?

Chapter Seventeen

Practice

Mia paced around her bedroom, closing drawers and picking up her clothes for the wash. The picture of her friends made her pause, and she picked up the gilt frame. She smiled at their faces, and bit her lip thinking of yesterday at the lake. True, they were all in the mortal world because of her, and she carried that guilt around every day. But was the answer to pretend to like someone as dangerous as Greyson? She sucked on her lower lip and sat down, the mattress squeaking beneath her. Ryder must think she was a better actress than she did, because she felt completely out of her depth. She was not Mata Hari, and Greyson was deadly. Had Ryder stopped loving her, because she felt as though he had thrown her to the lions?

Since her shooting walls of fire at Greyson in her head, he had been absent—which was good, very good, because it meant she had power over him. She was meeting with the others at the Warehouse today, but Mia couldn't dispel her fears. They were going to push their magic to the limits and see what they could do in the mortal world, but she missed Ryder's warm and reassuring voice. It made her strong. Now there was silence, and Mia felt all alone. *Damn Greyson!* Mia stood up and slung her back-pack over her shoulder. *You want me, then come and get me.*

Ryder's motorbike roared outside her window, and she ran downstairs to meet him. A smile broke out across her face at the sight of him. He smiled and it warmed her heart, making her feel like flying. She closed the door and ran to him. Mia stood in front of the bike almost afraid to get on until he held out the passenger helmet.

"Look Mia, about Greyson, if you don't want to do it, we'll find another way, okay?" His face revealed nothing of his feelings.

"I thought you'd explored all the other options," She said, grabbing the helmet.

"I have, but if we brainstorm, maybe we'll come up with something new."

"I've decided to give it a go."

He lifted his head up and pulled her closer. Mia dropped her bag and leaned into his firm chest. "I trust you Mia. It's *him,* I don't trust. I don't like any of this, but if he likes you, then you're his weakness and we have to…"

She pulled away to collect her bag, and pushed the helmet on her head, "Use that against him, I get it. I'm just not very good at deception, and I think he'll see right through me anyway."

"Get on. We'll talk about it with the others later."

Mia straddled the bike and leaned in close against his leather jacket, breathing in the scent of him. He accepted her hold on him without any jerky movements, and she tightened her grip around him, enjoying the close contact. Things were not as they had been—there was a hardness to Ryder, but he said he trusted her, and right now that meant everything because she wasn't sure she trusted herself.

Leaving the bike, they walked into school like always, holding hands. Ryder smiled down at Mia and rubbed his thumb against her wrist where the tattoo lay hidden from human eyes. Each stroke elicited an increasing need to scratch an itch on that exact spot. When they let go of each other and went to their separate homerooms, Mia turned and stared at her wrist. An inky-black menacing dragon throbbed boldly. Her cheeks erupted.

Did you miss me, Mia? That hated voice purred. *I was never far away. Just a few things at home I needed to check on.*

Mia's chest tightened and her head began to throb. She didn't know whether to respond to Greyson or not, but his words intrigued her.

Leave me alone! I hate you.

She sat down in her chair, searching around the classroom for Brianna, still scratching her wrist.

Mia, love and hate are very close bedfellows. I bet Ryder doesn't illicit such a response, does he? Never mind. The tattoo on your wrist is my family coat of arms. I belong to the house of Drakon, and because of the Claiming, it overrides his.

She gritted her teeth. This was too much. She let her wrist go and stared out through the window. There, dressed all in black, was Greyson.

Brianna appeared and sat down in the chair alongside her.

"Morning. Ready for later? It's all Tristan keeps talking about, you know—practicing and figuring out how to kick Greyson's butt."

Mia turned around and smiled at her, "Well, I have that covered. I'm going to kill him."

It isn't just Ryder I can hurt, Mia. You cannot win this. You're not strong enough. You don't really love him. You're not even truly his yet. Why? What have you been waiting for? I can tell you. You've been waiting for me. You've seen the visions, and they speak for themselves. You're going to belong to me. There's no escaping your destiny.

Looking out at where Greyson had been she saw nothing, but she could smell his strong cologne mixed with a scent of leather as if he had been stood next to her. She had no choice. She was going to kill him.

* * * *

Ryder shook his head. Mia was Greyson's weakness, but she was also *his*. For the last couple of nights, sleep had evaded him. Agreeing to enter the mortal world was a compromise on his part. Sitting in his Physics class, he didn't know if Mia even loved him. They had been getting closer, and he thought that maybe she was starting to trust him, but now it seemed hopeless. Taking a deep breath in, he sat back in his chair and closed his eyes.

The sweet fragrance of Annwn filled his lungs. It was the night that he had stood at the lake with Mia, Tristan, and

Brianna calling to Emrys. Before Emrys left, he had asked to speak to him alone.

His voice was low.

"None of this is easy, Ryder, I know. Your love is without question. You know the reason you're here is not to test the love you feel for Mia, but to test the love she feels for you. It has always been this way. Mia is young, she has to find her way. Love is not taken. Love is given. Maybe Greyson's the challenge? Be patient, for that's always been your strength."

But being patient, isn't that a challenge in itself?

"Mr. Mathews? Mr. Mathews!"

His name being called over and over broke his dream. He jerked forward, banging against his desk and opened his eyes. Mr. Grogan stood with his arms crossed, staring at him.

"I suggest an early night, Mr. Mathews."

He turned around and walked away. There were a few muffled wisps of laughter and then the bell rang.

How was Greyson able to exist in the mortal world without help? Was this all part of the challenge? Was Emrys behind all of this, or was the witch Rhiannon behind it? A cold twist of anger gripped his belly, and he ran his hands through his hair. This was not what he had expected—although, truth be told, he had not known what to expect. What was worse was that Emrys vowed him to silence, which meant he could not tell Mia. He stomped out of the classroom knocking the chairs aside. Ryder walked blindly, stumbling past people carelessly, walking until he barged right into Tristan.

"Where're you going in such a hurry?" Tristan said, grabbing Ryder's arm. Ryder stared at him and tugged his arm away continuing to charge out through the double doors to run down the steps. At the bottom, he sucked in the fresh air and some of his frustrations lift away into the clouds.

"Man, what's got into you?" Tristan said, catching up.

"Too much to explain right now, maybe later. I just needed to get out. Let's go and find the girls."

Mia and Brianna were leaning up against Tristan's blue Jeep. He was the designated driver.

"Hey, girls don't mess up the paintwork," he grinned.

"Yeah, right. There's more rust than paint," Brianna retorted. "Look, I can't stay long, Tyler's getting really moody about the amount of time I'm spending with you lot. He thinks I am into Tristan!" She frowned looking across at him. Tristan smiled watching Brianna, and then opened the door to let the girls in.

"I did always wonder about you two," Ryder said, as he punched his arm.

Seeing Mia lifted his mood, and watching her long hair brush across her flushed cheeks, he sighed. He loved her, and wished more than ever that he knew what she was thinking. Brianna and Mia slid into the back, removing the empty wrappers and magazines that littered the truck. Ryder sat down in the passenger seat.

"Tristan, your car's a mess. And, it's smells like something died in here!" Brianna said.

"Yup, that might be the Tuna sandwich from a couple of weeks ago." He chuckled.

"Man, that's disgusting," Ryder said, opening the window.

Tristan drove straight across town to the abandoned barn. The sun peeped behind a row of clouds, but in an hour they would lose the light completely. The car came to a halt and they all jumped out.

"Thank God, fresh air. You really need to clean your car," Brianna said.

"Honey, knock yourself out. That's a job for girls," Tristan said.

She walloped him across his chest and he doubled over pretending to be hurt. Ryder opened Mia's door and casually draped his arm around her shoulders. There was no scorching heat. No knife-twisting pain in his head. Just Mia. While Tristan drove, Ryder decided his task was to convince Mia that she loved him. He wanted to be patient, as Emrys had said, but they weren't in Annwn and this Greyson wasn't playing fair. If this was a competition to see who would win her hand, then he was pulling out all the stops.

Mia turned in his arms and lifted her head to stare into his eyes. "I'm not moving until you tell me what Emrys said to you. Please, you look as if you haven't had any sleep, and you're driving me crazy." Her fingers played with the buttons of his shirt and the warmth from her body made him respond with a need of his own. He longed to be closer to her.

"Mia, I ca—" Before he finished, Mia's hands wound their way into his hair and she was pulling his head lower. Ryder couldn't resist. He pushed her back against the truck and lowered his head to kiss her full on the lips. They tasted of her peach lip-gloss. She tasted so good. Her lips were soft and kissing him with as much need as his. Her back arched and she moaned against him.

"Ryder I need you—"

His back stiffened and a blast of cold air cooled his passion.

Be patient

Emrys's words hung in the air. He shook his head and backed away.

"I want you, believe me. I want you more than anything, but *you* have to be sure. Do you love me, Mia? Emrys is concerned. He can't see our future clearly anymore, and it concerns him," he said.

"I don't understand. What does this mean?" she asked.

"Emrys is a powerful seer—like you, Mia. He saw our future, or one possible future, but now there are several possibilities that weren't there before. Our future has changed," he stated. Ryder told Mia parts of what Emrys had said, to at least give her something. He winced, remembering Emrys words.

You know the reason you're here is not to test the love you feel for Mia, but to test the love she feels for you.

"I don't understand. I wanted you to make me *yours,* and then we could be together. What's happening? It wasn't meant to be like this!" she said.

Ryder turned away, but she flew in front of him and carried on, "What are you not telling me?"

"*You* aren't sure, Mia. There's a part of you that doesn't accept me, or Annwn. Having sex won't change that. Why are you pushing for it now?" he asked raising his eyebrow.

"Ryder, I—"

He watched her mouth open and her eyes widen. She shook her head, and he was certain tears weren't far behind. None of this was easy and yet he'd never doubted his love for Mia, but he was always terrified of losing her. She was like a butterfly, and to catch her would be unthinkable—you simply had to let her fly. Staring at her, he saw her grimace, and as she rubbed her hands, tiny sparks erupted.

"Owww!"

"Let me hold them. You're upset, tense. When your emotions fluctuate, your energy reacts—and it gets impatient. You have to release it. Emotions are powerful sources of energy, and when you feel sad or happy, your powers are magnified. Let it out, Mia," he said.

She exhaled and let her shoulders drop. Ryder stood behind her and held her arms out. A breeze rose around them and sent Mia's hair flapping around her face.

"Just breathe and relax." His words were soft and gentle. The air stilled, and pink blossoms filled the sky and rained down upon them. The sweet smell of Annwn floated in the air, and Mia laughed. The delicate petals covered their faces, and before they hit the ground they disappeared.

"But it's winter," she said.

"Not in Annwn," he said. "Come on, we need to go and practice or we'll lose the light." "Ryder, I need time."

"I know," he smiled.

Ryder grabbed her hand to pull her next to him, and they walked into the barn.

They were greeted with grunts and vigorous moans. Tristan lay face-down in the dirt, with his arms wrenched behind his back and held by Brianna, who sat astride his legs.

"Get her off me! She's a maniac," he spat out.

"Ask nicely, and I'll let you go. All you have to say is *please,*" Brianna smirked, her face flushing.

In one lightning move, Tristan broke free of her hold and rolled over, knocking her to the ground. He righted himself and grabbed Brianna, forcing her onto her back, lying on top of her, using his weight to hold her captive. He placed his arms either side of her body. "I don't think so. Keep trying," he smirked.

"You'd better let her go, before she stops breathing," Ryder said.

"I'm all right…" Brianna managed to get out.

Tristan sprang up and pulled her with him. His arm was still around her as they stood, and he pulled several leaves out of her hair. Brianna wouldn't look at him, and flicked his hand away. She walked away brushing the dirt off her clothes. Tristan stared at her back and grabbed a water bottle, knocking it back as if dehydrated. Mia and Ryder smiled at each other as they watched their friends.

"Our turn. We should practice some self-defense moves. I'm going to attack you, and you have to give me all you've got, okay?" Ryder said.

Tristan sat on a bale of hay and wiped his mouth as he watched the scene. Mia paced around looking over her shoulder at Ryder, her face expressionless. She walked through the barn and stopped as two strong arms grabbed her shoulders. Mia twisted and struggled to break free, but Ryder's vice-like grip whipped her around and he pushed her down toward the ground within seconds. Before Mia hit the ground, Ryder pulled her upright.

"You have to try. Use your mind to anticipate my move, and use the techniques I've shown you," he said.

"Sorry. I don't want to hurt you, that's all," she said.

"*Mia...* This isn't about me, it's about being prepared. Remember how scared you were when Greyson carried you away?" he said, striding away. Ryder huffed. She was not taking this seriously at all, and he wanted to throttle her. He watched as she walked toward the exit. Her small shoulders were pushed back, and her back was stiff. She was mad. Ryder crept with the stealth of a leopard. As soon as her hand touched the handle of the door, he grabbed her shoulders.

This time, before he could do anything, Mia pushed her leg back and her elbow hit him in the ribs, taking his breath away. Her body whizzed around, and she slammed her hand into his chin, forcing it upward. To finish him off completely, her knee plowed into his lower region. Shock-waves of excruciating pain tore through him, and he sank to the ground on his knees. Ryder blinked as tiny white stars swam around him and he wiped tears from his eyes. *Bloody hell!* He wobbled as he stood up.

"Oh God! Let me help you!" Mia wailed, rushing to his side. Her hand touched his chest, and waves of heat pummeled his body. The pain disappeared. He stared at her fingers splayed across his chest, and then up into her beautiful lilac eyes. She was truly magnificent.

Brianna ran into the barn, shouting, "What happened? I could feel someone's pain!"

"Just remind me not to think of Mia as helpless," Ryder said.

Mia stood up on her toes and kissed him. In an instant, his arms held her possessively. Her body fit snugly against his. They were meant for each other. This was where she belonged. Her eyes fluttered at him and he turned her wrist. The door of the barn slammed shut and the panes of glass in the side windows shattered.

"Mia—" Ryder let go of her wrist. She stood, her eyes larger than he had ever seen them before and her face pale.

"Aren't we going to test our magic?" She smiled, sweetly.

"Can you show some restraint? We don't want the whole world to know." He sounded harsher than he had meant to, but Mia unsettled him. Brianna and Tristan joined them.

"Well, first things first." Tristan gazed up at the exposed beams in the ceiling, and closed his eyes. The rest of them followed his gaze and lifted their heads. The roof disappeared, allowing them to stare into the night sky and the millions of twinkling stars.

"Beautiful," Brianna said.

"Hm, now we need some…"

Ryder stared at where they stood, and two soft leather couches appeared. The girls laughed and sat down. Brianna smiled—and a wooden coffee table appeared in the center, with cold drinks and an array of chips, crackers, fruit, chocolate and marshmallows.

"Okay, my turn," Mia said. Ryder sat next to her. His eyes fixed on her controlled expression. A fire-pit appeared and small flames leapt to life. Mia sighed and sat back into Ryder's waiting arms. The flames grew taller and sparks shot out catching fire to everything it touched. In seconds, the fire spread engulfing the walls and the beams.

"Mia, quit jerking around. Stop it." Ryder shouted, jumping to his feet.

"It isn't me." She stood glaring at him.

"The whole place is going to go up. Do something!" Brianna said.

Ryder grabbed Mia's hand and Tristan caught hold of Brianna's. They stood channeling their energy together. There was a rush of wind as each willed the flames to recede and stop.

"It isn't working. We've gotta get out of here," Mia yelled.

Ryder pulled on her arm forcing her to look at him. "Someone is using your magic. This isn't real. We can stop this, now focus." The flames trapped them in a complete circle and the heat burned against their faces.

"Mia, please." He wanted to shake her because she had zoned out. If she would trust him they could put the fire out. She stared at him and closed her eyes. Seconds later, the wind ceased and the flames fizzled and died.

"Okay, will someone please tell me what the *hell* that was all about?"

"Greyson," Mia and Ryder said in unison.

Chapter Eighteen

Mia knew that Greyson was behind the prank at the barn. He was sending a message. It irked her that he could interfere that way, and it was because he had kissed her and stolen her essence. Ryder explained that she was linked to Greyson and as such he could read her thoughts and feelings. He could also use her magic to strengthen his—basically, sucking her dry.

The thought chilled her to the bone. Ryder dropped her home and left in a stinking mood. Shaking her head, she couldn't blame him. Mia was beginning to despise herself. Pacing around her bedroom, she wondered what to do.

"Greyson…I know you can hear me. Show yourself, I want to talk to you right now."

Mia had never called out to him before. What had possessed her? She didn't know what she was even going to say if he turned up, which was highly unlikely. Moving away from the window, she bashed into a block of heat and muscle. Her breath caught tight in her throat.

Greyson.

He caught hold of her hands before she could escape, and calloused skin scraped against hers. Lifting her head, she stared boldly into a pair of steely-blue eyes and a mop of dirty blonde curls. A smug grin and white teeth flashed at her.

"Let me go, you great big oaf," Mia said, determined to stand her ground. Greyson held her gaze and let go of her hands.

"You called and I'm here. What is it you want, or have you already decided to give up this foolish challenge and come back to Annwn with me?"

His face was tanned from the sun, and she stared at him as he leaned against the wall, dressed casually in black pants and an open white shirt. For once he seemed fairly harmless, and this time, there was no fire-breathing dragon. Now that she had his attention, what was she going to say? She moved in front of him and stabbed a finger in his chest.

"So, despite the fact that you manipulated me, stole my essence, and that your mark is here on my wrist, I still have a choice in this?" Mia's hair whipped behind her and her cheeks flooded dark red. Picture frames, books, pencils, and perfume bottles rattled on her dresser. The whole room seemed to vibrate with her anger.

"What, no windows tonight?" Greyson ran his hands up and down her arms. Her body stiffened at his words and she wriggled away from his hands.

"What do you mean? You broke the windows, not me!" She stepped back pointing her finger at him.

"And why would I do that? You have so much to learn. It wasn't me. You shattered the windows, just like you made the room and everything in it shake. Whether through anger or fear, they're your emotions. You're a fire element like me, full of passion, but also temperamental."

Greyson moved toward her and she backed up, until her back hit the cold wall. His thumb touched her lower lip and stroked. Mia turned her head away, fearing any minute he would kiss her. Her heart beat rapidly and her chest rose and fell with each breath. He turned her chin to make her face him and he lowered his lips, kissing her softly. It was a gentle coaxing kiss. He wasn't rushing or plundering, but teasing and nudging her lips with his. Eventually, her lips softened under his and her hands wove into his hair and he groaned.

Mia moved her lips in sync with his, every now and then poking her tongue inside his mouth. At this point, she shifted her weight and held Greyson's face in her hands. She closed her eyes and while biting down on the tip of his tongue, drew his essence in. Her body twitched and the lights inside her room flickered.

Greyson shoved her hard, and she fell to the ground.

"Why, you conniving bitch!" he bit out, wiping the blood that smeared his mouth. Mia jumped up and wiped her mouth with the back of her hand.

"That was for taking my magic and my kisses. They belong to me, not you. And that's for the fire at the barn. Now get out. I don't belong to you, or anyone for that matter."

Greyson's eyes looked like jagged shards of glass, but rather than continue to glare, he laughed a deep belly laugh and wagged his finger at her.

"No one has ever tried to defy me because I would kill them, but with you, I find I really like it. It's such a turn-on," he said letting his gaze roam over every inch of her body, making her gasp and turn away.

"Mia, I never play fair. If I want something, I take it. That's who I am, and I never pretend to be anything different. You, on the other hand, pretend to be little Miss Perfect, but you have just proved you'll do anything to get what you want—proving how alike we are. I push all your buttons and it drives you wild, but be honest, it also makes you feel totally alive. And just so you know, the Claiming doesn't work if you have no feelings for the person at all."

His words lingered in the air. *It couldn't be true, he must be lying*. Mia swung around, her hands on her hips.

"You're lying." The air seemed to evaporate from her lungs leaving her gasping for breath. He stepped closer, his eyes narrowing. "This time, I don't need to. You don't know what you want. I'm giving you the chance to be queen—my queen. Your powers will know no bounds, and every day will be filled with excitement. Life with Ryder will be predictable and boring."

"You're wrong. The only feelings I have for you are disgust."

She pushed against his warm skin, but instead of moving, he lowered his head and lifted her fingers to his mouth, kissing them. He lifted his head and stared into her eyes. The iris of his eyes brightened and Mia couldn't pull away.

"Each kiss we share makes us closer. I know your heart beats faster when I'm here, and you're conflicted. How will Ryder feel about the fact we've shared another kiss, hmmm? Are you going to keep that a secret too?"

Before Mia could run away Greyson's hand held her head and he kissed her lips firmly. She twisted and thrashed against his chest until he let her go.

"Whatever you think, you're wrong. Ryder trusts me," she said breathlessly.

Greyson looked toward the window. "Well he won't for much longer, because when he sees my mark on you it'll be all over, baby." Mia twisted her wrist and sure enough, the dragon tattoo remained. She'd been sure, that if she managed to draw in some of Greyson's essence the tattoo would change. Big mistake. Close to tears, she racked her brain trying to grab at anything.

"There's something, you're not telling me. Why haven't you simply dragged me over your shoulder and taken me back to Annwn, then? What are you waiting for, because I'm never going to be yours of my own *choosing*—that's it! You cannot make me, I have to choose? Well that's never going to happen! I'd rather die first." Her voice sounded confident and sure that she had the right answer. She crossed her arms and waited for his reply.

Greyson stalked around her room and picked up two glass frames, and turned them to face her. One photograph was of her and Ryder at the gallery, and the other was of Cerianne.

"I've already told you, Mia, I don't play fair. I would never let you come to any harm, through your own hand or anyone else's, but I cannot say the same for your loved ones."

Ice filled her veins and froze her heart. Greyson the Darkshadow was back. His cold glare and raised eyebrows taunted her. "Don't mistake my wanting you for *love*. I have no time for such fragile emotions. Annwn is unstable, and that helps no one. My father is weak, his mind muddled, and it's time for a new leader with you as queen, the people will be united. Our betrothal will bring peace, and a power struggle will be averted. You cannot hide in this mortal world forever."

Mia couldn't shake off the darkness that was creeping around her heart. How could she fight him when he threatened her with those she cared about the most?

"Don't pretend to care about Annwn," she snarled. "You simply crave power, and if our home is unstable, it is of *your* making. You'll never convince me that our match is a good idea. Never! Now get out."

Mia took a deep breath and pushed her burning hands toward Greyson. Yellow-blue forks of electricity shot out of her fingertips and coursed through his chest. His body shook violently until he disappeared. She stared at the empty space and then at her fingers. This just keeps getting worse, was all she could think.

* * * *

Mia stood holding the microphone, waiting for her cue. She couldn't wait for rehearsals to finish. Today was Monday, but the school was closed due to a teacher-training session, and therefore the band was practicing for the Thanksgiving concert. Tristan also wanted Mia to meet his girlfriend Laurie. The news made her smile. However, watching Brianna and Tristan recently, she wondered how serious he was over this other girl. Mia was going to explain what happened with Greyson as soon as rehearsals were over. Several times it almost tumbled out, especially when Brianna looked at her as if already knowing what had taken place. Ryder smiled at her as she sang.

Holding the microphone and letting the music wash over her, she found it easy to believe in the words, and she wanted more than anything to be in love with Ryder. She gazed at his dark eyes, which looked almost black from where she stood, and longed to mess with his thick shaggy locks. The song ended, and Ryder and Laurie clapped. Leaving the microphone in the stand, she rushed to his side and kissed him. Tristan walked over and put his arm around Laurie's shoulders.

"I've been thrashing an idea around with Tyler, and I want to know what you think," he said. "We want to record a song from rehearsals and put the video on You Tube. Everyone's doing it. It's a way of getting our music out there. What do you think? Come on, Laurie's a media student. What do you both think?"

Tyler happened to walk over at just that minute, and his face twitched at Tristan's words.

"I think it would be cool to do a video of you guys," Laurie said. "You sound amazing. I think you should include some background of the band, and maybe some shots of you going over the lyrics. You know, like a docudrama. I'd love to have a go at filming and editing the video for you. It would be fun."

"Look, I just have one question," said Tyler. "Since when did Mathews get a say in any of this? I get it that you're all cool with the girlfriend thing, but this is bullshit, man. We're the band, not *him.*"

Tyler faced Ryder and Tristan, waiting for a reply.

"Look man, I'm not in the band, unless you're cool with me joining. However, I'm more of a singer than a football player. Give me a chance, and if you want me gone, then I'm gone." Ryder stared Tyler down.

"Well, that's surprising. You can *sing*? Let's hear you then." Tyler nodded his head in the direction of the microphone.

Mia gripped his hand and led him into the recording room. Ryder smiled back over his shoulder at Tyler and reached for the microphone. Mia picked up the spare and waited. Evan sat at the drums, Tristan and Tyler walked to pick up their guitars, and Brianna lifted her violin, ready to play.

"*The Promise*," Mia said, looking at the group. They nodded.

Ryder and Mia stood next to each other at the front. Laurie wandered in, holding the camcorder in her hand, and she started to film them. *The Promise* was a beautiful harmonic piece about everlasting love. Mia's voice was delicate, but strong enough to reach the high notes, and Ryder's voice was amazing. His voice was strong, and yet when the melody called for him to reach lower notes he carried it off. Ryder stood behind Mia and at the end sang the words over her shoulder, letting them flutter against her cheek.

The Promise we made
Binds us
Like a light in the darkness,
It guides us,
Across time and space,
It draws us,
One life, one love, forever more. "

The music stopped. Mia gasped, hugging Ryder, and for a moment there was silence. The song was full of emotions for Mia, and she wiped a stray tear from her cheek. As she wiped it away, Ryder caught her hand and gave it a squeeze. Her heart raced frantically, and her body burst with energy. There was a click as Laurie switched the camcorder off.

"Wow," Mrs. Tyler said, breaking the silence. She must have walked in while they were performing. Her presence unleashed a tirade of voices.

"That was amazing. You two were wonderful," Brianna said.

"Really?" Ryder and Mia said in unison. Ryder looked at Mia. Her heart melted. Singing with him felt so right. Standing with him felt so right.

"No, seriously, Ryder—your voice is amazing. Rocker, with a deep soft soul. Wow," Brianna said.

"I'm speechless, which means it was good. You were both good. Ryder, you knocked it out the ball-park," Tristan said, as all eyes turned toward Tyler and his serious expression.

"Well, I have to say… *Awesome*. You were freakin' awesome, dude. Maybe there is a place for you in the band, after all," Tyler said, grinning.

"It's all down to Mia. She's a witch you know, and she's cast a spell over me and Alex," Ryder said smiling.

"Don't give my secrets away," Mia said.

Laurie gasped and stared at Mia.

"I always knew you were a witch," Tristan said, laughing.

Everyone burst into laughter. Mia's eyes drifted to look over at Ryder as he spoke to the group. She watched his smile light up the room. She could not speak the words that he wanted to hear, because although she was certain she loved him, something held her back. But singing with him had exposed what was in her heart. His touch on her hand, his glance every now and then in her direction, proved her case. A quiver of fear ran through her. She let go of Ryder's hand and walked toward Brianna.

"You were great," she said. The boys disappeared into the control room to edit and make some adjustments to the video before they downloaded it onto YouTube.

"This is brilliant guys, come and take a look," Tristan shouted.

Ryder walked out from the control room and headed toward her, saying, "Will you take a walk with me?"

Mia nodded. They said their goodbyes and left.

In no time at all they were at the lake, where Mia felt equal parts of excitement and fear. The full moon cast its shadow upon the still water, a light breeze made the trees sway, and an owl hooted as they approached. Ryder placed a blanket on the ground and they lay down next to each other, gazing up into the night sky. She wanted to tell him about Greyson, but Ryder was being so tender, so kind. He was being romantic, and for once she was totally relaxed and at ease. He pointed out the constellations, with his hand.

"See there to the north, that's Ursa Major or the large bear. It's the third largest. See those seven stars?" Ryder pointed out the picture they made and Mia listened while her heart danced.

"This is like old times. Tell me more." Mia moved to rest her head against his chest and his arm wrapped around her.

"Well, in mythology they say that Zeus fell in love with a woman named Callisto, but when Zeus's wife found out, she transformed the women into a bear. The woman had a son and while out hunting he came across the bear, almost shooting it. Rather than letting the woman die, Zeus sent her and her son way up into the night sky."

He stopped and looked at Mia. The atmosphere between them changed and the warmth of his body left her and he sat forward. Staring at his back, she sat forward and gripped her knees.

"Ryder, I have to tell you something." She stared at the lake and turned her face away.

"I know what you're going to say. I just saw Greyson and you...*kissing*."

His words came out in a hiss and Mia gasped as if she had been stung. She was about to launch into an explanation when it occurred to her that they were reading each other's thoughts. Back at Tristan's house, she knew he wanted to talk to her in private. Her heart raced and she twisted her wrist. She sighed and then faced a very moody-looking Ryder.

"Look. Inside the space of a couple of weeks my world has been turned upside-down and inside-out. All I wanted for as long as I could remember was to be normal. Then, you turn up. I realize being normal isn't important anymore. I know deep down that I belong in Annwn, but I'm not the same Mia anymore. I've changed since living with the humans. I can't explain it, but I'm different. As for Greyson, he's playing dirty and I was trying to get my own back on him, but I'm making everything ten times worse."

Mia stood up, refusing to look at Ryder for fear of what she would see. Ryder stood and touched her shoulder pulling her around.

"I know you've changed. You resisted your memories and struggled with your feelings toward me. I know it's because of your human experience, but you seem so far away. The old Mia would never have arranged to see Greyson without telling me first. We would have discussed this and even if we disagreed, which happened a lot, we would decide together. Here, you're Miss Independent." Mia pulled free and couldn't help the anger raging inside.

"Let me get this straight. You're not angry about the kiss, but the fact that I can think for myself!"

"Really, Mia. We're meant to be a partnership. How can that be when you storm off and don't include me in your plans? Greyson kisses you and you kiss him back. What next? You let him believe he has a chance and that's all he needed. The reason his tattoo appeared was because you believed it was possible. You doubt our love."

He sighed and walked by the edge of the lake. The wind was rustling the leaves. Mia's anger turned into an embarrassing cringing. She did not know how to handle Greyson, and was blindly trying to fix things.

"I'm sorry. I've made such a mess of things, but he's not giving me a choice. He's threatening everyone I care about. I think he manipulated everything, so that while I was here he could wage war back home. He wants to make a show of bringing me back as his queen, striking the final nail in the Wise-Elders coffin, and I would be the way to strike a deal between his people and ours. He wants complete control or he'll dismantle Annwn piece by piece."

Ryder turned away from the lake and reached for Mia's hand.

"You cannot give into his threats, or he's won without even trying. Taking your magic by force doesn't last, and he must know that. Mia, you cannot give into him—unless that's what you truly want?" He brushed over her lips with his thumb, and tingles started low inside Mia's body.

"I will not let anyone be hurt, because of me. I *have* to go." She looked into his dark eyes as a twist of pain flashed across his features, and then she was in his arms.

"Mia, I'll be damned if I'll simply stand by and let him take you from me. This is about control and manipulation. That's all he's got. We'll sort this out together. *I'm* not going to lose you. I'd die before I'd let anything happen to you."

Mia nodded and laid her head against his chest. She knew Ryder spoke the truth. He would give up his life for her—but she wasn't going to let that happen.

Chapter Nineteen

Thanksgiving concert

Mia lay in her bed staring out into the night sky, watching the twinkling stars. She knew she loved Ryder, but was terrified as to what that meant—especially after his words, which shook her to the core.

I'd die before I'd let anything happen to you

Could she say the same? Would she be willing to give up her life to save him? At the lake, she promised that she would not give into Greyson. At this point, besides giving into him, the only other option which she had not discussed with Ryder was to kill him. The thought of Greyson hurting those she loved made her want to rip his head off. Dark Magic was completely outlawed, but unless she could find another way, what option did she have. Thinking of killing someone was way different to actually committing the act. No matter how much she hated him that would make her just as bad as him, confirming his statement that they were alike, which brought her back to her only option, to go to him willingly.

In the chaos that was her life, Fusion was the only normal part. Fusion's video was becoming an overnight sensation. They had already received over two hundred thousand hits, plus Mr. Fitzgerald was playing their track on the air. The band was getting stronger, and its newest member, Ryder, settled in as if he belonged. Rehearsals had been every night because the Thanksgiving concert was tomorrow. For the past two weeks Greyson had been suspiciously absent. Mia tried not to worry that this meant he was up to something, but a part of her was curious to know if she had actually hurt him. Last time, she used such force to harm him, maybe she had already killed him? Was it possible? There was a tap on her door and she turned as Cerianne walked in with Samson following close on her heels.

"Mia, I know it's late, but it's your birthday soon and I wondered if you wanted a party?" she said. Mia had forgotten about her eighteenth birthday. With everything that was going on, her birthday didn't seem important.

"Maybe just a dinner." Mia gave a small smile.

"Don't you want a party? I could ask at the gallery," she said.

"No, nothing big, really," Mia said.

"Okay. Mia, you and Robert—is it serious?" she said, sitting on the bed.

"Mom…" Mia said.

"You see him every night. I just worry."

"Then don't. I am serious about him, but we've been rehearsing too. Robert joined the band, and it's been crazy trying to get him ready. You know the concert is tomorrow," she said, playing with her necklace.

"I know. I just wanted to check. He's your first real boyfriend, and I want you to be safe and sure before you take the next step."

Mia stared at her mom. This talk was old, but now it was different. She was in a real *bona fide* relationship, and a hot flush warmed her cheeks. Cerianne stood up and left her to finish her work.

Just thinking about Ryder and his kisses made Mia's insides quiver. She traced the outline of her tattoo with her finger. Ryder's family seal lay there once more. Her heart swelled. Lately she'd been certain of her feelings, and now his mark was there. Oddly enough, seeing the mark did not scare her as it once did, and although she had mastered hiding it from human eyes, she left it there for all to see. Mia yawned and closed her books. Her brain couldn't deal with anything else, and she fell asleep.

A cool breeze touched her cheeks. She lifted her head, and there he stood. Greyson. He stood dressed in dark pants and a white tunic, and a wool cape surrounded him. She held her breath, and at first he didn't move. She watched, as he simply stood staring over the stone wall of the castle, looking at the fog-filled forest below and gazing into the distance. The sky was a misty-gray, and the sun was about to rise. It was dawn in Annwn. Mia stepped closer not wanting to disrupt his serenity.

"Come here, before you freeze." Greyson turned and beckoned. She moved, and her skirts swished behind her. As she drew next to him, he caught her in an embrace, wrapping his arms and cloak about her. She nestled against him, feeling warm and secure. His hand rubbed against her belly and a movement deep within her, stirred. A kick. She stared down her gown at his hand and the rounded bump beneath it.

"Mia, a new day begins." Clear blue eyes twinkled at her. It was Greyson, and yet his face was older and softer than she remembered. There was an air of calmness about him. His whole demeanor was different. Another stronger kick ricocheted through her, and Greyson gasped. He turned her around to face him.

"He's very active today. Does it hurt when he kicks you like that?"

Mia rubbed her belly and the baby she was carrying responded with another forceful kick. "No, silly. He's simply strong like his father."

She lifted her head to stare into his blue-topaz eyes, staring at the fine lines that surrounded them. His blonde locks peppered with white streaks.

"You've given me a gift that I can never repay, but I'll spend this lifetime and the next trying." he said as he caressed her cheek with the back of his hand. A wave of love flooded her and she turned to stare at the sky awash with streaks of burnt orange and cerise. The sun rose, evaporating the mist.

"And you've given me this child. What more could I ask?" Mia said.

* * * *

Not again! Greyson was manipulating her visions, Mia was certain. Last night, she saw a time when she was pregnant with Greyson's baby. Chewing her nails, she forced herself to get up. She was going mad. Greyson must be behind this. He *must* be manipulating these visions. Her blood boiled at the thought of being with him—and yet, remembering the tenderness he had shown, she was shocked. Whatever version of Greyson appeared in her dreams, it was not one she had ever met or thought possible. She decided no one needed to know about the vision. There was far too much other stuff that demanded her attention. Today was the Thanksgiving concert.

Mia grabbed her bag and headed to Brianna's house. Ryder called to say he was sorting out a few things and would meet them at the school. Trying to touch base with his thoughts was still difficult. It did not help that he was being deliberately vague. Brianna was ready when she arrived.

"Come on, I have some pink spray to match your top," she said.

Mia wore a short ballerina skirt and black leggings with a black fitted T-shirt. In the center of her top was a bright pink sequined heart.

Half an hour later they arrived at the school. It was dark outside and snow fell to the ground forming a thick layer of white icing. Stepping out of the car, Mia skidded on the icy road and grabbed hold of Brianna. "This is a mess. Is it going to stop?" She stared into the sky as the snow swirled around. Snowflakes fell on her face.

"I have a very bad feeling about this," Brianna said

Mia nodded, and they locked arms, walking together for support. The hall inside was warm, and the band's equipment was set up on stage. Tristan wanted everyone here early to go over the songs one more time before the concert. Tonight, Mia was going to sing around eight songs. She gulped as shivers cascaded down her spine. Even with the make-up and her hair now sporting bright pink streaks, Mia could not stop the nerves. Tristan, Tyler and Evan were strumming some notes on their instruments, and they stopped as Mia and Brianna walked in.

"Any sign of Robert?" Mia said.

"Nope, but he'll be here," Tristan said.

I'm worried about him, and I cannot sense him at all. Please Tristan.

A jolt of panic shot through her.

What if Greyson's hurt him? You know his threat?

Tristan and Brianna stared at Mia.

I'd know if there was a problem, trust me.

Tristan's words were so certain that her shoulders relaxed, and she smiled at Brianna. Dumping her coat on a chair, Mia walked on the stage. The bright stage lights glared down on them. Mia gulped down some water, picked up the microphone and took a deep breath. Everyone stood ready as Evan started to tap the beat on his sticks.

"One, two, three, four!"

He thrashed against the drums. Brianna glided her bow across the violin, and the guitars joined the melody. Mia took a deep breath and began singing. The songs were so familiar now that as the words left her mouth, her fears dissolved.

After about an hour, Mia finished the last song and opened her eyes to find that Ryder stood before her in the hall, his hair wet and covered in snow.

"Sorry it's been crazy. It's um, really coming down out there." He nodded his head toward the window. Tyler hung up his guitar and jumped off the stage, followed by the rest of the band. They stared out the windows. It was a whiteout. Several inches had piled up since they had arrived.

"Freaking snow!" Tyler yelled.

Mia walked over to Ryder, "Where have you been?" she said, trying to gauge his thoughts.

"I'm sorry, but I had to sort something out." His arm curled along her shoulders and he pulled her in against him. Despite the warmth his body now provided Mia sensed he was hiding something.

I was scared.

He raised his eyebrows, lifted her chin and kissed her lips.

There was no need. I can hear you, and I have all morning.

She raised her arm to show her tattoo. He smiled and was about to kiss her again, when Principal Grayson walked in shaking her head. The school janitor Mr. Murphy walked next to her.

"I am very sorry. I meant to come by earlier, but we have been busy. Tonight's performance has been cancelled. The weather station is reporting at least a foot of snow. I am so sorry," she said.

"*What!* You can't!" Tristan cried.

"I don't have a choice, sorry. Mr. Murphy's here to close up." She smiled sadly at the group, and then headed back the way she came. Mr. Murphy stood glaring, his keys jangling.

"Damn it. I cannot believe it," Tristan said, glaring at Ryder. Unspoken words passed between them and Ryder shook his head.

Mia watched the scene and wondered what they'd said. He was on edge, but over what she could not tell. Did he know about the dream? He turned and gave an uneasy smile.

"What a nightmare. It didn't look like much earlier, but damn," Tyler added.

Ryder, what is going on? Mia pulled on his arm as the others moaned about the concert. She wanted answers.

"I cannot believe it, all this hard bloody work… Well, who's up for coming to mine?" Tristan said.

Ryder refused to say anything. Mia turned away.

"Me," Mia said along with the others.

"Er, Mia, I think…" he started to say, but someone entered the hall, and everyone stood speechless.

Tristan opened his mouth and gazed at Mia. "Come on guys, gather you're stuff. We're outta here," he said

Mia stood unable to process what she was seeing.

Brianna and the others grabbed their equipment and left. She stood still, turning her head as each friend passed by. Staring in disbelief at the ground, Ryder stepped closer and gripped her hand. He kissed her cheek and let her hand fall.

"I'll wait outside, but I'm not going anywhere, okay?" With that, he walked out of the hall. With everything that was going on, Ryder had brought her father home. Mia did not know whether to scream or cry. Her father, whom she had not seen for years, stood shuffling his foot awkwardly.

"Mia, are you okay?" he said.

What had possessed Ryder to do this? She lifted her gaze to stare directly at her father. He looked older. Hell, he was older. She looked away but quickly turned back to face him.

"What are you doing here?" she bit out.

"It was time," he said.

Mr. Murphy swung his keys, and without saying another word, they strode toward the exit. She took big steps wanting to put as much distance as she could between them, but he pulled her arm, which she tugged free walking out the door.

"Mia, stop. We need to talk."

A hot churning sensation rose inside her. She had to control her temper. The last thing she wanted was to start a fire or thunderstorm. This time, her father would lock her up for good. Her back stiffened, remembering his look that day, years ago, when she told him about the plane crash. Fear. Hate. Despair. Anger. She did not know what his thoughts were exactly, but he had not protected her or made her feel that everything would be all right.

Mia, calm down and let him explain. Ryder's words were a balm to her rising temper and cold water to her fire. She turned, searching for him.

I'm in the car when you're ready

She looked at her hands and then at her father.

All right.

Taking a deep breath she willed herself to be nice. "One hour, you've got one hour."

Outside the snow continued to fall and they both ran toward Ryder's Range-Rover. She opened the door and sat down next to Ryder. She turned to check as her father sat down in the back. She turned back and stared at Ryder's profile.

Why? Mia wanted to understand.

You needed closure. You need to understand. Ryder placed his warm hand on hers and drove as safely as possible in the blizzard-like conditions. *Don't worry. Cerianne knows.*

This must have been something they had been plotting for a while, without her even realizing it. Dad chatted away in the back, explaining that he was going to stay for a couple of weeks and that he wanted to be here to celebrate her eighteenth birthday. In no time at all they were parked in her driveway.

Mia jumped out and chased after Ryder, catching his jacket before he could escape. "What are you doing?" she said, shaking—from the cold or from shock, she didn't know.

"Cerianne asked me to stay, and I thought once you settled down, you might want me around, but I can go—" he said, catching hold of her hand.

Heat rose inside her chest. She truly did not deserve Ryder—he thought of everything. The last thing she wanted was to face her father alone.

"Come on," he said, and they went inside.

Cerianne stood in the hallway, and after a few awkward moments, coats were shed and Mia and her father walked into the living room where a healthy fire blazed. Ryder let go of her hand, promising to return after helping Cerianne in the kitchen. Her father walked to where she stood next to the fire to warm his hands.

"Mia, you've grown up so much. I hardly recognize you. Hearing you on the stage was amazing, I never expected—"

Mia could not stop herself, "What, that I could sing? Well, if you had been around, you would've known." Something shifted inside of her.

"Mia, I know I've let you down. Please, let me explain," he said, looking at her.

She stared at the lines that creased his forehead, and the graying hair. There was nothing he could say that would change the past five years, but Cerianne was being amicable, so the least she could do was to try. Tears fell as Mia listened to her father explain away the past several years, explaining his regrets, apologizing for his past behavior leaving Mia shocked. The hurt that had held her heart captive disintegrated and suddenly she was desperate to run, bursting with happiness that she did not know what to do or what to say. Ryder was right. Her father did not hate her. He simply did not know what to do, and bailed.

"I'm sorry for hurting you, but I never stopped loving you or your mother. We just could not be together anymore, and I left," her father said, as they hugged.

Later that night after dinner, Mia smiled and stared at Ryder. She pulled his arm, dragging him into the living room and in front of the warm fire.

"So how do you feel?" he said.

"I've felt so many things about him over the years, but today…just seeing him and listening to him, none of that mattered. I've missed him, and I didn't realize how big I had let that hole in my heart get. You were right, he's not perfect—no one is—but I felt his love," she said, staring into his dark captivating eyes. Tears fell down her cheeks as Ryder cradled her in his arms. The tears soaked through his shirt, but instead of moving away, he stroked her hair.

"We all make mistakes," he said, kissing the top of her head.

Ryder sounded so wise. Mia made mistakes on a daily basis, and yet for some reason she expected more of her father, placing him on an impossibly high pedestal. Her father was back in her life because of Ryder. He knew all her weaknesses, all her strengths, and still he held on. Her hand rested against his chest as his heart thumped strongly against it, and hers beat in time. Warmth spread through her and her heart beat loudly in her ears. She trusted him implicitly and loved him without question. Yes, she would give up her life to save his.

* * * *

Yesterday, with her dad showing up, it was as if any last remnants of fear about loving Ryder had been washed away. All the anger, disappointment, and hurt that she had carried around about her dad was gone. Today, she couldn't stop smiling. Even thinking about Greyson didn't scare her as it had. Today she could manage anything, and it was because of Ryder. Despite it only being seven-thirty in the morning, she needed to see him. She tip-toed down stairs in her pajamas and headed for the living room, but the quilt that she had given him last night was neatly folded and the couch empty. On top of the quilt was a folded note.

> *Your dad loves you, Mia. Anyone can see that. He deserves a second chance.*
>
> *Yours Ryder.*

She smiled and decided that she would cook breakfast. Her heart ached just knowing how much Ryder loved her, which made her feel invincible and capable of anything. Maybe love was worth the risk after all. She cracked eggs and tipped them into the frying pan, where they sizzled as they hit the fat. Mia busied herself juggling the eggs, bacon, and toast, while brewing some fresh coffee. Her head snapped in every direction to make sure that nothing burned. A wave of churning made her bend, and she gripped her belly.

No.

A sharp twist of gut-wrenching pain exploded inside her belly. She drew in a large deep breath and blinked. *Please, not now...*

Ryder!

The smell of coffee tickled her nose and the machine beeped, signaling it was ready. She took one step in front of the other, and then she was gone.

As soon as Mia took a breath, she coughed and spluttered with the foul air. Beads of perspiration trickled down her back, and she covered her mouth. Thick gray smog surrounded her, and she was in the middle of a village with an exploding volcano on the horizon. The wind blew violently, and in the snatches of clear air she saw palm trees bending and snapping. She moved, unsure of her direction, but was soon swept along with the tide of men, women, and children who were running for their lives, covered in ash, and their faces gripped with fear.

Screams ripped through the air.

This time Mia was ready. She searched around, looking for any clues as to where she was. Bikes, trucks, and the injured, lay on the dirt roads, abandoned. Everyone was running, but to where? A wave of dizziness hit her, and her head spun. Any minute she was certain she would lose consciousness. Searching the skyline, she saw that huts lay burning from the hot fiery orange and golden rocks that dropped from the sky. Plumes of smoke and ash continued to steal over the village like a blanket. Destruction and death lay everywhere. The dizziness swamped her. Mia stood frozen. What was she to do?

Alone and terrified, she was about to run after the others, but there was a whimper and Mia's hand was pulled. A filthy hand lay inside hers. A small child of around seven was tugging her hand and pulling her away. The little girl was covered in ash, barefoot, with torn and dirty clothes, and yet her brown soft eyes pleaded and gave Mia such a sense of strength that she nodded. The girl's matted hair flew back over her shoulders, and together they ran. Mia could feel the heat from the little girl's hand, and it jolted her heart as she ran. Fearing the little girl would fall, she grabbed her up into her arms and ran, not daring to look behind. Explosions shook the ground, and it trembled beneath her feet, almost making her fall. Fiery balls dropped from the skies, and pain scorched her back, making her scream. She fell, dropping the child who landed on her feet. They stared at each other before the girl darted away. Mia watched her as she raced away, and saw a sign. The words were hard to read, and she strained to pick them out as cries sounded around her. Pain slammed into her taking all thought and understanding away until there was nothing.

Mia gasped. The smell of burning filled the air, and for a moment she thought she was still inside the vision—until Mia peered through her lashes, and her father stared back at her. His eyes narrowed revealing the lines and wrinkles of concern. She was lying on the couch in the living room. Her head throbbed along with her chin.

"Owww."

"Careful, I think you hit the table as you went down, and I'm not sure what else. I felt your head but couldn't feel any bumps. You were on the floor, passed out. You gave me such a scare."

She sat up and rubbed the lump on her chin. Mia looked away unable to face her father's knowing glare.

"You had one of those episodes, didn't you?"

The moment of truth that she was dreading—until now, it had all been about him and Cerianne. It was like all those years ago, when she blurted out about the plane. He moved away from her so fast, as if what she had was catching. His mouth was open and his gaze watchful. He was disgusted. At least he seemed that way to her. She forced herself to stand.

"I'm sorry. I was making breakfast."

He stepped closer gripping her shoulder to make her look at him, "Mia, I made mistakes, some pretty big ones. I hope one day you will forgive me, but I want you to know that what you have is…a gift. I just didn't want to believe it, didn't know how to help you. You see, you were such a beautiful surprise. One we never thought we would have, and I knew when I found you on that doorstep that you were *special*. I just never realized how until it was too late."

Mia couldn't breathe or move. She was scared the spell of this moment would shatter and her father would regret what he was saying. She didn't trust his words to be real or the truth.

"I'm sorry—I was scared. Cerianne and I were both scared," he said, shaking his head, and walking to stand by the doors overlooking the garden. "That night you came into our lives was a mess, but everything changed overnight. We were about to split up, things hadn't been right for a while. Cerianne couldn't get pregnant, and then you arrived like a miracle. We were in awe of you. You brought love back into our hearts. I've made mistakes, I know, but can you forgive me?" he said, tears filling his eyes

Mia sighed. None of this was his fault. After all, he did not know who she was, but he loved her. It was time to put the past where it belonged. He smiled, biting his lip, waiting for her to reply. Mia stared at her father and for the first time realized how fragile the human existence was. She could not put her father in danger, and letting him know just how much she was gifted was dangerous. The fact he knew she was gifted was enough. All the hurt she had carried around melted. She grabbed his hands and stepped up to kiss his cheek. As she did so, she closed her eyes and placed a block around his memories of this conversation. The moment she stepped away, he would forget everything he had said and, more importantly, any memory of her special gift and the trouble it had caused. She let him go. "Dad, I hadn't eaten and I fainted, that's all. I'm sorry about breakfast. I wanted to surprise you both, and now's it's ruined."

Nicholas Childs stared at his daughter and shook his head, "Mia, I…I can't remember what for the life of me I was going to say, but as long as you're all right, let's go out for breakfast."

She smiled, "Great." Her cell-phone beeped and Mia knew, before she picked up, who would be on the other end and so did her dad.

"Tell him to come along too."

She nodded and ran upstairs to the privacy of her room. He was phoning about the vision.

"Mia, are you all right?" Ryder said.

"I am now. I had the vision while I was making breakfast for my parents, and Dad found me on the floor." She walked around her bedroom looking through her closet trying to decide what to wear.

"I'm coming over," he said.

"No, I'll explain later. We're all going out to breakfast. Can you check out a place called Dakarta? If you find anything, bring it with you." Snatching a pale pink wool jumper and leggings, she threw them on her bed and turned toward the shower.

* * * *

Cerianne, Nicholas, Mia, and Ryder sat in the booth next to the front window at Felicity's diner, and Mia couldn't help but laugh. Ryder gripped her hand, rubbing his thumb over her knuckles in a gentle rhythm. Cerianne and Nicholas talked, and Ryder pulled out his iPad.

"I brought the research you wanted, and think you should check through it," he said, pressing the electronic tablet into life.

"I wasn't sure if anything would come up, but there's so much here. What do we do?" Mia clicked on the icon for Dakarta, and saw several pages listed. She turned her head toward Ryder. The first one she clicked on appeared on the screen. The article was in the *Scientific Journal* dated six months ago—"Dakarta on Brink of Disaster." Clicking on each article, Mia nodded as Ryder mentioned something about breakfast, and she kept reading. Each article talked about the volcanic activity at Mount Enrapi, near the town of Dakarta in Indonesia. It was clear from reading all the information that everyone knew the volcano was going to erupt. The village was even preparing for evacuation. She sat back and sighed.

"I ordered you the full-works breakfast. Hope that's all right?" Ryder said.

She did not care that her parents were there and looking at her. She grabbed his chin and kissed him, making him blush.

Afterward, they walked out the diner holding hands, and Mia turned to Ryder. "It's all documented, it's all there. I don't understand what I'm meant to do. They are taking measures, so why am I getting the visions?" she asked, watching her parents as they talked jovially and walked ahead.

"I said once your gift was a curse, and I meant it. You feel what they feel, and I hate it. You suffer what they suffer…" He shook his head, "and I cannot take it away. Sometimes, there is nothing we can do. This is nature, Mia. We cannot stop the planet from changing. This is not for us to meddle with. I'm sorry." As the words left his lips Mia knew he was right.

"In the diner, I helped Mrs. Fielding. Do you think I'm meant to do the same for the little girl?"

Ryder brushed her hair behind her ears. "Mia, I think we established that the diner incident was a setup. We can't go around saving people's lives if that's changing the course of history, and every time we use magic there is a consequence. Anyway, with Mrs. Fitzgerald that happened before your eyes. The girl is across the ocean. I don't see how it connects. The visions will keep coming, and so will the clues. As it gets closer, we'll figure it out—as we usually do!" He kissed her and held her in his arms, and she inhaled his scent.

"I was there, and she saw me. We connected physically. That's never happened before."

Chapter Twenty

Happy Birthday

A week passed, Mia was no closer to solving the puzzle of her vision, and today was her eighteenth birthday. She sat up in bed and watched the blinds gently bump against her windowsill. Seconds ticked by. *Time,* she thought—and every second she sat here, time passed. She turned her head and stared at the clock. It was seven-thirty in North Littleton. In Dakarta it would be six-thirty in the evening. She wondered if the people there had any idea of what was to come. Reading through all the news reports from the last week, they seemed to be evacuating. However, remembering the vision, she knew it was not going to succeed, and there was nothing she could do. Ryder was right—seeing the future was a curse, and really sucked.

Not wanting to sit around a minute longer, she bounced out of bed and headed for the shower. It might help clear the fog that clouded her mind.

As she opened her bedroom door, several large and brightly colored balloons with the number eighteen on them hit her squarely in the face, and she laughed. Cerianne or Ryder, she wondered.

She crept into the shower, letting the hot water pummel down her back, and shut her eyes. Ryder said they would discover the meaning of the vision together, and that word *together* sounded so good right now. Five minutes later, Mia was wrapped from head to foot in fluffy towels—and no sooner had she stepped on the creaking floorboards than Cerianne appeared, her face full of smiles.

"I couldn't wait any longer. Happy birthday!" Cerianne said, wrapping her arms around Mia tightly as she sobbed.

"Mom, don't," Mia said, and Cerianne stepped away. "I meant don't cry, not the hugging bit. I love you, mom," Mia said, hugging her mom back, "Can I get dressed now?" she added, starting to shiver.

"You okay?" Cerianne tilted her head back, staring at her.

"I'm fine, just dripping." A small puddle was forming around her feet.

"Oh, yes. Go get dressed. I'm cooking breakfast, and there are presents to be opened," she said, smiling. "Dad is coming over later, and we thought we'd give you our present together."

Closing her bedroom door, Mia leaned against it and smiled. Celebrating her birthday was not a priority right now, but Cerianne was not going to let it pass without some kind of recognition, and she loved her mom for it. Dropping the towel to the ground, she winced as the cold air hit her. Goose-bumps erupted along her skin, and a growl of fury escaped her mouth as she tried to snatch up her towel to cover herself, too late to save her modesty. Greyson stood there, ogling her nakedness. Without lifting her gaze to his, Mia imagined herself dressed in leggings and a T-shirt. She tried not to respond to him, but her cheeks scorched with embarrassment. The last couple of weeks had been Greyson-free. Now he stood there, leaning up against her wall, drinking her in with a grimace on his face that showed he remembered exactly what she looked like moments before. Even his usually ice-cool blue eyes seemed warmer as they fixed on her face.

"You're so beautiful Mia," he said, with a voice that sounded oddly strained.

Mia's heart was beating like a hammer, and she wanted to strangle him. He laughed, and she knew he was aware of her thoughts. Greyson took a deep breath and circled around her like a hunter stalking prey. She turned, watching him as he moved until he stopped in front of her. The corners of his mouth lifted slowly as he wet his lips. A cold puff of air touched her cheeks, and she shivered. She wanted to scream, to push him away, but was terrified of what he would do. He was so controlled and determined. He lifted his hand and skimmed his fingers across her collarbone, making her step back.

"I've been more than patient, but I'm warning you, my patience is about to run out. If you don't make the right decision, then I will not be able to stop what happens next. It isn't just me. I come seeking a peaceful end, but there are those who desire death, blood, and vengeance. I can give you all you desire and keep those you love safe. What more could you want?"

Nothing had changed. Greyson was not going to disappear or give up. Her attack on him changed nothing. He stood determined and more dangerous than ever.

"I need love." She flicked her hair over her shoulders, and turned away as a lone tear fell down her cheek.

He moved up close against her, and she could feel his heart beating against her back. "I don't know how. Perhaps as my queen you could teach me?" His voice was lower and softer this time. An idea burst into life and she shut her thoughts off, unwilling to let anyone know what she planned.

"If you want me to come freely, I need more time. I know nothing about you or your home, and I can't make a decision until I know it is the right one."

He pulled her around to face him, "You're just trying to delay the inevitable. You saw the vision of us, standing together, just as I did. I stayed away, but no more. You were carrying *my* child, and you were content."

There was a part of her that acknowledged his words as the truth. Remembering the vision clearly, she was filled with joy. Staring at him, Mia saw his veins throbbing in his neck as his teeth bit out the words. She mentally made notes of what made him angry or yielded a softer response, "You've manipulated and tricked me. That vision was just another trap."

His hands weaved their way through hers, "I didn't create that vision. I wouldn't do that…" Without another word, he vanished.

Mia let her breath out. She was never going to be free of him. Her idea bounced around in her head. If she could show him what real love was, if she could make him fall in love with her, then surely he would let her go, knowing she loved another. Was that the answer? The smell of bacon wafted into her room, and she pushed thoughts of Greyson out of her mind.

Breakfast and presents.

Mia left her room and walked into the kitchen, where there were yet more balloons and streamers. A pain where her heart was stopped her. She couldn't let anything happen to her family, because they meant the world to her—and Ryder. Underneath all the roughness and sharp edges, Greyson must have a heart—and if she could get him to acknowledge it, then maybe they would have a chance of defeating him.

As if on cue, her cell-phone rang.

"I am going to kill him—and *No*, absolutely not, Mia. I wanted to wish you a happy birthday, but instead it's stay there and don't move. You're going to be the death of me!"

In his usual style Ryder gave no option, and ten minutes later he showed up at the door with her dad. Her father kissed her on the cheek, and handed over a box wrapped in shiny pink paper with a big bow. "Happy Birthday," he said.

Cerianne appeared from the kitchen and walked over to join them. "Honey, happy birthday. This is from both of us," she said as she kissed her on the forehead. Mia held the box, sniffing back tears. She tore the paper off. Inside was an Apple laptop.

"We thought you would need one for yourself in college. It has all the latest gadgets, and we can Skype, so we'll be able to talk—" Cerianne started crying in earnest now, which made Mia cry as well.

"We wanted to get you a gift that you would actually use, this time. Unlike the car!" Dad said

"I haven't left yet, and really this is too much. You spoil me, but thank you—and I will use the car," she said, between sobs.

"I know, but you're getting so grown up, and it won't be long before you're gone for good," Cerianne said.

"Awww, Mom, I'll never be far away."

"Cerianne, she can't stay home forever. She has to make a life for herself," Dad added.

"I know, I know."

For the next hour they all sat around talking, but all the while Ryder was arguing with her in her head. Not being able to stand it any longer, Mia made her excuses to her parents and they left the house.

"Seriously Mia, what the hell were you thinking? Greyson's pulling out all the stops, and here you are again being swayed. Do you want to be with him? Is that what you want?" Ryder was pissed. She knew that he had heard her planning how to win Greyson over, but she was not sure if he had heard Greyson's threat.

"Of course not, but Greyson's made it clear that he isn't working alone—and he's running out of patience." She waited for him to reassure her. He sighed and grabbed her hand.

"Let's get out of here. It's your birthday, and he isn't going to spoil it anymore." Ryder reached inside his black jacket and produced three small packages. "Open this one first," he said, handing her the first gift.

Tearing open the delicate tissue paper, she sighed, "They're beautiful. I love them." She held up a pair of crystal earrings in the same color as her necklace, and placed them into her ears.

Mia leaned into him and kissed his lips. "They're perfect, thank you, but you've already given me my best gift—my dad," she said, hugging him.

"This is just a little something," he said, passing over the second gift. Her fingers ripped the paper and a red dragon key ring dropped into her hand.

"Hmmm," she said.

"Come on, time to get behind the wheel." Ryder fished inside his pocket and pulled out a key—her car key. He was full of surprises again. She laughed, looking back at the house and catching her parents peering at her through the window. She smiled and waved the key ring at them, then attached the key to it.

"Do you still remember how to drive? Just take it slow, okay? I'm a nervous passenger," he said, laughing. She could tell he was loving every minute of this, and so was she. Mia sucked on her lower lip. The Volkswagen beetle had remained unused because she was convinced her dad had only bought it out of guilt. Now she knew it was love, and there was no longer any excuse for her not to drive it. She took a deep breath and unlocked the door. The smell of leather and lemon hit her straight away.

"It probably won't start," she said looking across at him uncertainly.

"It will. We gave it the once over yesterday. Drives like a dream. The tank is full, I topped off the windshield-wiper fluid, the oil is new, tires all pumped, and the battery is charged. Come on, I'm right here and I don't want to die either. If you don't give it a go now, you never will." He arched his eyebrows as if to dare her. For a second, Mia wondered if she had held off driving because she was actually scared. One look at him, and then she sat down in the driver's seat. She turned the key and the engine hummed to life. As Mia placed her hand on the wheel, Ryder covered it with his.

"Last gift."

It was a small square package wrapped in silver paper. She tore the paper off, and inside was a CD. On the front there was a beautiful drawing of a sunset, and handwritten at the top was the word *Secrets*. Her hand shook as she tried to put it into the music player and she held her breath until the music played. It was the song she had heard and could not get out of her head. It was Ryder. He was singing the song. Being confined in the car was as frustrating as hell at that moment, because she wanted to launch herself at him. Instead, she settled for unbuckling her seat belt, clambering across to straddle his lap, and grabbing his face so she could kiss him. Pulling back, she opened her mouth, "I love you," she said.

There was silence and neither spoke. "Did you hear me? I said I love you." She waited, gazing at him.

He gave a smile and touched the tip of her nose. "It sounds like something you would say before you going hurtling off a cliff or something. Are we? I know you haven't driven for a while," he said, almost laughing and she punched his arm.

"Ryder, I'm serious. I don't have any more hang-ups. I trust you more than I trust myself. I love you."

He pulled her chin closer and brushed his thumb across her lips, "Finally. Now I wish more than anything we weren't in this damn car, but I'll take it for the moment. I love you too, by the way. Now drive," he growled.

Mia hopped back into the driver's seat and replaced her seat belt. Despite how the morning had started she was floating on air. She loved Ryder, and could not deny it any longer. Even though she knew she faced impossible decisions, for now she was giddy and euphoric with the love that filled her heart. She put the car in reverse and slowly backed out of the driveway.

Mia drove around town for about an hour—and then a car pulled suddenly out from the side road. There was a squealing noise from the brakes as she slammed her foot down, and they jolted forward.

"You okay?" Ryder said.

"I'm fine, but I'm sure you're regretting your decision to let me drive now, aren't you?"

He laid his hand over hers, which still gripped the steering wheel. "*You* stopped. He was the jerk who pulled out. This is where the real learning begins. Come on, pull over and I'll drive from here. I want to take you somewhere."

Ryder was a confident driver, and after twenty minutes they arrived at Wingaersheek Beach in Gloucester. Even though it was early December, today was like spring. The sun and its hazy mist shone, and a warm breeze brought the smell of the ocean with every deep breath. The beach was not entirely deserted, because a few people were walking their dogs. Mia held Ryder's hand, and as they walked her worries seemed a million miles away. They stopped and sat on a large amber-colored boulder, staring out at the aqua-blue ocean.

"I want to contact Emrys again. I thought he might know what we're meant to do about Dakarta," she said, staring ahead.

"Mia, he won't be able to give you the answers you're looking for. You know that. I know it's frustrating, but you have to be patient. Anyway, we need to talk about Greyson. I was wrong before about trying to get close to him, to find out what he wants."

Mia sat bolt upright. He moved and let go of her hands, shaking his head furiously.

"No, I absolutely forbid it." She put her hand on his knee, and he pushed it away. "No. I read your thoughts about trying to pretend to love him—and once you go down that route, there's no turning back. He'll take what you offer and won't give a damn about anything else. I won't stand by and watch." He stood up and stormed off.

The waves crashed against the shore, and Mia's head bowed low. Why did everything have to be so complicated? She wanted to explain why she believed that showing Greyson what love was would be the key—that in making Greyson fall in love with her, she could make him let her go, and his threat to hurt those she loved would be an idle one because he would love her. If she could get Greyson to experience what real love was, he would have to see reason—but the only way she could achieve that would be to lie and pretend that she loved him. Reading Ryder's mind, she knew the hurt and fear that consumed him. He did not deserve that after everything he had done for her, but what was the alternative?

"Ryder, please," she called, running along the sand to reach up to him. The wind was picking up, and as he walked his jacket billowed. He dug his hands in his pockets as if not wanting to be touched, and he didn't acknowledge her calls.

As she pulled up next to him, she tugged on his sleeve. "Ryder, please stop. This is tearing me apart. Today, I told you I love you. Does that mean nothing to you?"

He whipped around to face her, his face blazing with fury. "Not if you go to him and play happy families."

She winced at his words and the memory of the vision. "You're jealous, and you have no reason to be. I love you. Don't you trust me? I would never give myself to him." Her hand reached to smooth his cheek.

"I do trust you, but he doesn't play by the rules. How are you going to convince him you love him if you don't kiss him—and do other things? And when he wants more, what'll you do then? Will you succumb, because in your eyes you're protecting those you love? Well, I won't be around, so don't stop on my account."

He grimaced as he twisted around cursing out loud at the roaring surf and the seagulls that squawked above. Finally, he stopped and faced her.

"Look, Emrys said this challenge was to test your love, not mine—but I'm not sure about that anymore, because this is testing me. You are the most infuriating girl ever, and I love you, but we have to find another way to tackle Greyson. You can't play games with him. You're innocent. He'll make you do things you'll regret. Promise me that no matter what happens, you won't go to him."

He towered above her, the wind blowing his dark hair over his forehead, and he raked it back to no avail. Her heart raced. Ryder was right, convincing Greyson that she loved him would be nigh on impossible without entangling herself in a web of deceit she might not be able to get out of. "Okay, but we have to come up with something soon."

She pulled his shirt toward her and breathed in his scent. Resting her head against his chest, she heard the rapid beating of his heart as his arms held her. She didn't want to move, or face anything without him.

Later, Ryder drove her home and left, promising to meet at Felicities at seven. They were having dinner with her parents, to celebrate her birthday low-key and quiet, exactly what she wanted. As she walked through her front door, her parents both popped out with smiles on their faces.

"Well, how did you get on?" Nicholas Childs asked.

"Pretty good. I actually drove, and didn't hit anything or anyone," she grinned, thinking of how Ryder made her feel so comfortable and confident. Mia chatted with her parents for a while and then ran upstairs to get ready.

She was giddy and dizzy with the feelings that swamped her. After spending ages in front of the mirror, and several changes of outfits, Mia was finally ready. She wore a lilac gauzy top with spaghetti straps, black leggings and her converse sneakers. With her heart beating in a frantic rhythm, she didn't notice the coolness of the night as she rushed to meet her parents.

Ten minutes later, she stood outside the diner. Ryder's bike was parked out front, so she knew he was already inside. Mr. Childs pushed open the door, and the bell tinkled. Warm air, the aroma of coffee, and freshly made bread greeted them along with silence, except for the ghostly music from the jukebox. Mia followed her dad inside and stepped into an empty diner, and shivers of apprehension twisted in her gut, even the lights were dimmed.

Ryder, what's going on?

Before Mia could utter those words to her parents, the lights switched on and a rush of people emerged from the kitchen. Ryder, Brianna, Tristan—the diner was filled with her friends from the band, school, and the diner.

"Surprise! Happy Birthday!"

With the bright lights now on, Mia saw the streamers and balloons that filled the diner. Party poppers exploded, and clouds of confetti flew through the air toward her and she laughed.

Sorry, I couldn't stop them. Just relax and enjoy it. Happy Birthday.

Ryder's voice was comforting, and she searched through the crowds for his face. At the edge of the diner, and possibly furthest away, Ryder stood soaking up the scene. He smirked as their eyes met. He was so handsome her heart melted. Straight away, she longed for the crowds to vanish and for it to be just the two of them. It was so unfair that just the sight of him made her heart race. She turned, and smiled at her parents to mouth the words *thank you.* Then she was swallowed up by the wave of people wishing her a happy birthday, and carried away. Pastel colored confetti rained down on her like snow and it tickled her face. Strong arms moved around her waist and pulled her. Sucking in her breath, she faced a very happy looking Ryder.

"You keep surprising me. How do you do that?" she said.

He smiled and nodded, "Your parents wanted to do something special, and so did I." Lowering his head, he leaned his forehead against hers. Then he placed a soft kiss on her lips before pulling away.

Your parents.

Ryder stepped back to reveal her parents. A surge of happiness took over and she hugged them both. "Thank you for making it so special," Mia said.

Cerianne started to cry, and Nicholas placed an arm around her shoulders. "Come on, no more tears. Let her enjoy tonight." Nicholas pulled Cerianne away, and moved to where people were dancing. *What a Wonderful World* by Louis Armstrong was playing from the juke-box. Mia watched as they hugged each other, amazed they could be so happy and relaxed. Brianna and Tristan appeared as Ryder went to get some food. Sam and Sylvia both came over and gave her a hug.

"We've bought you a present and put it on the table over there. If you don't like it, sweetie, just let me know, and we'll change it."

Mia took note of the word *we,* and smiled at Sylvia. She smiled at everyone until her cheeks ached. Everyone had been involved in organizing her birthday party, and it occurred to her that, despite everything that had happened recently, she was surrounded by people who cared about her. Ryder was by her side physically and mentally. For the first time, as she stood and straightened her back, she was not afraid of anything anymore—even Greyson.

She lifted her head and looked at the news report from the overhead television. A ripple of *déjà vu* exploded down her spine and she clasped her arms.

The footage showed a volcano spewing its orange lava, and thick gray clouds covered the town below. There were snatches of shots of villagers running away from the disaster, and then another scene appeared showing the devastated town and the injured that had been rescued. The reporter stated that at the moment, one hundred and sixty people were confirmed dead, but that there were possibly many more. The evacuation from

Dakarta had been extremely difficult, and the volcano had erupted in the very early hours of the morning, catching many unaware.

A close-up of a scene inside a makeshift hospital appeared on the screen, and Mia's stomach nosedived. She gripped the table for support, almost knowing what was coming next. Another reporter was telling the story of a little girl, and there staring back at her was the girl from her vision. She was five years old and had been severely burnt. Mia suddenly could not breathe. Her throat tightened, and she gasped for air. Whirling around and pushing past people, she headed for the exit.

Outside the coolness hit her, and she inhaled a lungful of air. She'd known that the volcano was going to erupt, and that people would die, but it still didn't make it easy.

Another sensation swept through her, and she turned her head, knowing he was there.

"Happy birthday, baby."

Mia whirled around, fury flaming her insides. She hated him calling her that, it was so intimate.

"I'm not your baby!"

Greyson walked around her, eyes devouring every inch of her body. His hand swept across her shoulder and trailed a finger downwards, and stopped just above her breasts. Mia's chest was rising and falling in a fast rhythm and the pulse in her neck pounded loudly.

"I can help you in ways you'd never imagine. You only have to ask." His words were unexpected and confusing. How could he help her? She didn't know what he was referring to, and stared at him. "You're sad because of the child. There's no point in denying it, because I can read it clearly in your thoughts. You really should learn how to hide them."

Mia shivered, and Greyson breathed against her skin, sending a heat wave throughout her body.

"As a birthday present, I saved the child."

She was astonished and puzzled, "*You* saved the child? Why?"

Music poured out from the diner into the street. Mia could see people swaying to the music, unaware of her dilemma. A rough hand stroked her neck and lifted her chin. Staring into midnight blue eyes and tawny blonde curls she froze, waiting for what he would say next.

"And so the game continues. I saved the child, because for some unfathomable reason you care about her. I saved her to show you that I can show mercy. But the people of Dakarta have you to blame for their plight. I warned you. People will die, and you're dragging your heels. If you choose him, more will die." He let go and walked a short distance away. Mia gasped and raced after him, pulling him around to face her.

"*You!* You were responsible for that destruction! You killed all those people! Why?" Her hand was on his sleeve and she dropped it as soon as her words were out. He brushed his hair back and gazed down at her, frowning. An owl hooted nearby and Mia stepped closer.

"You're not meant to be here. You came because you wanted to find a way to help the humans, but also to help the people of Annwn. You think there's a cure here, a way to stop the infertility that will spread and kill the human race. But you're wrong. Every human civilization dies. You cannot save them. Their time is over, and we've simply helped things along. The volcano was going to explode—I simply tipped the balance. As for you, I can give you what you wish for. I'm a Darkshadow, and of pure blood. I can give you a child, whereas Ryder never will. The fate of Annwn is in your hands. Our people must be joined."

He was evil with no thought for life, and the humans were playthings to him. An ache low in her belly, cried out to her. She let out a scream. The wind whipped around her and everything was blurry. It couldn't be true. Cold words whispered against her ear, and she wept.

"If you don't come to me, more will die—and that includes Ryder. Love holds little interest for me. I'm not a soft touch, Mia. Don't believe that for one minute. I'm ruthless, and always get what I want. Humans are fragile and easily crushed. Do you really want that?"

A blaze of fury and hatred pierced her and she raised her hand to slap him across the face, but he caught her wrist and bent it behind her back. He dragged her against his chest. She whimpered as he twisted her arm.

"This is the real me. I'm not some love struck puppy you can wrap around your finger, and don't ever think you can fool me. Make your decision, and soon, or I'll kill him and make you watch."

He released her arm, and she fell to the ground. There were no words, no ways to outmaneuver him. Greyson was manipulating events in the human world. He was bringing disaster and chaos, and he was using it as a way to get her to do what he wanted. There were other voices now, but she was empty and drained. Everything that happened was because of her, and there was no way out of this. Blinking, she saw hazy figures approach and shook her head, but the lights faded.

"Quickly, she's coming around. Brianna, get some water. Tristan, keep a watch on her parents will you." Ryder's voice threw out orders with an impatient tone.

"She'll be all right." Tristan's voice was softer.

Mia blinked and sat up. Tiny stars floated around, and she felt sick. Ryder had her in his arms and his hand was rubbing her back. She gave a weak smile.

"Not enough excitement in the diner?"

Remembering what Greyson had said, she gasped. "He did it! He killed those people, and then bragged about it. He said he saved the girl from the village, the one from my visions, because it was my birthday. What are we going to do?" She brushed his hands away and stood up, wobbling as she did. His face creased in concern and Brianna stood wide-eyed.

"What do you mean, he killed those people? What am I missing?" Brianna looked across at Mia and then Ryder. Tristan returned from the diner breathless and panting.

"What did I miss? Mia, are you all right? Okay, will someone please explain why you're all looking like that?"

Mia explained everything she could about Greyson and all his threats. Ryder placed his arm around her shoulder and stared at the diner. Every now and then he squeezed her shoulder or winced as she went over everything. Brianna and Tristan shared looks of shock and bewilderment. It was quite some time before anyone spoke. Mia told them what Greyson's parting words had been, *Make your decision and soon or I'll kill him and make you watch.* Ryder let go of her hand and paced around like a dog with a bone.

"Not if I kill him first," he growled.

"We have to go into warrior mode, I agree," said Tristan. "Greyson is not backing down, but he's a bit of a coward if you ask me. I mean, he only appears to Mia, scaring her and making threats. I wonder if he would be so fearless if he faced us all?"

Mia stared at Tristan. He was right. That night when she had pushed him away with her hands, it must have had some effect. What if they were all to go against him? What if Ryder was right, and the only answer was to kill him? Could they really do that? Killing wasn't how they solved problems in Annwn. Surely, there was a better way…

"I know what you're thinking, Mia, but he's threatening everyone now, and it's about time we fought back. We just have to plan how and when." Ryder's dark eyes looked almost black, and his face was stony as he glared at her. "He's using every trick in the book to make you feel that you have no choice, but I won't let you sacrifice yourself for me. Do you hear me? He's knows how to touch you where it hurts. He's a bully, and we will find a way to overcome him," Ryder said.

"So, we're going to *kill* him?" Brianna said, sounding worried.

"I'm going to protect those I love at whatever the cost. If it's a fight he wants, then that's what he's going to get." Ryder said, hissing the words out.

"Ryder, we don't kill people. That's not what Annwn is about. Now who's letting their emotions get the better of them? Emrys said, we mustn't forget who we are and where we came from. We're Children of Annwn, and there has to be another way."

Chapter Twenty-One

Ayesha

Mia kept thinking about the many faces of Greyson and how he knew exactly what buttons to press to get a reaction. He'd said he had shown mercy by saving the child in her vision—only to take pleasure in telling her that he had allowed many to die, and that it was her fault. He was evil, pure and simple. All of this was some kind of twisted game, and the humans merely pawns. Yet, he saved the girl—and true it was, because Mia had connected with her, but still he could have let her die. She was curious as to why. Greyson held all the power in his hands, and yet he was still trying to win her hand and not simply take it. Surely that must mean that, as much as he was evil and denied that emotion meant anything, underneath that darkness there lay a heart. Mia was certain Greyson could change if he was shown what real love involved.

Since her birthday, no one talked about killing Greyson. Every day, she watched the news reports about Dakarta and the girl called Ayesha, who remained in critical condition. Every night Mia met with all the members of Fusion to discuss the band and rehearse. Out of the blue, Tristan announced that his father had arranged for them to go into the radio station and perform. He was doing a new segment on local bands and upcoming talent in the Boston area, and he wanted Fusion to come in. There was a buzz now when they met, and nothing else seemed to matter. The idea was that they would perform a couple of songs live and answer a couple of questions—easy enough.

The YouTube video was taken up by the media, making headlines on the news for reaching over twenty million hits in the first day. Ryder and Tristan both swore that they had not used any magic, but Mia was not so sure. The *Today* show wanted an interview as well as *The American Teen* magazine. They were in the middle of media frenzy, and it was crazy and exhilarating too. However, Mia dreaded the night. Since her birthday, visions were plaguing her—and they all centered on Ayesha. Staring at her face in the mirror, she knew she looked bad. Her eyes looked a dull grey compared to the normal blue-lilac they normally were, and silver shadows surrounded them. Maybe tonight she would sleep. Letting her head fall into the soft pillow, she closed her weary eyes and exhaled.

Hot flames licked around her, and she couldn't breathe. The child with matted black hair was clasping her hand, and she stole a glance behind. Fiery orange balls hurtled through the cloud-filled sky. Beyond, a screeching and flapping of wings made her stop dead in her tracks. Her heart pounded, and she stared in complete fascination. The sky was a thick sea of billowing gray smog, and yet a shriek filled the air. She knew that sound and what it meant. Turning around she looked at the child.

"Ayesha, no matter what happens, don't let go of my hand. Okay?" The child couldn't possibly understand her words, but she nodded, and as Mia gripped the tiny hand and squeezed a flash appeared inside her head.

A tall lady dressed in a white doctor's coat was walking with a group of doctors. She was chatting, and they were smiling. In her hand she had a clipboard, and she entered a room where a young woman sat in a bed.

The girl smiled like the midday sun. "Dr Mosabi. I cannot believe the news. I'm pregnant." The doctor sat on the bed and gripped her hands. Mia stared at the doctor's face and blinked. It could not be. She blinked, and the image vanished. She was left instead to gaze into the eyes of the child in front of her. They were the same eyes of the woman in the doctor's coat. A wild beating of her heart. This child was important. She took one more step.

The wind around them withdrew. Wings the size of houses flapped into view, and a dragon's face burst through the clouds, roaring and snorting flames from its nostrils. Great wide black-and-orange slits for eyes zoned in on her, and the dragon charged directly toward them. The gray and purple dragon screeched and soared through the air as Greyson sat upon its back, riding like a rodeo star. His hand was raised high up in the air as the dragon swooped and ducked. Mia clung to Ayesha. She had to protect her because this child might be the key to solving the problem of human infertility. Mia had to make sure she was safe. Greyson called.

"Get on, before this whole place goes up, if you want to save the child."

Mia clenched her teeth and held the child against her chest. The world around her was full of destruction. The dragon swooped alongside her and the rush of air blew her backwards, but strong arms gripped, and before she could say anything, she and the child were on the back of the dragon with Greyson's arms wrapped around them both. In seconds, they were ripped away from the ground, flying straight up until the air cleared, and they could breathe.

Mia woke clutching her chest. *Ayesha.* She leaped out of bed and ran toward the window. Greyson stood in the moonlight on her front lawn.

I said, I could help in ways you'd never imagine. Well, you've seen for yourself. Not only can I give you what you desire, but I can stop the humans from their own self-destruction. The Darkshadows have been helping nature along for quite some time, helping to rid the Earth of these parasites you care so much about. Look, I will show you.

Mia couldn't stop the onslaught of pictures that assaulted her brain. A room was filled floor-to-ceiling with skulls and bones. In the center lay an altar with a large gold cross.

For years, humans have waged war upon each other, and we merely helped tip the balance.

More pictures flashed countless faces of dictators, Presidents, Kings and Queens, battle-fields littered with the dead and wounded, volcanoes, earthquakes, and tsunamis. Bodies lay scattered all over the world, death camps with children walking in rags, dirty and crying, disease-ravaged and war-battered scenes filled her head until she couldn't take anymore and sank to the ground.

You did all this.

It was not meant to be this way. In Annwn she had been certain she could help the humans and the people of Annwn, because with Ryder everything seemed possible. When he held her hand and smiled, strength filled and warmed her heart and there was no fear. Now, listening to Greyson rattle on and laugh over the Darkshadows secret plans, everything was different.

We have been visiting for centuries, and mankind has not changed or learned from their mistakes. In the beginning my people merely observed, but over time our reasons changed. We want the humans to die, and they are hell-bent on their own destruction anyway. We simply added a few sparks to the fire. We have never started a war or created a disaster that was not going to happen anyway.

Mia remembered standing in the cold sea before they left that fateful night, promising Ryder that she would love him forever no matter what happened. She wiped away the tears that fell and stood up. It was true, she would always love Ryder and that would never change.

So you have manipulated disasters and incited wars, killed innocent millions throughout history. What else is in store?

Mia figured she had no other choice than to give in, but if she could discover anything more that could help, she was going to try. A whoosh of air and Greyson stood before her dressed in tight-fitting black leather pants and a dark-gray shirt. He was always Greyson, whether he was in the mortal world or back in Annwn. He looked strong, powerful, and capable of anything. Narrowed steel eyes gazed at her. He pulled her off the ground and she glared at him.

"There are many ways to toy with the humans. We manipulated their DNA, exposing them over years to a poison that will stop them from conceiving. It was put in the food and water. Loxus made them promiscuous, and that increased sexually transmitted diseases, which also prevented males from being fertile. Do you need me to go on? We want to cleanse this disease-infested world and claim it for ourselves. Annwn is too small. Your visions made you dangerous. At some point, you would have realized the truth, and we could not afford that, so we lured you here. The game is over, Mia."

Ryder was right about the Loxus, but Greyson did not mention the name of the poison used in the food and water supplies. Mia would have to consult Brianna, who knew most of the herbs and plants from Annwn. She was certain it was not a substance that was easily found in the mortal world. Mia inhaled a sharp breath.

"If I agree to your terms, then you must not only promise to keep those I love safe, but you must help Ayesha!" Mia stared directly into Greyson's piercing eyes. The magic that he had used in the human world would leave a signature, and that signature could easily be traced. A plan was forming as to how to make that possible. However, changes to human DNA—even if created in the beginning with magic—were harder to put right, and Ayesha was undoubtedly the key.

"Check-mate. I have to admit I'd expected more." His mouth curled into a gloating smile, and Mia dug her nails into her hand rather than around his throat, which was what she wanted to do.

You may have won the battle, Greyson, but you have yet to win the war, she promised to herself. Shutting down her thoughts was becoming as easy as switching the lights on and off. Mia was never going to let anyone rummage through her mind unless she wished it. Instead of showing her hatred, she pouted and gave a half smile.

"Christmas. Give me until then, no more games. I'll leave here and return to Annwn as your queen."

His eyes narrowed as he bent and shook his head. Greyson did not move. It seemed that he was waiting for something. He needed convincing. Mia moved next to him and lifted his hand, smoothing her fingers over his palm feeling the rough calluses. There was a moment of hesitation, but that was it, as she stepped onto her tiptoes and ran her hands through his hair pulling him down toward her and kissed him. He did not move except to hold her around her waist. She lifted her head and stared into his midnight blue eyes. The shade of his irises seemed to alter with his mood. The corners of his mouth lifted, and again, she kissed him, until she teased his lips apart and then his hold on her was like steel. Ryder was right. He took what she offered. She pushed at his chest and pushed again, yanking herself away from him. He gave what sounded like a snarl and turned away.

"'Til Christmas and no longer, or so help me, I'll kill them all," he said, his voice hoarse.

* * * *

Ryder knew Mia was plotting something, and that he was not going to like it. Since her birthday, several things changed. She was secretive, retreating inside herself, and blocking all her thoughts to him. Each time they met, when she was not aware of his gaze, he caught a look upon her face of utter despair. It was killing him. She was his to protect, and he would do anything to save her from this fate she was determined was hers. He wanted to reach out, hold her and tell her everything was going to be all right. Gazing at her, as she looked like a deer caught in the headlights, was going to be his undoing. Many nights, he had imagined killing Greyson with his bare hands, and his fists automatically balled at the name. *Emrys, where are you?* His question went unanswered. *You said this was not a test for me, but you lied, and I am done playing games with this monster.*

He shook his head. He would try one last time to convince Mia to listen to him, and failing that he was going to take matters into his own hands. He always knew he risked losing Mia, but this was not how he imagined it would be. Mia loved him. He knew this just as surely as he knew that she was everything to him. Maybe loving each other was not enough—but that was crazy, it defied everything they believed in.

They were all at Tristan's house rehearsing and discussing plans for a concert to raise funds for Ayesha and her Aunt to visit the United States for her surgery, Mia's latest project. Could she really be the answer to their problems? A shout dragged him away from his worries. Tristan sat next to Brianna messing around with the song sheet.

"No, Tyler again. What's up, Brianna?" Tristan taunted as she snatched the sheets of paper from his hand and sat back.

"What, no Laurie?" She gave him her sweetest smile, wiping the smirk off his face.

"So, about this concert, the interviews next week with the *Today* show and the radio station will really help get more tickets sold. We've certainly got the media's attention." Ryder smirked at Tristan, shifting in his seat to collect Mia's hand.

"Yeah, Dad said he'd help with everything. You know—tickets, venue. He knows all the people we would need, and he says he's calling in a few favors. Making it a fundraising concert will definitely draw the crowds, and it'll be good for the station. The coverage about Ayesha has been relentless, everyone's talking about her." Tristan smiled back at Ryder. Mia caught the look that passed between the two. "Did you have anything to do with this?" she asked.

"We may have helped things along somewhat, but it's for a good cause," Ryder said, observing her expression, which revealed nothing of the turmoil he was certain she was feeling. An hour later, Mia and Ryder were alone back at his house. Tristan wanted to discuss all the details of the concert with his dad, and Ryder wanted some alone time with Mia. They sat in his back room that overlooked the garden. A simple thought, and a burst of roaring flames brought the open fire to life. Mia settled next to him on the leather couch, cuddling against his chest.

Her face was flushed a soft pink, and her lips beckoned to him. Without another thought, he cupped her face with his hands and kissed her. As his lips touched her skin, he could not hold back any more and groaned. His hand reached under her soft woolen top, and Mia gasped. Her skin was so soft and warm. A scorching heat filled him, and when her hands touched his chest, he pushed her against the pillows. His lips moved from hers, and he dropped tiny wet kisses along her jaw and then along her neck. Mia shivered and made a noise that made him smile with triumph. He wanted her, all of her, and whispered in her ear, "You're so beautiful, you're driving me wild."

Mia fumbled with the buttons on his shirt, and Ryder moaned. Any minute now he was going to lose control, and there would be no holding back. A powerful need rose up inside him, a need to claim her and make her his. He lifted his head to stare into her lilac eyes, and knew she felt the same. He planted a soft kiss on her lips and sat back.

"Mia, I know what's in your heart, but if we take this step now what we're trying to do may get sidetracked. If we keep going, I won't be able to stop."

She stared at him with wide and misty eyes. He waited, unable to breathe, knowing if she as much as moved, he would not be responsible for his actions. Mia ran her finger down his tight abdominal muscles and sucked in a sharp breath. She wanted this, and now. He pressed closer and was inches from her lips—when his cell-phone rang, and then so did Mia's. They looked at each other and for a second ignored the ringing, but as the noise continued. Ryder finally answered the call.

"It's Tristan. His dad wants to come over and talk about the concert. He has a few suggestions, and he wants us to meet someone." Ryder said, tucking his shirt back into his jeans. Mia's face was bright red, and she simply nodded at his words.

"Mia, there'll be a time for us," he said, reaching for her hand.

* * * *

Mia tried to hide her disappointment. She wanted Ryder as she had never wanted anything before in her life. The phone call pulled her back into the harsh reality of her situation with Greyson. She could not give herself to Ryder and then leave. It would kill him and destroy her. It would be better to keep a distance between them. Being this close would only make matters worse. Biting her nails, she watched him. An idea of making Ryder hate her formed in her mind Hell, he would hate her once she was gone anyway. That dissolved all the feeling of seducing Ryder like the flames in the fire that dwindled and died.

"I'll just go and freshen up, then." She turned to walk out the room.

"Mia..."

She turned and gazed at his crumpled face, forcing a smile. "I'm fine. You're right. We have time."

As soon as the words left her mouth, she headed for the restroom to throw up. Tears and pent-up emotions gave way, and so did her stomach. She vomited into the toilet and sank to the floor. Mia wiped her mouth and stared, unable to move. It took a while to regain control, but as she leaned against the wall calling to the earth spirits, calm descended upon her. Minutes later, Mia stood by the now roaring fire chatting to Ryder about the concert. The front doorbell rang, and Ryder left to answer it. She stood, her back to the fire feeling the warmth on her skin as strong male voices and laughter echoed from the hallway. Ryder walked back in smiling. Behind him was Tristan, Mr. Fitzgerald—and *Greyson.*

Mia's jaw dropped. It was impossible. The room swirled, and Mia wobbled. She felt the blood drain into her feet, and she was sinking. Strong arms rushed out and grabbed her. Her head dropped forward, and as she lifted it, she stared into Greyson's icy-blue eyes. His hair was cut short and was sleeked back. As Mia gazed at him, his straight slim nostrils flared, and his mouth pressed together in a firm line.

Now, don't make any more of a scene than you already have. You asked for my help and that's why I'm here.

After letting him help her to stand, she moved away as soon as possible and just glared. Her heart was pounding, and she tried to settle its rhythm, aware that Ryder was watching her closely. Greyson was dressed in an expensive and tailored black suit with a crisp white shirt open at the neck underneath. He stood as tall as Mr. Fitzgerald, and with his broad shoulders and impeccable outfit, he oozed self-assurance and confidence. Every inch of him screamed money and power. He looked even more dangerous dressed in human clothes, and she moved to the back of room, as far away as possible, even though she could feel his gaze burn her skin. At that moment she could scream, but instead she smiled. Ryder whispered, "Are you okay?" She nodded, not taking her glance away from Greyson.

"I have that effect on women, but not usually quite so spontaneously."

Mr. Fitzgerald and Tristan laughed.

Ryder placed an arm around her shoulders. "Usually only I have that effect on you. Do you need to eat?" Ryder whispered while rubbing his hand up and down her arm. Despite the warmth it created on her skin, Mia shivered.

"Yes." She looked up at Ryder and then back at the group. Mr. Fitzgerald was talking to Greyson.

"Mia, are you okay? Because I would like to introduce the man who came to your rescue. Michael Christian. He's my secret weapon, a friend I've made over the last couple of years and well known in the music industry. He manages several bands, and has had phenomenal success. I played some of Fusion's music, and here we are. He wants to get to know the band and help with the fundraising concert for Ayesha. What do you think?" Jonathan Fitzgerald tapped Greyson on the back. Tristan and Ryder were smiling but speechless. Greyson shifted his stance and moved closer smiling.

"I know exactly what you're thinking…" His eyelashes flashed at her.

Mia snorted and looked away.

"I know you look at me and think *he'*s too young, how can he help us? But I'm confident that as with The Crows and The Ladykillers, I can. I have the money, the knowledge of the music industry, and I have an ear for raw, fresh talent. That's exactly what you are, and I can give you what you want—fame, fortune. Everyone will know your music."

Ryder turned his head swiftly to look at Mia. He was beaming. Greyson's statement had the boys drooling and giving each other high fives. The boys talked to Mr. Fitzgerald about the concert, and Greyson slunk his way over to Mia.

"Well, Mia? I told you, I could help you in more ways than you could imagine. Your agreeing to my proposition allows me to be generous. What I said is true—I have many connections, many doors that are open to me. Money and power has that effect. I like your music. Your voice is both ethereal and bluesy. It has a gentle strength, and it's as pretty as you," he whispered against her ear. Mia wanted to slap him across his all too happy face, so she did the next best thing. Greyson inhaled sharply and raised his hand to his cheek, which sported a very large red imprint. As his hand touched his skin, the mark faded and he simply glared at her.

That's for ruining my birthday. I may not be able to win, but I'll never make it easy for you. I'll fight you to the bitter end.

Greyson walked away and stood next to Ryder. Mia tensed and bit her lip. Greyson smiled at the conversation and then let his eyes rest on her as he laid his hand on Ryder's shoulder.

I could kill him right here with my bare hands, or I could make Tristan kill him. Mia, I really don't think you know who you're up against. That's twice you've struck out at me. I won't tolerate a third.

"If you agree then, we need to get to work. I want to hear you sing. The song that's all over YouTube, who wrote it? The mix is good, but I think it needs a few tweaks and it could be your first number one. I want you all in the studio, middle of the week. Tape a few songs and we'll see what you've got. There are many bands out there that would kill to get a chance of airtime, let alone to be given the opportunities you're about to be given. But I need an answer today." Before Mia could open her mouth—and she tried—Greyson glared at her, and both the boys said in unison, "Yes."

"We'll do it," Tristan said. "Whatever it takes, we'll do it. The song on YouTube, Mia and Robert wrote together, but I write most of the songs with Mia. In total, I think we have around eight solid songs." The boys were smiling and Mr. Fitzgerald was positively beaming. Greyson stood back and seemed to dominate the room. His lips curled upwards and his cold eyes sparkled like diamonds.

"Well, Mia, what do you think?" he said.

"I'm not as easy to convince as the boys, but I want what's best for Ayesha. At the moment it seems you're the answer. All the proceeds are to pay for her surgery and whatever she needs to help her recover. I want her to have a future. As long as that's agreed, then we can be in the studio for Wednesday." Mia did not take her eyes off Greyson. She shrugged her shoulders and waited. Ice filled her veins, and she didn't care how she sounded or what the others thought. He must agree. He was playing a sadistic game, and now he was *here*. If the boys knew, it would be all-out war. Greyson was more dangerous than anyone she had ever met, and he was not working alone.

"Deal." His voice was triumphant, and his lips curled into a menacing smile.

Chapter Twenty-Two

Greyson was manipulating them like puppets. His cocky smile and oozing confidence laced every word that tripped off his tongue. He was a snake. Mia wanted to wipe his smugness off his face by lashing out at him, but her hands were tied. He had no conscience, no remorse over anything that he did. Greyson threatened Ryder, right in front of her. No, she was not in a position to act impulsively. Her insides were empty and hollow. She did not want to face Ryder or Tristan, but there was no choice. Today there was no school because of another teacher-training day, and they were meeting at Tristan's house to rehearse.

Even the dream of Ayesha from the night before did nothing to make her feel better. The dream showed the girl as a grown woman. Vivid images showed her at university, achieving award after award for her research into infertility, as a doctor of fetal medicine researching genome mapping, traveling around the world and helping women conceive. Knowing that made what was happening bearable. As for the poison that Greyson was using, she had a plan, but needed to discuss it with the group and this would take some careful lying. Cerianne was up early, and for once Mia did not want to rush out the door.

"You have a busy week with everything going on. How come you're still here?" Cerianne asked. Mia stroked Samson's belly as he lay on the ground begging for attention. His tiny legs wiggled in response and his pink tongue flopped down the side of his mouth.

"I'm going."

Cerianne sat down and lifted Mia's hand, "Is everything all right? I mean, you seem far away. Are you worried about you and Robert?"

Mia flicked her gaze back at her mother and noticed her hooded stare. She smiled and then exhaled.

"Mom, I'm fine. You're coming to the concert, aren't you? It's been booked for Christmas Eve. It's going to be at the Blues Club in Boston. I should go." She pushed away from the table and grabbed her bag. Before she left, she bent to give her mother a kiss and hug.

"Mia, you've changed so much in the past couple of months. I feel so privileged to watch you grow into this beautiful woman, because that is what you are. Of course, I'll be there. I wouldn't miss it for the world." Cerianne smiled and Mia walked away.

"Love you," she called, before walking out the front door. Mia stepped into her car and turned the key. Staring up at her house she thought of her mother, Ryder, her friends and family. She'd never had a choice. How could this be happening? None of her visions gave the slightest hint of Greyson. She banged her hand against the steering wheel and reversed. Her wheels squealing, she drove off.

Mia walked into Tristan's house, and the air was laced with waves of heightened emotions—panic, excitement, exhilaration. Brianna was laughing hysterically with Tyler. Evan was banging his drums, and Tristan was playing on his guitar. Her gaze wandered over the group, and she searched for Ryder, catching sight of him as he walked over to meet her. He reached for her hand and tried to pull her into his arms.

"Not now, please." She wriggled her hand out of his and stood back unable to return his gaze.

"Mia, I need you to sit, please." She looked at Brianna, who smiled, and Tristan nodded with his guitar in hand, as Ryder motioned for her to take a seat on the stool. The air stilled and everyone waited silently. He looked across at Tristan and nodded, picking up the spare guitar. Ryder began to serenade her. Mia gasped and her heart squeezed inside. He took her breath away. His deep voice sang a sweet melody. The song was called, *A Time for Us.*

Ryder's rich dark eyes pierced her soul, and she blinked. The song, which he must have written, was about her.

With eyes that sparkle like amethysts
And a smile that lights up like the sun,
She leaves me breathless
Desperately wanting
Like flowers crave the rain
But there will be a time for us.
Oh, yeah a time for us.

Mia held her breath as he performed, and was unable to take her eyes off him. He was full of passion, raising his voice up and dropping it low, as if he wanted no one else to hear his final words of love. When he finished, the band yelled and clapped. Mia, could not hold back the flow of tears.

"I had to write it," he whispered to her. "After yesterday, I just wanted you to know that I feel frustrated, but I want to wait—not because I don't love you, but because I love you so much. I worked on it all last night, and maybe the melody isn't quite right—"

Ryder's words floated around inside her head, but all she could visualize was Greyson. His threat reverberated around inside her mind. Despite Ryder being so close, Mia jumped up, pushed past him and ran outside. She took several deep breaths and forced the tears back. The biting wind blew through her thin jumper, and a million goose bumps erupted on her skin. Instinctively, her hands clasped around her. She was shivering and desperate to pull herself together.

"Mia what the hell is going on? I thought maybe the song would make you cry, but to have you running off.... Have I upset you?" He stood with his hands on her shoulders, turning her to look into his eyes. Her heart gushed with love for him. She wished more than ever that they had made love the other day, because now she feared they never would.

"Ryder, don't be silly. How could you upset me? It's a lovely song." She smiled and blinked, forcing herself to remain calm.

Ryder sighed and removed his hands to his sides. "Then what's wrong?" His gaze fixed upon her face. She moved to walk back inside, knowing they needed to rehearse and to leave would be foolish, but he grabbed her arm.

"Let me go. I'm fine. Now, we have to practice, or it's going to be a colossal disaster."

She tugged her arm out of his grip and, holding her back stiff, marched away—not wanting to be near him. How on Earth was she going to pull off any of this when her body ached for his touch? She knew if she let him, she would end up telling him everything. Holding her head high and sniffing, she strolled back into the basement. Ryder wandered in behind her, and before reaching the bottom step, he pulled her arm and pushed her against the wall.

"I'm done playing dumb, you're lying and you need to tell me why? Something's wrong, and you're going to tell me, right now. I may not be able to get inside your head, but I know you love me and something's changed."

She pulled herself away from his grasp and stepped up in front of him.

"Don't do this, not now." Her voice was soft as velvet, but the tone was ice cold.

"Don't do what, Mia? What the hell is going on with you? One minute you're all over me, and then today you're the ice maiden from hell."

She laughed and swiveled away. "Well, that's me, and you should know that, as you're always telling me how well you know me—when the truth is, you don't know me at all. You see what you want to see, but that isn't the real me. Not anymore."

Ryder ran his hands through his hair and stared at her as if for the first time. Mia knew he was confused and angry he had every reason but she had to stay distant or she would never be able to hide what was going on with Greyson. Unfortunately, their shouts had drawn the attention of the others, who stood in the living space looking awkward, along with a frowning Mr. Fitzgerald.

"Whatever is going on with you two, it stops now. There's too much at stake to be messing around. You have to focus on the band, or else we'll call it quits right now. I know it's stressful, but this is when you need to pull together, not rip each other apart. Is that clear?" Mr. Fitzgerald stood dressed in his shirt and pressed pants. He sighed and loosened his tie, "*Is* that clear?"

Mia moved away from Ryder and nodded. "Yes, and I'm sorry. I just haven't been sleeping well lately." Her gaze flickered toward Ryder and away. Ryder frowned, and stared over at Tristan.

What the hell is going on, man? I've never seen my dad so freaked out, and I've never seen Mia so angry.

Ryder shook his head and rubbed his temples. How could she have changed so much since yesterday? Or was Mia right, and he didn't know her at all? Yesterday she was as hot as the desert, and today she was frigging Iceland. He scratched his head.

Something's going on with her, and I need to get to the bottom of it.

After that the band settled into rehearsals, going through all their songs, singing each one before Mr. Fitzgerald so that he could organize them from most popular to least. He made suggestions for tweaking the sound or upping the beat in one or two of the songs, and it was eleven-thirty before they called it a night.

"Okay, so let's just recap. The songs you have are great, but there are one or two I think still need work. I think *Dream Lover* and *The Promise* are the strongest. Add those to the others, and it should be enough. I think that Michael has a few ideas as well, but that's good. Now tomorrow, you're at the station with me—that'll be fine, no problem. Wednesday, you're at the recording studio and then it's Channel Seven's interview with the *Today Show*. Remember, pull together."

One by one, everyone left with barely a word. Ryder nodded his good-byes and nudged alongside Mia as they strolled out of the house and toward her car. "Mia, don't just go." She turned around. Her hair flew over her shoulders, but she wasn't smiling.

"Ryder, I'm really tired. I tried to tell you that earlier. I need to go." Her hair swished behind her and after unlocking the door, she got inside. Being heartless when Ryder looked so lost, concerned, and full of love brought stinging tears into her eyes.

She had to give him something. Mia stared into his eyes and then down at her lap. "I know how Greyson is hurting humans, and I have a plan to undo the magic by using our music. I want to weave a spell into the music, so that when it's played it will stop them reacting to the Loxus, forever. They'll be immune, but we have to ensure that Greyson doesn't find out."

He leaned his hand against her car and shook his head before sighing.

"Hm, we can do that—a small incantation, a subliminal spell, so humans won't even realize that anything has changed. That would work, but I know you're not telling me everything and why are you being such a bitch?"

Mia explained in an even voice about the night Greyson had let slip perhaps more than he had intended about the Darkshadows and the humans. Ryder nodded and gave a quick smile as if pleased that she was finally sharing something of her plans. Later, as she drove home, she knew that keeping what Greyson had said a secret was protecting Ryder, and she would do anything to keep him safe, even if he ended up hating her.

* * * *

Fusion had two honorary days off from school, so that they could perform live on the radio station in Boston and attend the sit-down interview with Mindy Peterson from the *Today Show*. The charity concert for Ayesha was in three weeks, and every time Mia realized that, her throat constricted. The day after the concert was Christmas Day. The day, she had promised Greyson that she would leave. Mia stared at the walls in her bedroom and the pictures of her friends and family. How could she leave? Her mother would fall apart again, and this time it would be because of her—but at least she would be alive, along with everyone she cared about.

The media was covering the story of Ayesha like a rash. There were daily updates as to her progress. The latest headlines stated that an anonymous donation had been received to help with her surgery, and that plans were afoot to transfer her to the Children's hospital in Boston. The newspapers covered the story from every angle. The story was getting caught up in a mounting frenzy of media attention, and some nasty headlines were appearing concerning Fusion. Mia shook her head as her fingers ran over the newspaper print.

"Oh Mia, love, I wouldn't read that. They're simply printing what sells. We all know you're not trying to become famous on the tail end of Ayesha's media hype." Cerianne lifted the newspaper off the kitchen table and put it away on the dresser.

"Mom, people think the only reason we're doing this concert is to get attention and become famous. It's all become so twisted." Mia pushed back her chair, and it scraped against the floor. She picked up her bag and stormed out of the kitchen. She was certain this was all Greyson's doing, and she let the door slam as she walked out of the house. Mia drove silently over to Tristan's house to join her friends hoping that today would be easier with Ryder. She parked outside and nodded at Tristan who was loading equipment and their instruments into Evan's camper-van along with Tyler and Evan. Looking around, Ryder was nowhere to be seen.

Ryder's talking with Brianna inside, he'll be out now, but take it easy on him Mia. Whatever is going on with you, he's hurting.

Mia swiveled around and caught Tristan's glare, he was in a mood with her as well as Ryder. She nodded, but couldn't say anything she was too choked with emotion. Ryder and Brianna walked out from the house chatting deep in conversation, which stopped as soon as they saw her. She gave a forced smile and swallowed her sorrow as she walked over to Ryder.

"Hi," she said weakly knowing it was a really lame thing to say, but she needed to pull herself together, or she would be a mess. Mia looked up at Brianna and saw a tentative smile, which let her know she was there for her as well. Ryder didn't try to kiss her. He stood stiffly with his hands in his pocket as if not wanting to touch her. *We need to talk about Greyson, Mia. I need some answers.*

"Come on, get in or we're going to be late," Tristan said before Mia could respond. She gazed at Ryder's pale and taut face and nodded.

The drive to the radio station was a loud and boisterous one as excitement spiraled into almost hysteria as they laughed and joked about being interviewed. Boston 104.5 FM, was housed in an classically designed brick building right down in the bay area of the city, overlooking the Charles river. Tristan's dad had explained they could park in the radio station's car park. With the van safely tucked away in the underground car park, they collected their instruments, and made their way to the elevator. Few words were spoken, and the bell tinkled announcing they had reached the correct level.

Mia stepped out through the doors and the others piled out behind her. Tristan pushed in front and walked over to the glamorous female receptionist that stood alone at the black granite and cherry wood front desk. Mia hesitated for a second, waiting for Brianna and Ryder to catch up to her before making her way across the pale granite floors. The dark haired receptionist smiled at them and lifted the phone announcing their arrival. Several minutes later, Mr. Fitzgerald appeared and introduced them to the station manager, Alan Parson, and to Sandra Wilkins, who would look after them for the rest of the morning.

A couple of other bands were also here today as part of the segment on local talent. After the introductions, Sandra showed them to the waiting room because Mr. Fitzgerald's show was about to begin. The room was long and wide. Along the side wall was a buffet table full of drinks, fruit, muffins, and bagels. The wall that faced them was made of glass, and it gave a spectacular view of the boats on the river. They walked in, and the boys started helping themselves to the food. Two other bands were already munching and chatting away. They nodded as they entered the room.

"You must be Fusion! We're Atomic Rocket, and the girls are The Kittens," a gentle quiet voice said. Mia looked, and smiled. Everybody shook hands and started talking about their music and where they were from.

The boys in Atomic Rocket had matching blonde Mohawks. The sides of their heads were shaved and the hair in the center was sculptured to stand up straight as if electrocuted. They were dressed in ripped jeans, tight T-shirts, and their arms were painted with colorful imitation tattoos. Compared to their looks, their polished and private-school voices were startling.

The Kittens were an all-girl band—blonde girls, tall, skinny, and very pretty. Each girl wore a face full of make-up, and their hair was coifed and styled to perfection. Their skimpy bustiers and short black skirts left little to the imagination. Mia stared at them and then looked at her own ordinary clothes. Today, she was wearing a comfy white T-shirt, tucked into a pair of faded boyfriend jeans, and her converse sneakers. Ryder, Tristan, Tyler, and Evan could not stop smiling and admiring the Kittens' long legs and lacy stocking. The Kittens eyed both Mia and Brianna, instantly dismissing them to chat with the boys.

"I wouldn't be able to walk in those heels," Mia smiled and looked across as the prettiest girl moved closer to Ryder. She whispered in his ear, and he stepped back looking around the room. His gaze settled on Mia, and the girl glared across at her, obviously annoyed and not wanting her company. Mia had no right to feel jealous after the way she'd been treating Ryder, but she couldn't help herself and grabbed Brianna's hand striding over toward them.

"Are you the lead singer then?" the girl asked, staring at Ryder as she chewed her gum.

"Mia and I are the main singers," he said nodding at Mia as she approached, and he reached down to clasp her hand in his.

She stared at him, needing the closeness of him. His warm touch spread across her palm and rippled up her arm. Instinctively, she moved closer to Ryder and glared back at the girl.

"Would you sing with me?" the girl challenged, twirling her finger in her curly mass of hair.

"Sure." Ryder said, smiling and glancing at Mia as if to check it was all right. Mia slipped her hand away and braved a smile.

"Do you know *Need You Now* by Lady Antebellum?" she asked

He nodded, staring at Mia as Tristan walked over to stand next to her and Brianna.

"The girl's called Simone." He stood holding his arms across his chest, looking entranced. Brianna and Mia stared at him, laughing

Close your mouth, Tristan. You're drooling like an idiot.

Jealous are we, Brianna? I'm simply admiring her outfit.

Her barely-there outfit?

Brianna was speaking to Tristan, but Mia could hear their heated internal exchange. She smiled and her gaze wandered over toward Ryder and Simone. Simone was older, maybe in her twenties, and her blond curls fell below her shoulders. Her big blue eyes twinkled like sapphires. Yes, she was very pretty, very seductive, and it was killing her to watch them together—because not only was she gorgeous, but she could play the guitar and sing. Her voice had a scratchy and husky quality to it, and Ryder's added a power and depth that she could not. The duet was good. They looked as sexy as hell together, and it stung. The song ended, and everyone clapped and cheered. Even Mia clapped. Susan Wilkins appeared at the door with a bright smile.

"Kittens, you're up next. Come on. "

Simone rushed forward, grabbing Ryder's shirt so that she could plaster a stinging kiss on his lips before he could object. Before she darted away, she whispered something in his ear and then headed for the door. Mia's insides seethed and her hands itched. She wanted to rip the girl out of his arms, but looked away instead. Looking back seconds later, Simone turned at the door and gave a spectacular smile to Mia as she left. Ryder cringed and wiped his mouth free of the pink glossy lipstick as he walked over to Mia. He opened his mouth ready to speak but Mia nodded.

"There's nothing to say," Mia said, attempting to be indifferent. She couldn't help the mixed messages she was sending and knew at some point it was all going to end badly.

He touched her arm, "Mia, don't be like that."

She turned around, "Like what? It was a kiss, Ryder. That's all."

Everyone in the room started weighing in with their opinions of Simone.

"She's a tart. She's like that with everyone. Don't let her get to you," said Stevie, the lead singer from Atomic Rocket. "She does it to cause trouble. This is a very competitive business. Every gig is a gig, right? And you never know who's going to be here, or hear you. She's been around the circuit for a while, and it's hard to get a break," he said.

After that, time evaporated. Atomic Rocket was called and then it was Fusion's turn. Susan arrived with her chestnut-brown hair bobbing along at her shoulders and waved them over toward the studio.

"It's been good so far, there's been lots of response. Good luck." She opened the door, and they all entered.

Mia froze.

Greyson sat in the black leather swivel chair next to Mr. Fitzgerald, with his arms bent on the table and leaning against his chin. He looked at them all, until his gaze finally rested on Mia. Taking off his headphones, Mr. Fitzgerald explained that for the interview, they would only need Ryder, Tristan, and Mia. The others could set up their instruments in the adjoining room. Then he passed the headsets around.

"Okay, we have a two-minute break. First off, you need to place those on so I know you can hear me, and we'll clip on some microphones..." They all nodded and he continued," I'm going to start by introducing you, and then there'll be some questions. Just relax and follow my lead. Michael is here to watch, and he wants to have a word afterwards. Ready? Now, just relax." He sat back down and swiveled in his chair, looking at them as they sat across from him. He signaled the engineer and started speaking.

"Okay, so next up is a new band called Fusion. Yep, you've heard their song *The Promise* because it's being played everywhere since they downloaded their video onto YouTube. They've become a sensation overnight, with the media recording their every move. They're here today to talk about a fundraising concert on Christmas Eve. It's to be held here in Boston, at the Blues club. The money from the concert is going directly to the Ayesha appeal. Now Robert, Alex, and Mia are here to take your calls and tell you their story. They're also going to sing live. Our number is 879 347 9987."

He paused, and listened to his earphones.

"Okay, ready, the calls are coming in. Let's see what we have," Mr. Fitzgerald, winked.

Mia sat in between Ryder and Tristan. Despite trying to remain distant with Ryder, she reached for his hand. At her touch, he lifted his gaze to meet hers. He smiled and gave her hand a squeeze. No matter where she let her eyes rest, Greyson was staring. Mia swallowed, uncertain if she would be able to speak at all.

"Okay," said a caller's voice. "Hi, Jonathan. By the way, I love your show. My name is Leanne and I'm from Charlestown, and I wanted to know what inspired the band to write their song *The Promise*."

"Okay, Cathy, who would you like to answer that question?" Mr. Fitzgerald asked.

"Mia," she said.

Mia took a deep breath and swallowed. She stared at the microphone and began.

"Hi, Leanne. The song *The Promise* originally started out as a letter that I had written a while ago. Really, it's about falling in love and the promises you make, and how sometimes you're faced with challenges. Sometimes, the love is strong enough to survive and sometimes… it…isn't." Mia coughed and picked up the glass from the table pretending her mouth was dry, but really, she was close to tears.

Mia, are you all right?

Ryder's arm wrapped around her shoulder and his eyes were hooded with concern. She nodded.

"Okay we have another caller. This time it's Andrew from Beverly"

"Hi. I wanted to know how the band came together, and how long have you been playing, and I don't mind who answers."

"Okay. Well, I'm Alex, and the band was my idea. I play bass guitar. I started to play when I was about seven years old, and originally the band was me, Tyler and Evan. Over the last year Danni and Mia joined, and then Robert. We all love music, and wanted to create a unique sound. The songs are a mix of efforts, really, and the band as a whole has a say in every step of the process. We're called Fusion because, even though we're all different, it's only when we are all together that we can make great music and there's a band."

"Okay, we have time for one more, and it is going to be Scott from Boston"

"Yes, I wanted to know why you would use this girl from Indonesia to gain headlines for the band. Isn't the music good enough on its own?" The radio station quickly killed the call, but it was too late. The question caused uproar. Tristan and Ryder both tried to give an answer, but Mia pushed them back.

"I want to answer the call if you don't mind, guys. Ayesha is a little girl whose story has affected us strongly. We felt we had to help her and her family. It has nothing to do with the band gaining attention. Our band will either sink or swim on its own merit. However, if the media hype around us helps this little girl get the care she needs, then that's great. Ayesha nearly died. She's already lost both her parents and her brother. The town she lived in has been destroyed, and her only living relative is a distant Aunt. Her story simply reached our hearts, and we knew we needed to help. All the money raised will go toward her medical costs, for the skin grafts and whatever further treatment she'll need." Mia sank back glad that she was able to explain their side of the story.

"Okay, well that does it for the questions. I understand you're going to sing two songs, one obviously *The Promise,* and your new one *Dream Lover*? Is that right?"

"Yes," they all said together.

They left their seats and joined the rest of Fusion. Mia and Ryder sang the two songs and the segment ended. Jonathan closed the show and, after taking his headphones off, came over to join the band.

"Well how did that feel?" he said, looking at them all.

"Great," said Tristan.

"Well, that guy Scott was a jerk, but I think Mia gave a good answer," Evan said.

"Yeah, man it was cool," Tyler said.

"There's always one, but I think you handled it well, Mia. People will decide for themselves," Mr. Fitzgerald said.

Greyson had been silent throughout the interview. Now, he walked into the recording room, shook Evan's hand and nodded at the rest of the band. "Great session, guys. I've arranged for a photo shoot, and you're also booked into my studio this afternoon to record some of your songs. It'll be a long couple of days, but we need to get it done. I'll be with you for the interview for the *Today* show, because I want to make sure you're ready for some of their questions," Greyson said, standing there in a navy pinstriped suit that hugged him and a gleaming white shirt. His dirty-blonde curls were sleeked back at the sides. "Just to let you know, The Kittens are going to support you, and I have Reckless as the headliner for the concert. We need an established band to draw the crowds and sell tickets," he added.

"Wow, man! Reckless is amazing," said Evan, as he banged his drums. Greyson smirked and Mr. Fitzgerald slapped him on the back and shook his hand.

"Great! Well, I'm going to finish up, and I'll meet you at the studio," Jonathan said. With that, he left them. Greyson leaned against the table in the room as the rest of the band gathered their equipment.

"Well, I'll see you all there," he purred. "You sounded good live. I was impressed. Does anyone need a lift?"

"No, we all came together, so we can meet you there," Mia said. The boys were already carrying out their equipment to put in the back of the van.

You can cling onto your friends as much as you like but they cannot help you,

Mia swirled around and glared at him. He took pleasure in needling her all the time.

At least I have some.

Chapter Twenty-Three

Mia was on auto-pilot, putting up a front, trying to convince her friends and Ryder that she was fine. Staring at the reflection of her tangled mess of hair and dark–shadowed eyes, she knew it was only a matter of time before she caved. She was jumpy, irritable, and tears pressed behind her eyelids. Yesterday, having Greyson around her all day was torture, but in the recording studio they finished the songs, enough for him to create a CD. Lifting her brush, Mia tried to smooth through the knots that her constant tossing in bed had caused. With each stroke of her brush, she sighed and stared at her reflection. The mirror lost its hard sheen, and the surface rippled like water. Mia blinked and gasped. Her brush clattered to the floor.

Mia stood in a cream silky blouse, soft leather pants and boots. She was in a golden field of wheat, and the sheaves moved with the wind. Screeches and cries filled the air as serpents played and soared across the sky. Brightly colored butterflies danced in front of her face, and she smiled, lifting her hand to touch them. They stopped and turned. She gasped, as tiny perfect faces stared back at her.

"Mia, you're home. You must come with us."

A gust of wind hurried them away, and deer leapt out from the forest. Startled and nervous, they ran following the fairies. Rabbits, fox, badgers, mice, and all manner of animals darted in the same direction. Mia stared in fascination as the sky darkened and the wind sent her hair flying around her shoulders.

Mia.

Ryder's voice called to her, and she ran. As the sheaves of wheat moved back and forth she caught glimpses of dark wispy hair. She ran, calling his name. Eagles swooped up in the sky, their long wings flapping overhead. She had never seen so many. Her heart pounded. Something was coming. As she was running fast and heading for Ryder, a blast of heat reached across her back.

An ear-piercing screech ripped through the air, and she covered her ears. Loud snorts blew against her, and she kept running, knowing what was behind her.

"Where are you running to, my love? There's no escape."

Panting and heart pounding, she carried on. Ryder stood several feet away, his hand outstretched, in seconds she would be with him. She licked lips, ignoring the puffing and panting behind her. There was a whoosh and urgent flapping above her. Mia raised her hand to her forehead and stared into the sky. Above her, she could see the underbelly of the dragon, and flames hurtled out from his nostrils, his claws digging into the air pushing him farther and farther. Upon his back was Greyson. His ice-cold eyes glared toward her. In one swift motion, he jerked the reins and the dragon turned, landing in front of her. The flames stopped and small puffs of white smoke snorted as the dragon breathed. The animal lifted its head and yawned, revealing large sharp teeth that drooled. Greyson jumped to the ground.

"Come, it's time."

The ground shook beneath her, and she turned around. Hundreds of ferocious beasts were charging forward, huge saber-toothed tigers, salivating wolves, behemoths the size of trees and goblins with evil smiles. They were armed with axes, swords, and a taste for blood. In the center, a woman with flowing raven hair was sitting upon a powerful black horse. She was surrounded by an army of warriors, all dressed in brown leather, with swords ready in their hands. Their pale faces and glowing eyes fixed on her.

"Mia, the war will never happen if you come now. Let Rhiannon have her will."

Whirling around, Mia stared at Greyson, as he beckoned for her to join him. Her heart battled inside, and she trembled. The decision was hers to make. Ryder's voice rose across the distance.

"Don't do this! We'll fight."

Blinking back tears and refusing to look at Ryder, she walked toward Greyson and gave him her hand. He kissed it. The dragon kneeled, and he and lifted her onto its back and then sat behind her, his arm holding her waist. A swift kick and the dragon rose, squealing, and lifted into the air. Once in the clouds, dragons of all colors and sizes joined them and squealed in delight.

"My queen."

Mia awoke sprawled out on the floor, her brush next to her. She wiped her blurry eyes and sat up. *Rhiannon!* Emrys was right—Rhiannon was behind all of this. Mia had only heard tales of the beautiful witch, and how as her power grew she turned to the dark side. Greyson and Rhiannon must be working together. Rhiannon wanted war. She wanted Annwn. She wanted revenge, surely.

Mia finished getting ready just as a sleek black limousine drove up.

It was exactly seven-thirty in the morning.

A chauffeur stood and opened the door. She ran to the car and smiled as she sat down. Inside, the rest of Fusion sat giggling and enjoying the comforts of the limousine. Mia sat next to Brianna. She noticed that Ryder had chosen to sit the farthest away. He did not even acknowledge her, simply staring out the window. What did she expect? She played with her fingers, smiled at Tristan and started to talk to Brianna.

You two have to sort out what's going on Mia, because Ryder's in a bad place right now.

Mia turned her head in surprise and stared at Tristan, looking at his pale face and raised eyebrows. He nodded toward Ryder. Mia stared at Evan and Tyler as they poured themselves some sodas, and then at Ryder. She focused on his slow breathing and listened to his heart beat. It was slow—too slow, and heavy. She gasped and closed her eyes. Thick angry waves emanated off him. Swallowing, she suppressed her rising nausea. Ryder quickly turned his head and glared at her. His dark eyes were hooded and he pulled his mouth into a tight line.

He was ready to burst with anger, and it was aimed at her. This was what she had wanted. She'd wanted him to hate her, to make it easier when she left. But, as his heart fluttered and missed beats, she realized she might as well kill him herself, because she was ripping his heart out. He had not shaved, and looked terrible.

Ryder

Mia bit her lip and laughed at one of Evan's jokes. Ryder turned away and Tristan shook his head. The rest of the trip they didn't speak or look at one another. When they arrived at Channel Seven news station, they were greeted by the producer Paula Smith who explained what would happen. After a quick walk through the building, Paula directed the girls into a room for make-up and took the boys next door. After what seemed like hours of hair styling, eyebrow plucking, make-up application and styling, the girls huffed and puffed at themselves in the mirrors.

"What do you think?" Mia asked, looking at Brianna.

"Shit, we're The Kittens," she said.

They laughed. The boys walked in, dressed in faded jeans and shirts with T-shirts underneath, and started to whistle. Mia and Brianna both wore shimmery vests, short skirts, lacy stockings, and thigh-length boots. Martin Lloyd and Shirley Cummins, two presenters from the morning news segment at Channel Seven, came and discussed how the interview which would be broadcast live would run. Each person was fitted with an earpiece, and they all sat in a row on the large sofa. The cameras were set up and there was a huge screen in front of them, so they could see Mindy Peterson in the *Today Show* studio in New York. They were going to show the YouTube video first, and then the interview would start. Their instruments were set up in the corner ready for them later. Mindy Peterson sat in her New York studio and smiled.

"Well that was the YouTube video that rocketed into space within twenty four hours, and now stands at a staggering one hundred and seventy million views. All the money earned is going to the Ayesha fund, along with the money raised at the concert on the 24th of December. Welcome Fusion, and thank you for joining us. The song and the video of *The Promise* are truly captivating. Congratulations on its success so far. Can you tell me, did you have any idea that the video would receive such a phenomenal response?

In unison the band answered and laughed together, "No."

"Absolutely not," Tristan said. "In the beginning it was to see what kind of an effect it would cause. The video was a combination of us recording and rehearsing. There were parts that showed us arguing and fighting and in the background there's this very gentle love song. So what started off as a sort of shouting match ended up in silence as everyone watched Ryder and Mia sing. The rest was just plain crazy."

"Now you have a CD that's going to be released, and the concert. Are you ready for this kind of exposure?" Mindy crossed her legs and smiled.

"We've been working toward this, but our coverage has all gone crazy. Its wild, man, but we're working really hard, so we're ready—and we're lucky we have a lot of support from family and friends," Evan said.

Mia stared at Evan. He was usually the quietest of the group, but he was lapping up the attention and really focused. Ryder still refused to look at her directly and she looked away.

"Now there's a lot of hype circulating that Robert and Mia are a real-life couple. Is that correct?" Mindy asked. There was a pause and several members of Fusion sat back and stared at them.

What are you two going to say?

It was Brianna's voice. Mia stared across at her and leaned forward to catch Ryder's glare. She dipped her head and then answered, "No comment. We're all friends and have known each other a while. Certain songs bring you closer. *The Promise* was a love song, and as you can see, it moved us both. It's a powerful song."

Mindy asked several more questions, and then the interview finished with the band giving a live performance.

Standing next to Ryder this time was different and awkward, especially as he would not even look at her.

Whatever is going on you two have to pull it together. Remember why we're here.

Tristan's gruff voice shook Mia awake. Reaching for her microphone, she walked next to Ryder and held his hand.

Ryder, please look at me.

For a second, she pictured herself and Ryder standing in the glossy blue shimmering waters the morning they left. They were kissing and hugging each other as if their lives depended on it. Pushing her images into Ryder's mind, she willed him to see them.

Ryder.

She squeezed his hand and smiled into his dark soulful eyes. The corner of his mouth lifted, and he stared at her for a long time before he kissed her lips briefly and squeezed her hand back. The band started to play, and the melody lifted them both. The studio vibrated with the strings of the violin, the strumming of the guitars and the crashing of the drums. Ryder and Mia sang together, never letting go of the other's hand. They stared into each other's eyes as if no one else was there or mattered. As the music ended, Mia stroked his face and smiled, full of happiness.

The people in the studio clapped and the camera's rolled away. Greyson walked over to the group scowling. "Declaring your love for each other is sweet, but it will put a lot of our audience and potential customers off. The audience wants to believe you're obtainable."

Mia tried to pull away from Ryder's clasp, but he was not having any of it. His hand held her, while his other arm wrapped around her waist. He kissed her cheek and then inhaled.

"The reason we're here is because of our feelings for one another, and we're not going to hide it. The video has had over a hundred millions hits, so quite a few people, it would seem, like the way we are together. I think you're wrong." Ryder gritted through his teeth.

Mia had never seen him so angry and strained. He stood his ground with his shoulders back and his jaw muscles twitching. He glared at Greyson in a challenge. He might not have recognized Greyson yet, but he really did not like him.

Well, well, well. Your little boyfriend has a bit of a temper it seems. I'd hate to see that get the better of him, especially around the media.

Mia gasped as soon as the words filtered into her brain, because, as if Ryder had heard them, he reacted. His swiftly dropped his hold on her and charged at Greyson. There were shrieks and gasps. Brianna and Tristan both screamed as Tyler and Evan grabbed Ryders' arm. Before Mia could react, the world paused and everybody froze, except for Greyson.

"You seem a bit confused as to who is in control, Mia," Greyson said aloud. "You're setting your little lap dog up against me, and I'll crush him like an ant. Is that what you want?" Greyson walked around the still statues of her friends and the staff from the studio. Again, he was immaculately dressed and his razor sharp eyes swept over her as she backed away. There was no escape. He would crush everyone with a mere flick of his finger.

Was he really that powerful?

Mia strode toward him, until she was in front of him looking right up into the dazzling shards of glittering ice for eyes. Right next to his lips was a small nondescript mole that disappeared as he smiled.

"Is Rhiannon behind this?" she said.

He tapped his finger on the end of her nose. A curious frown appeared on his face and he headed toward the exit. Everyone started to wake up and move, completely having forgotten what happened. Ryder smiled at her as he walked toward her.

You cannot win this, Mia. Love isn't the answer, trickled back to her.

* * * *

The last two days drained Mia. Greyson was prowling around like a hunter, and Mia was the prey. However, at the mention of Rhiannon, something had shifted. She sensed it. For whatever reasons, Greyson was uncomfortable at the mere sound of her name. Either he didn't know what to say, or he was scared that he might say something he should not. This very notion delighted Mia. Since Greyson started playing this game of cat and mouse, he was always in control—until now.

Today was Thursday, the ninth of December. Two weeks from tomorrow would be Christmas Eve, and the concert. Then it was D-Day. The news on the television was good about Ayesha, between the mysterious benefactor and the money Fusion raised from their YouTube video. Next week, she was going to arrive in Boston for the start of her treatment. Ayesha was heavily sedated because of the pain from the burns, which covered a large portion of her back and legs, but she was doing as well as could be expected.

Mia, I'm outside. I want to talk to you.

It was Brianna. Mia grabbed her bag and left her bedroom. The house was empty because Cerianne was already at work. Mia walked out the front door, and Brianna slung her arm through hers and pulled her away from the house.

"Now, will you tell me what's going on? For days you've been on edge, and I know it has to do with Greyson. Ryder is as moody as hell because you won't talk to him, and yesterday at the studio you used magic. Why? Now, talk." Brianna swiveled around and stood in front of Mia. Her jet-black hair was sleek and straight, devoid of any of color, and her hazel eyes glowed with streaks of gold. She was furious.

"Brianna, stop it," she said and pushed her away. The force of her pushing sent Brianna falling to the ground. Mia rushed to help her up, but Brianna shoved her hand away.

"Don't. This is typical of the human side of you, Mia. You won't let anyone in. When will you realize we're in this together? Whatever is going on, we're a team. Ryder wanted to be here to get you to open up, and Tristan wants to force it out of you, but I said I would talk to you first."

Mia cursed under her breath. How dare they all plot behind her back? And yet that was exactly what she was doing. She stormed past Brianna unsure of what to do. They reached school, but it was the last place she wanted to be. She wanted to be in Annwn.

"Cerianne is worried about you. She said, you're not eating properly or sleeping. Mia, talk to me." Brianna squeezed her eyes together and pushed her mouth into a tight line. She stared at her friend. Mia tried to move, but her feet were stuck.

"Brianna," Mia growled, as she faced Brianna and she called forth her energy from the earth—knocking Brianna off balance, and breaking the spell she'd cast. Mia carried on.

"Stop it, we have to sort this out!"

Mia turned to check on Brianna.

Just as she grabbed her hand, the tree-lined street and saltbox houses vanished. The smudgy gray sky disappeared.

As Mia blinked, the scenery changed. A watery sun stared down upon her and the air was sweet. Mia whirled around and Brianna stood next to her. "How dare you?!" she snapped.

"I dare because I care, and this hard bitch standing before me isn't you. We're a team, and I miss my friend." She reached for her other hand as a hushed silence surrounded them.

"Well, now we're here we need to go into the temple," Mia said. "Come on."

They walked through the tall grasses and stepped into the garden of Ashwar. Smooth green grass stretched before them like thick carpet. A multitude of colorful flowers edged the borders, and fruit trees swayed heavy with their bounty. Mia stepped onto the grass and charged toward the alabaster dome temple. Brianna panted behind her as their feet tapped against the granite steps that led up toward the giant oak doors.

"Mia, why here?" Brianna stood up one step higher than Mia, looking down at her as she caught her breath. Mia bowed her head.

"We're here, because I need information on Rhiannon. Greyson's threatened to kill everyone I care about. He's manipulating everything—my dreams, my visions. I don't know what's real anymore. Michael Christian is Greyson, and, I have until Christmas Day to beat him at his own game or I have to leave with him. I've promised him, I'll go. I love Ryder, but I cannot let Greyson kill him, or anyone else." Mia lifted her head and looked at Brianna, who placed an arm around her shoulders.

"Wow, Michael Christian is Greyson! Oh, my god, he's been there the last several days! How could you not say anything, and he's behind the concert? How did we not realize or sense his magic?" Brianna stared at Mia, her eyes wide and her nostrils flaring.

"I know he's a powerful caster, and he manages to mask himself pretty well. I'm not as strong as he is, that's for sure, and I suspect Rhiannon is helping him. The Darkshadows have been instrumental in shaping the humans' demise throughout history, and he triggered the volcano explosion in Dakarta. Yet he saved Ayesha. Yesterday, when he was taunting me at the studio, I mentioned Rhiannon and he left. I had a vision and Rhiannon was there. I know it was her, because I remember her portrait with her raven hair and her unusual eyes. She was sitting on her black charger, leading an army into Annwn. I think I'm a pawn in a much bigger game, but I don't know why. I just know I have to find out about Rhiannon, and that means we have to go in the temple."

Mia pushed up and strode up toward the giant doors. The gold handle was rusty and old. It took several goes before Mia heard the handle click and the door creaked open. A rush of stale dusty air greeted her. She spluttered, and before she could take another step, Brianna tugged on her sleeve.

"You know this place is run by soul-catchers?" Brianna held her arm.

"They won't bother us. Coming?" Mia smiled back at Brianna, her belly tingling with anticipation. Mia sensed she was exactly where she needed to be. She wet her lips and stepped forward. Each step she took, the torches that lined the walls lit themselves, and the dark shadows blossomed into a yellow light. The ceiling was domed, and at its center, a large black chandelier containing hundreds of candles swayed back and forth. Shiny cream granite covered the floor and pillars of white alabaster ran off in a row either side of the large granite desk under the dome. Beyond the desk, there were rows upon row of tall wooden bookcases. Looking around and above, she saw two floors whose stillness suggested the place was deserted.

"Brianna, come on. There's no one here." Mia turned around to encourage her to follow, but instead found her backing away and shaking her head. The hairs along Mia's neck tingled and stood up, and a shiver of fear rocked down her back. Brianna was terrified of something behind her. Mia slowly turned back around, and there stood two elderly librarians arguing.

They seemed harmless enough. She stepped forward and held onto the edge of the cold stone desk. Both ladies immediately stopped arguing and turned to face her. A breeze from nowhere rolled through, and the candles on the walls went out. In the muted light, the once sweet–looking old ladies, with their neat little buns and glasses, growled like rabid dogs. Their motherly features changed into sharp and gruesome ghouls, their white hair fell loose and flowing around their scary faces. Mad, glowing, red eyes stared at Mia, and crooked, stained teeth were revealed as the ladies lifted their fingers to their mouths. Mia shuddered, but instead of moving, gripped the desk tighter.

"Please, I need your help," she whispered. "I promise to be quiet, but I really need your help." The wind died down around her and she pulled on her lower lip, never taking her eyes off the two ladies. The candles lit up once more and they nodded at each other.

"Of course, dear. How can we help?" Both ladies answered together, their faces restored and smiling.

Mia looked back over her shoulder and beckoned for Brianna to join her. "I, um, I need some information on the witch Rhiannon."

There was a joint inhaling and mumbling from the librarians, who covered their mouths and whispered. They nodded, and one of the ladies walked away.

"All the books about the dark witch have been locked away," said the other. "Nobody has asked to see them for centuries. My sister has gone to get the keys." She opened a large registry book that slammed as it fell against the desk, and dust floated into the air. Mia coughed. "Sorry, but we don't get many visitors. What's your name, dear?" The lady pushed her glasses back and squeezed her eyes staring at Mia's face.

"Mia."

The lady paused, took off her glasses and scowled at her. "Your whole name, dear." She replaced her glasses and poised ready to write her name. The other librarian returned holding a large set of iron keys which jangled as she walked.

"Sorry. Mia Childs."

The old lady glared at her. "That name is not registered here. Do you have another, dear?" Her lips pulled back, her jagged teeth drooled and a long tongue flicked outwards. Mia shuddered.

"Try Mia Leronde."

The keys clattered on the floor and both ladies' stared at her. They immediately curtsied.

Mia stifled a laugh, and reached down to grab the keys.

"Mia, come on. Let's go," Brianna said, standing next to her. Mia nodded and held the keys tight.

"Um, thanks," she said, before darting up the winding wrought-iron staircase.

"Our pleasure, your highness," the librarians called after them. "Just remember the books remain here. Once you get to the second floor, turn left. There's another spiral staircase. Take that right to the top."

The words faded as they climbed higher and higher. Brianna was racing to get to the top. Mia glanced back over her shoulder, but the ladies had vanished.

"Did you hear what they said? What was that all about?" Mia called out, and her voice echoed around the walls. The candles on the walls around them lit as the candles below went out.

"I haven't a clue, but this place gives me the chills. Come on, let's hurry," Brianna said.

At the top of the second narrow and twisty staircase there was a small oak door. There was only one candle on the wall at the top, and all the others below had gone out. Shadows flickered across the walls. Mia looked behind her and then at Brianna.

"Do you feel that?" Mia passed the keys to Brianna as she beckoned for them. She pushed one of the long keys in and tried turning the handle. Nothing. She picked up another one and tried again. A sudden chill surrounded them and as Mia exhaled tiny white clouds escaped from her mouth. She shivered. Brianna's hands shook and the keys dropped to the ground with a clatter. Cursing, she bent to retrieve them. The last candle extinguished plunging them in darkness. Brianna was on her hands and knees along with Mia in an effort to find the keys.

"I've got them," she said, and they both jumped up. Brianna shoved the key into the hole.

The solitary candle lit again.

"Come on, open the door."

There was a squeak, and the door opened. Standing in the doorway, they both stared around. The room was about ten feet in width and length, and each wall contained dark wooden bookcases. Each shelf was filled with dusty books. In the center there was a small brown table with four chairs. A chandelier holding multiple candles swayed from the ceiling and lit up as they walked in. Cobwebs hung in between and the sudden intake of air disturbed them, and they floated down. Everything inside was covered with at least an inch of dust. Mia sneezed, and then Brianna.

"I can't stay in here, with the dust and probably spiders too. Do you even know what we're looking for?" Brianna said, sneezing. Mia twirled around—and in a flash, all the dust vanished. A fresh smell of lemon hung in the air.

"Ooh, much better. So, what are we looking for?"

"I really don't know—anything that sheds some light on Rhiannon," Mia said, staring at the various books, waiting for her instincts to take over. She let her fingers touch each book until a tingle started after she touched one. It was a small leather-bound book tied with straps. Her hand hovered, and the book lifted into her palm. Mia sat down at the table and flicked through the pages.

The leather-clad book was simple. Inside were pages of parchment, and the words were hand-written in black ink. It was Rhiannon's diary. There were drawings, a lock of hair, poems and entries that she had written herself about her life in Annwn.

Mia inhaled deeply and her heart began to race. She looked across at Brianna, who was leafing through a book as well. She turned back to stare at the pages and to study the drawings. On one of the first pages was the drawing of a distinguished man. Underneath the drawing was the name Emrys. She jumped in her seat. The air chilled again and the door creaked.

"Brianna—" She stretched her arm across the table and gripped Brianna's hand. A sudden whisper of wind snuffed the candles out, plunging them into darkness. Mia's heart soared like a rocket. Books hurtled off the shelves, flying across the room, smashing into the bookcase and dropping to the ground. Mia covered her face to stop getting attacked by the books, and ducked as one whooshed toward her—but one hit her shoulder, and she winced. Brianna tugged on her arm.

"We need to leave, now." As she had pulled them into Annwn, she was responsible for getting them home. The room shifted and disappeared.

Mia sat upon the grassy yard, up against a tree, and next to her on the grass lay Brianna. Still clutched in her hand was the diary, which she hid in her backpack. Brianna stirred and shook her head.

"Wow. We're going to be so late." Brianna stood up and pulled Mia with her. "Did you find anything?"

Mia sucked on her lip and pulled the dairy out from her bag. She opened it on the page where Rhiannon had drawn a picture of Emrys. “Look.” She pointed at the drawings and the name.

Brianna stared and gasped. “Didn’t the old ladies say we weren’t to take the books?” she said, frowning.

“I didn’t intend to—it kind of stuck to me. Anyway, I think it’s Rhiannon’s diary, and look, there are pictures of Emrys in here. I think they were in love. We have to talk to him—there’s a history between those two. He knows more than he’s letting on.” Mia let Brianna look at the pictures, watching as she flicked through a few pages and then stared at one.

“Hey, have you seen this?” Brianna turned the book around and pointed at the drawing.

The picture was an exact replica of her pendant. Mia snatched the book back and let her fingers touch the drawing. The drawing vibrated underneath her fingers as she touched the ink. A tremble ran through her, and she slammed the book shut. Studying the front and side of the book, she could not find a title. Mia put the book carefully into her backpack.

“My necklace—it was the first thing that Greyson tried to take from me. Does it belong to Rhiannon? Why would Emrys give it to me? Rhiannon wants control. She wants war, but what has my necklace to do with any of this?” Mia slung her bag over her shoulder, and headed down the tree-lined street with Brianna following.

“Mia wait. You told me about Greyson, now you have to tell Ryder.”

The trees were bare, and the streets mostly deserted, as they ran the rest of the way to school. Mia knew that after telling Brianna there was no going back, but everything was going to explode in their faces. The concert was two weeks away, and if Greyson discovered that the others knew, what would he do? Mia’s heartbeat hurtled into the near supersonic, and her hands trembled. Had she sentenced everyone she loved to death, including the human race?

Chapter Twenty-Four

Ryder was fit to burst. It was Friday afternoon, and patience was a swear word. He needed answers, and fast. Mia was at his house to talk, but controlling his frustration was proving difficult. He wanted to pick up the coffee cup from the table and smash it, or punch his fist into the wall. Instead, he forced himself to be calm. Screaming, shouting, none of that would help. The weight of her carrying around these secrets was telling. Her face was pasty, and her energy lacked any conviction. She was physically and mentally drained and all because she chose not to confide in him, so why the hell did he feel guilty?

He ran his hands through his hair and hooked them around his neck. Staring across at Mia, he cursed. Gray shadows smudged her violet eyes, and yet she still looked so damn beautiful. For the last hour, she explained that Michael Christian was none other than Greyson. His blood pumped through his veins and arteries at such a rate, he was sure his heart would explode. A twisting hatred for the man was threatening to drive him mad. By all accounts, Greyson was sadistically taunting Mia and playing on her emotions. Even so, he could not understand, after everything, how she could agree to leave with him. Was he that disposable? He kept his distance, because he wanted to shake her and yet hold her and never let her go again. Instead, he stalked around the den.

"I wanted to tell you, but he threatened to kill you and everyone I care about. I know now that I'm only a piece in a much bigger plan, and I don't trust him. I think he'll hurt you anyway. Everything is a disaster." Her hands reached up to cover her face. As angry as he was, he just wanted to hold and comfort her. If Rhiannon was involved and war was coming, they should return to Annwn. He pulled her hands away from her face and sighed.

"Mia, I love you, and that means you're never alone. When will you get that in your head? All along Greyson has scared, intimidated and threatened you. You've already let him win? What's more, I know you love me—but that doesn't give you the right to make decisions for me. This is my life, and I'd rather die trying to save you than to let you sacrifice yourself for me. What kind of life would I have? It's time we faced Greyson together, because we are a team. This is not just your fight, but ours. No more charging off on your own, or am I fighting a lost cause?"

Mia's eyes sparkled like tanzanite and a hesitant smile lit her face. His heart flamed with the need to hold her, and he pulled her into arms and kissed her. He was not going to lose her, no matter what. Emrys had told him that he wouldn't be tested like Mia, but staring at her, he knew that wasn't true. He had lied, but why? He let out a deep breath, everything about being in the human realm challenged him. It was all alien to him, and when he first found Mia, he had battled with his insecurities about her feelings for him.

His head throbbed, and he rubbed his temples to ease his tension. Since the moment that he'd collided with Mia in the human world, he'd been a thorn in her side, always disputing him. First, it was out of fear of him and over what it meant for herself, but then she had taken the truth and gradually accepted it. Coping better than he imagined after everything that she had experienced as a human, proving yet again how strong she was. Her ability to sift through the mess and keep trying all in the pursuit of what was right, was why he loved her so much, and he could do no less for her.

Standing here watching and listening to her, knowing everything she had suffered at Greyson's hand was because she loved him. She would give herself to the despicable man if it meant he was safe. Knowing that, made his heart swell and soar, but it also filled him with a sick dread. Ryder didn't fear much and could tolerate many things, including torture, but the thought of losing Mia would mortally wound him. *Was he meant to simply let her go?* An idea formed in his head, and he called to Brianna and Tristan.

We need to go to Annwn.

* * * *

Half an hour later, Ryder and Mia joined Tristan and Brianna at Lake Cochichewick. A light snow dropped from the sky, a thin layer of ice covered the entire surface. The moon lay hidden in the cloud-filled sky, and birds squawked, as they stood in their familiar spot. Night would soon be upon them.

"So, we have to pretend that we don't know that Michael Christian is Greyson, and carry on as normal. He must not realize that Mia has told us," Ryder said, gazing at them all.

"He's just one, and there're four of us. Why don't we strike at him before he has the chance to hurt anyone? I reckon I could take him down." Tristan said as he cracked his knuckles, and Mia hissed.

"He's manipulated and helped millions die throughout history. He's outsmarted us every time. You were in the recording studio when he *stopped time,* and there was nothing we could do. He comes and goes at his leisure. He has money, position, power, and he has Rhiannon. Do not underestimate him." Mia was in Tristan's face.

Ryder gripped her hand and pulled her away. He pushed her gently onto a red blanket that lay on the grass and the others joined as well. A cloud passed by, and a slice of the moon gazed down on them as small flakes of white snow floated down on them.

"Killing him is very tempting right now, but Mia's right—it isn't the answer. If everything that Mia believes is true, I vote we return to Annwn. If war is coming we need to be there, but we need to speak with Emrys first. Mia, bring the book." They linked hands and Mia's pendant glowed like the sun.

Soft snowflakes were replaced with bright sunshine and the roar of waves crashing against the shore. The four of them stood at the edge of the ocean. The salt tang of the clear aqua water greeted them. Tristan dipped his hand in the water and splashed the girls. They giggled and retaliated by splashing him back. Howls, carried along by the breeze, lifted Ryder's gaze away from the playful scene. He stared up at the surrounding jutting cliffs. His eyes darted back and forth as several more howls filled the air. Tristan came to stand next to him.

At the cliff's edge, five black wolves peered down over the beach. They lifted their noses into the air and howled in unison.

"Quick, over here!"

Emrys stood at the cliff's foot, in black leather pants and a soft white cotton shirt, signaling with his hand for them to follow him into the cliffs. Mia, Brianna, Ryder, and Tristan ran over the golden sand until they reached the base of the cliff. As they reached the jagged gray rocks, an opening appeared behind Emrys and they entered. As they stepped inside, the damp cave walls sealed behind them. The roar of the ocean was dimmed, and the cave was silent apart from the drip of water from the ceiling. Light came from a huge roaring fire and candles floated everywhere.

Ryder jumped straight to the point, "What do you know of Rhiannon?"

He stared at Emrys, whose face crumpled at the sound of her name. Ryder beckoned to Mia and she came forward with the book which in turn he passed to Emrys. He sighed and stood against the cave wall leaning his arm against it.

"You have to understand, we were all young once—young and in love. At least I was, but Rhiannon wanted more. She started to use dark magic. She convinced my brother, Prince Elgin, she loved him and was crowned as his queen. My brother was besotted by her beauty. Once they were married, I entered the mortal world. After the war in the mortal world I returned, because Elgin was no longer capable of ruling. Rhiannon was behind the thefts of artifacts from Annwn. The death of our people lay in her hands. I condemned her to the pit at Drakensberg. She sought to destroy the humans and claim power for herself." Emrys paused, haunted by his memories, and shook his head violently. He turned and stared at Mia, his deep-set eyes ablaze.

"I lost them both, and what was worse, I covered up a terrible secret—for years." Ryder listened to Emrys, but stared at Mia. He walked to stand in front of Emrys.

"There was a child, wasn't there?" Ryder knew the answer before he spoke. He gazed at Mia, and then back at the others who sat on the wooden benches warming their hands against the flames of the fire. Emrys kept his eyes on Mia.

"Rhiannon was pregnant, and as soon as the child was born I—we—took the baby from her, and then bound her to Drakensberg. She cursed me and everyone involved, but I could not leave the child with her. If the Wise Elders knew of the child's existence, they would have condemned her too. I took the baby and hid her in plain sight, in the village with a reliable family. She was well cared for."

Mia started to back away. A chill was reaching up inside her, twisting, and she cried out, "Nooooo!" She turned frantically, looking around the faces that gazed back at her. Suddenly the reason Rhiannon wanted her was crystal clear. She had always been told a freak accident had claimed the lives of her parents at a young age, and Emrys had practically raised her. Before, she could take it back, she slapped Emrys across his cheek. She shook with anger.

"How dare you play god with so many lives! Oh my God, I can't believe it! All this time, and you knew. That means we're related, that she's my…oh my God."

"Great-great-granddaughter, actually."

There were too many implications of this knowledge. It was too much to bear. Brianna cried out to her but she whirled around until Ryder caught hold of her arms and pulled her against his chest. He ran his hand up and down her back and spoke words of comfort into her ear until she was quiet. Over her shoulder, he spoke to Emrys.

"How did the bookkeepers know, at the library? I'm presuming they knew, since they addressed Mia as her highness once she gave her full name. It doesn't seem it's been much of a secret, Emrys." Ryder gripped her hand and stroked his thumb across her palm.

"No one goes into the temple anymore. It hasn't been used for years, and the librarians were never told, but all the birth and death records are kept in there. The dead have a lot of time on their hands." Emrys slumped into a heap as he sat down and stared into the embers of the fire. The howls of the wolves broke through the silence.

"Rhiannon has managed, over the years, to kill all her descendants—taking their magic to rebuild her strength. You see, when she was bound she was barely alive. Her magic was stripped from her—at least most was, but she is the most powerful witch I have ever encountered. Her daughter Ami disappeared after giving birth, and ever since it's been a battle to hide her bloodline. Mia, you are the last in that royal line, and the most powerful descendant to date. I formed the Guardians not only to protect our world and the humans, but to protect you. She's using Greyson to get what she wants because her life-source is not strong, and she's still bound here." Emrys shook his head. "Greyson must be stopped. He must be sent back to Annwn. You can do that if you link your powers. Mia, I did what I did to protect you…you must understand." He lifted his face toward her, but Mia could not speak. A million thoughts raced around her head, primarily that she was related to the evil witch, Rhiannon. Ryder held her and would not release her even when she pushed against him.

"How do we send him back?" Ryder stared at Emrys who stood up and came to stand next to him.

"When you're all together, use the pendant and focus on sending him back to Annwn. The pendant is more powerful than you realize. It always allows me to find you, it opens doorways, and it calls to me. Now, you must go. Rhiannon's hounds are close."

Emrys came to stand next to Mia, raised his hand and then lowered it. "I watched over your mother as closely as I could. She never knew the truth, and was happy. When you were born, it was obvious from the moment you drew breath that you were different. Certain abilities skip generations, but you were special. I took you when you were just six weeks old. Your magic was overpowering and Rhiannon would have found you—but the huntsmen came, and killed everyone within reach. Your mother gave her own life to save yours, and Rhiannon believed that the bloodline was lost—until she discovered you."

An instant picture formed in Mia's mind of her real mother, with dark flowing hair, the telltale violet eyes, and a wide smile. A bright white light surrounded her, and in her arms was a tiny baby, in whose eyes images of the world appeared.

"Your essence is stronger than hers or Rhiannon's. Maybe, it's even stronger than mine. I did the right thing Mia. I did." His hand ran across his furrowed forehead and walked away.

The waves crashing against the rocks broke the silence. Mia shivered. Her head ached as she tried to understand everything that Emrys was telling her, but she could not get rid of the chill that had invaded the very marrow of her bone. She did not know what to believe anymore. Her entire life was a lie. She was Rhiannon's descendant. Rhiannon was a real *bona fide* evil witch, a murderer. What did that make her?

Tears blocked her vision. She lifted her hand to her head, gazing at Emrys and Ryder. He hadn't known of her legacy until now. Was this going to change things between them? How could it not?

"Mia, you are not Rhiannon. Do you understand? We make our own choices."

Brianna and Tristan huddled around Mia and Ryder. They clutched each other's hands, and the pendant glowed, lighting their way home. Mia kept her eyes averted from Emrys. She didn't know what to say. But there was a question.

"You said that Rhiannon didn't know I existed. When did she find out?" Mia asked, controlling her voice.

"Rumors, I suspect. From the moment your visions started playing a significant role, there were whispers. A feeling, a connection as she gains strength, maybe she has an awareness. I sent you into the human world as a test and to hide you until I knew what was going on. I suspect Greyson has been on your trail for some time. I'm not sure." He stood and rubbed the bristles on his chin.

"If you formed the Guardians to protect me, did they know who I was all along?" Mia broke free of Ryder, feeling the answer before he spoke and backing away from everyone.

"Mia, you have to understand. If you had known, you would—by that knowledge alone—be in danger. Your friends were only told that you were of royal descent, and sworn to secrecy. Do not blame them for loving you and protecting you. I have to go, but one day you will realize your destiny."

The light in the damp cave dwindled, and like a candle blowing out Emrys vanished.

* * * *

Waking up, Mia found herself lying across Ryder's lap. She jumped up as he and the others woke. Ryder, Brianna, and Tristan stared at her waiting for the explosion of bitterness and confusion she was generating and hurling in their direction. She turned her back on them facing the lake, and the water rose like a tidal wave, Ryder shouted as the wind rustled the leaves and bent the trees back, almost snapping them. Tears escaped down her cheeks, and she dropped to her knees. As her knees touched the ground, the water crashed and resumed its place, splashing them with a cold spray. How could they all hide such a secret for her?

"Mia, it's all right to be upset," Ryder said, "But you have to acknowledge that Rhiannon is only half of your bloodline. The other half is Emrys. We all have a dark side, but we're not royalty—although I always thought you acted like a *princes*s."

"Stop thinking that. I was always your friend, and it was never a job to be," Brianna said. Mia looked over her shoulder at Brianna, smiled, and accepted Ryder's outstretched hand. "How do you know Emrys is my great-great-grandfather, and not Prince Elgin—and Rhiannon was not always evil?"

"Mia, stop thinking about Monica Goldman. You were protecting yourself—rather clumsily—and as soon as you realized you had gone too far, you stopped. You're not evil, okay? Rhiannon has no conscience, even killing her own." Ryder moved close, but held off touching her.

"You knew about Monica?" She stepped closer, her cheeks flushing pink.

"When you told me you loved me, on your birthday, a whole bunch of emotions and memories poured out, and that was one of them. I didn't want to bring it up until you were ready. You're not a bad person, Mia. This changes nothing. We have to get rid of Greyson and undo the spells he has cast over the humans," he said.

They left the lake and walked out of the forest. The clouds had rolled on by, and the moon glared brightly.

"It doesn't change anything, Mia," Ryder said, picking her hand up to link it with his.

"You're wrong, it changes everything. I'm not who I thought I was. Hell, I'm back at the beginning, only now my real life is a total lie as well. How do you think I feel?" she said, snatching her hand away.

"I get that you're angry, but—"

"But, we don't have time for this, I know," she said.

"Emrys did what was best to protect you, knowing that Rhiannon will stop at nothing to gain what she wants. You're surrounded by people who love you, and have always loved you. That has not changed and there isn't a single harmful bone in your body."

Mia leaned in close. "That's not true. I *punched* you, and kicked your ass."

Ryder and Tristan laughed. "True, maybe there is a bit of evil witch in you after all. I love you. Now, we have to work together to send Greyson back to Annwn. It'll have to be the night of the concert," Ryder said as they leaned against Tristan's car.

"Then home?" Tristan nodded at Ryder.

"I don't think we have a choice. By then the concert will have raised enough for Ayesha, and her future should be all set. Once we get the CD out with the reversal spell for Loxus, everything will be set in motion to change the Darkshadows predictions for the humans. And if war is coming to Annwn, we need to be there."

Tristan lifted his arm and laid it across Brianna's shoulders. She smiled at him and Mia smiled at them both. She sighed, returning her thoughts to Annwn. For some reason, though it didn't seem possible, Ryder was right. War was coming, and they needed to be part of that battle.

Chapter Twenty-Five

Mia wished there was more time, but it was Christmas Eve and the concert was hours away. Last week Mia had accepted that Emrys had hidden her past for good reasons, but a part of her still felt lost and adrift. She sighed and shook her body to pull herself out of the deep pit she was sinking into. Ryder was at her side constantly, going over the plan to send Greyson back to Annwn. He wouldn't know what had hit him, and once he was there, Emrys was going to imprison him. Just as Emrys opened a portal allowing them into the mortal world, he was going to reverse it and pull them all back into Annwn. At least, that was the plan.

Easy, right?

Flicking the blind up, Mia stared out the window. A light sprinkling of white snow floated and glided, until finally it fell to the ground. The last time it snowed, the concert was canceled. Not tonight.

Mia grabbed her bag and left her room. Her father's laughter reached the landing. He'd arrived two days ago and was flying out Christmas evening. By then, she would be gone and the human world would return to normal. What that would entail, Mia did not know. She hoped that her parents would find happiness. As she stepped down the stairs, the smell of pine and cinnamon filled her nostrils from freshly hung garlands draped over the handrail and around the living room fireplace. Mia walked in the room as Cerianne and Nicholas finished the final touches to the Christmas tree. The Frasier Fir tree stood six feet high and was overflowing with silver and purple ornaments. This was the first Christmas they had shared together in several human years. Mia swiped away a tear. None of this was real, but she would miss them.

"Aw, honey, are you all right? Have you been crying?" Cerianne moved from the tree and came over to hug Mia, who wrapped herself around her mother and rested her head against her chest.

"Just some last-minute nerves, I guess. The tree looks lovely." Cerianne looked back at the tree and at Nicholas. He gave a guarded smile and came to join them.

"Your mom always did know how to dress the tree. When are you leaving?" He was dressed casually in blue jeans, a dark T-shirt and a denim shirt. His hands he shoved into his pocket.

"He'll be here soon. A limousine is picking us all up, and I'm the last one." Her parents were treading carefully, sensing her nervousness, but they didn't guess the truth. If only they knew! Instead of normal fears, like whether she would forget her words, Mia was worrying about saving those she loved from Greyson. His name conjured up so many waves of emotion, none of them good. Today she must act normally around him, and keep her thoughts blocked—easier said than done.

Greyson had put together an official timetable that Fusion had to follow today. His management team was going to be on site to co-ordinate the concert and ensure it all ran smoothly. All Fusion had to do was turn up and—as if on a conveyer belt—they would be preened, styled, and polished to perfection, ready to perform. The concert would kick off at seven o'clock. Glancing at her watch, she saw that left several hours. Mia could not stop her growing anxiety. She just hoped they could pull it off.

Now remember, Mia, I have made certain that Ayesha survives and will be well cared for. I've also promised to leave Ryder and the rest of your loved ones alone. Do not renege on your promise. It would be most unwise.

Mia gritted her teeth and fixed her stare on her parents, giving them a cool smile.

I'm about to leave, but you're making me more nervous than I already am. I won't break my promise, but if you keep taunting me, I'm going to mess this up. Now leave me alone.

The front door bell chimed. Her parents kissed her and walked her to the door. Mia opened the door, and there stood a chauffeur dressed in a black and white suit. The back window of the limousine descended and Evan's head popped out, along with several waving hands. She glanced back at her parents.

"Mia, break a leg."

With tears threatening, she wrapped her arms around both her parents and then fled into the waiting limousine. Ryder pulled her into the vacant spot next to him and she snuggled against his chest, inhaling his clean citrus scent.

Greyson isn't going to back down. He was taunting me this morning, reminding me of all that he's done, and will do if I back out.

Mia stared out of the tinted windows. Ryder's turned her chin toward him with his hand and kissed her lips.

We can do this. "Have you heard the news about Ayesha?" he said.

"No." Mia's thoughts consisted of the concert and Greyson.

"They're moving her to Children's hospital in Boston next week." He held her hands and smoothed his thumb over her palm. Ryder stroked her palm making circles, and it elicited a need to move closer. She kissed his lips and stared up at him.

"I never expected that. I wish…I wish I could've met her," she said, her voice quick and breathless. Ryder raised her palm and kissed it. A delicious wave erupted deep inside Mia. They were in the limousine, but it was just the two of them lost in their own desires. She kissed his lips again, a soft needy kiss. Nudging him and pulling him against her.

"You two, cut it out." Evan's voice was sharp and Tyler tugged at Ryder, pulling him off the seat and over to the other side. Mia laughed and wiped her mouth. For a moment all thought of Greyson or what was about to happen had been forgotten, and that was Ryder's plan. She smiled at him as her heart bounced along and her cheeks burned.

"This is going to be awesome, if you two can keep your hands off each other," Evan said. Ryder pushed against Evan.

"Mia's nervous, and I was trying to distract her." He winked over at Mia and she smiled. Brianna sprawled next to her and laughed.

"Well, I'm psyched. I can't wait to get on stage. After tonight everything's gonna change." Mia looked at Brianna, Tristan, and Ryder. After tonight, everything would indeed change. No more Fusion, no more Evan or Tyler, and they would be back in Annwn.

"Well, we don't know what tomorrow will bring, but for now, here's to Fusion," Ryder said, lifting his hand into the air.

"Fusion!"

Everyone yelled and piled their hands on top of Ryder's.

The limousine drove across the Tobin Bridge, and Boston's skyscrapers dotted the horizon. Tyler pushed the button and the window descended. He stuck his head out the window and howled like a wolf. It was Christmas Eve and they were performing in front of their biggest audience to date. The limousine shook with music from Katy Perry and their whoops of laughter.

Remember, together we're stronger.

Ryder's words comforted Mia, and she nodded.

The sky in Boston was a freezing dark gray. The car wove through the afternoon traffic, and turned down a side street to the back of The Blues Club. At the back door of the three story brick building, two hefty bouncers dressed in black suits and dark glasses stood on guard. The Blues Club was a well-known cellar bar where many artists performed.

"This is it. Dad said the tickets for the show sold out, so this place is going to be rockin," said Tristan.

The limousine stopped, and the chauffeur stepped out to open the back passenger door. Mia stepped out first and the others followed. Sprinkles of snow floated down on her and she brushed them off her face. The bouncers ushered them all inside. Mia could smell Ryder's woodsy scent behind her. Leaning up against the walls were life-size posters of Fusion. Mia stared at the girl that was supposed to be her. Gone was the reserved girl from several months ago. Standing before her was a pouting temptress, in a figure-hugging tiny black leather dress that finished way too high above her knees and long leather black boots. She looked like Catwoman, and all that was missing was a whip. Brianna was dressed in a similar outfit. The boys had barely been touched up, and were dressed in ripped jeans and T-shirts. "Fusion" was slashed across the front. Brianna coughed and burst out laughing.

"Oh my God, Mia, I have to get me one of those. We look like warriors, with the hair swirled back. Wow, the dark eye shadow really makes your eyes stand out," she said as she studied the poster. The boys stood gaping at it too. Ryder slung his arm over Mia's shoulders.

"That's not me. He's made us all look so different," Mia said. Ryder stared at her and pulled her around to face him.

Mia, you may not like it, but that is you. You're beautiful and strong and that poster, well, it shows us how Greyson views you.

"Wow, dude, I think it's amazing. Girls, you look like sexy assassins—like Lara Croft. The poster gives the band a kind of fantasy look. I think that's cool," Evan said.

"Mia, it's like acting. It's you underneath. When you're on stage, you come alive. You have such power, such confidence," Ryder said.

Mia blinked back her tears and drew a deep breath. She wanted to kiss Ryder—but Greyson strode down the hallway. His face twisted into a stony glare aimed right at her. His eyes flickered toward the posters, and he gave one of his sly smiles.

"So do you like them? I had one of my graphic designers working on it. They're fresh from the printer." Greyson turned his head and stared at the group. Evan and Tyler were ecstatic. The rest nodded. Mia simply glared.

This is how I see you, Mia—lethal, focused, self-assured, and sexy as hell.

His words unsettled her. Greyson could be sadistic, but there were times—like now—when he revealed a side of himself that, no matter what he said, showed he *liked* her. Was he really as ruthless as he made out, or was it Rhiannon's influence? She shook her head. *Impossible,* Mia sighed.

Greyson moved away and called for them all to follow. "Well, come on, you need to go through to the dressing rooms and get ready. Then you need to do some warm-up vocals and go over the routines. Any questions?"

Mia walked through the hall and into the grand foyer alongside the others. An enormous golden, glittering, crystal chandelier hung from the ceiling, dominating the entryway. Thick red carpet covered the floors. The surrounding walls were decorated with embossed wallpaper in a *fleur de lis* design, and the woodwork was painted in a rich gold. The overall effect was elegant and sumptuous. They were directed through more doors and quickly found themselves in the hands of the make-up artists and stylists in the back rooms.

An hour later, Mia and Brianna stood admiring each other. Mia glanced over her shoulder and stared into the full length mirror. She had a black long-sleeved top that was low-cut in the front, revealing far too much cleavage for her liking. The top was also cropped and stopped short above her belly button. She shivered. From below her waist she wore a black skirt that had multiple slits, and beneath it black sheer tights. Every time she moved, her long legs flashed. Mia looked over at Brianna her outfit was similar, but as she would be sitting down for most of the performance, she would not be as exposed. Her hair had been brushed until it glistened. Subtle strands had been sprayed with gold that twinkled as her hair moved. The make-up artist had covered her face in a barely-there foundation, and covered her eyes in a smoky brown eye-shadow. Her lips, which she pouted, were covered in a plum color the make-up artist had sworn would not wear off while singing.

Mia stared at herself. There was nothing familiar about the girl staring back. She straightened her shoulders and blinked. The girl facing her looked confident, older, and very sexy. The boys wandered in and gawked, then began whistling.

"Danni, you're smoking hot," Tyler said, promptly throwing her a kiss.

"Mia, you look beautiful," Ryder said, his voice hoarse.

"I feel different. Maybe it's the make-up?" she said. Tristan and Evan stared at the girls with open mouths.

"Well, even The Kittens don't match up to this transformation," Tristan said.

Evan went on to explain that the other band had arrived, but they hadn't seen anything of the headliner for the concert. Mia glanced once more into the mirror, and then grabbed Ryder's outstretched hand. Walking into the empty hall was surreal because, in a matter of hours, it would be filled with people here to listen to Fusion. The surrounding tables were covered in simple white tablecloths, and in the centers were tall pillar candles in large glass hurricane lamps. There were three bar areas, two on the ground level and one above. The stage stood before them. Long red silky curtains adorned either side of the stage and were held back with gold sashes. On the stage various instruments, speakers, and microphones lay in wait. Bright lights highlighted the ghostly scene, and an eerie silence echoed around them as no one spoke. Mia wanted to get on stage and start performing, and at the same time she wanted to vomit.

"Wow it's huge," Evan said, gazing around,

"You okay?" Ryder said.

"I will be," Mia said, holding Ryder's hand. Brianna and Tristan watched and listened.

We need to stay linked and to channel our thoughts, she transmitted. *Keep the block on Greyson until the last minute. We will have to act quickly and focus all our energy on him and Emrys. Ten minutes into our performance, at exactly ten o'clock, we will triangulate him. Okay?*

Feeling the hairs along the back of her neck stand up, Mia turned swiftly away from the stage. Greyson walked in with several of his stage crew, dressed immaculately as always. His steel-gray eyes zoomed in straight at Mia, and his smile was far too confident. She shivered.

What if he knows? Brianna's mental voice sounded fearful and unsure.

Mia stared back at her and glared. There was no place for uncertainty. This must work. *It will work.* She spoke with more conviction than she felt, and balled her fists. Ryder's hand touched the small of her back, and she unfurled her hand. Together, they could do this.

"What a transformation. You look exactly as I imagined you." Greyson looked straight at Mia, but addressed them all. "Are you pleased with the results?"

Tyler poked Evan and they laughed.

"I've never smelled so fruity," Evan said. They all smiled.

"Time for last-minute practice." Greyson ushered them toward the stage.

Evan started banging on his drums, and for the next hour everyone focused on the music and getting ready for the concert. Even on stage, Mia could feel the heat of Greyson's stare on her. He stood in front where the audience would be, chatting with the stage crew and Mr. Fitzgerald. There were smiles and waves, but all the while Mia knew that Greyson was studying her.

There's something different about you tonight. What is it, I wonder?

Mia willed her mind not to respond. She shook her hair and twirled around on the stage as she sang the words to the song, but in the end she spoke—worried he would suspect something if she ignored him.

There's nothing different about me except the outfit, which I have to admit I quite like, and I'm getting ready to perform. Now stop distracting me and leave me alone.

Mia gazed at him as she moved to the rhythm and beat of the music. Greyson folded his arms and moved his thumb across his lips.

The way you look calls for salacious stares.

The back of Mia's throat was dry, and she looked up, glaring at Greyson. His voice sounded deep and husky as she smoothed her hand through her hair and swirled to the music.

They practiced for another thirty minutes, and then Reckless came out to rehearse. There were whoops of delight from the boys, and lots of hugs and shaking of hands. Mia and the group stayed to listen to Reckless perform, and then were ushered away.

Night descended and the snow stopped. People filled the club, and Mia sensed a rising energy in the air. It crackled with excitement and nervous laughter. Brianna chatted with Tyler. Tristan and Ryder laughed as Evan tapped his sticks in the air and mimed words as if already on stage. Loud rock music filled the hallways and people rushed past with headsets and sheets of paper. The Kittens popped in, and Simone gave a wide sweeping smile before disappearing to perform. Ryder stood next to Mia stroking her arm.

"Ready," he said.

Mia nodded. She just wanted it over. The stage manager appeared in the room, his forehead creased, and he was wiping his brow with the back of his hand.

"The Kittens are just finishing up, you're on next. The crowd is crazy, and the hall is maxed out. Like I said in rehearsal, smile, relax, and enjoy." He waved the itinerary and gave them the thumbs up. Mr. Fitzgerald walked in as the stage manager walked out. He nodded at everyone.

"Good luck guys. This is your night, enjoy it," Mr. Fitzgerald said. Mia looked around expecting Greyson to appear, but he didn't. She stared at Ryder.

Don't worry, he's probably busy. He'll be on stage, just stay calm.

Ryder lifted her hand and they walked out into the corridor following Mr. Fitzgerald toward the stage. Mia's heart bumped erratically against her ribs and her breathing came in quick pants. Her eyes darted everywhere and her hands felt clammy. Nervous bubbles rose and then stopped. Ryder cupped her face, "I love you, Mia, no matter what happens. Do you hear?" he said.

Blinking at his words, Mia wondered if he knew something she didn't—but as she looked into his large dark, still eyes, he showed no fear—just concentration and determination. Strength flowed over her from him. He was not afraid at all, and it made her feel powerful too.

"I won't lose you," he said, pulling her against him until she could hear his beating heart against her cheek.

"I love you. I always have," she said, smoothing her hand across his cheek. Mr. Fitzgerald stopped and waved them forward. The stage manager rushed forward beckoning for them to get on stage.

"Come on! After the introduction, you're on."

Just above her churning stomach and hammering heart, Mia heard the screaming audience. The presenter introduced Fusion as The Kittens ran off stage, huffing and puffing. Simone strolled by Ryder and blew him a kiss. Mia glared at the girl, wishing she would trip over her feet—and instantly Simone stumbled almost falling, but at the last moment found her balance.

Ryder glared at her and tugged her hand to walk up the short flight of stairs that led to the stage. The curtains were drawn in front of them, but they could hear the crowd. Heat from the lights instantly warmed Mia. She swallowed and took her place by the microphone, watching as everyone else took theirs. Everyone was quiet. Mia turned her head back and forth—still no sign of Greyson. Evan sat waiting, his forehead was shiny from a light layer of sweat. Brianna stood next to Mia, and winked over at her. Mia smiled back. Looking to her left she saw that Ryder stood there, and he reached to squeeze her hand.

Ready.

Mia scanned left and right, then back toward Tristan. Everyone was focused and ready.

This is it!

She couldn't answer him, not just yet. Greyson stood in front of the curtains introducing the band. Mia listened as he explained about Ayesha, and he sounded *so* convincing. There were shouts, yells, and then silence. The curtains drew back, and a sea of waving arms and unknown faces covered in semi-darkness flowed before them. Bright lights streamed down, dazzling them, and Mia blinked. Ryder stooped forward into the microphone and introduced the first song, *The Promise*. His gaze washed over Mia, and she willed her heart to slow.

I'm ready.

Brianna lifted her bow and started to serenade them, delicately caressing the strings of her violin, and automatically Mia came alive, singing the words she knew so well. Mia and Ryder's voices blended together. The urgency of the guitar and drums pushed them forward until everything else was forgotten. The music took over. Halfway through the song they separated, each striding away from the other. The guitars and drums whipped up the music into a frenzied crescendo. Everyone in the audience moved and swayed to the beat. Mia saw Cerianne and Nicholas dancing and smiling. At the end of the song, Ryder and Mia came back together in each other's arms at the front of the stage. The music slowed and softened, bringing the piece to its conclusion. Applause ripped throughout the hall.

After that Mia settled, forgetting about Greyson. She sang song after song easily. Apart from the odd missed beat, Fusion performed as if they had been doing it for years.

Ryder sat down on the stool. It was their final song, and Mia's to sing alone. *Dream Lover.* She ran a hand across her brow as sweat trickled down her spine. It was nine fifty-five.

The lights seemed impossibly bright now, and an uncomfortable sensation clutched her insides. Her mouth was dry. She glanced sideways at Ryder and soaked in his beautiful smile. A hush swept over the audience as the soft strumming of the acoustic guitar started. Evan's skillful tapping on the drums lifted her away, and before she could analyze the sensations, she was singing her words to the needy crowd. Her voice loud and clear, but behind her eyes and above her temples, a persistent throb increased. Mia squeezed her eyes shut and forced the pain away.

Mia, are you all right?

Moans and screams sounded off in her head. She heard Ryder's frantic concern, but Mia was trying to decipher what was happening. A loud popping sound ricocheted around in her head. As the music reached a furious momentum, she gasped. Inside her blood turned to ice, and she trembled.

A gunshot! I heard gunfire!

Her wild eyes searched Ryder's intense stare. Blind pain scorched her head, and she snapped around to stare into the crowd. The words to the song automatically left her lips, but her mind wandered over the crowd of onlookers. Mia froze when she saw Greyson, standing right at the back, chatting and laughing with her parents. Her heart quivered and she stopped breathing, holding the air in her lungs. Greyson stared right at her. Voices invaded her mind, attempting to get her attention. She shook her head, still singing the words of the song, smiling at the crowds. The pain eased enough for Mia to finish. As the last word left her mouth, she hung her head into her hands and wept. The crowds loved the performance, screaming for an encore. After the roars from the crowd the atmosphere, changed. Prickles started at the back of Mia's neck.

Ryder, we need to do it now!

A commotion broke out by the bar and people dispersed like scurrying ants. An ordinary man, dressed in a white shirt and khaki pants, with short gray hair, stood there muttering. He swore in a thick Boston accent—while idly waving a large gun around in his hand.

He has a gun.

Mia stood at the front of the stage, watching the man as everyone backed away from him. There was an eerie stillness and silence, apart from the man's ranting. The man's face was brick red. He was shaking his head, but as soon as a bouncer tried to intervene, his head lifted and with both hands, he steadied the gun and fired. The popping sound reached Mia and she screamed. Glass smashed, and screams tore through the hall.

Pop! Pop! Pop! More shots were fired randomly around, and everyone started screaming. It was utter chaos. Ryder and the band rushed to the edge of the stage.

Where the hell is Greyson?

Tristan and Ryder scanned the crowds. People pushed and shoved each other to escape. Tables crashed to the floor, and people fell. A massive stampede headed toward the narrow exits. Everyone was scrambling and clambering to get out, running haphazardly in every direction to get away from the gunman. The middle-aged man continued to yell, while a crowd of bouncers circled him as they talked into their headsets. Greyson stood there in front of the man, and he seemed to be trying to calm the situation down. The man screamed, "Get it out of my head! Get it out, or I'll keep shooting."

Greyson backed away and the man followed him. Each step Greyson took brought him closer and closer toward the stage. Evan pulled on Mia's sleeve and Tyler ran off with Brianna, but Mia could not move.

We have to triangulate Greyson now and send him back.

Mia insisted, shouting out her silent message to Ryder, Tristan, and Brianna. The man raised his arm, seconds ticked by. The gun pointed at Greyson, but he shifted at the last moment and the barrel of the gun was suddenly fixed on Mia. A shout sounded out by her side, and there were urgent pleas in her head, as she eyed the man, but everything stilled. None of this made sense, Greyson could freeze time and yet he stood by watching and waiting. *This is Greyson's doing.*

He must know of their plans, and was using this as a distraction. Mia flicked a gaze at Ryder and then back at the man. She tried to reach into his mind to get him to stop—but she found nothing, and she shook her head.

Ignore the man. He'll never let him hurt me. We have to focus on Greyson.

Greyson's head snapped around, his face like white granite, and his eyes sparkled like diamonds. Thump. Thump. Thump. Mia's heart beat against her ribs as she held her breath. She met Greyson's glare and leaned forward to touch his shoulder. She fixed her stare on the man with the gun but called to the others.

Now!

Brianna shouted along with several muffled voices, but she would not let go of her grip on Greyson even as he struggled. It was now or never. A soft popping noise whistled in the air and she was knocked sideways to the ground. For a second, she could not see anything. More gunshots filled the air and frantic screams. Around her there was a delayed reaction everything seemed to happen in slow motion. Sitting up, Mia shook her head as people slowly moved and she stared at the unmoving figure lying next to her on the ground.

"Noooooo!"

Mia leaned over Ryder, listening for the sounds of his heart. There was nothing. Her hands touched his mouth, and then his chest, while tears ran down her cheeks. Blazing heat poured out from her fingers and surged into his body. She trembled and shoved Brianna away as she tried to move her.

Ryder had to die, she heard. *In time, you'll accept what is. You were never going to hold up your end of the deal, and I'm done waiting.*

Tears cascaded down her cheeks and she let out a wild scream. She was beyond reasoning even as Tristan and Brianna pulled frantically at her arms to hold her back. The cold metal of her necklace bounced along her collarbone.

Greyson is going to hell. Work with me. Hold him in our circle.

Mia flashed her eyes at Tristan and Brianna and then at Greyson. In her mind, she drew in the energy from her pendant and focused on Greyson, Emrys and Annwn. Ryder could not be dead. She sucked in a deep breath. Her heart battered against her ribs. She pinned Greyson to the spot with all the force she could gather. His face twisted as his arms slapped down against his sides and he could not move. Ice-blue eyes blinked at her as he fell to his knees. His head snapped up, but Mia pushed through, squeezing, twisting, and pummeling his body with wave after wave of excruciating pain. A force she had never felt before filled her and she let it flow out at Greyson.

Where's Rhiannon now, you bastard?

Greyson face shook and twisted in pain as he struggled to break the hold.

Mia…you…cannot…hold…me.

His voice came in clipped phrases. His essence was weak. Mia braced herself. Her hair flapped against her back and she glanced around the hall. Everybody froze, except for Greyson, Tristan and Brianna. She closed her eyes and called to Emrys.

Her body shook and her hands trembled as she stretched them toward Greyson.

I tried to get you to see reason, Greyson, but you would not. I am not one person—I am many and we will always beat you. Now.

Beams of light flowed out from their fingers and the glow bathed Greyson in a milky-yellow haze that turned a white-blue. Mia's gaze held his face. A howling wind whipped around Mia, Tristan and Brianna. A golden fan of light broke through what looked like a crack in the air. The fan of light opened like a creaking door. Emrys was working alongside them in the Otherworld—she could sense him, and his face flashed inside her mind.

Mia, you can do this.

Pictures of Ryder flicked through her mind. The bright light sparkled.

Greyson's desperate eyes watched her as his cheeks rippled and were pulled back from his face revealing his gleaming teeth. His body was sucked away into the whirling vortex, the light vanished, and the door closed.

Mia closed her eyes, ignoring the throbbing pain, and pictured a dark, damp place, high in the mountains, deep out in Tregenith. A soulless place. *Drakensberg*. Mia fell to the ground in a crumpled heap.

In the darkness, a glittering outline walked toward her, calling her name. Ryder. Mia jumped up and ran over to his still, lifeless body. Blood covered Ryder's shirt and pooled in a congealed mess on the floor. Tristan crouched nearby, his head low. Tears filled his eyes and he cursed. Brianna touched Mia's shoulder.

"Mia, he's gone. It's been too long, and there's no pulse," she said.

The hall, which had emptied, was now swamped with armed police carrying rifles, shouting out commands. Mia took no notice.

"You will not die. Do you hear me? You will not leave me," she sobbed against his chest, blood smearing her pale skin.

As she lay on him, her pendant dipped in Ryder's blood and mixed with her tears. White light flamed into life and Mia sat up, pulling the glowing crystal toward her. Gripping it close, she inhaled. Her body shook and the pendant fell away. Mia placed her hands on Ryder's chest and it buckled under her touch shocking him.

Don't die, please don't die.

Two hefty paramedics glanced at Mia. Tristan clasped her shoulders and pulled her away. Without another word, she watched as the medics worked on Ryder to stem the bleeding and restart the heart with a defibrillator. Unable to bear the sight any longer, she turned in Tristan's arms and wept. Pictures of Ryder filled her mind. The first day they crashed into each other. Their first kiss. The night of the homecoming. The first trip to the lake. The paramedics sat back and shook their heads as police surrounded them.

"No!" Mia pushed off Tristan, and ran over to Ryder. She could hear a weak heartbeat. His. And his voice.

Be strong Mia...I will always love you.

"No." Mia dropped to her knees, leaned over his body and kissed his lips. The paramedics tried to remove her, but Ryder's limbs moved and twitched. The older paramedic instantly felt for a pulse and restarted resuscitation. Mia stood up, watching as an oxygen mask was put over Ryder's face, and then the stretcher was pulled away and out of the hall. Mia stared, unable to hear anything but a slow, steady heartbeat—and then she collapsed.

Chapter Twenty-Six

Ryder and Mia laughed as they strolled along the soft, golden sand. She raced ahead, glancing over her shoulder every now and then to check his distance from her. Powerful strides brought him up against her back and he tugged her against him. They fell into a heap on the soft sand. Rolling off her, he pulled her around to face him. He laid her gently back on the sand with his body hovering above her. She touched his lips with her outstretched hand and then trailed her fingers down his chest. There were no marks from the bullet. Ryder looked as he always looked—perfect. He smiled, and Mia smiled back.

Dark clouds rolled across the sky above, blocking out the sun, and Mia shivered. Ryder followed her gaze. A horrifying screech filled the air and she turned to look at Ryder, but he was gone. Mia was alone.

"Did you really think it would be that easy to get rid of me?"

The high-pitched squeal was getting closer and closer. Mia jumped up and ran as fast as she could, not daring to look behind.

"Drakensberg cannot hold me—and when I'm free, I'm coming for you, Mia. There will be no bargaining. No warning. It will be checkmate."

Mia opened her eyes and sat up, but a wave of dizziness hit her and she fell back against the pillows. A strong whiff of antiseptic swamped her senses as she inhaled. She was in hospital, but why? Ryder was the one that was shot. She clutched the sheets and tried sitting forward once again. An intravenous infusion stood next to her bed, and the plastic tube was taped to her hand, but she moved, despite feeling as weak as a kitten. Cerianne was in her face, speaking soothing words and attempting a smile.

"You were having a bad dream. Don't move," Cerianne said lightly pressing her hand on her arm to push her back.

"Ryder. Where is he?" Mia asked.

"Mia, honey, you must stay still, who is Ryder?" she said frowning and running a hand across Mia's forehead. Mia swallowed a lump that had formed in her throat. She hadn't meant to use his real name it was just so automatic.

A nurse entered the room, checked the intravenous infusion, and wrote on the charts before she smiled.

"I'm glad you're awake. You're going to be fine, you just need to rest," she said, lifting Mia's wrist to take her pulse.

Mia sat up and pushed aside her thumping headache. She yanked out the tube in her hand and moved her legs over the edge of the bed. Horrified, the nurse tried in vain to get her to settle back into bed. Blood trickled down her wrist and Mia grabbed a tissue.

"I meant Robert, where is he…please," she asked, stepping off the bed. Mia was not sure if he was alive or dead.

"Your friend was in a pretty bad way when he arrived here. Bullet penetrated…lost a lot of blood…Intensive care unit—" The nurse kept talking, but all Mia heard was the intensive care unit. No longer listening to the pleas of the nurse or her mother, she pushed past them and charged toward the elevators.

Once she arrived on the second floor, she was greeted by two burly security men and anxious looking nurses. She gripped the wall to steady her wobbly legs. A nurse approached and placed an arm around her waist, guiding her toward a side room. Mr. Mathews was sitting in a chair next to a sleeping Ryder. Mia breathed a sigh of relief. Ryder was attached to a spaghetti-junction of tubes and machines. Blinking away tears, Mia stared at his expressionless and pale face.

"Mia, you shouldn't be out of bed. Come on, sit here," Mr. Mathews said, moving out of the chair.

"Please don't make me go. I just want to sit here for a while, please?" Mia said, not taking her eyes away from Ryder.

"Five minutes. I'd better let Cerianne know you're here," he said, walking away.

Mia touched Ryder's warm hand and squeezed her eyes shut. She could hear the lub-dub of his heart, and as she rubbed his hand, his pulse rate increased.

I love you, do you hear me?

Today was Christmas day, and knowing that Ryder was alive was the best gift Mia could have hoped for. A choir stood in the foyer and started singing, Oh come all ye faithful. Mia laid her cheek against Ryder's arm and let the tears wash against his skin.

Twenty-four hours later, Mia was discharged home. Her parents fussed over her, and she let them. Mr. Childs had stayed on because of the shooting, but he was leaving today.

"Mia, you have a beautiful voice. Don't let what happened put you off using it. It's a gift. You cannot live in fear, and you have to live your life." He kissed her forehead.

"Dad, I love you—"

He stood back and held her hands. "You mean the world to me. If you ever need anything, just ask." he said. "Robert… You love him, don't you?" he said.

She nodded and looked away.

"Well, be careful," he said, walking into the waiting taxi.

* * * *

At the hospital, Ryder's condition improved daily. He was awake, breathing on his own and getting stronger. The doctors said he could be discharged next week. Mia arrived at the hospital and walked onto the surgical ward that Ryder was now on. Walking into his room, she smiled at all the cards and balloons. Since the shooting, the media reported daily on his progress and that of the five other people who had been injured. The gunman had died. Tyler had fallen while running away, and needed several stitches. Evan was quiet and refused to talk about that night at all. Ryder lay in bed with his eyes closed, but his mouth spread into a huge smile and he opened his eyes. The warmth of his gaze hit her and tears dropped onto her cheeks.

He patted the space next to him on the bed and she sat down brushing her lips over his, kissing him softly.

"It's going to suck to be you, for a while," Mia said, running her hand across his chest and instantly his face relaxed.

"Why, because you're going to yell at me again?" He brushed her hair away from her face and a tear touched his finger.

"You don't know what it was like seeing you there, all covered in blood. I thought you were dead. Hell, for a moment you were. Promise me, you'll never do that again. I don't want you to die for me. You are my life." She glared at him. Ryder lowered his head and looked out the window.

"Mia, I would not wish for your life to end, simply because mine had. I would never be that selfish. I want you to live a long and happy life, no matter what," he said.

"What kind of life would I have, if you were not in it?" Mia pulled his face around to look up at her. Tears bubbled and her lower lip trembled. She'd almost lost him, and knew he would risk his life again to save hers. Her head lowered. How could she expect anything less, because she was willing to give her life for him?

"I could never just stand by and let you get hurt. Did you think I would've just let Greyson take you? You're my life too. I know you love me, and I know what you'd sacrifice for me, so don't expect anything less in return." Ryder pushed himself forward, frowning, and lifted her chin.

"If I had gone to Greyson, I would have been alive and so would you. You must promise you will not put yourself in danger for me again," she said

"I can't. It would be like asking me to stop breathing. I simply couldn't do it." He kissed her lips, and her arms immediately went around his neck and held him there. She released his lips and leaned her forehead against his chin.

"Ryder, I don't know if next time I could help you or anyone. What if I couldn't?" she whispered.

"Death is just another part of life. Anyway, knowing you love me and would be willing to be with Greyson to save me would be like ripping my heart out. So what's the difference?" he sighed.

Mia exhaled sharply. They would never agree on this.

Breaking the silence, Tristan and Brianna marched in with smiling faces. Brianna placed some grapes on the small table, and immediately began eating them.

"Dad has given the go ahead for us to stay at his friend's cabin next weekend, when you get out. It's up in the mountains in Maine, away from everything. I think it's what we all need. What do you think?"

Ryder glanced at Mia, smiling. "Sounds exactly like what the doctor ordered. However, Mia is right—it's gonna suck to be me for a while. I have a pretty impressive scar after they removed my spleen." Ryder winced as he wiggled himself back against the pillows.

"Well, if Mia can keep her hands off you, I think I can manage the driving. We need some space and we need to speak to Emrys, so I figured this was as good a chance as any. Look, I'm not sure what's going to happen from here on in, but Evan is in a really bad place right now. He wants to quit the band." Ryder shook his head and Mia nodded. She'd been so focused on Ryder for the last week that she hadn't given the band or the others much thought.

"I can't think about the band right now. We need to talk to Emrys and figure out our next move. We should've all returned to Annwn with Greyson, but it didn't work out that way. And I'm not sure what comes next," Ryder said. Brianna stopped eating the grapes and looked up, moving closer to the bed. Ryder, Tristan, and Mia stared at her knowing she wanted to say something.

"I didn't say anything before because it wasn't the time and there was too much going on, but the night of the concert—when Mia saved you—the paramedic was watching you intently, and so I dipped into his thoughts. He saw your magic, and he was telling the other one about the bright light from your hand." Brianna stared at Mia.

"Oh my God. I never stopped to think—"

Ryder squeezed her hand. "Mia, a couple of months ago you were adamant that you were not the girl that I knew, and yet, at the concert, you took over. You took control. *You* sent Greyson back. I told you once that you're stronger than you realize. We'll just have to deal with whatever comes our way," Ryder said.

Mia nodded, realizing she had let their secret out. Not once had she believed a human would be able to see her magic.

* * * *

The doctor's said Ryder's recovery was remarkable, which made him smile. He knew that Mia's healing hands had been working to ease the pain and heal his muscles. Rubbing his chest with his hand, he inhaled and shifted his position in the car to ease Mia onto his shoulder. The shooting was two weeks ago now, but it felt like a distant memory. He was weaker than ever before, but Mia's healing powers helped to make him feel his energy returning. New Year came and went, and despite Brianna's announcement that the paramedic witnessed Mia's magic, there was nothing in the papers or on the news, which was good. He gazed at Mia as she slept, and smiled as she made little huffing noises. Brianna switched places with Tristan as he was being sarcastic about her driving skills. Their laughter was infectious, and he had to hold his ribs as he winced after laughing so hard.

It was January, and thick snow fell in clumps. The weather report said a foot of snow was likely to descend upon them tonight. Ryder hugged Mia, letting her warmth soothe his stiff body. Tristan's dad arranged for their stay in the mountain cabin in Maine. Since, the concert, not much was said about the future of the band or the disappearance of Greyson. Ryder stared out the window at the passing, tall, snow–covered, fir trees and impressive mountain ranges that ringed the skies. The car pulled up a long tree-lined road and stopped. Ryder gently prodded Mia awake and gripped her hand as they stepped out of the truck. Boxberry House was more of a mansion than a log cabin.

"Wow. It's very Last of the Mohicans up here. Perfect," Ryder said, taking a lungful of fresh air.

"Guys, come and check it out! It's awesome," Brianna yelled.

Mia grabbed Ryder's hand, and together they walked into the house.

A wood-burning smell invaded Ryder's nostrils as soon as he entered. The downstairs was spacious and open-planned. A small, fully–equipped, stainless-steel kitchen lay to the right as they walked in, and on the counter was a welcome basket. Looking back into the main living room, they saw two long couches in a soft red fabric that sat in front of a stone fireplace. The view of the impressive mountain ranges was virtually brought into the living room through the floor to the ceiling wall of glass, which extended across the back of the house. It was amazing. Beyond the glass wall was an equally impressive deck, that matched the length of the house.

"Well, I'm more than happy to call this home for the next couple of days," Ryder smirked, holding Mia at his side. Before everyone settled, he wanted to reach out to Emrys. Afterward they could relax and enjoy some privacy. He smiled and met Mia eyes as she looked up at him. Her thoughts were the same, and he quickly called the others.

"Before you go in the hot-tub, we should talk to Emrys," Ryder said.

Tristan stared at the open fireplace and instantly a huge roaring fire blazed into life. The four of them stood and held hands. Mia's pendant glowed brightly and bathed them in an impenetrable golden field of light. Ryder called to Emrys. A hazy outline tried to form in the center, but it flickered and faded. The room shifted and the sharp lines distorted, but they remained in the living room.

"It's not working," Tristan addressed them all.

Still they held firm, and the figure in front of them thickened and started to speak. It was Emrys but the figure was weak and hazy.

"I'm sorry, but it's not safe." His voice was small and weak. "You cannot come back as you did before. That door is now closed. Go to where it all began, use Rhiannon's book, and don't lose what's most precious to you. War is inevitable. Everything's changed. Greyson's not in Drakensberg. He knew—you must find your own way home."

Mia pulled to move forward, but Ryder held her, and the weak outline of Emrys faded. They each tried to call him back as questions raced around their minds.

"I don't..." Brianna stared wide-eyed at Mia, as Tristan wrapped his arm around her and moved her closer against him.

"You're cold," he said and she nodded resting her head on his chest.

"Emrys brought us into the human world through a portal, and when Mia sent Greyson back that door closed. There are others, but I don't know where. Emrys would have said if he could, so it's up to us. There may be clues in Rhiannons' book," Ryder said, standing and walking over to stare out at the falling snow. The mountains were ghostly shadows in the distance. Mia jumped up and pulled his arm back.

"Ryder, how did Greyson get out of Drakensberg?"

He turned to gaze into her misty violet eyes. "He must have known what you would do. Anyway, Greyson isn't our biggest worry. If the portal has been closed, chances are he's stuck in Annwn. The portals are known to only a few. What did Emrys mean, that everything's changed? It struck me as odd." He cocked his head sideways, staring at Mia and then toward the others. Mia hugged herself, shivering.

"I thought he was referring to the fact that war would change everything in Annwn," Tristan said, joining Ryder and Mia.

"But we're not in Annwn, and for some reason I thought he meant here. Look, there's no need to panic. We're all together, and nothing's changed. It just means we'll need to go on a bit of a road trip," Ryder said.

"I'm sorry, but I'm not on the same page as you lot. Emrys said it wasn't safe. Did he mean for him, or for us? And where *did* it all begin?" Brianna walked to join the group. Mia looked at the ground and then across at her.

"I think we have to return to Wales," she said, biting her lip. "Emrys is right. The book talks about a doorway into the human world."

Tristan stared at Brianna. "Tomorrow, we'll figure it out. Today, it's time for the hot-tub," he said, whisking Brianna away.

Mia laughed and turned toward Ryder. Before the words were spoken, he nodded in agreement.

"They're made for each other. Sooner or later, they'll realize it too. Here, put this on. I want to show you something." He fished in his pocket and groaned. "Wait on the deck, I have to get something. I'll only be a minute."

Ryder turned away, and then back, as if he had forgotten something. He pulled the thick gray parka that was wrapped around Mia, closer toward him. Mia lifted her head, smiling, and their lips touched. She nudged hers against his until Ryder pulled back. "I love you," he said. "Don't move."

Out onto the deck, white fluffy snow swirled around her. The cold air froze in her lungs as she breathed, but it was good to shake away the disturbing feeling that was gnawing away inside her. Ryder rushed through the doors and closed them quickly behind him. As soon as he stood next to her, he pulled a small black box out of his pocket and opened it.

A sparkling gem sat innocently on crushed black velvet. Mia gasped and looked into his eyes and then at the sparkling gem. A shiver rippled down her spine, and she blinked.

Greyson's haunting voice whispered. *Congratulations. Check, Mia, but it isn't check-mate. You've merely won the battle, not the war.*

Mia smiled at Ryder. She would fight anyone who threatened those she loved. After all, she was a Guardian of Annwn, and that made her exceptional.*Bring it on!*

The End

About the Author

Jennifer Owen-Davies writes YA and adult romance. Her first YA romantic fantasy The Promise:Children of Annwn is the first in a trilogy about Mia Leronde and Ryder Blackwood who are from the mythological realm of Annwn where falling in love comes with a price. The second book, The Battle is coming soon.

Jennifer developed a penchant for romance by reading novels by Dame Barbara Cartland as a teenager. After reading her books, she fell in love with the certainty of the happy ever after stories she created. Her reading tastes have grown since then and vary from Nora Roberts, Catherine Cookson and Jane Austen to Jodi Picoult, Deborah Harkness, Cassandra Clare, Suzanne Collins, P.D.James, and many more..

She developed a thirst for writing rather late in life, but is ever thankful that she made such a fulfilling discovery.

Jennifer Davies has been married for nineteen years to her best friend, and the keeper of all her secrets. Mr. D encourages her to keep reaching for the stars. They have active family life with four mostly happy and healthy boys each with very different personalities. Her oldest son lives in Wales and works in the communication industry. In his spare-time, he acts in workshops at a local theater. Her "teens" are in high-school and the greatest challenge is balancing their social and academic lives. Whilst, her youngest is in elementary school, and he loves swimming, basketball, and Minecraft.

Jennifer Davies and her husband are originally from Cardiff in Wales, but they now live on the East Coast of America with their family and two cats.

Website: http://www.Jenniferowendavies.com

Coming soon, the second book in the Children of Annwn series The Battle.

Made in the USA
Middletown, DE
26 November 2018